Praise for *We Know You Know*

"A practiced hand at inducing pleasurably creepy reading experiences . . . In [Kelly's] capable hands, what begins here as an alarm-bell-ringing deception of a husband by his wife evolves into an unabashedly dark tale that throws into sharp relief some of our most critical contemporary issues as well as those of the all-too-recent past."   —*The Seattle Review of Books*

"The reader will be exposed to institutional horrors that make *One Flew Over the Cuckoo's Nest* look as inviting as Disneyland. It's disturbing to the max, but hey, that's what we read thrillers for, right?"   —*BookPage*

"Erin Kelly messes with your psyche once again with [*We Know You Know*]."   —Women.com

"It is a tale of maternal nurturing and neglect, blackmail, distrust, and titillating suspense."   —Bookreporter.com

"Twisting back through time, [*We Know You Know*] is the story of how a covered-up murder will never lie quietly . . . A genuinely surprising twist that turns assumptions neatly on their heads."
                                        —*The Guardian* (UK)

"A beautifully dark, gothic story of characters haunted by their past: poignant and tragic, full of unexpected shifts and twists, addictively scary and thrillingly audacious."   —Nicci French

"Warning: may induce whiplash. So many novelists merely maintain altitude with each book; Erin Kelly tops herself time and again. [*We Know You Know*] is the best and boldest novel to date from one of the very best thriller writers at work today: a sinuous, slippery thriller as ingenious as it is absorbing."   —A. J. Finn

"It is rare when exquisite plotting and damn fine writing come together, but Erin does it every time, seamlessly. [*We Know You Know*] is an absorbing, humane, and intriguing story that will have readers enthralled."
—Liz Nugent

"Gripping, moving, impossible to put down, and fiendishly readable . . . She's done it again."
—Laura Marshall

"[*We Know You Know*] is an incredible work of psychological suspense!"
—*Book Nook*, WOSU Radio

"[*We Know You Know*] is a vibrant and nonstop mystery brimming with high drama."
—*Manhattan Book Review*

"[*We Know You Know*] is a truly skillful, beautifully written novel."
—*Marilyn's Mystery Reads*

"I can't recommend this book highly enough."
—*A Bookish Type*

Praise for *He Said/She Said*

"A tour de force—a gripping, twisting, furiously clever read that asks all the right questions, and keeps you guessing until the very end. I loved it."
—Ruth Ware

"Haunting. Mesmerizing. Unforgettable."
—Gillian Flynn

"It's a tribute to Kelly's sleight of storytelling hand that the disclosures are incremental but relentless in their chilling effect. Here, as in her other mind-blowing works, she concerns herself as much with her characters' emotional baggage as with precise, engaging plotting and adrenaline-bursting twists. Just don't get too complacent when reading Kelly: She's always got extra cards up her sleeves."
—*The Boston Globe*

"*He Said/She Said* is a thriller to savor, and should be one of the highlights of the summer."
                                                                —Associated Press

"Heart-pounding . . . The panic of her heroine practically rises off the page. [Her prose is] always energetic, encompassing an abundance of inventive descriptions and striking metaphors."
                                                                —*The New York Times*

"Kelly weaves a story with emotional weight. A pair of twists rotates guilt and absolution between characters." —*Paste* magazine

"The shocker twist is a jaw-dropper."   —*Good Housekeeping*

"Author Erin Kelly will have you questioning everything, and asks: Who do YOU believe?"   —*HelloGiggles*

"Kelly delivers another tale full of lies, obsessions, and richly drawn characters. This is a sure bet for readers who like their psychological suspense heavy on character and full of twists."
                                                                —*Booklist* (starred review)

"This first-rate psychological thriller and deft exploration of the delicate dance of marriage and the secrets people keep works on multiple levels, and the passages about the early days of Laura and Kit's relationship—filled with the gossamer promise of new love—make what's in store for them even more harrowing. A stunning conclusion will take more than a few days to fade from memory."
                                                                —*Kirkus Reviews* (starred review)

"This riveting psychological thriller from British author Kelly explores the extremes to which people will go to conceal a lie. . . . Readers will be rewarded with airtight plotting, mounting tension, and shocking twists. . . . This is an affecting tale of infatuation, desperation, and betrayal."   —*Publishers Weekly*

we know you know

ERIN KELLY

 MINOTAUR BOOKS   NEW YORK

Published in the United States by Minotaur Books, an imprint of
St. Martin's Publishing Group

www.minotaurbooks.com

The Library of Congress has cataloged the hardcover edition as follows:

Names: Kelly, Erin, 1976– author.
Title: Stone mothers / Erin Kelly.
Description: First U.S. Edition. | New York : Minotaur Books, 2019. | First
    published in Great Britain by Hodder & Stoughton, an Hachette UK
    company in 2019.
Identifiers: LCCN 2018047634 | ISBN 9781250113719 (hardcover) |
    ISBN 9781250225641 (international, sold outside the U.S., subject to
    rights availability) | ISBN 9781250182838 (ebook)
Subjects: LCSH: Family secrets—Fiction. | Psychological fiction. | GSAFD:
    Suspense fiction.
Classification: LCC PR6111.E498 S76 2019 | DDC 823/.92—dc23
LC record available at https://lccn.loc.gov/2018047634

ISBN 978-1-250-24823-7 (trade paperback)

Our books may be purchased in bulk for promotional, educational, or business use. Please contact your local bookseller or the Macmillan Corporate and Premium Sales Department at 1-800-221-7945, extension 5442, or by email at MacmillanSpecialMarkets@macmillan.com.

Originally published in Great Britain by Hodder & Stoughton,
an Hachette UK company

First published in the United States under the title *Stone Mothers* by Minotaur Books

First Minotaur Books Paperback Edition: 2020

10 9 8 7 6 5 4 3 2 1

For Owen Kelly, whose trespass inspired this book

In its first year of operation we are pleased to report that this asylum has no equal in the Region or beyond. The building is equipped for the most modern treatments and tranquility is promoted by its healthy locality, its spacious rooms and galleries. The sun and the air are allowed to enter at every window. The propensity for female insanity is recognized in the design, with eighteen female wards and fourteen male. Indeed, many women committed due to domestic discord or excess of childbearing request to stay.

Sir Warwick Chase, Chief Inspector of Asylums
and Advisor for the Commission of Lunacy
Extracted from the first Annual Report on
The East Anglia Pauper Lunatic Asylum, 1868

PART ONE

park royal manor
2018

I

The blindfold hurts. His inexperience shows in the knot. It's tight but crude, and has captured a hank of my hair. Every time he takes a corner too fast, I rock to the side, the seatbelt slicing my shoulder and the tiny needlepoint pain in my scalp intensifying. He brakes without warning: I'm thrown forward. A loosening of the purple silk near my right temple lets in a little light but no information.

He has gone for full sensory deprivation. There is no music, only the rhythm of my breath and his, the bassline of the engine, the key changes of the shifting gears. The radio would help. An accumulation of three-minute pop songs would let me measure time. If forced to guess, I would say that we have been traveling for an hour but it could be half an hour or it could be two. I know that we drove out of London, not deeper into it, and that we must be far out of town now. For the first couple of miles I could track our route by the stop-start of traffic lights and speedbumps. It takes ten minutes to escape Islington's 20-mile-an-hour zone in any direction. I'm sure I smelled the barbecue restaurant on City Road but I think he circled the Old Street roundabout twice to confuse me and after that I was lost.

Once we were out of the city and moving fast, my nose caught a couple of bonfires—it's that time of year—but they had the woodsy feel of a domestic pile rather than anything agricultural or industrial. Sometimes it feels like we're in the middle of nowhere, winding through lanes, then he'll go smooth and fast again, and the rush of passing traffic will tell me we're back on an A-road. If we were heading for an airport, I would have expected the boom as the jets graze the motorway. I will not get on an airplane.

"Shit," he mutters and brakes again. The last few strands of caught hair spring loose from their moorings. I can feel him shift in the seat, his breath skimming my cheek as he reverses slowly. I take the opportunity to put my hand up to my head, but he's watching me as well as the road.

"Marianne! You *promised*!"

"Sorry," I say. "It's really getting on my nerves now. What if I close my eyes while I retie it? Or while *you* retie it."

"Nice try," he says. "Look, it's not far now."

How near is not far? Another minute? Another thirty? If I twitch my cheek I can see a little more. What light I can sense starts to flicker rapidly through the violet gauze. Sunlight through a fence? The pattern is liminal, more irregular than that. We're in a tree tunnel, which means a country lane, which means—

"Sam! Have you booked us into a spa?"

I can hear the smile in his voice. "I think I've done better than *that*."

My shoulders relax, as though the masseur's hands are already on them. I can't think of anything better than two days being pummeled floppy by muscular young women in white tunics. It must be that organic place on the Essex coast I've been longing to try. I could relax in Essex. I could get to Mum in an hour and to Honor in two. Maybe, when Sam says he's done better than that, he's even arranged for Honor to *be* here.

The road is uneven now, all potholes and gravel, and I put my hands up, ready to unwind the scarf.

"Two more minutes!" Sam's voice vaults an octave. "I want to see you see it." The tires crunch. I wait patiently with my hands in my lap as the parking sensors quicken their beep. "OK, now," he says, undoing the knot with a flourish. "Welcome to Park Royal Manor."

The name is familiar from the brochures and so is the image but shock delays its formation.

I see it as a series of architectural features—crenellations and gables, fussy gray stonework, tall forbidding windows—but I can't take in its breadth.

"I'm too near," I try to say, but it comes out in a whisper.

Nazareth Hospital, or The East Anglia Pauper Lunatic Asylum as it originally was, wasn't designed to be viewed up close like this but as a whole, from a distance, whether you were being admitted to it or whether it was one last haunted look over your shoulder as you left or ran away. The last time I saw the place, and the way I still see it in my dreams, was from afar. It seemed to fill the horizon. It is perched on what counts for a hill around here, its width a warning to the flat country around it. Built to serve three counties, it is too big for modest Suffolk, its soaring Victorian dimensions all wrong.

I can drive from London to Nusstead almost on autopilot so how did I not recognize the journey?

Sam rubs his hands together in glee. "How much d'you love me right now? Come on, let's have a proper look at the place." He reaches across me and thumbs my seatbelt unlocked. I cannot get out of the car. A scream claws its way up the sides of my throat.

The pictures in the brochure didn't do the changes justice. The floor-to-ceiling paneled windows have been unbarred, hundreds of uncracked panes in new frames. The ivy and buddleia that sprouted impossibly from tilting chimney pots and rotting lintels has gone, replaced by a Virginia creeper whose remaining deep red leaves are neatly trimmed to expose silver brick. The vast double doors have been replaced by sheets of sliding glass with "Park Royal Manor" etched in opaque curlicue. My eyes refuse to go any higher.

"What . . ." I begin. "What are we doing here, Sam? What are we *doing* here?"

5

He mistakes panic for surprise. "I got you a little pied-à-terre. No more crashing on Colette's sofa or shelling out for a hotel."

I look down but that's even worse. No, I can't see the renovated clocktower but I can see its shadow, like the cast of a giant sundial, a dark gray finger pointing right at me. For all the fancy ironwork of its clock face the tower was only ever a lookout post in disguise—Nazareth ran on its own time—and I feel watched now. I pull the blindfold clumsily back down over my eyes, the hem of the scarf catching in my mouth.

"Marianne?" says Sam, staring at me. "Marianne, what's the matter?"

It isn't a scream after all but its opposite, a dry desperate sucking in of air that contains no oxygen, only dust. "I can't go in," I manage. "Please, Sam, don't make me go back."

2

"What the hell's the matter?" We are parked under a huge cedar, far enough around the curved driveway that the place is out of sight. The needling leaves are a black canopy above us. I'm embarrassed by the force of my reaction and trying desperately to downplay it but it's too late. Sam's face has changed. Gone is the eagerness of two minutes ago, replaced by the expression I saw when he took the first call about my mother, or the one I see when Honor's back in the Larches and he's waiting for me in reception. He hands me a bottle of water. The cedars make a soft susurrus.

Jesse carved our initials on one of these trees, JJB & MS surrounded by a heart. Sometimes these carvings grow more pronounced over the years as the trunk spreads and the scarring expands.

"I'm so sorry," I say, and that's all I can manage because I am seventeen again, in the echoing wards. Words going up in flame, lives reduced to checklists and doctors' rounds. Keys turning in locks. Smashed glass and running. The things that define me fall away; mother, wife, work. The title in front of my name and the letters after it erase themselves, and I am made of my past. The thought of reentry feels like—the comparison makes itself before I can help it—an electric shock.

"I mean, I thought you'd *love* it," Sam says. "I thought I'd be carrying you across the threshold now—there's champagne in the fridge. If you don't like this place, why did you have all the estate agent's brochures under the bed? I wasn't snooping; they weren't hidden." It's a bloody good question, it's *the* question, and one I can never let him know the answer to. I feel the need to keep tabs on the place, much as I do on Jesse. Relationships with people and places can be intense and reluctant at the same time. I have read those brochures on my own, my secret bedtime story, turning the pages slowly as if I could catch the lie, as though only care kept the dark truth of then from emerging through the gloss of now. Sometimes, when the masochistic compulsion to keep looking was at its worst, I had to take something to knock me out, something so powerful that it was all I could do to slide the pages down the side of the bed before passing out. "I thought it must be your dream home, the way you stashed it all away. The hoops I've had to jump through to get a mortgage without you knowing. All right, maybe I shouldn't have surprised you, but you're acting like I've done something *bad*."

For a wild second I consider telling him the truth, but, "It's a phobia," I say to my lap. My shame isn't feigned: I'm lying to someone who doesn't deserve it. "A childhood phobia. I just . . . this place. I wasn't expecting it."

"But you can see it from Colette's house. It's never bothered you before."

"It's three miles from Colette's," I say, on the defensive but at least regaining control of my heartbeat, of my head. "When I was little, Nazareth Hospital was the local haunted house. It's what you'd make up stories about on camping trips. Escaped lunatics running out across the fens with their manacles still around their ankles, out to get you in your bed. I used to have nightmares about the place." That much is true: only the tense is a lie.

"Oh, darling." There's laughter in his voice. "Sorry. But—it is ironic. You've got to admit it. A History of Architecture lecturer with a crippling phobia of an *old building*."

"I know, right?" I smile weakly. Of course it's not an irony or even coincidence. My whole career has been a way of trying to understand, and control, this place.

"And then the first time you ever actually come here, I spring it on you like something out of a bloody Hammer Horror. Even when I try, I can't get anything right, can I?"

It suddenly strikes me what Sam has done: the time and effort and the money that goes into buying a property, that he has done all of this without ever asking for my help, in the middle of a huge project, and that he has done it for me, to make life easier for the wife he thinks he knows and the family he married into.

"God, you must think I'm such an ungrateful bitch. Thank you, Sam. It's one of the kindest things anyone's ever done for me." I force a smile. It feels like it's going to split my lips but it works: Sam looks pleased with himself again.

"Good. I know it means a lot to your mum."

This gets my head up fast. "You told my *mum* about this? Did she even understand?"

"Well, Colette can remind her."

"*Colette* knows? I don't know what's more astonishing: that you went behind my back or that she kept a secret." My sister is the biggest gossip in Nusstead; my mother's old mantle, it fits her perfectly.

"I'm a man of hidden depths." Sam's joking, but I don't like it. Hidden depths are not what I signed up for. Amanda, my head of department, once rhapsodised about her complex, enigmatic husband, saying that she had married him because she knew she would never get to the bottom of him. I can't think of anything worse. Sam is not a shallow pool but he is a crystal clear one. Initiative is for his drawing board, not for his marriage. He is solid, in character as well as in body. We agree on everything, except, occasionally, how to manage our daughter. I trust him. Not enough to tell him of course, but in the sense that he won't hurt me. Anyone who thinks that predictability is a poor reward for security cannot have known real fear.

The sun dips behind the hospital roof and the temperature drops suddenly. It always used to do this, I remember: night would fall on the forecourt hours before true sunset.

"It's getting cold," says Sam, rubbing my arms. "Let's go and unpack. I mean—it was just the shock of it, right? Now you know what to expect, we can go in. You'll feel better once you've unpacked, made it your own. You know what it looks like inside, if you've seen the brochures. It's not at all spooky." His tummy growls loudly. "We can get a Deliveroo," he suggests.

"Sam, you're in rural Suffolk. There's only one takeaway round here and even they don't deliver. Let's go out."

Anything to get the place behind me. Anything to play for time.

3

Sam keeps one finger on the switch that dips and raises the head-lamps. When I was a girl you could go for five minutes and not see another vehicle and it isn't much busier now. Asylum Road—or Regal Drive, as I see they have renamed it—is a dead end. Naza-reth to Nusstead is only three miles as the crow flies, but the road must take into account the impassable Nusstead Fen and winds an asphalt oxbow around the wetlands. Images flash in and out of the beam: branches, verges, hedgerows and occasionally a pair of tiny eyes at bumper level. A pink farmhouse looms up and is in-stantly gone. There's a little church on the corner and beyond that, in the flat dark, the glittering marshy fenland where Michelle's ashes were scattered. Suffolk is a sparsely populated county anyway but this shallow valley, just a few miles south of the River Waveney that's an informal border with Norfolk, is as remote as it gets.

"There's nothing spookier than a country road at night," says Sam. "I always expect a teenage girl in a bloodstained nightie to stagger out in front of me with her arms outstretched."

"That's your standard Saturday night out in Nusstead." Lo-cated: one sense of humor. Maybe I can do this after all.

Sam indicates right as we approach the Crown. "Not here," I say. "They'll have Sky Sports on, you can't have a conversation. Keep going into Eye. We'll eat at the hotel." Sam brakes but doesn't turn. "I really can't be arsed to drive all the way to Eye. The whole point of the flat is that we don't *have* to stay miles away."

In fact, we have never *had* to stay at the hotel. Before Colette moved Mum into her front room, her sofabed was always at our disposal. It's not them I'm keeping Sam away from. They come from different worlds, my grammar-school husband and my left-school-at-sixteen sister, but they get on: they have the same instinct for family, a certain straightforwardness. Any rift is one I've created, my insistence that we never stay at Colette's implying that Sam thinks her house is beneath him, or that she doesn't want him in her home. Nothing could be farther from the truth. The fallout from my past dusts everything.

No, I keep him tucked away in the Eye Hotel, more like a secret lover than a husband of twenty-five years, because I live in fear of the scenario where Sam, on the real ale trail, sees Jesse in the Crown. Jesse wouldn't be able to control himself: at best, he'd let slip a sly insinuation, at worst, a full-blown confession. And Sam *would* run into Jesse. When I come home, he's everywhere I go. The Brames were never good at staying in and it's passed to the younger generation. I can't remember a recent visit to Nusstead without seeing Mark pushing Trish's wheelchair, or Madison her pram. Clay's latest motorbike will always be propped outside the Crown. Jesse's younger kids, the three who actually live in Suffolk, I have never formally met (although their mothers know me, of course), and have not seen often enough to recognize. In my more paranoid moments I wonder whether Jesse has organized his family into some kind of patrol rota, so that I can never walk the streets of my hometown without human reminders of my guilt, or of who I might have become. But I can't explain this, so I simply say: "Jesse drinks in the Crown."

"Ah." Sam releases the brake. I have introduced him to Jesse, in the spirit of hiding in plain sight. It didn't go well. Each man has the exact qualities the other lacks, and it picks at both their senses of inferiority. Even if Jesse had money he'd never have Sam's easy social confidence; and women don't look twice at Sam.

We pass Main Street and the house I grew up in, the two-up two-down whose front door opens onto the street. To our right is the war memorial, its size and its roll call out of proportion with this tiny town, early poppies already at its base. The co-op is half shuttered, the library in darkness. A minute later Sam slows outside Colette's redbrick semi. Bryan's car is parked on the street, resting between long commutes to the power station on the coast, and the light in the front room is off, meaning that Mum's asleep. If Colette and her family have an evening to themselves then the last thing I want to do is intrude upon it. I shake my head. "Not on an empty stomach."

"I did think about buying one of these, but only absolute wrecks came up and I didn't want a project," says Sam, nodding to another little ribbon of terraced cottages. "I think they're quite charming, though."

"I suppose they are." They'd go for close to a million in our end of Islington, where cottages and mews houses are at a premium. Here, they'd fetch maybe an eighth of that. They were built for the hospital workers back in the 1870s. Whole generations of families worked in the asylum. It was a big place, built to serve the whole region. When Nazareth went there was nothing to replace those jobs; the tourism that was supposed to come in never materialized after the Cunniffe scandal. The second-home boom never reached Nusstead. The reason gentrification has passed us—them—by is the estate that borders the Victorian cottages on three sides. Pebbledashed boxes, hurriedly thrown up in the 1950s to house staff when overcrowding in the hospital got so bad they had to turn nurses' accommodation into overspill wards. They were built for an expansion that never came. Nussteaders still call them the "new" houses sixty years later. Their ceilings are low and their proportions mean. They are warm and do little to trouble the horizon but they will never attract the out-of-towners; they will never be quaint.

"What about there?" says Sam, pointing to the Social, where the lights blaze through plate-glass windows. "We could go for sushi, maybe? Or tapas?"

The joke is clearly meant to put me at my ease but I resent it. The Social is chicken-in-a-basket and chips-with-everything and he knows it. It's a one-story prefab, thrown up along with the estate, a kind of workers' club for the nurses and orderlies, and when there were more unemployed than working the community took it over. Mum was on the cleaning rota then; Colette helps out now. It is still as familiar to me as my own bedroom; the carpet, orange and green, was worn to a sheen, while the wooden blocks of the dance-floor only shone when they were wet. It is a big part of my past. To insult it is to insult my hometown, which is to insult my family, me.

"Don't be such a snob." I didn't mean it playfully, but Sam laughs it off. It's stupid to think of him in that way. If he really were a snob, he wouldn't have married me.

4

The Eye Hotel is all Georgian sashes, tasteful planting and gleaming AA stars. They know us well and panic at first, thinking they've mucked up a reservation.

"Marianne!" says Nancy, from behind reception. "Did you book? I don't have any vacancies . . ."

"Just here for dinner tonight," I say. "Can you fit us in?"

Relief widens her smile. "For you, anything. How's your mum?"

"More of the same, really. Thanks for asking."

In the restaurant there's heritage paintwork and ten-quid starters catering to tourists and the Up From London brigade; popped Ralph Lauren collars and red chinos as far as the eye can see. Sam and I blend right in. Jesse would never come here. If I am keeping Sam out of Jesse's way then I'm also shielding Jesse from the way I live now. I mean, of course he knows what I do but I don't want him to know the extent of the difference; that I am, certainly by the standards of our childhood, rich. *You owe me,* he said years ago. That was before I had money but his conviction holds, as does my perceived debt. These days it's about guarding Jesse's pride, the downplaying of my comfort and nodding in sympathy about the difficulty of paying all that child support to all those different women on a paramedic's salary. Jesse gets obsessive and defensive, stews over offhand remarks and imagined slights for years. For our gossamer trust to hold, he needs to think of us as equals. Our relationship is crosshatched with the fault lines of money and sex, complicity and guilt. It all comes down to this. The life I have now, the life that Jesse is at once a huge and tiny part of: you can trace it back to the fact that I used the money to leave him.

Of course, anyone with a drop of business nous could have looked up the turnover of Thackeray & Khan, but Jesse never had that kind of initiative; it was one of the things that came to frustrate me about him. One look at our place in Noel Road and he'd have known how far apart we have grown, but Jesse hates London too much to visit even me.

"I'm going to have the dressed crab," says Sam, setting down his menu in a show of decisiveness. I order the beetroot and feta salad and a large glass of Cabernet Sauvignon. When Sam nips to the loo I motion for Nancy to refill it. Sam never checks the bill in restaurants, whereas I can't help totting it up as we go along, a throwback to my childhood watching my mother mouth the sums before putting anything in her shopping basket. I check my phone, flipping open the case Honor customized for me, the words "Daddy Issues" tattooed in copperplate on baby blue calfskin. Out of habit, I check her Instagram before my own emails. She has shared two new pictures with her 5,000 followers: a map of this morning's run, 6k along the Thames path. It's a good distance, indicating neither mania nor a slump, although I don't like the route she always takes through the estates and back streets of Kennington. There's also a heavily filtered picture of avocado smash on sourdough, with a cigarette ground out in the middle of it. She's hashtagged it with her own name, which means it is a Work and I roll my eyes even though there's no one there to see. Anyone who thinks I'm incapable of perspective regarding our daughter need only ask me what I think of most of her art. Still. There is nothing concerning tonight. She is "settled," as her psychiatrist says.

Aside from a handful of memoranda, my work email inbox is empty. I never used it for personal emails anyway, and all student messages will be diverted straight to Amanda. It's strange to be halfway through a term and not know this year's undergraduate intake, or to think about the post-grad students quietly plowing on without my supervision.

I set the phone face down and take a deep breath. I can do this. I can go back into Nazareth. Why not? They will have stripped the place back to the brickwork when they did it up. The character's all on the outside and it must have given up any remaining evidence. The clocktower will be difficult for me, depending on where the flat is, but I'll only have to see it from the outside twice a day. If Sam's driving I can close my eyes and if I'm behind the wheel I'll just focus on the driveway and not look up.

Sam sits down, sips his half of bitter like it's a fine wine. "You look loads better," he says. I swallow an acidic burp and he clocks my glass, refreshed but already half-drained. "I take it I'm driving."

"Thanks," I say. "I feel a bit silly now." He holds out his hand for mine. Very few men have beautiful hands but Sam does. His nails are one of the reasons I fell for him; he has them manicured and buffed once a week. In fact, his hands were the first part of him I ever saw, in the high-ceilinged hush of the RIBA library in Portland Place. His fingers brushed mine as we reached for the same book, a dry cloth-bound brick about structural rationalism in Europe. I was a few months into my doctorate, besotted with Art Nouveau and the Paris metro: Sam was in the immersive early stages of creating a new church and looking for inspiration in the curves of Gaudí's Barcelona. "Ladies first," he said, handing it to me, and remained polite when, seconds later, I dropped the 2-kilo volume on his foot. "No need to cripple the competition," he said. As he handed it back to me, I noticed the shiny square tiles of his nails and as the day went on I saw those same hands curl carefully around a coffee cup, support the stem of a wineglass, cradle a brandy bubble. Weeks later, his fingers closed around the handle of my bedroom door. In Sam's well-kept hands, in his considered touch, I caught sight of a life of order and care that was mine for the taking. It felt like finally being able to sit down after a lifetime on my feet.

In a rare moment of drunken clarity, Mum told me that she'd also fallen for my father because of his beautiful hands, although I have to take her word for that.

"So," I say, pulling my hand away. "This isn't like you."

"Ordering crab?"

"That is very maverick of you, yes, but . . . you know what I mean. Being spontaneous." I bury my irritation in money talk. "Can we afford it?" I have worn my good fortune well but never quite trusted it.

"If we're careful, yes. It's not that much more than we've been spending here." He gestures upward at the hotel bedrooms. "And it means no holiday this year but once you're back at work, it'll easily pay for itself. You won't be on sabbatical forever." He realizes what he's said. My open-ended career break lasts for as long as my mother does. "Oh, God, Marianne, I'm sorry. That was clumsy." I wave it away. He knows I know what he meant.

"Maybe my sabbatical was a bad idea." I know that it wasn't: it was a way of making official all the days of compassionate leave, of an end to students waiting outside my study door while I'm already halfway to Nusstead, or wherever Honor might be that week. "I can ring tomorrow, see if Amanda will have me back on a two-day week?"

"Marianne. Your work isn't going anywhere. But you've only got one mum. Stay here with Debbie. Give her these months." The crying reflex is strong but so is my counter-reflex: I keep the tears where they are.

The food is set before us. Sam cracks his crab's claw and it smells of the sea, of rare childhood trips to the coast. My salad seems thin and unappealing.

"If you say you've ordered the wrong thing and ask to swap with me I'm leaving you," he says, without even looking up.

"We could do half-and-half?" With resigned practice he forks half his food onto my plate and I slide a sludge of carmine, white and green onto his.

"Oh, hang on." A realization drops like a stone. "Family therapy."

"I've taken care of that," he says. "Dr. Adil reckons six weeks off won't hurt us. Might even give us time to let what we've covered so far percolate. She'll keep seeing Honor for her one-to-ones, of course. I thought you'd be relieved."

Relief isn't a strong enough word for the soaring inside me. For the past couple of months all three of us have been sitting in a treatment room turning over concepts such as *codependency* and *enmeshment* and other euphemisms for my perceived inability to relinquish control.

"OK," I say. "No more unilateral decisions though, all right?"

He knits his eyebrows at the irony; one emerging theme in family therapy is my habit, formed in Honor's early childhood when Sam was off building into the sky and I was at ground level, of steaming ahead with big decisions without consulting him. This is my own medicine he's spooning into me. Honor is our common ground but also our battleground. If I say the wrong thing now, tonight will be hijacked by this endless circling argument.

"How's the build going?" The real question: please, can we drop this? In his dry-swallow I see that he is as relieved as I am to talk shop. Or rather, as I currently have no shop, Sam talks and I listen. He sees himself as an engineer as much as an architect. He does function and his partner Imran does form. They design the kinds of institutions that even Damian Greenlaw would approve of. They're currently working on a "needs-led" special school in Finland and are, I learn at great length, at a stand-off over the precise angle of a skylight.

The mains come: steak for Sam, seared salmon and zucchini fries for me. "I've been there before, you know," I blurt suddenly. It's the understatement of the year but the truth encloses the lie. "To the hospital. That's where Mum worked before Ipswich. And my nanna before her."

"Marian with one n," nods Sam, referring to my namesake: the working-class name was given a frill on the end for me. Mum puts frills on everything: tissue boxes, duvet covers, names.

"That's right. They had a garden party for some anniversary or other." How old would I have been? Colette wasn't born yet but Jesse was there with his brothers, all three of them, which means that Butch was still alive, so . . . "I must have been about six."

"So you can't have *always* had this phobia, then?"

He's only taking an interest in my childhood, but it feels like an interrogation.

"We didn't actually go in that day. It was all in the garden."

"So you've never actually been inside."

"No," I lie, twisting my napkin in my lap.

"What I don't understand is, why keep all those catalogues if you're scared of the place?"

"Morbid curiosity; professional interest. I'll be all right. It was the shock earlier, that's all." I set my knife and fork down. "I haven't even asked you if it's a flat or a house." Some of the low-rise villas have been turned into cottages. Whatever ghosts lurk *there* are not mine, although I might be able to see the clocktower from the window.

"Couldn't quite stretch to one of the cottages, I'm afraid. But the apartment's lovely, I promise you. Two bedrooms, so Honor can come down whenever she wants."

The apartments. They are on the old wards, then. Where the patients slept, where the machines were. "How lovely!" I force out. "Where's our flat? I mean, do you know what it used to be?" The old signs flash through my mind. *Occupational Therapy. Gymnasium. Shop. Physical Rehabilitation. Electrotherapy.*

"I do, actually. The marketing suite isn't wild about promoting the grislier aspects of the hospital's history but I looked up the plans online. Actually went down a bit of a click-hole, found the original floor plans. I forgot myself a couple of times and looked it up on the iPad then panicked in case you found out what I'd been doing. Other men are deleting their internet history because of porn,

I'm wiping blueprints of Victorian asylums. Is that the right plural? Shouldn't it be asy*la*?"

"Sam."

"Oh, sorry. Our little flat was in the old women's wing. A general ward lined with seclusion rooms."

The waitress passes and I thrust my empty, trembling glass at her. "The Victorians used to call their mental hospitals stone mothers," I say, to distract Sam, whose only interest outside his family is architecture, from my nerves. "They had such faith in architecture back then that they thought the design of the building could literally nurse the sick back to health. I mean, I know that's what you do too but they were working on poor psychology from the start. Most of the big Victorian asylums were finished toward the end of the nineteenth century and of course then along came the First World War and shell shock changed everything they thought they knew about psychiatry, and those places were all wrong for it. It was a complete philosophy, you know; nothing about the way they're built is an accident—the segregation and all the bathrooms to literally wash away your madness. They were built like workhouses, not hospitals. Really, they were obsolete within years of opening."

"And yet it took nearly another, what, ninety years to shut them all down." Sam speaks lightly: the closing of the hospitals is a footnote in history for him, not a pivot. "I never realized thingummybob was behind it. You know, that hectoring MP with the space-age hairstyle who's always telling old people to run marathons or whatever." He looks at me expectantly, apparently blind to the blood that's flooded to my cheeks and pounds there. "Looks like a shark in lipstick. What *is* her name?"

"Helen Greenlaw." I get the name out, say it like it's nothing, with the kind of cool self-control Greenlaw herself would be proud of. Sam's description is spot-on, although it's not her mouth I recall but her eyes, bright Tory blue with a disfigurement in the right iris, a dash of navy pigment, as though the border of the pupil had been breached by a hook and the darkness tugged out.

"That's the one. Never liked her," he says absently, sawing at his steak. My face is on fire. If Sam has noticed, he's clearly put it down to a hot flash, which he's tactfully ignoring. "Christ knows how they got that pool in the old chapel past the planners—I take my hat off to the developers. They've made the old pulpit into a hot tub. Almost sacrilegious but it's a shame not to, isn't it? Residents get free membership, by the way. You can swim every day. You can sign Colette in, maybe, if she needs a break."

"I like the sound of that." I press my palm flat on the cotton tablecloth and try to absorb its coolness. As far as Sam is concerned, nothing just happened. Helen Greenlaw's name has passed through a conversation and out the other side without the sky falling in, something I did not think possible. My cheeks drain: my thoughts order themselves, return to home. If I have a base down here, Colette might actually have time to go swimming, stretch out in a spa, read a book on a lounger. She has put her own nursing career on hold for as long as Mum needs her. It's been a 24/7 shift with no breaks. Sam has done this for her as much as for me, I realize.

I eat slowly to put off our return. Nancy is discreetly folding new napkins for breakfast as I order another coffee "for the road" but eventually we must either drive back or sleep in the car. I chatter nervously all the way back to what I suppose I must learn to call Park Royal Manor.

"What does Park Royal Manor even mean?" I say, as we turn right at the illuminated sign promising LUXURY LIVING IN THE HEART OF THE SUFFOLK COUNTRYSIDE. "There's no royal connection around here that I know of."

"They could hardly call it Nazareth Mental Hospital, could they?"

"They dropped the 'mental' when I was a kid," I tell him. "It was just Nazareth Hospital then. To get rid of the stigma, I suppose."

"I suppose they wanted something a bit more neutral. Even Nazareth's a pretty loaded word."

The black cedars touch above us, a second, starless sky. I prattle on as the car curls toward the place. "Did you know, the phrase 'going round the bend' refers to asylums? They used to design the driveways in a curve rather than a straight line up to the front door so that the patients had a sense of privacy and seclusion from the outside world. So if you were driven round the bend, it meant that they were taking you up to the asylum."

That thought propels me to another. When I was at school, we wouldn't say anyone behaving eccentrically was going round the bend but "getting the number six." Back in the day, the number six bus was the one that, after they closed the railway, ferried workers and patients alike from Nusstead and beyond to Nazareth. I'd assumed it was a universal idiom. It was only when I went to Cromer Hall that I understood that the phrase was something I'd have to censor, along with my history, and my guilt, and the accent I shed like a shell.

5

At night, the facade is floodlit, a single beam of pale gold light trained on the clocktower. Before it collapsed, the tower was braced with iron bars that were supposed to deter suicides and I wonder what it looks like on the inside now, whether it still serves any kind of security purpose or is purely ornamental. The creeper glows scarlet. It must need trimming once a week to frame the windows but never infiltrate the old brick.

"OK?" Sam says, holding my hand. His palm is dry and warm. Mine is clammy. "God, this is a really big deal for you, isn't it? The human brain and its irrational fears. I had no idea."

The huge glass front doors open automatically onto the atrium. If you didn't know better you'd think this a grand hotel, thumbing its nose at the surrounding rural poverty. The old admissions desk is reception now, lilies and oleanders elegant in a fishbowl vase. On either side are the doors that led to the wings and the words WOMEN and MEN are still carved in stone on the left and right lintels respectively.

The grand staircase has been restored, wide wooden steps that give on to the landing where the old administration rooms were. The wood is restored to gleaming perfection. It's easier to imagine a bride or a debutante gliding down those stairs than it is a patient marched up to an interview with her consultant. The guilt, and the cruelty of what I have done—what *we* did—charges through the decades and bends me double.

"OK?" repeats Sam. I can only nod.

The liveried manchild on reception—Oskar, according to his badge—all but tugs a forelock.

"Good evening, Mr. Thackeray," he says in a thick Polish accent.

"Oh, for goodness' sake, call me Sam. This is my wife, Marianne."

"Good evening, Marianne," says Oskar, clearly uncomfortable with the familiarity.

I growl a "Hi."

The lift is mirrored with soft, foxed glass that throws us out of time. My teenage self is so present tonight that I almost expect to see her reflected but no, there I am, all forty-seven years of me. Suspiciously smooth brow but downturned eyes, beer-brown hair that magazine journalists would say is a few inches too long for my age. If you didn't know me, you might be surprised that I have a grown-up daughter. I was twenty-seven when Honor was born, a London anomaly. You can take the girl out of Nusstead . . . Round here, the generations are closer together. When Colette had Jack at twenty-two, she'd already been in work for five years, married and mortgaged for two. On my street in Islington there are women my age raising six-year-olds. I assumed that having my child early would free me up, later, when my peers were off starting their own families. I didn't anticipate the second informal maternity leave of Honor's teenage years. Next to me, Sam—teddy bear build, curly graying hair in need of a trim—checks his perfect teeth for spinach. "What's the service charge on this place?" I ask.

"Marianne. Don't worry. We'll find a way." Am I being paranoid, or is this a step down from the *we can afford it* of earlier? "Right, it's a bit of a walk. You're sure you're not spooked?"

I force myself to look. Fire doors now partition the corridor. The service corridor on the floor below was once the longest in Europe, half a mile end to end. It was a source of bizarre local pride that Nazareth was wider than Buckingham Palace.

They've gone for reproduction rather than restoration. In place of the school radiators thick with decades of paint stand smooth, powder-coated replicas. Even the glossy parquet is new. Rothko prints replace the patients' crude Occupational Therapy paintings and the photographs of them basket-weaving and turning shoes on lathes. Here and there, they've framed original plans of Nazareth and aerial shots. Viewed from above, the main building looks like the blade of an old-fashioned key with large square teeth running its length.

I notice they've kept the rounded-off walls and curved skirting, thoughtful touches that were supposed to prevent the patients in-juring themselves, but they've plastered over the honeycomb ceiling and fitted spotlights in the smooth arch. Where there was peel-ing plaster are metro tiles, sleek white bricks that are everywhere now—you can't order a coffee without being reminded of an old-fashioned municipal swimming pool. They're supposed to add authenticity but I find them grotesque; originally these tiles were in horrible places: derelict public lavatories, creepy regional train stations, neglected hospitals. Tiles like these bricked in the poor and desperate. Tiles like these witnessed the worst of me.

"Our place used to be the show home so it's not decorated to our taste yet," says Sam, shouldering yet another fire door. As if there's any such thing as *our* taste. I can't name one thing in our house Sam chose.

"OK, here we are. Welcome to our humble abode."

The lock is silent, and I'm glad. I remember too well the grat-ing of the old keys. The apartment is a wash-out of beige and taupe, oatmeal and mushroom. Show-home neutral, decorated not to offend anyone, a blandness an insult in itself. I have to look at my red coat to check that color can exist in here. The living area is twice the space covered by the bedrooms and the ceiling is double height. A spiral staircase winds around one of the iron pillars that used to run down the center of the wards. Only that and the windows, thirty-two conjoined panes overlooking the old airing courts, give away its institutional history. There are metro tiles in the kitchen, naturally. I will bet our second mortgage they're upstairs too. Today's beloved interior trend is tomorrow's avocado bathroom suite.

"What do you think?" Sam's eyes beg my approval. "I know it's a bit plain, but . . ."

"Well, you'd certainly never guess what it was." I go to the window and stare out onto the fen. Nusstead is a cluster of sequins on the horizon. One of those pinprick lights is my old bedroom window. Movement behind me pulls my focus back to the window. Sam has a flute of champagne in each hand.

"I hope it doesn't feel crass, to drink a toast to the new place," he says. "I wish you didn't need to come back. But I hope having a base here can—I hope it can take the sting out of what's to come, somehow."

I turn to kiss him. "I love you for it."

Sam drinks his champagne too fast and wrinkles his face as the bubbles go up his nose.

"I don't know whether to say this," he begins. "I was going to say it in the pub and then I bottled it but it's better to get these things out in the open. I did a bit of snooping and—I know about the murder."

Over the years I've learned that my body has a very specific reaction to bad news. It wants to get away from the source. The involuntary step I take away from Sam is a violent lurch that gets me halfway across the room, fizz slopping everywhere. He's mortified, for the second time this evening. "I'm sorry, sweetheart, I didn't think it would get to you like this. You were so young I didn't think it'd bother you. But listen, it's OK. It's in the past." He catches me up, produces a tissue from his pocket to mop the spillage on my dress. "You know Darius Cunniffe is dead, don't you? He died in

Broadmoor in 2013. I remembered the case from the news, I just didn't know it happened *here* until I looked the place up."

Relief is a drug better than alcohol: it floods my veins, bubbles of it pop inside me. Sam's talking about the infamous killing, the one that people know about. He doesn't know about the other one, the last secret Nazareth Hospital ever had to keep.

6

Colette slurps a latte made in the machine that came with the flat. My mother drinks Ribena through a straw from a carton. They are so alike, birdy little women in leggings and scrunchies, shrunken in the double-height room. I feel like a double-height person next to them, strapping and outsized thanks to the strand of Viking that twists through my DNA.

"We could get used to this," says Colette, raising her mug. "Couldn't we, Mum?" Colette talks for both of them now. Debbie Smy, ward sister, Olympic-level gossiper, barely speaks from one hour to the next. I haven't had a proper conversation with her since the first stroke, which wasn't the first stroke at all but merely the first one they identified. Vascular dementia works by stealth, a series of tiny strokes, each one wiping out a little more dignity and memory.

"Sam not hanging around then?" She tilts her nose; I wince. This is my doing.

"He had to go back for work. I dropped him off at the station this morning."

I don't add that we missed his train by three minutes, a road closure in Stradbroke and the lights at the level crossing in Hoxne flashing for a good ten minutes before the train came past. Nusstead is in a kind of public transport Bermuda Triangle between three stations, each allegedly a forty-minute drive but it took an hour to get to Diss, over the border in Norfolk, this morning. Nazareth used to have its own branch line, ferrying patients straight from Ipswich, running through Nusstead to pick up workers on the way, but the tracks were pulled up a century ago and Nusstead Halt station was built over in the fifties. Maybe I should've gone south to Darsham or even direct to Ipswich. I'll need to develop some kind of internal algorithm to calibrate the length of the train journey versus the state of the roads. Which reminds me:

"When did Asylum Road get renamed?"

"When they started building. I don't know why they bothered. Everyone I know still calls it Asylum Road." Colette blows on her coffee. "I don't know how you can sleep here on your own. You know Kim Wittle from my year at school?" I don't, but nod anyway. "She went to London for a conference and the Airbnb she stayed in was made out of an old church they'd carved into flats. Overlooked a graveyard. Big old stained-glass blond Jesus on the cross over her bed, eyes following her around the room. She didn't get a *wink*. Went and checked into the Premier Inn in the end. I can't say I blame her. It's the same in here. I wouldn't be able to sleep, all the people who went mad over the years." She realizes what she's said. "I don't mean anything by it."

"I know."

She turns to face the window. "I mean. Look at all that lot down there with their racquets, acting like it's the most normal thing in the world to be playing tennis where that poor woman died."

I look over her shoulder. She's miles out. "Actually, those were exercise courts when it was built. Airing courts, they called them, for the patients to stretch their legs. That's probably one of the only places still being used for its original purpose. There's a proper memorial to her in the grounds. A rose garden."

"Her son must be, what, thirty-odd now, mustn't he? Poor sod. Doesn't bear thinking about." Colette doesn't like to hold an uncomfortable thought for long. She strokes the kitchen splashback.

"You've got those nice tiles. I want mine done like that, if I get the money. It's a rollover this weekend."

"If you won the lottery you could buy a place here," I suggest. "One of the villas, maybe." According to Oskar, very few of the units here have sold to Nussteaders. The locals are mostly priced out. The rest are incomers, commuters. A handful of second-homers like us.

"No thanks." Colette shudders. "You all right there, Mum?"

Our mother is staring out of the window, cloudy brown eyes fixed on the horizon. "One of those is our old house," I say. "I'll bring my binoculars from London next time, we should be able to see the village quite clearly. You can make out the war memorial if you really try."

"Did I ever tell you about when I was a kid, and the alarm went off?" It's the longest sentence I've heard my mother utter in months. Instantly, Colette and I fall silent. She told us this story countless times when we were young; like all good fairytales it's a warning wrapped in narrative.

"No!" I say. "Tell me now."

I hit the "record" button on my phone so that I can keep this story forever. Colette understands. Her face shakes with the effort of trying not to cry.

"I must've been about four," says Mum, squeezing the air out of her Ribena carton and watching in fascination as a bubble forms and pops on the end of her straw. "Some pedo, or a child molester as we called it in them days, got over the wall. He was still in what they used to call strong clothes, these awful sacking trousers they made the worst ones wear. God, the sound of that siren. You had instructions from your mum, whatever you was doing, whether you was in the street or out on the fen, as soon as you heard that noise you just *pelted* home. Like: awooooo . . ." She starts to imperson-ate the siren, her voice going slowly up, slowly down, a familiar sound from black-and-white films about the Blitz. It goes on for too long but neither of us have the heart to stop her. "You're lucky, you girls, you've lived a life without that noise. It chills you to the bone. They had an actual helicopter overhead, it was the first time most of the kids in the village had seen one and so we stopped running and started waving up at it. We was more excited about that than we was scared of the madman. Even then, nothing ever happened around here unless it was to do with the hospital."

The straw falls out of her carton and she tries unsuccessfully to push it back in through the little hole in the foil, screwing up her face in frustration as she misses. "Did they catch the man?" says Colette, even though we know that they found him in the Scout hut within the hour.

"What man?" asks Mum. It's as though the last couple of minutes never happened. "What man?" She tries to insert the straw again, then glares at Colette with a child's frustration. I end the recording, knowing that if there ever comes a time I can bear to replay this, I'll have to stop a few seconds before the end.

"Nothing," says Colette, tucking the straw back in its hole and squeezing Mum's shoulder. While I've been lecturing on the Queen Anne revival or the Garden City movement, Colette's been cleaning and wiping and comforting. Sam's right. I need to be here. I should have been here months ago. It's not only my mother who needs looking after.

"Hey, Marianne, speaking of lock up your daughters," says Colette, "Jesse was asking after you in the pub last night. He's single again, as of last month."

My heart rocks. "Oh God, really?" Jesse is always more dangerous when he isn't tethered to a girlfriend.

"Well, as far as I know he managed to get out of this relationship without getting anyone pregnant, so that's progress."

"Ha." Then it hits me. "*Please* tell me you didn't tell him about this place."

I can tell by her face that she has. That's that, then. This isn't just downplaying where I went on holiday this year. You can't hide a second home. I sip my coffee and wish it were wine.

"Jesse knew I had a flat down here before *I* did?" I groan. "I thought Sam swore you to secrecy."

"Yeah, from *you*. What's the big deal? He was glad you'd done so well for yourself. I'm sorry." For a second she is not a capable nurse, wife and mother but my baby sister again, hiding her hurt in a sulk. She resented not *that* I left—youth unemployment in rural communities is even worse now than when I was kid; so many people have to leave Nusstead to find work that the primary school is constantly threatened with closure—but *how* I did it.

Then she relents and even giggles, so I see a flash of her girl-hood crush on Jesse. "He got me tiddly. He must be flush at the moment, he got a round in for once in his tightarse life." I should be relieved but whatever he's done to come into money, it won't last long. If he won the lottery, he would be all over the press with the giant check for seven figures, then a year later he'd be selling his riches-to-rags story to the same papers for £500. "Anyway, what did you expect? That you'd be living round the corner and he wouldn't find out?"

Ideally, yes, but this is Nusstead where the downside of community is the forfeit of privacy. She's right. And maybe it's better, after all, that he heard on the grapevine. This way he can work through his grudges on his own.

"I think it's sweet, really," says Colette. "The way you're still fond after all these years."

There is nothing I can say to that and I'm almost glad when Mum interrupts.

"I can hear you and him, you know, fumbling around on the sofa downstairs." She's back in the room, if not the present. "You're not as quiet as you think you are. I wasn't born yesterday. Are you using protection?" I look at Colette in half-amused horror. Thank God Sam isn't around for this. "Mind you," she continues as Colette bites her lip to trap the laughter, "he tries hard, I suppose. I think he felt like he had to, after what happened to the brother. Feels like he's got to make up for it. You know the one that went to prison, him that looks like a potato, you know he got done for selling drugs? As for whatshisface who works on the cruise ships, have you *seen* his hairstyle? Promise me you won't end up with him,

Marianne? You want to get yourself a career, get out of Nusstead and get yourself a proper boyfriend."

I squeeze her bony little hands in mine. "I will," I say, because I want to make her happy, and because it's easy to make a promise you've already kept.

7

"Just a crack, let some air in." I open the window even though I know Mum will shut it the second my back's turned. There's an institutional fug in Colette's house. It's only twelve degrees outside but the heating's on so high it's hard to breathe. Maybe Mum likes it warm because our old house was so cold but as a Londoner it seems like an insult to the beautiful fresh air round here not to breathe in as much as possible.

Colette is out shopping, acting as though I've handed her a week in Ibiza. I didn't realize it had got to the stage where going to Aldi on her own counts as a treat. I help Mum wash her hands, clean the toilet after she's missed a bit, check she's wiped herself properly and get the place tidy before parking her in front of *Come Dine with Me*. I can power through these jobs because I'm not worn down by them like Colette is. I've got time to put on a load of washing, clean the inside of the fridge, put the Dyson round and even get dusting. Mum has her own shelf on the living room unit, above Colette's books and underneath Maisie's and Jack's sports trophies. It's crammed with porcelain knick-knacks and our childhood pictures in silver frames. There's one of me the summer before I got together with Jesse, all freckles and rosy cheeks, not so much about to bloom as to burst.

I take a break to check in with Honor online. She's posted some arty shots of the Royal Vauxhall Tavern at sunrise. They're beautiful photos but I can't enjoy them as I know she can only see the pub if she hangs out of her window at a death-defying angle. There's a new artwork too and for once I love what I see: she's made a human brain from old pills and blister packs. I write underneath it, *Proud of you sweetheart! Mum. X*

She texts me by return.

Can you please stop commenting on my Instagram? It looks really unprofessional. I had to delete it.

I *literally* have a degree in History of Art! This is a professional opinion.

At least stop signing them Mum.

She signs off with a smiley emoji, an embarrassed emoji and an old woman emoji to show she doesn't really mean it.

According to Colette's page-long instructions, twelve noon is time for lunch.

Be strict—make sure she eats at least 2/3 of what's on her plate.

Mum's tastes have reverted to those not of her childhood but of mine: she lives on a revolving menu of Heinz tomato soup, Fray Bentos pies and, today, fish fingers, which I burn under Colette's unfamiliar grill. Mum still sits up straight and holds her cutlery like she's eating at some kind of state banquet. I wonder how many times I was reminded as a child that manners cost nothing. She's proper, my mother: born a generation earlier and she'd have been donkey-stoning her doorstep every morning. Now, she dabs at the corner of her mouth with a sheet of kitchen roll like it's an Egyptian cotton napkin, a tiny dignity that breaks my heart. When she's finished she pushes her plate away. I peel the top off a child-sized yogurt. Mum holds the spoon and doesn't know what to do with it. She can switch between capability and helplessness a dozen times in a minute. After some brief marveling, she holds it in her fist and looks at me, her hopeful blink asking for confirmation she's doing it right. I nod my encouragement. "It's strawberry flavored."

"Don't patronize me," she barks. "I'm not a complete fucking idiot."

Anyone who tells you caring for someone with dementia is like looking after a baby doesn't know what they're talking about. Babies are fat little balls of possibility. Here, the opposite is true. All the drudgery with none of the portability and none of the potential: just an impossible parcel of grief in the post.

As Colette opens the front door I wonder how she is still sane. The clue is in the shopping bags she dumps on the worktop: a liter-bottle of gin, green with promise.

"Thanks, love," says Colette, untying the tea towel round Mum's neck before I have a chance to.

"Don't keep saying thanks. It makes it sound like she's your job. The whole point of my coming down here, surely, is that it's *our* job."

I can see from Colette's face that this *is* her job; that actually she's reluctant to share. I get it: I was like that when Honor was born. This is one comparison with raising babies that does stand up. The night feeds were *mine*.

"Where's your car?"

"Up at the hospital."

Colette laughs. "How long are you going to keep calling it a hospital? It hasn't been a hospital since the eighties."

"I can't bring myself to call it Park Royal Manor. It's such estate agent wankiness."

"At least call it the flat, then. There's enough talk of hospitals in this house without you throwing another one into the mix. Anyway, why *did* you leave the car there? D'you want a lift?"

"I fancied a walk, through the fen." Colette looks at me like I intend to nip to France by swimming the channel. "I just want to clear my head, OK? See you tomorrow."

Outside I take a deep, cleansing breath. There is more sky in this part of the world than seems possible, as though the earth itself must be super-convex to show you this much all at once.

When I was a child, you could not walk from Nusstead to Nazareth. The wetlands were a natural moat between the asylum and the town. A few years ago, the fen—one of only three in Suffolk—was made a nature reserve and wooden sleepers were laid end to end to make a three-mile path through it. It feels like cheating, almost, to be able to tread this path: to be so high above the reeds. The boardwalk is just wide enough for two adults to pass, but for all the campaigning for its construction, there is no one else out walking. Reeds gossip in hushed tones. Black eels writhe alongside me, ink that shapeshifts from comma to dash and back again.

I loosen my hair to get rid of the smell of Birds Eye fish fingers. I take the air deep into my lungs, thinking, I'll bank this for when I go back to London. When will I go back to London, though? If Honor comes to me, if we can make that a regular thing, there's no need to return this side of Christmas. To walk this landscape, whose lack of features is a feature, is a homecoming. *I live here again*. Despite everything, there is a rightness to being here, a completeness. Just as my feet have found their rhythm, a shallow rise lifts the land out of the fen and into stubbled fields, the sleepers replaced by dirt tracks. I pass under a buzzing pylon. Knee-high grass flattens at my tread and there isn't a footprint before me. Every now and then I see a little acorned sign that lets me know I'm still on the public footpath, as though there isn't a hulking great tower pointing the way. I steel myself and raise my eyes to the horizon. I manage to keep them on the clocktower for ten whole seconds. It helps, of course, that it's a reconstruction, and foolishly I feel that I have the advantage by approaching from the rear, as though I'm getting one up on the place. Stupid, really. A place can't be out to get you and stones don't tell stories.

My thoughts turn back to Jesse. Next time I see him I won't have an excuse to cut the conversation short before intimacy rears its ugly head. I've tended to shuttle between Eye, Ipswich Hospital and Colette's house. We have wound down our relationship to snatched conversation on the street. For a while, every now and then, one of us would turn to the other for a favor, a quality-control test for our blood pact. There have been tiny things, like when my car ran out of oil on the A11, and big ones, like the fiasco with the DNA testing. But that hasn't happened for years now. It looks like an organic drifting apart of two old friends: it is not. I have been pulling away for years, so slowly that I don't think Jesse has noticed.

Colette is wrong. What binds us is not fondness, not residual teenage tenderness. We keep each other sweet because we have to. On a bad day, I worry he'll casually let the whole thing slip to his brother or a colleague over a pint. Other days, I would trust Jesse's silence over even Sam's fidelity or Honor's need for me. But it's a three-way pact of course, a sick little eternal triangle with Jesse and I at either corner of the strong base and Helen Greenlaw, the real monster under Nusstead's bed, the unknowable third point. And when I think of her I realize our foundations are as solid as the fen.

8

I'm getting used to the place. I can approach it now without feeling sick. It helps that those huge warped wooden doors are gone. I like the transparency as well as the practicality of the sliding glass. There's a straggle of women coming through now, yoga mats under their arms. They part to reveal a man, his back to the entrance, dressed head to toe in black, and my heart loses its balance. I twist the rings on my left hand so that the diamonds are on the inside and the platinum bands can pass for silver. He's losing his hair. His pate catches the light between strands so raven-black they must be dyed. I'm not surprised: I never thought he would go gently into that particular dark night.

OK. So. I'll tell him that we're only renting this flat for a couple of months, that if Colette told him it was a second home she was mistaken.

"Jesse." He turns round slowly and for a split second we're both seventeen again. The ruled lines on his brow have deepened but his smile is still youthful; he always had the whitest teeth, the pinkest lips. I used to know that mouth better than I knew my own.

"Babe." No one else ever called me that and I wish he'd find a new term of endearment. It's what he called Michelle. I close my eyes against the image of Michelle's face, of her bright colors; orange, pink, blue, so out of place against the washed-out grays and buffs of Nazareth.

Jesse chucks me under the chin, a weirdly paternal gesture that's more intimate than a hug. I don't know what to call the pang I still feel when I touch him: even our desire is unevenly weighted. The mercy fuck after the funeral set a precedent, made Jesse think it was always on the table, but I wouldn't do that to Sam. It's bad enough he doesn't know what his wife is capable of without making a cuckold of him too. Jesse, of course, would relish this ultimate one-upmanship. I would only have to say the word, only have to undo a single button, to have him again.

"You look beautiful," he says, and I love him for not using the word *still*. Oskar is all ears behind his elaborate floral display. Jesse opens his mouth then closes it again, an old habit that means he's working himself up to saying something important. He gulped air like this before all his big declarations: *I'm in love with you* or *I've got this mad idea* or *Please, babe, please don't leave me to deal with this on my own.*

"Aren't you gonna ask me in?" I think for a second it's something he's saying for old times' sake, because it's what he used to say to me outside my old house on Main Street, before I realize he needs my permission to enter. "Couldn't get past this jobsworth. It was easier to get in here when it was an asylum! He's only a fucking glorified receptionist. He's not even *from* round here."

"Sorry, Oskar. I'll sign him in." Declaring it makes it feel less clandestine. I log Jesse's car, a red Audi TT parked in one of the guest bays. Colette was right; he must have a few quid at the moment. He's about the age to have paid off his mortgage. Park Royal Manor aside, houses round here are affordable even on a modest salary, and Jesse has never been out of work.

We wait for the lift. He smells like he always did. Soap and leather and engine oil. He's done himself a disservice with the dye job; gray hair would suit him. When he was young his coloring was almost too high—only his strong features stopped him looking like he was wearing makeup—but sprinkles of white in his eyebrows and stubble have softened the effect.

"I always knew you'd come home eventually."

"It's not forever, it's just till my mum . . ." the words dribble out.

"Oh, babe, I know. We're at the age for it, aren't we? Every other conversation I have is about someone's parents dying. Circle of life. I mean, grandchildren take the edge off it. I'll show you a picture of Madison's littl'un later. Corey. He's two now, into everything."

I should ask after the rest of his children, but I can never remember who he still sees and who is estranged. The arrow on the lift display swivels from up to down.

"How's Clay?" It's a name I drop gently.

Jesse blows out his cheeks. "He's a nightmare, isn't he? Seems to be on an even keel but you never bloody know with him." It's a bitter irony that despite Jesse's job—he might not be a mental health nurse like his own father, but ambulance crews regularly ferry sectioned patients to hospital—when mental illness strikes close to home, his attitude is more "snap out of it" than "talk it out." Our background, of course, might have something to do with that.

"And Mark and Trish?"

"Mumanddad?" He has always run his parents together in a portmanteau as if to underline how tight they are as a couple. It was what he expected for us. He blames the breakup on what happened rather than on me, and it's a fiction I indulge in a way that's equal parts kindness and cowardice. "They're all right, all things considered. You know she's basically housebound now? They'd like to see you, I reckon, while you're down. You can't use your old flying-visit excuse this time."

I can't believe he's asked me this. How could I look them in the face, after what I did to their son? "I—ah—I don't know, that might be a bit weird?"

"Suit yourself. The kettle's always on round theirs." The lift doors sigh open. This might be my home but he ushers me into it, still a vestige of his proprietary feelings over this place, and over me. We meet each other's eyes in the mirror and with little mouth-only smiles acknowledge the softening and thickening of our reflections. I know what he's thinking: we still make a good couple.

"How's Honor?"

"Also on an even keel. She's doing a BA." I realize as soon as I've spoken that the acronym is lost on him but to explain would be condescending. "Goldsmith's college, in south London. She's doing an installation where she tattoos bits of leather. Still, if she's dragging a needle through an old leather handbag, she's not cutting herself. Colette told you she was in the Larches?" Jesse nods. I don't need to explain what the Larches is. It's like the Priory or the Betty Ford Clinic; a household name, the place you pretend you're going to end up when you've overdone the prosecco at Christmas, the number six bus for our times. "She had a few awful years but her new medication seems to agree with her and she's been out for six months, no sign of a relapse, so . . ."

The lift lets us out into the gleaming corridor. Jesse steps out first. "Ah, that's brilliant," he says, although it's not clear which achievement he means. "Good girl. And what about Now That's What I Call Sam?" Jesse came up with this nickname after seeing the chart compilation CDs in my glovebox. Sam buys these instead of original albums. He has actually used the phrase *down with the kids* to explain this habit. I grant Jesse the thrill of contempt.

"Sam's fine." I don't mention the special school or last year's award.

"Let me get my bearings. Which side is this, anyway? Men's or women's?"

I stare at him. "Are you serious?" I can't believe that the layout of this building isn't imprinted on his brain like it is on mine. The thought of holes in Jesse's memory ought to comfort me, but it doesn't. I need to be known.

He checks the window. "I can see the villas from here. Which means this would've been the old seclusion room where . . ." The smile he drifts into is lascivious and I return a dilute version of it, keen to bury the bad memories under good ones. Once Jesse's through the door, though, and he takes in the high ceiling and all that awful bland bling, he seems to lose a couple of inches in height. The flat feels ready to further betray my wealth, as if the sprinkler system will suddenly start raining liquid gold. "This in't even your main house. Bloody hell, babe."

It tips the balance of power and although it should be in my favor, I feel like I'm the one on the back foot.

"Sit down," I say. "Let me get you a drink."

The sofa swallows him whole. A phone falls out of his jeans, an old-fashioned Nokia 8110 of the kind that Honor keeps threatening to get.

"Bloody thing," says Jesse, stuffing it back into his back pocket.

"That's a real museum piece. Haven't you got a smartphone?"

"Don't need one," he says. "I've got enough to look at out the window without staring at a screen all day. I can't get my kids to make eye contact as it is."

"Fair enough." I wonder whether it would have been different if we'd had the internet at our fingertips when we were kids. The obsolete teenage experiences of boredom, curiosity and naivety were a big part of it. Not that that excuses us. Nothing could excuse us.

"Tea?" I offer. "Coffee? I've got Nespresso."

"All right, Starbucks. Got any tins?"

I show him the toy soldiers of Becks in the fridge door. Jesse takes two, uncaps the first with a bottle-opener I hadn't noticed, fixed to the wall, and downs it in one. He peels at his label.

"Are you actually millionaires now, then?"

Here I go; a proper lie, but to save his pride. "It's only rented."

His cheeks lose their flush. What have I said? His hand is so tight around the bottle, his knuckles are white. He turns his body to the window, faces across the fen to Nusstead. "No it's not," he says quietly. "Madison's ex worked here as a sales negotiator. They sold the show home to an architect from London. Don't patronize me, Marianne."

Too late, I see that it would have been better to hurt him honestly.

"I'm not, I didn't . . ."

"All those times I've whinged about money and you've joined in, like we were both in the same boat. God, you must have been having a right laugh at my expense."

"Jesse, no, I never would. I just—I didn't want you to feel weird because I was living a—" I nearly say *better* but catch myself in time. "A different life to the one I'd have had with you."

A vein swims up his neck like an eel. "That's even worse!"

"Well, here you go—now you know, and you *are* being weird."

"I don't like being lied to by the *only* person in the world I can trust, all right? I mean, Jesus, the stuff we've kept between us. Even a little lie is big coming from you."

"I know. I'm sorry."

"However much you have, you'll always be Marianne Smy from Nusstead to me." He takes the glass out of my hand and puts his face close to mine. Heat pulls us together. I know Jesse's face when he's turned on and this isn't it: this is about power, a return to the one place we could still be equals. There is a desperate, frightened part of me that considers, for a second, offering myself up as an apology. When I put my hand on his chest, I can feel his heartbeat, fast as a child's. Before I notice him move, his hand is between my legs and there is our old attraction, proved in the pulse. It would be so easy. It would get him back on side. Then I think of Sam, and Honor.

"You know we work better as friends, now."

"We got too much dirt on each other not to be, I reckon," he says, but doesn't pull his hand away.

"Jesse, for fuck's sake!" At my push, he takes his hand away but my rings have slid around to the front and my biggest diamond has snagged on a hole in his sweater. We both watch as navy wool is tangled then pulled taut by the flashing stone, unraveling to expose the flesh underneath. There's an excruciating moment where he sucks in his belly while I disentangle myself. I wait for his apology but there's only challenge in his eyes.

"I want you to go."

He holds up both hands in a mockery of defeat and backs away, letting himself out. There's a tuft of dark wool caught between two tiny diamonds in my eternity ring and my hands are shaking too much to pull it out. What the hell just happened?

9

Honor's face fills the screen, rainbow disarray behind her. Her new place is in Vauxhall, a tatty little enclave between new developments two minutes' walk south of the Thames. Even vulnerable students don't quality for halls of residence in their second year, and the hours Honor keeps and her need to control her environment means it suits her to live alone. Her hair is a baby blue this week, there's steel in her nose, rose-gold in her septum and her eyebrows. It is always uncanny to see my own face rejuvenated and then defaced.

There's something strange hanging from a clothesline over her shoulder: I'm about to tell her that bedlinen will never dry folded up like that when I realize the dirty pink "pillowcase" is made of leather, and that it still has its trotters and a tail.

"Honor, what the *hell* is that?"

She deflects the question with concern of her own. "You've been crying!" It's not a tactic; her concern is genuine, and unexpected. After Jesse stormed out of the flat without apology, I howled. I thought I'd done a good job covering my red eyes with makeup and low lighting.

"Just a bit tired, that's all." I never let Honor see me distressed; the tiniest thing can trigger a downswing. "Honor, is that a *pig*?"

"I'd be the same if you were ill," she says, her chin puckering.

Guilt stamps down hard; of course she thinks I've been crying for my mother. "Poor Mum. Do you want to talk about it?" How many times have I asked her that question, through keyholes, over bad phone lines, at hospital bedsides? I shake my head. Honor chews her lip for a bit then changes tack. "Let's see the new flat then." She rubs her hands together. "Is it Gothic as hell? Padded cells and straitjackets, dungeons, manacles dangling from the ceiling?"

"Hardly." I turn the iPad face-out and scan across the sitting room and kitchen.

"Oh, this is *very* disappointing. They haven't even left the bars on the windows. That sofa is disgusting. *Disgusting.* How can you live with that repro painting, Mum? It's dreadful, take it down *now,* it's going to give you cancer."

I start to laugh. "No can do. It's nailed to the wall."

"I like the lights, though, and the coffee machine. Oh, you've got those awful bougie metro tiles. What a wasted opportunity to let the character shine through."

"I don't think they'd shift many apartments if they'd left the bloodstained walls and rotting floor struts."

"*I'd* live there then."

"You're not their target market. It's a bit . . . footballers' wives."

"Is it full of nouves?" she asks gleefully. Honor is very keen on *authenticity.* Her world is all original this and artisan that, in an inverted version of the snobbery she perceives in me. I wanted the best of everything for her but still worried I'd breed a little snob, with the posh school and the piano lessons, but if anything she's swung the other way, delighting in what she calls her "working-class" roots. She can take or leave Sam's solidly middle-class family but loves her country cousins. It's a luxury born of privilege—she was never cold or hungry growing up—but I don't lecture her. With Honor, I choose my battles. When you know that some weeks it will take three hours to help your daughter to shower, when you have held her wrist so that she could type her coursework, when you've slept across the threshold of her bedroom so that you'll be there if she wakes and goes searching for sharp objects in the night again, social graces take a back seat.

"Honey, how many times? I'm a *massive* nouve. *You're* half-nouve." Honor laughs. I love it so much when she laughs. I lean in conspiratorially. "There's a lot of new money at Park Royal Manor. Some of them have even had to *buy their own jewelry*."

"Heaven forfend." She wrinkles her nose. "You'll be telling me they don't inherit their silver next."

"You look happy," I say, and it's the wrong thing: she doesn't like to think that her mood is being monitored.

"I'm fine," she says. "Don't waste your energy worrying about me. Save it all up for when I need it." She brushes her hair away from her face and bangles clank. Years of what she calls "therapeutic" cutting have left a pale cat's cradle of scores on her forearms. She's tattooed over the worst of them, and I can see them now without flinching, even the one on the inside crease of her right elbow where she sliced through a freckle that healed into a grotesque chocolate smear.

"You promise you're telling the truth?"

She returns my gaze so levelly that I wonder if the screen has frozen.

"Don't start."

I have told her, since she was old enough to understand, that she can always tell me the truth, that she *must* always tell me the truth. I'm aware of my gross hypocrisy. I interrogate myself about it; why do I insist she divulges everything when there is so much about me she can never know? I think the answer is this: if I foster a spirit of honesty then whatever happens, she can tell me. I am not a naive parent who thinks their child incapable of wrong. My experience shows me that anyone is capable of anything and I would forgive her anything. I would forgive Honor what I did, even though I can't forgive it in myself.

"Honor, can we talk about the skinned pig hanging about two feet behind you?"

"It's fine, the skin's been treated by a taxidermist."

"That's hardly the—" I give up. It'll be something else this time next week.

"Listen, Hon, your grandmother wants to see you." It's not true: she might not even recognize her. What I mean is, *I* want to see you. I *need* you. "Daddy's driving down on Friday night. You could get a lift."

"Love it. We can get busy with the CD player. I'll see you then."

She draws in to kiss the screen and for a moment her face is directly over my reflection, the same bone structure with all the padding of collagen. When she cuts the call the illusion is gone and I'm a middle-aged woman staring at her own sagging face. It takes me by surprise, the wave of grief I feel for Honor's early years; makes me catch my breath. Not just because she seemed happier then, but also because it was the one honest relationship I have ever had. If intimacy means being profoundly known and loved anyway then it can't describe my marriage or even the uneasy truce I have with Jesse. I have had four lovers in my life but the only true intimacy was with my baby daughter, the euphoria of knowing her essential needs and being able to fulfill them. Whatever I had with my own mother can't have been the exclusive, deliberate closeness I had with Honor. She was back at work six weeks after she had me. There was no maternity leave or compulsory child support in those days, even if my father had known of my existence.

People talk about apron strings as your child grows up but this image of a cotton ribbon doesn't capture the visceral wrench of a child who talks and then walks, inevitably away from you; when they go it's more like they're pulling out your veins through your wrists.

I still know her better than anyone and to understand what she goes through is to hold up a mirror to hell. I wondered, when Honor first fell ill, if madness was in my milk, but that thought was short-lived. Guilt is the poison in my bloodstream. My daughter is my karma, a flesh retribution. Not just that she is ill at all but the *nature* of her illness. Jesse was the superstitious one, the one who believed in heaven and hell and reincarnation but even I have to admit it doesn't feel like a coincidence.

When she attempted suicide, she didn't slash her wrist but took a cold new razor to the brachial artery. *Wrists are for pussies,* she said in hospital. The vertical slash shows you mean it; you'll bleed out a lot quicker that way. That's Honor: bright and focused and always with one eye on style, even in suicidal ideation.

The how was easy, the how she was almost proud of.

The why took longer, tangled in shame, drip-fed to me from a hospital bed. She'd read a text from Jesse on my phone, about DNA testing kits—always an issue when your progeny is as chaotic as his—and became gripped by the conviction that Sam wasn't her real father and I'd lied to them both her whole life. Her image of me shattered, and out came the blade.

"It was bad enough thinking I wasn't who I thought I was but the idea that *you* weren't who I thought you were was even worse."

Her reaction was out of all proportion, I know, but it was a fore-taste of what she might do if the worst truth ever came out. The suspicion of a lie had her reaching for the razor; the truth could, literally, kill her. And so I protect her at twenty, just as—more so—I did at two, ten, twelve. Colette and Sam call it smothering but they weren't there, they only saw the bandages. The world is full of sharp objects, and pain and secrets run red and blue under soft thin skin.

IO

The Crown hasn't changed since I was a teenager, with its frosted windows that wives can't see through, etched with a brewery logo. I'm sticking to the dress code in my hoodie and tracksuit bottoms. I feel surprisingly at home. Or perhaps I stick out like a sore thumb and I'm just deluding myself, the way that no one thinks *they* have an accent.

I'm sitting in the "beer garden," six picnic tables on a concrete forecourt. From here, Nusstead is pretty and quaint. You can't park on Main Street, and only the satellite dishes on the terrace betray the century. The "new" houses, where Jesse grew up and still lives, and the old Social, lie low behind tall chimneys. A couple of teenagers are snogging in the poppies on the memorial. The fishwife tut on my tongue is pure Debbie Smy.

The text that summoned me here said *I've got something important to say* and I should think so too. Jesse's at the bar buying me a half of Suffolk cider. I can see him through the open door, clearly rehearsing his apology as he waits at the bar, foot on the brass rail, tenner rolled up in his hand. I wonder how he'll phrase it: *I'm sorry for coming on to you,* perhaps, or *I don't know what I was thinking.* And I ought to offer one of my own. I can't deny I was clumsy and I don't mind backing down if it re-spins our web.

"Some things never change," says Jesse, nodding at the teenage couple. "Brings it all back, innit?"

Does he mean us? I never kissed Jesse in public like that. I wonder if he's remembering Michelle, or if I'm remembering Michelle and Clay. For all Clay's resemblance to Jesse, it's Michelle's face that haunts, her body that made me shiver and turn away at the time. I remember how Clay raked his fingers through her hair and my hand goes to the threads of gray at my own temple. Michelle's bright red hair never had a chance to fade.

"I suppose so." I want to thaw the frost but find myself returning it. "What did you want to say to me?"

"I'm sorry for—you know." He slides his hand, palm up, across the table and for a moment I think he expects me to hold it, but then he beckons in an imitation of goosing me. It's an inelegant apology, but I accept with a smile.

"I'm sorry too. Not for buying the flat, but for lying to you about it. I won't do it again."

"Good." I can tell he respects my honesty. "Because we have to be straight with each other, you and me. I've lied to every woman I've ever been with, and you're not exactly upfront with Sam. This is supposed to be, like . . ." He motions a circle on the table.

"Safe space?"

It's clearly the first time he's heard this hackneyed expression. "Exactly. Safe space. Yeah. That's what I texted you about." He drops his eyes. "It's what I came to tell you about yesterday and then it all went weird. I had a thought; more than a thought, really. About Greenlaw."

The words are bullets, tearing through thirty years of scar tissue. It feels like this has come out of nowhere but of course there's no such place as nowhere. Helen Greenlaw has been the subtext of every conversation we have ever had since the last night in Nazareth.

"What's happened?" My heart is a lab rat, my ribs its cage.

"She's still going to the House of Lords. Did you know that?"

Why can't he ever answer me straight? "Of course I know." There can't be a political journalist in this country who has followed her stellar career as closely as I have. I know everything she's done, every clueless bullying public health initiative she's launched, her cynicism in crossing the floor. I'm trying to compensate for failing to pin down her first crime—her original sin, as I think of it. There's that saying about politicians, that anyone who craves political power should by default be excluded from office, only in her case it's truer than the public knows.

"You *know* I know. Jesse. What's happened?"

My mind trips to doublethink: theories I believe in even as I know they can't be true. Something was uncovered, something was found during the development of Nazareth. Or someone has spotted me and knows. Someone has seen old records, old names, and put two and two together to make the four that implicates the three—me, Jesse and Helen Greenlaw.

She would write off our lives to save her reputation. That much I *do* know.

"She's still voting on things." Jesse slaps the table, seemingly oblivious to my rising panic. "That fucking woman, still making choices from her fucking throne that affect the real lives of real people. Still playing at politics."

She was never playing. "Jesse! Will you get to the point. Has Greenlaw done something? Has she contacted you?"

"No. She wouldn't, would she? She's got more to lose than either of us."

"So someone outside the three of us knows."

"No, babe." He's almost scornful. "How could they?"

"Will you *stop* all this mind-game bollocks? Because unless there's literally a direct threat from her, Helen Greenlaw is the last person I want to think about right now, to be honest with you. I don't know if you've noticed, but I've got quite a lot on my mind."

I might as well not have spoken.

"*She's* a millionaire."

"A lot of people in the House of Lords are." I intended it to soothe: it comes out airily, and I've tipped him back into bitterness again.

"I suppose you move in that world now." He prints a caterpillar with the base of his pint glass.

"I really don't. Jesse, where's this going?"

"You've *changed*. Money's changed you." He is, as my students would say, *othering* me. It suits us to believe that poverty desensitizes or that privilege insulates but only someone who has had both can understand that is not the case. "You're hard," he says. "Like *her*."

It's the worst thing he could throw at me and he knows it. "I am not—I'm *nothing* like her! How can you say that?"

"Prove it, then. Prove I can trust you. Prove you're still on my side."

"How?"

"We were idiots to stop when we did. I think we can tap her again." I feel suddenly very weak, as though I want to put my head on the dirty table and fall asleep. "And I need your help, babe. You knew the right words before."

"Have you gone *mental*? Jess, no, of course not." His face clouds over. He expected me to say yes; this has hurt him.

"You said, that night, that we were bound together forever."

Did I? "What I would have meant was that we're tied together by the secret, and whether we like it or not, we're tangled up with her, too." I lower my voice, lean in close. "You pull one string, it all goes to shit. We'd *all three of us* go to prison. And then there's the small matter of proof. We don't *have* any. Don't you remember what happened?"

He loses focus for a moment, so obviously remembering the flare that I can almost see it reflected in his pupil.

"If you've got money problems . . ." I know it's stupid as soon as I've said it. The Brames were always incredibly proud; they wouldn't even buy from catalogues. Jesse explodes.

"I've always provided for my family, don't cast aspersions on my ability to do that. It's the principle. Redistribution of wealth." He illustrates his point with a sweep of his arm; his glass tips onto the concrete, the smashing glass parting the teenagers at the war memorial. The girl, I realize with a shock, is Maisie. She sees me, blushes and runs. Jesse lowers his voice, compressing anger into every velvet word. "Helen Greenlaw, right, lives in luxury at the expense of the working man. And she destroyed a *town*."

"It's exactly this line of thought that got us into trouble in the first place. What are you going to do this time, doorstep her at the House of Lords?" I laugh, but he doesn't join in. He is just as entrenched in his vendetta as he was as a teenager.

"I'm going after her again, Marianne, and if I mean anything to you, you'll come in with me." Tears in his eyes undermine the threat. A few years ago he said I was still the only woman who'd ever seen him cry and I jump on that vulnerability. He's got as much to lose—not materially but in terms of family—as I have.

"I want you to do one thing for me," I say. I take his hand and stroke it. It seems to anchor him. "I want you to picture your parents' faces when the police come for you, and they have to lose another son. OK? I want you to imagine Clay finding out. Madison. *All* your kids. Picture their faces. Imagine playing with Corey in some shitty family room in prison." He twists his face up and turns it away. "Jesse, *promise* me you'll leave it."

He snatches his hand away. "All right. Forget it, babe. Forget I said anything. Forget I asked you. God! How can one woman have so much to answer for?" He sweeps his hand toward the pub. "All these men'd be in work if it weren't for her. *We'd* still be together." His assured tone presumes an agreed, self-evident truth but still I'm stunned to hear him say it; I thought it was on the list of things we knew but never talked about. My face changes shape—I feel the air in my mouth—before I can work out an appropriate arrangement of my features. Will a wistfully tilted head, a long slow exhalation, even good old-fashioned dropped eye contact get me off the hook? While I'm running through the options, I am wide open for Jesse to read. "Wouldn't we?" he says, in a voice that sounds like someone's got his balls in their hand.

Too late, I snap on the wrong sort of smile. "Of course we would." My words are pale, pathetic. Jesse can't dissemble in time either. He looks punctured, from the hollowing of his cheeks to the way his body retreats into his leather jacket. I can read his thoughts as clearly as if he had spoken them. My slow reaction has undone something he has believed for over half his life and I can see now just how much he has built his life on that belief. If he can't blame Greenlaw for my leaving, then he has no choice but to blame me, and it hurts more, not less, for the years that have passed.

11

The lasagna I made from scratch bubbles in the oven and I'm crushing Mum's yellow pill to put in her yogurt when the kids bring the house back to noisy life. Jack, bumfluff beard and long hair up in a man-bun, dumps a stack of books on the kitchen table; he's doing all three sciences at A level. He wants to be an engineer like his dad. Maisie's hair is wet from swimming and she won't meet my eye.

"All right, Nan?" Jack squeezes my mother's hand.

"Look at you!" Mum says. "So handsome."

Colette brings up the rear. When she drops her carrier bags on the worktop, there's the telltale chink of glass on glass. I don't miss the look that passes between Jack and Maisie. Colette watches me rock the teaspoon from side to side; she doesn't quite trust me to get the powder fine enough. "Did you catch up with Jesse?"

"Mm-hm. We had a drink at the Crown." I wink at Maisie to tell her I'm going to keep her secret. She blushes scarlet. Good. My silence buys hers. This isn't the kind of thing I want her to let slip to Honor on social media, or to Sam next time she sees him.

"Anyway, I ask because I just saw him in the *library* of all places," says Colette.

"I thought they shut the library down." I vaguely remember signing an online petition a couple of years ago. Colette is always for-

58

warding petitions about our hometown and I always sign them: raise funds for the fen walkway, get a proper barrier at the level crossing, save our school from cuts.

"No—well, they did, but then volunteers opened it up again," she says, taking the spoon from my hand and stirring the yogurt through. "He *really* wants to sort his hair out. It's turning into an actual comb-over, you could see Big Ben through the gaps in it. There comes a time when men have just got to buzz it all off, d'you know what I mean? When Bryan started to recede—"

"Hang on—Big Ben?"

"The Houses of Parliament, whatever it's called. That's what was on his screen," says Colette. "When Bryan started thinning I bought him a pair of clippers for Father's Day and he hasn't looked back since."

An early warning system goes off somewhere inside me, as unignorable as the old Nazareth siren. I remember my own words: what are you going to do, doorstep her at the House of Lords? He wouldn't. Not after I told him how much it would devastate the Brames if we got found out. Not after everything we said about trust.

"Colette, have you got any wine in for supper?" I ask, knowing that she hasn't.

"*Supper!*" she says. "Listen to yourself. It's tea in this house. And the answer's no. Got six kinds of gin, though."

"Mother's ruin," says Jack.

"I'll ruin *you* if you don't start your homework."

"I fancy a glass of wine with that lasagna," I say. "I might go and pick up a bottle of rosé from the co-op."

It's a two-minute walk to the library, a prefab shack built at the same time as the estate and the Social. On the way, my breath mists in the dark. It could be anything, I tell myself; it could be a coincidence that he's online looking up the Houses of Parliament.

The poster advertising free Wi-Fi is hand drawn. A yellow mountain bike is propped against the wall. The rider hasn't bothered to lock it. The plate-glass window frames a bank of computers.

Jesse has his back to me, close enough for me to read the screen over his shoulder. Colette's right. Under the harsh striplight of the library, his hair is a series of rope bridges across his crown. He's on a web page entitled *House of Lords: They Work for You*. His hand is curled around a pencil and he's shielding his page like a child who doesn't want his classmate to copy his spelling test. I wonder why he can't just look it up on his phone like a normal person, then remember he doesn't believe in smartphones. Unless he doesn't want this search showing up on his home computer . . .

Baroness Greenlaw of Dunwich's fine-boned face is in the corner of the screen. I step to the left, the better to read the screen, and knock over the bicycle. It clatters to the ground and I back against the wall just in time. Jesse comes and presses his face to the window. I'm sure that the trail of my breath must give me away. He looks and looks but sees nothing, eventually returning to his desk. He shuts down a screen extolling the virtues of 10,000 steps a day and replaces it with a street map of Westminster.

How *dare* he accuse me of betrayal and then do this? He is jeopardizing *my* family, *my* future, as well as his own, not to mention Greenlaw's. His hypocrisy is staggering but his stupidity is worse, and there is no one I can talk to about it, no one I can ask for help. I slide down the wall until I'm sitting on freezing paving stones and after a minute's self-indulgent crying it hits me that of course there *is* someone I can turn to.

Whatever is wrong with Greenlaw—and there is plenty—she will go to great lengths to keep her past a secret, and she only becomes stronger when cornered. I can either side with the woman whose instinct for self-preservation overrides everything else, even human life, or the man who says he loves me but who is hell-bent on self-destruction. Jesse acting alone changes everything. She was public enemy number one, and then our private conspirator. Now, either I am Helen Greenlaw's savior or she is mine.

12

There was only one explicit term of our agreement with Helen Greenlaw: we should have no contact afterward. I'm about to break a vow I made a lifetime ago, with no real sense of what I hope to achieve in doing so. The transgression of getting in touch feels big enough for now.

I know she keeps a London flat—famously, she still walks to and from Westminster every day—but according to the electoral roll she pays council tax at Greenlaw Hall on the coast. It appears that Damian and his family live there too; evidently their estrangement is over. He must have one eye on his inheritance. Of her London address, I can find no trace. In a phone call to the House of Lords I'm informed by a receptionist with the kind of voice that suggests he'll carry an umbrella and wear a bowler hat as he commutes home on the Clapham omnibus, that I'm welcome to leave a note for Baroness Greenlaw. It will be written on a piece of paper, pinned to a messageboard that all the peers pass daily. It is suggested, however, that email is the fastest way to contact a peer these days although they vary in their responses to "the new software." I find Greenlaw's email address in three clicks. The message I compose takes me very much longer. Jesse was wrong about the right words coming easily. They must be both precise and vague enough to tell her who I am without fixing myself to the crime scene.

Dear Baroness Greenlaw,

My name is Marianne Thackeray, née Smy. We met near Nusstead in 1989. There is something important I need to say to you. Please can you email me as soon as possible?

Will that be enough? I know *I* would know from the wording exactly the night in question. It depends how close to Greenlaw's surface the past lies.

Yours sincerely,
Marianne Thackeray

I press send, want to throw up, rise from my chair, stretch, and click a coffee pod into the machine. I wonder how frequently an eighty-year-old woman checks her emails. I'll give it until the weekend and then I'll . . . what?

My inbox pings before the coffee has brewed.

I will see you for tea at the House tomorrow. Meet me at the Peers' Entrance at 3 p.m. My mobile telephone number is below. Please reply with your own.
Sincerely,
Helen Greenlaw

I wouldn't expect warmth from Greenlaw but the terse authoritarianism still pulls me up short. There are not enough lines to read between, but the rapidity of her response is both reassuring—she is taking this seriously, she hasn't dismissed me—and unsettling—she is too ready to agree. I feel another wave of fury that Jesse has driven me to this.

I accept her invitation, add my number and send the message, and only then remember that Honor is coming down tomorrow and I've made Sam take the afternoon off to drive her. I don't think I have ever canceled plans with Honor and if I do so now my family will know that something is wrong. Not the truth of course, but they might think I'm unwell, that I'm traveling up for some kind of test or treatment. Amanda did that when she had breast cancer, didn't tell her kids for the first six months. We had to cover for her if they called her at work.

The memory gives me an idea.

"Good timing," says Sam when at last he picks up his phone. "Just this second come out of a meeting."

This is how it begins, the first shot of silk for a new web of lies. "Bit of a change of plan for tomorrow," I say. "Amanda's asked me to come into the department for a staff training day."

The silence on the line is as close as Sam ever comes to losing his temper. "You texted literally yesterday saying we had to be there for six. I've rearranged the whole week for you. I moved a client meeting for—you said it was . . ." His office door clicks behind him. "Marianne, you'll have to miss it—you're supposed to be on sabbatical. I've half a mind to ring Amanda myself and tell her to leave you alone."

"No!" I make a mental note to brief Amanda about the lie, which means inventing a cover story for her too. "I'm sorry. But they're introducing a completely new system and there's only this one training day. You know what it's like. If I don't get up to speed now it'll take me days when I get back. You and Honor can still come, we'll just eat late." If he insists on driving, I might even be there and back by the time they get through the traffic.

I can hear the effort it takes Sam to control his voice. "Marianne, the whole point—the whole point of my sinking every penny we have into this place is so that you can look after your mother without being stretched by work as well. You're making yourself sick. You can't do this."

I scoop up my anger at Jesse and throw it at my husband. "Are you *forbidding* me?"

I picture Sam in his glass office, pinching the bridge of his nose. "Don't be ridiculous, of course I'm not. I didn't think you'd be racing back up to London at the drop of a hat, that's all. I'm *worried* about you."

"I just want to keep my hand in, all right? I want a career to come back to, after all this is over. You said yourself we can't afford to run two houses indefinitely."

Another low blow that puts the onus back on him.

That evening, sleep is elusive. The floodlight from the old airing court shines through a gap in the curtains and picks out the ceramic brickwork in the en-suite. The cold, utilitarian feature no longer seems like a design cliché but offensive, grotesque, mocking. A tile for every frightened woman, a tile for every cruel nurse, a tile for every tablet they made the patients take, tiles and tiles and tiles building to a wall that's too high to vault, wider than Buckingham Palace and no matter how fast you run you can never get to the end. I get up and slam the door on them but in the true dark of my bedroom the tiles continue to move and shift about like blocks in a game of Tetris. They brick me into a shallow sleep from which I flail awake, at 2 a.m., by the thought that perhaps Helen Greenlaw is so keen to see me because Jesse—somehow—has got to her already.

Now, in the charcoal dark, I understand completely why I am going to see Helen Greenlaw. I need to know what she will do: whether she will join me in ensuring we take our secret to our graves, or whether she intends to let Jesse tear it all down. I can no more see her siding with Jesse than him making good on his threat in the first place, and yet. If we are to be exposed, then I must come clean to Sam and Honor before the police come for me. The only thing worse than seeing Honor's face when I tell her what I have done, and what I have covered up, would be not being there to soften the blow with explanations and love. I kick off the covers, walk to the window and look out upon the dark fen that stands between Nazareth and Nusstead, and for the first time in years, in the place where everything happened, I start to rehearse my confession.

13

London is performing well for the tourists, the spikes of the Palace of Westminster shining gold against a blue October sky. Long before I had studied Augustus Pugin and Charles Barry, the Gothic points were familiar from bottles of brown sauce, and it was a long time before I could picture the place without thinking about pork chops and boiled potatoes. Armed police patrol Parliament Square and Millbank but the Peers' Entrance to the House of Lords is almost comically twee; a policeman in full dress uniform sits in a little black wooden tollbooth. I'm dressed in my most conservative clothes, a navy wrap dress and nude court shoes. Today I'm wearing my diamonds on the outside.

It's dim in the entrance hall, after the brightness of the street. I'm aware, as so often in my work, that this is a public-owned place that most of the public will never see. Once through security the atmosphere is more like a sixth-form common room than a seat of government. Slats of dusty sunlight paint lucent stripes on coatracks and cheap wire hangers.

Greenlaw is waiting for me, hands clasped in front of her, railthin in a royal blue suit. Her blonde hair is still teased into a perfect bubble around her face, which has gone from pert to pinched since last we saw each other. She is of the vanishing generation of women that still have their hair set rather than blow-dried.

I'm used to walking in heels but my knees wobble as I approach her.

"Dr. Thackeray." Her term of address lets me know she's been Googling. "Kind of you to come at such short notice." Years ago, her eyes were blue with that one distinctive navy streak in the right iris. They have faded now, getting that watery look of the elderly, so the dark fleck is less pronounced, but the years haven't softened her voice: she still speaks with the old robotic lack of inflection. She's a circuit board with a chip missing.

"You're very welcome," I reply.

"Have you been here before?"

"I haven't," I say. I worked very hard, at Cromer Hall and ever since, to ensure that I am confident in any social situation. I thought I'd finally shrugged off the insecurities of my upbringing. Here, my roots grab me by the ankles.

"Well, I shan't have time for the tour, I'm afraid." She checks her watch. "I'm expected in the Chamber at half past." I'm glad we're against the clock. It will stop me filling the gaps with nervous conversation and let me get down to the exchange of information. It will help me speak Greenlaw's sparse, efficient language.

"You'll have tea?" she says archly.

"I will." I appear to be playing the yes/no game of my childhood.

We walk through corridors crawling with Pugin's manic profusion of detail. Pattern is almost alive in the flats of the fan-vaulted ceiling. Bookcases line one wall and paintings of a thronged chamber the opposite. I am reminded again how male the iconography is in these places. Most of the art is from the days before women were allowed in. A relatively recent oil painting features Margaret Thatcher, her bright blue suit a splash among the monochrome men. Helen must be in there somewhere, another of the spots of feminine color, but she doesn't stop to point herself out. No one pays me any attention as I trot along behind her. She walks faster than I do. Someone as censorious about health as she is can hardly let herself go. A memory wriggles to the surface for the first time in years, of the front-page photograph of her out jogging, in Reeboks, legwarmers, a toweling headband and full makeup, the corpse barely cooled. I hold that thought so tightly that it shatters in my hand.

The Peers' Dining Room—I recognize it from books—is a rich, red tea shop of a space hung with screens showing the debate in the Chamber. On the famous oxblood benches, jowly lawmakers snooze through a mumbled discussion about broadband. Numbers, meaningless to me, scroll along the bottom of the screen.

"I would never have recognized you," says Helen, when we're seated at the round table with its immaculate white cloth and fussy cruet set. I shake out my napkin from its ring and at last force myself to meet her eyes. Something passes between us before we can stop it; an understanding, and an irony. I am one of the only two people in the world Helen Greenlaw can relax in front of, and her me. There should be a dark freedom in this conversation. But she blinks and it is gone.

She orders tea and scones for two. Silver pots and bone china arrive in seconds. This will all be heavily subsidised; here's another irony. "I have a duty to the public purse," she said after the murder. That was the phrase that did for her; her admission that her loyalty was to her ledger first and people second.

Helen pours; neither age nor nerves unsteady her hands. But mine are shaking. As soon as the waiter is out of earshot, Helen says, matter-of-factly: "I suppose you're here for money."

She genuinely thinks I want cash and she thinks it *having met me*. Jesse was right, then. I'll always be Marianne Smy from Nusstead. Did he know I would do this? Or, worse—"Jesse's already asked you."

Her quirked eyebrow gives little away. "Jesse? I haven't heard from him."

So his threat was empty. I can't allow space for the idea that I have come here for no reason and I can't relax. I must act, not react.

"Right. Well—I have money now." I want to tell her that I have money in the way she understands. The kind of assets that take time to turn into cash. Jesse is right in this respect, if nothing else. "But Jesse has decided he wants another pound of flesh, and he's going to ask for some soon. That's why I wanted to talk to you. To get to you before he did. If he hasn't made contact yet, it won't be long."

Helen blinks mechanically. "I should have thought he would have wanted to keep his own connection to Nazareth firmly in the past, for his own good."

Two men in suits sit noisily down at the next table. If I can hear them, they can hear me: it makes an already stilted, coded conversation even more awkward.

"Well, yes. I told him that." I hear the Suffolk in my voice then: it comes out *towd*, that unpronounced *l* the only inflection I can't shake off. "If he lifts the lid on that, then what's to stop it all coming out?"

She looks at the men in suits before answering, so softly I can hardly hear her, "Detection has moved on, of course. In the unlikely event that anyone talks, it is as well for us that the body was cremated." It is not just the words' confessional content but the flatness of her delivery that silences me. "But I know what you mean. I thought that our . . . participation, I thought that ruled out him ever doing anything this stupid again." She's dishing out hard logic. It is as though she has found a way to take humanity out of the equation. I almost envy her. No wonder she is so efficient. What would a modern psychiatrist make of her? Sociopath? Borderline? She is Honor's opposite in many ways, all analysis and control where Honor is pure impulse. Honor is a different kind of superhuman, too many emotions for one soul to contain. Helen is unmoved by anything except her own advancement.

"He gets ideas in his head." How can I explain the tangled subtleties that Jesse has interpreted as betrayals? He replays events until they fit his thinking. For her, there is strength or weakness, duty or dereliction thereof, not this swirl of emotions the rest of us have to lug around.

"What are you going to do?" I ask her. "Will you go to the police? Because if you do . . . I mean—it doesn't look good for any of us, but . . . I have a daughter." At this, Greenlaw regards me with amusement, as though the notion of family life and wanting to protect someone you love is an interesting weakness.

A waiter sets the food down. Helen saws at a scone and trowels on a thick layer of clotted cream before answering. "How can I expect to hear from him?"

I mirror her actions, but place my scone back on the plate. I know I couldn't swallow it.

"I don't know," I have to admit. "I suppose the same way as me, but we're very different people now, we live different lives. Once I would've been able to predict his behavior but I think those days are long gone. I've *told* him not to make a move. I don't want anything to do with it. Please, can you give me an idea of what you're going to do?" Even as I beg, I wonder what the point is. I might as well appeal to one of the statues in the lobby.

"Do? Well, I shall pay him, of course." She shrugs, lightly. My jaw drops. "I have worked too hard for too long to be brought low by this. I do good. I'm *needed*." She holds my gaze even though we both know she shouldn't be in any position of responsibility, let alone sitting in government. "What did you expect?" she asks and I realize that of course this is exactly what I expected from her. "I did it before."

She can clearly afford it. The money doesn't matter to her. I need to make her see how important this is, to appeal to her on the only consequence that matters.

"Honor—my daughter—she has . . . look, I don't like the word disorder and all the judgment that comes with it, but just, she's ill and incredibly vulnerable. She's exactly the sort of person you say you care about. She's an extraordinary person, she lives life so deeply but everything hurts her, it's like—she's got splinters in all of her fingertips and glass in her feet. If this comes out, even by accident, if the police come for me and she finds out—she's been in hospital before, she's tried to . . ." If I say the words, tears will follow. "It took a lot, you know, for me to come here today. But I would do anything to protect Honor from this. As a mother, you know what that's like."

Nothing. I should have known it was no use appealing to her on *those* grounds.

It suddenly feels imperative that I justify my own inexcusable place in all this. "It would have ended there. I've never forgiven myself, you know. I was only seventeen and I didn't know the first thing about how these things work and," my voice catches but I will not cry in front of her. I want to say *poor* but the word won't come out, so I say: "I was so hungry, I was so bloody *cold*."

Cowd seems to echo around the room. Helen's face is expressionless. Why should she care about my excuses? She never made any.

An electronic bell makes me jump.

"Ah," she says. "It's time for me to go back to work. I'll walk you out."

I have made myself vulnerable before her and got steel in response. What was I hoping for? Some kind of sisterhood?

"Is it going to be all right?" I plead with her.

"Thank you for your time, Dr. Thackeray."

I emerge blinking and confused into the autumn sun. A family of Chinese tourists ask me to take their picture; the phone the father hands me is the same model as my own but after five attempts I've only produced some blurred pictures of feet. "I'm sorry," I say, and thrust it back into their hands. Unable to face the Tube, I hail a taxi to take me back to Liverpool Street. The river is to my right as we chunter past Embankment, Temple, Blackfriars until the river road ends and the buildings rise on either side, stealing the sky from me.

I have no idea whether I have just made things better or worse.

14

Against all odds, against a signal failure at Manningtree, a grid-lock in Diss station car park and that bastard level crossing, I make it back to Nazareth—to Park Royal Manor—for 7:45 p.m. The buffet car was shut and I've only had coffee and one bite of a scone since breakfast this morning. I'm shaking with hunger by the time I get back. Mum doesn't usually eat this late, so when I smell the cooking from the corridor, I'm grateful that Colette's managed to make her hold out this long. The dining table is set for five, but there are only two faces around it. Sam's is weary and Honor's is tear-stained.

"Sweetheart!" The chronic remorse of the past is replaced by the acute guilt of the moment.

"She didn't know who I was, Mum. She didn't recognize me."

"Colette had to take Debbie back," says Sam, hair bobbing. His face is framed by a babyish aureole that has crossed the line from genius mad professor to unkempt. It won't do him any favors with clients. I hadn't known until we began to spend time apart that he has become the kind of man who needs his wife to tell him when it's time for a haircut. His eyes go to the kitchen, where smashed crockery nestles in a dustpan. Mine go to Honor: he sees the conclusion I'm jumping to and heads me off before I can land there. "No, it was Debbie. It all got a bit much for her."

I don't know what's worse: the distress my mother must have felt, being seated in this strange house opposite the blue-haired freak, or Honor's horror at seeing her grandmother's deterioration. Either way, I should have been here.

"Oh, God," I say. "Come here, Honor." I stroke her back. My fingertips read her: well-covered ribs tell me she's eating enough.

"I'm so sorry," I say. "We should've all gone to Colette's. I should never have gone in, I should've said tomorrow instead."

"I thought work said it had to be today?" Sam looks up sharply, spotting the bad join in my stories, but I know he won't say anything in front of Honor.

"Yes, I know, that's what I meant. Sorry, I'm all over the place. I should eat. Is the food spoiled?"

"I'll dish up," says Sam.

Honor fills a wineglass for me as I empty my bag out; keys in the bowl, phone on the worktop. "I love that you still use my case," she says, picking it up and sliding her thumb under the flap. I had it on silent while I was in the car but there could be a message from Jesse on the screen. There could be a text from Helen. I go to snatch it from her hand, knocking the glass at her elbow. She catches it by the stem; it sloshes but doesn't smash.

"What a save," she says, her achievement distracting her from the grab that caused it. Sam has noticed, though. Something in his face has folded closed.

The food is nice—some kind of casserole, chicken and olives—and the wine takes the edge off things. Sam seems to have relaxed, too; and if he calls me out on my edginess I'll blame it on stress.

As I decant the leftovers into Tupperware, Honor and Sam settle down on the sofa, each plugged into a device. My two favorite faces glowing Facebook blue in the dark; a picture of what I stand to lose.

What would Sam do if he knew where I'd been today and why? I don't think he would leave me, not if I could make him see how that would derail Honor. He would stay with me, but the love I know, that deluded, dependable love, would be gone, and that would be the second greatest loss I could imagine.

"Look at us, ignoring each other in favor of screens like a proper family," says Sam.

"Actually, I'm going to deactivate all my social for a bit," Honor replies. "I read that it can be as harmful for mental health as smoking skunk. It literally reroutes your nervous system, it makes you dependent on the next dopamine hit; it's like crack. Or sugar. I really want a clear head for this term."

I know she's right, but Instagram is my baby monitor.

"Go for it," says Sam. "I checked Twitter last night. Glanced up and I'd lost an hour."

"I might start not even turning my phone on till like 4 p.m."

This is a step too far. "But what if I need to check you're all right?" The thought of her being in London, incommunicado, sends a flare up inside me. "What if you need me?"

Honor looks at me like I'm an idiot. "Then I turn on my phone and ring you."

But we all know that when she's low, she doesn't reach out. "We can pay for a landline, can't we Sam, in case we need to reach you."

"Mum." From Honor's eye roll you'd think she'd never had a day's vulnerability in her life. "The whole point is not being reachable. Not having to answer to anyone else. Just being on my own. I thought you'd be happy for me? I honestly think in years to come we'll regard internet use the way we think about cigarette-smoking in the olden days, we'll look back and think, how did they not know what they were doing to themselves?"

Sam shoots me a warning look over his iPad that condenses so many conversations we've had. Stop smothering her. Respect her wishes. I know he's right, but I can't stop myself from talking. Not least because any big shift in Honor's behavior patterns can be a flag.

"But the landline would only be for us to call. You wouldn't have to give out your number to anyone else."

"Mum! *You count as other people,* don't you get it?"

She doesn't want me. I hide my grief in humor. "OK. It was just an idea. I'll back off." I hold my hands up and walk backward across the kitchen in mock surrender. It breaks the atmosphere and makes Honor laugh.

"Anyway, since I'm having a binge before I go cold turkey, want to see what I've found?" She pats the seat next to me and I'm so grateful to be invited back into her space that I nearly fall over in my haste. "You might be able to explain some of it to me; I'd like to get your take on it. It's actually harder than you'd think to find pictures of what this place used to be like," she says. "You've got to wade through pages of property websites and bland interior shots before you can get anywhere, but I've come up with some gold. This place was *wild* back in the day." She tilts the screen my way. Sam mouths *you OK?* at me and it takes me a few seconds to remember my fabricated phobia. *Fine,* I mouth back. A Victorian daguerreotype leers up at me in ghoulish sepia. I only know she's a woman from the frilly dress: her features are coarse and her hair's been hacked off.

"She was epileptic and they locked her up for it. Can you imagine?"

"No," I say weakly.

"Fucking hell. Here's a list of why women were put away the year it opened." The yellowed facsimile on her screen doesn't look that different to the notes they were using well into the twentieth century. "Death of sons in war, medicine to prevent conception, eating snuff, religious mania, scarlatina—whatever that is—domestic abuse, alcohol, melancholia—and these are just the ones I can read! Congenital defect ascertained, ill-treated by husband—can you *believe* this shit?"

"Ooh, hello," says Sam, tapping his own tablet. "You'll like this, Honor. Some artists got into the hospital after it was abandoned and took loads of photographs. Look." He shifts along; the three of us have re-created the bedtime huddle from when we used to read her *Peter Rabbit,* but instead of turning the page on watercolors, Sam's swiping through a seemingly endless bank of images.

"*Wild,*" says Honor, as a slideshow of fallen debris, fluoro murals and dismembered mannequins plays before her. There's a picture of the abandoned pharmacy, shelves swept clean, nothing left for Clay to steal and sell on. "They're incredible shots and not a filter in sight," says Honor. "Back then you would've had to really know what you were doing to get pictures like that. They're not credited. I wonder who took them?"

Images scroll past: there's the doorway where I first saw Michelle through the grille in the door. It's unlocked in the photograph and swinging wide. Honor swipes left onto the ward where I lost my virginity. It might even be the same bed. I can't look anymore.

"Anyone else want some more wine, or a G&T? I fancy something a bit lighter."

"I'm good thanks, Mum."

"Not for me, darling."

I have my back to them as I busy myself with glass and ice. Three fingers of Bombay Sapphire and a clumsy splash of Fever Tree.

Then Honor says, "Christ," and goes deadly silent, and then, "Oh, her poor son."

She holds it up for my inspection but I don't need to see it. They always use the same picture of Julia Solomon, those lovely dark eyes staring across the decades, one slender arm around the nuzzling toddler. "Did you know about this, Mum?"

I halve my drink before answering. "Yes, of course. I was a teenager at the time. It was on the national news but it was a huge story around here for years. It's really sad."

"Sad? It's an abomination! How could it have been allowed to happen?" Her eyes flick from side to side. God knows what blog she's reading, what archived tabloid rant or broadsheet opinion piece, but you can't get very far down this click-hole without coming across Helen's picture or her name. Chin tucked into her neck, face creased in indignation, for a second Honor looks like I do now. If she sees anything, though, she doesn't make the connection. Why would she?

15

Dirty brown leaves tumble against a white sky and bounce off my windscreen. On the roadside verges, stripped hawthorn branches are keep-out spikes for the fairweather visitors. Autumn returns Suffolk to those of us who live here all year around.

"Just remind me," says Mum, in the too-bright tone she reserves for covering the gaps in her memory. "Where were we, again, this morning?" The question costs her. These are the most heartbreaking moments: when she knows that she doesn't know. Heartbreaking because this stage too will pass and it will mean the loss of the last of her.

"We were at the hospital, in Ipswich," I say.

"For work?" This is a leap sideways: when we were at geriatric outpatients this morning she didn't remember she had ever worked there.

"No, for your check-up."

"Of *course,*" she says, so cheerfully I know she doesn't remember. Is there any part of her that knows that hospital is the reason I exist? Morten Larkas was a Norwegian neurologist over for a conference who took a pretty young nurse out for a drink on his last night in Ipswich. By the time I found out his name he was married with children; by the time I found out his address he was dead. I glance at Mum, scrutinizing her reflection, a light, vacant smile on her face. The air in this car seems to throb with conversations we'll never have now. Why didn't she want a relationship with my father or Colette's? Why was she too proud to ask them for support? It's not as though she had some unorthodox parenting ethos that a man would've interfered with.

I suppose I should be encouraged that she's never mentioned my father in all the time she's been ill. I worry daily about my own old age, about a lifetime of care and control undone as I blurt something while Honor ferries me around, crunches my medication into yogurt. The thought of ever being a burden on my daughter twists at my guts.

Instead of talking I shove the *Now That's What I Call the 90s* CD into the player and let Boyzone carry us home.

Colette's waiting at the door for us. She's had her hair done while we've been out. A soft, reddy-brown dye, flicky at the ends. I tell her I love it, then update her on this morning and add the latest notes to the box file of medical records.

"Stay for a coffee?" says Colette, filling the kettle.

"If you can spare me, I fancy an afternoon on my own." I want to wallow in my weird mood, to spend the afternoon lolling on the sofa chain-watching *The Good Wife* and eating a whole wheel of Brie on an entire packet of crackers.

"Give me a hug. I love you."

I pull the front door closed behind me. As I pop-pop the car open, my phone vibrates in my bag.

"You were right," says Helen Greenlaw. I sink into the driver's seat and close the door behind me. I don't have to ask what I was right about.

"How did he do it?"

"He approached me as I was walking along Millbank. I suppose it's known from my ten thousand steps initiative that I commute from Pimlico on foot. It comes up in interviews and profiles and such."

I make a mental note: Pimlico. One stop on the Victoria line away from Honor's beloved Vauxhall. She lived there while Robin was an MP, three white stucco stories of super-prime real estate in St. George's Square that she sold after he died; I checked. It's something to go on.

"Was he in a state? Did you tell him I'd been to see you?" My heart pauses while I wait for the answer.

Does she hesitate here, or is paranoia playing tricks on me? "No. It was very perfunctory, the whole exchange over in moments. He introduced himself, told me what he wanted, said he needed cash and then gave me a rendezvous."

My heart resumes, double time for the skipped beats. Behind my fury there is something approaching admiration: I didn't think he had it in him; the research, the trip to London. Underneath *that* lurks something bigger and darker. I had underestimated everything about him; how he felt about me, how hard he has taken my "betrayal," how serious he is about scaring me.

"Right." I'm not sure what I'm supposed to do with this information. "Well, thanks for letting me know."

"No, I haven't finished. I need you to do something for me." There is no question mark in her sentence and no coaxing in her tone. I am being given an order from a superior. "He wants cash, naturally. Getting the money won't be a problem but the delivery is concerning. He won't come back to London, doesn't want it happening anywhere near a camera, so he's asked me to deposit it in a location somewhere on the eastbound carriageway of the A12." When she describes the meeting point I know it instantly. It was a little old-fashioned petrol station but it's just a mess of rubble now, concrete stumps where the pumps used to be, the odd trucker parked up for a sleep, only visible if you know when to look up. They pulled it down a few years ago and built a BP garage and an M&S Food on the other side of the road. "I can't go alone." It's a statement of fact, not an expression of fear.

"Jesse's not *violent*," I say, realizing only then that I'm afraid to be alone with him.

"In fact it's more of a practical reason than that," says Helen briskly. "I have cataracts, I can't drive and this assignation naturally isn't something I want to advertise. I can hardly have a taxi driver deposit me somewhere like this." It takes a few seconds to process what she's asking of me. If I don't help her, anything that makes her vulnerable to discovery also puts me at risk. She clearly takes my silence for someone working up the courage to refuse her. "I did not ask for these floodgates to be opened any more than you did, but since they have been, you must act in self-preservation."

Well, she's the expert in *that*.

"Marianne."

For the first time in my career I feel like insisting someone addresses me as Dr. Thackeray, but I bite my tongue. "I'm here, I'm thinking, just give me a second." I can't disguise the plea in my voice; knowing this is panic, not defiance, she lets me think.

I take a deep breath. "I'm not getting out of the car," I say. "I don't want him to see me with you."

16

Helen emerges blinking from Diss station. She is dressed casually in slacks and the kind of flat shoes with a Velcro fastening you see advertised in the back pages of *The Telegraph* magazine. I go to search her eyes for the milkiness of cataracts but reactor lenses in her glasses turn gray-brown in the low autumn sun.

The money must be in her hard black handbag. Diss is hardly a criminal black spot but nowhere is mugger-proof and I find myself walking on the side of her, then finally offering to hold it. For all its bulk it's surprisingly light.

"How much did he ask you for?" I say, once we're in the car.

"Ten." She keeps her own eyes on the road.

It's a small fortune—certainly more than I could have laid my hands on at that kind of notice, even if I could explain it away to Sam. Helen Greenlaw sits next to me in what I think of as Mum's seat. There's a deceptive vulnerability in her tiny frame, the easy-on shoes. She looks doddery, even sweet: old age reduces all of us to innocence, on the surface at least.

"Whereabouts in Pimlico do you live?"

I see her weigh up the pros and cons of guarding her privacy; the fact that she tells me I take as a sign of trust, or rather resignation; we have got her, now. "A little mews house, off St. George's

Square," she says. She may have downsized but she hasn't gone far.

"That sounds nice."

I abandon my unconvincing small-talk for the familiar press of unsaid words. I want to ask Helen about right now and what happens next and I want to ask her, this might be the only chance I ever have to ask her, about then, about her life before it crashed into ours. But guilt stops me, guilt and the brittleness of this silence. I open the window an inch. I am a coward, now as then. I have the words, and I let them go.

I turn off the dual carriageway and drive past the ROAD CLOSED sign. On the old slip road weeds shoot through chinks in the tarmac and flatten under my tires. The old garage's concrete footprint is only just visible under a forest of buddleia. I check over my shoulder like a getaway driver. The drivers below are going too fast to register us. The litter bin is half full of old waste, and Helen drops her envelope into it with distaste.

"Right, let's get you back to the station," I say when she's back in the passenger seat. "If we leave now, you'll make the four sixteen to Liverpool Street."

"I want to stay until he gets here."

You almost have to admire her stubbornness.

"No. If he sees me here, he'll explode." Jesse wouldn't understand that he forced me into this. All he'll see is the greatest betrayal he could conceive. I would be frightened to be near him. But that's not all. I am ashamed to be plotting with this awful woman. I still hate what she has done.

Helen gives that slow blink again. I'm sure she only blinks once a minute or so. "I need to know he has it."

I sigh. If it were my £10,000, I would want to see it too. I cross the bridge, park around the back of the services, tucking my car behind a white van. At the counter I order myself a latte.

"What's your mum want?" says the salesgirl. She's nodding at

Helen but the word "mum" sparks a reflex of tenderness in me, immediately extinguished by the way Helen flinches at the thought we could be related. I remember another flinch, another insult, and harden against her.

"I won't, thank you," she says.

The milk in this latte constitutes the only calories I've had today. Since I came home I've been either buzzing, crashing or drinking. It's showing in the loosening of my waistband but in my putty skin and my dry eyes, too, and the constant low-level shake of my hands.

We stand side by side on a grass verge and wait.

"Here he is." I don't know what route he's taken but he must be tired because he's on the yellow bicycle from outside the library and it's a good half-hour's cycling from Nusstead to here. He swings one leg boyishly over the crossbar before gliding to a halt next to the bin. I squint, and wonder if my eyes need lasering again. "Can you see him?"

"I came prepared." She pulls something out of her handbag that it takes me a few seconds to recognize as a pair of little red opera glasses. Nice woman-of-the-people touch, there. Even with the naked eye I can see him put his hand in the bin, pull the bag out and open it. He pads his chest with bundles of cash and tears the envelope into tiny pieces which whirl and eddy and blend with the autumn leaves. Helen keeps the glasses raised as he cycles away, her eyes staying on him long after he's out of my vision.

"Well," she says. "I hope that's an end to it."

17

I have the pool to myself. I never spent time in the chapel, so it's conjecture that makes me think of all the desperate prayers said here, for patients and by them, over the century it served. I stand at the deep end, hands pointed, but to shatter the surface feels, as Sam predicted, almost sacrilegious. Rattan recliners line the old transepts. The water is a mirror, leaded-light saints reflected unrippled. I can't help but think of that other room, its flooded floor. The spa bath is turned off; there's a vague rumble from the plant room and occasionally the steam room, which is in an old vestry, lets out a hiss. I execute a perfect dive, as they taught me in Cromer Hall. I don't so much swim as fight the water, throwing punches instead of strokes.

In the steam room, lights slowly change color, making rainbows in the mist. I stretch out on marble, legs crossed. I raise my arms above my head. The weight I've lost since being back in Suffolk has left me feeling baggy rather than lithe. I wonder how many good summers my upper arms have got left.

The door clicks open and a figure in the haze is an alien disembarking a spaceship.

"This must be one of the few rooms we never christened. Ironically."

I scramble up, slip and my elbow cracks against hard stone. The pain sings through my body, stealing my breath. How did he get in here?

"They've got an offer on," says Jesse, as though he's read my mind. "Three-day off-peak pass to the gym. They're trying to drum up a bit of trade, off-season. Didn't think they'd let the chavs in here, did you?"

"Don't be like that."

"Why? It's what you think."

He's got me in checkmate. I can't deny it without condescending to him again. I stay sitting up while he lies on the slab opposite, his body making a slapping noise on contact with wet marble. The machine puffs new steam. Jesse shifts and displaces it, his long limbs carving fan-shapes in the whorls.

"Bad news," he says. "Greenlaw said no. Wouldn't give me any money." I laugh out loud, the way you do when you can't believe your ears. The sound echoes. "I ain't joking, babe."

The shock seems to turn down the ambient noise so that all I can hear is my breathing and his. Calling him out on his lie is to tell him that I was there with Helen. I have no idea *why* he would lie but I think—and I'm thinking fast, here, in a panic—I think I should cut this one off before yet another untruth spirals out of control. There is anticipation in his stillness, until it seems he is barely breathing at all. I thought bringing his family into it would work but I was wrong. I don't know what else to do but call his bluff.

"So does that mean you're going to go to the press?"

"No," he says. I relax, exhale, and the world seems to start spinning again. The spa starts to bubble, meaning we're not on our own, and the relief of that loosens my shoulders another inch. Jesse senses it too, takes the steam deep into his lungs before releasing it slowly, almost like he's in a yoga class, and then he moves, fast as a young man, and grabs my upper arm: "You'll have to make up the shortfall."

"Jesse, you're hurting me." The pain of his grip delays the impact of his words. He is asking me for money. Demanding it.

"It's only what you owe me."

"I what?"

"Who stayed in Nusstead and cleared up all the shit? *I* dealt with it. Everyone crying and wondering and never saying a word. Where were you, then?" he says. "You din't pay *anything* toward the funeral."

"You never asked me to!" No one expected Jesse Brame to provide the free bar at the Social: booze flowing in as fast as the tears could flow out. "You did that for your own benefit, to assuage your own guilt."

"Yeah, well, you done a runner." Is it sweat or remorse that loosens his fingers around my arm? "Let's call it ten grand, with interest, in today's money. That's still less than you owe."

"What do you take me for, some kind of criminal injuries compensation board? You can't get a lawyer to work out loss of bloody earnings or whatever in a situation like *this*. And anyway, compensation is for victims, Jesse. Not the people who caused the problem in the first place." He doesn't answer. Some essential oil's being pumped in, juniper or menthol, cold and clean in my windpipe and lungs. It forces me to measure my breath and I'm grateful. "And even if I wanted to give you money, I can't, not a lump sum like that."

"Marianne, you've got *two houses*. How dare you sit there and tell me you're skint?"

"I'm not saying anything till you let go of me." He loosens but doesn't let go his grip. I turn my face to his. "I'm not going to insult you by telling you I'm poor. You know I'm not. It's tied up in things." I hear myself and am disgusted. So much money that we have to lock it up in property, in shares and stocks and ISAs to get the most out of it. But that doesn't take away the fact he's lying to me. He's had Helen's money.

"Don't threaten me," I say. "I'm sorry, all right? I'm sorry I did a runner and I'm sorry if I misled you about my life but this is— we've kept it together all these years, Jesse. You're breaking my *heart*."

My heart gets through where logic met a stonewall. Jesse lets go suddenly and drops his head into his hands.

"I thought I could count on you," he says. I find my hand skimming his silhouette, the comfort reflex strong, but our old license to touch each other with tenderness is surely revoked. I let it hover over his shoulder.

"You can, Jesse, you can, for . . . normal stuff, that doesn't rake up the past. I'll always care about you."

"But?" he asks. But I won't love you and I would have left you. Us both knowing it doesn't mean I can say it.

He drops to kneeling at my feet: I close my legs and slide them to one side before he can try anything. There's a crack as the forehead that he clearly expected to bury in my lap makes contact with marble. I wince, and lay one hand on the back of his neck. He shrugs me off and staggers to the door, shouldering it open. The temperature drops and the air clears. He's outlined for a moment in the doorway, stained-glass windows in the background, only the slightest slackening around his waist marking his age, so different to Sam's silhouette that there's a seismic shifting inside me before I can help myself. "I wish you'd never come home," he says, and he is crying.

I wait a long time to be sure he's gone, longer than you're supposed to spend in the steam room. When I come out, light-headed, the pool is full. I don't know what's the matter with my face but everyone stares and a man heaves himself out of the spa and helps me to a lounger while his partner gets me a glass of water and says, are you OK, you really should sit down, you look like you've overdone it, are you sure you don't need a doctor?

18

My wet hair is in a turban, skin feeling squeaky clean, insides feeling anything but. The fish pie in the oven smells good now but I know I won't want to eat it once it's on the table.

Sam will sleep here tonight before his flight, even though Stansted's probably closer to London than Nusstead. I check the car park for his silver Prius, my subconscious scanning for a red Audi or a yellow bike.

I pace a bit, try Honor, but her phone's off, even though it's long after 4 p.m. I check her Instagram: nothing for a few days. My pulse accelerates. I can't escape the idea that Honor is reclaiming her mental health at the expense of mine. I know better than to share this opinion with Sam.

Before he gets here I want to check whether I was telling the truth when I told Jesse I didn't have the money. I fire up the laptop, line up the various online banking widgets and log in one by one to our accounts. I wasn't lying to Jesse: all our capital—and as the word forms in my mind I hear Jesse's voice sneering that only rich wankers call it capital—is tied up. This place has cleared us out. Where we used to have savings there's nothing. The company is more than healthy but I'm a minority shareholder which means I can't withdraw funds without Sam's signature. There's nowhere I could get cash that Sam wouldn't see and I cannot think of a way to explain away £10,000. My current account is barely in the black, and in another month I'm going to be the kind of woman who has to start asking her husband for money for a new dress. I did not think in those terms when I gave up my salary, but then I could never have predicted this mess.

I go back to the window for a while and two glasses of wine later, when it gets too dark to tell the cars apart, I break another promise to Sam and log in to the department intranet and browse the dissertation subjects for this year's Masters' intake. I check in on a handful of students I taught as undergraduates, noting again my soft spot for the former comprehensive kids, of whom I see fewer every year. Amanda's got some interesting theses to look forward to this year: Queer Space in 20th-Century London, Cuba Before Castro, Reexamining the Victorian Prison. I dip into the proposal for Queer Space but can't concentrate even on something I'd usually find fascinating. My inability to focus beyond bullet points makes me realize that I don't miss the work itself so much as the structure it gave my thoughts. As it is, my only refuge from the stress Jesse's causing is stress about my mother.

I fidget through my phone, double-check that I've deleted all messages from Jesse and Helen. My finger hovers over her number.

Do I owe her anything? Ought I to warn her about what just happened with Jesse? I have to hope he stops here but if it comes to it maybe Helen would lend me money, to save herself.

J behaving very erratically. Denies getting your—I tap out *money*, but then go back and retype *letter*—*If he contacts you please call me asap. M.*

I've been staring at the screen for so long I've dropped my watch over the car park. The bang of the apartment door makes me scream and drop my phone.

"Bloody hell, Marianne," says Sam. "I thought you were over the ghosts of the asylum." There's annoyance rather than sympathy in his voice. He has that gray, exhausted look he always gets in the middle of a build.

"I didn't hear you come in, that's all." The tears come from no-where.

"Oh, darling." Pressed into Sam's jacket I can smell his after-shave and his coffee and the comfort of him. If Jesse is a stirring inside me then Sam is a settling. To be held by him is to be suspended in warm honey. I could happily stay here all night, I could sleep standing up. "You've been swimming," he says, inhaling my hair. "God, I need a drink after that drive. Red or white?"

We can't both drink, not when one of us might need to go to London at the drop of a hat. "Whatever you want. I'll give it a miss."

Sam sees through me. "I saw her only three hours ago, Mari-anne. She's fine."

"You *saw* her!"

"Yes. Had a meeting in Victoria so I popped by. She's getting used to people visiting apparently. Something about this being a more real way of living." He rolls his eyes, but affectionately. "The flat was a tip but not in a mad way. The pig's still there, unfortu-nately."

"Did she keep her appointment with Dr. Adil?"

"As far as I know. I didn't ask. She's at 1G." I force a smile: as a teenager, Honor explained that her state always seems to have a corresponding gravitational pull. 1G is neutral, enough to anchor her to earth without pinning her down. Zero gravity means no sleep or food; 2G means she can't get out of bed. "She won't need either of us tonight."

He uncorks a bottle of Malbec—he still insists on corks—pours a glass and hands the bottle to me, but I'm a dog with a bone. "I want to get her down here for the week."

"What, and have her miss a week of her course, just to justify your paranoia?" Sam swills the wine in the bowl glass out of habit. "Let her *breathe*, Marianne. She's *steady*. Her medication is actu-ally making her better instead of worse. How long is it since we've had one of those phone calls? Ten months, a year?"

"Then she's due a relapse, isn't she?"

Sam purses his lips for a moment. "And honestly? I think your mum needs you right now; Colette does too. You'll never forgive yourself if you lose these days." His chin quivers just for a second. His father passed away when he was on a work trip and he's never made peace with it. He stares at the wall behind my shoulder, blinking too fast. Sometimes I'm so busy holding up other people that I forget who's holding me.

"You're right. It'll draw a line under my day," I say, and I fill the glass myself. "Where's the build at, anyway?"

"A month behind, thanks to that bloody skylight," he says and then he's off and it's a relief to listen to him talk about beams and joists and access. I wait for his face to uncrease as he dumps his work stress on me, but it doesn't. I force down a few forkfuls of fish pie, realizing for the first time how absolutely disgusting a dish it is. Still, it dampens down the acid in my guts.

It was always going to be an early night but conversation is stilted—which never happens with us. At around ten we stiffly climb the spiral stairs. Sam folds his trousers and lays them neatly over the mezzanine banister with the rest of the morning's clothes. What bulk he ever had at his shoulders has slumped to his waistline and the comparison with Jesse is a guilty reflex. "Oh yes," he says, still with his back to me, in a voice that isn't quite his own. He straightens the trousers that are already valet smooth. "I bumped into Amanda in the library at RIBA today."

I go cold. I never did brief her about my fictional staff-training day.

"Did you have much of a catch-up?" I ask with unconvincing lightness.

"No, ships in the night. You know Amanda. Always on the way somewhere. She sent her love." He lines up the hemlines on his trouser legs. "Funny thing. She didn't remember seeing you the other day. Said she hadn't seen you since your leaving drinks?"

How tentatively, how hopefully he volleys the ball into my court.

"No, she wasn't there," I say. "It was an IT thing. She did it the following day."

"But you said it was only one day. That's why I changed everything."

"I'm sorry. I'm all over the place at the moment."

I go to his side, rest my fists on the banister. Sam is rigid beside me; the apartment a dark void below us. "Hey," I say, and turn him to face me, tilt my chin for a kiss, raising my eyebrows. I feel the moment when he chooses to believe me.

As we settle in for fifteen minutes of maintenance sex, he sees the mottled handprint on my upper arm and stops, shifting his weight off me as though my whole body is bruised. "How did you get that?" Panic freezes me. "Was it Debbie?" The doctors have warned us about this: there comes a stage where the patient becomes so frustrated that they start lashing out at their carers.

"She couldn't help it, she didn't know what she was doing." The idea that my mother's little hand could make that huge bruise is absurd. Is there anyone left I won't lie to, or about? I feel sick even though she'll never know.

"Christ." He winces.

"It looks worse than it feels. I'll be on my guard now."

Sam traces the skin around the bruise with a gentle forefinger. "I wouldn't have thought she still had it in her. She's got a big grip for such a little woman, hasn't she?"

I couldn't feel more guilty if Sam had found one of Jesse's hairs in our bed. With that thought, an energy rises that I haven't felt between us in years. I close my eyes and wonder why my body chose now to come to life under Sam's hands. Is he igniting a fire that being close to Jesse has laid? Is it everything that's been poured into me in the last week finding an outlet at last, or the fear that Jesse's about to blow my life up and this could be the last time?

Sam finishes before I can get there and afterward, while I smile and wait for the longing to subside, to reabsorb the frustration, he strokes my cheek and says, "You're still beautiful."

We don't need the alarm. The phone shocks us out of sleep. It's Colette, calling from the back of an ambulance. Mum's had a fall, probably as the result of another stroke. If she hadn't sent a vase flying and woken the whole house, she wouldn't have survived. As it is, the paramedics say I should get to Ipswich Hospital now.

19

The machines beep and wink. Mum could come round any second or she might stay like this for weeks. The nurses who wear her old uniform and walk her old corridors say talk to her, read to her. Tell her about your day. Read her books from her past.

The accumulated possessions of a life boil down to that shelf in Colette's house and an old metal trunk in one of the lock-up garages around the back of the estate. It's not somewhere I like to go at the best of times, but I braved it for this. My throat swelled at things my mother couldn't bear to part with: my exam certificates, a bundle of yellowing baby clothes, a 1,000-piece jigsaw of *The Hay Wain,* a pot of dried-out markers and the ragged copy of *When We Were Very Young* that's currently spatchcocked on my lap, the spine held together with cracked Sellotape.

I am so tired I am almost hallucinating. When I was doing my finals on a diet of caffeine pills and brewer's yeast I saw eels sliding all over the ceiling. They're back again now, swimming around Christopher Robin and Winnie the Pooh. When I close my eyes it is not against hallucinated eels but the unbearable tenderness of my childhood. Sleep attempts to rescue me but I dream about the tiles again, bricking me in and then cracking, falling like bad teeth. I hear a hundred-year-old key scraping in a lock. A black eel sidewinds toward me and it has Michelle's face.

I come round rather than wake up and there's Honor, perched on the edge of the bed. "James James, Morrison Morrison, Weatherby George Dupree," she whispers. "Took great care of his mother, though he was only three."

I watch them through my eyelashes as I calculate how I might straighten my neck without necessitating a visit to a chiropractor. Honor has thrown down the detritus of her journey on the little nightstand—tickets, phone, coins—but only has a day bag. I lift my head up; something deep in my shoulder crunches.

"Hey," says Honor, keeping her voice low. "You've been out cold."

"I feel worse now than I did before I went to sleep. Jesus, my *neck*. How's Mum?"

"No change." Honor holds up the book. "Thought I'd give this a go. She used to read it to me when I stayed with her, when I was tiny."

"She used to read it to *me* when *I* was tiny." Honor holds my hand, joining three generations of women. In the bubble of the moment I think with a pang of the ghost links in this chain. My own grandmother, Marian with one n, and of any daughters Honor might have.

"Did you get a cab from the station?" I ask.

Honor sniffs long and loud. "No, I walked."

"It's a long old way."

"Five miles. Just felt the urge to move, y'know? Before we sat down here for God knows how long. I'm on the three thirty back." I've only got a couple of hours with her now.

"You know what this reminds me of?" I gesture around the room.

Honor smiles. "Me being in the Larches?"

"No! Not at all. It reminds me of waiting to have you. Waiting for an ending, it's like waiting for a birth. There's this sort of hush that falls. This edgy anticipation as you wait for a . . . passing from one dimension to the next." Sam would scoff at this, I'm talking like Jesse now, but you can never be too melodramatic for Honor.

She just nods. "Everyone tells you, it'll happen when it happens. I couldn't relax about it then and I can't now."

"Oh, Mum. It might not be an ending, you know what they said. Why don't you go and get some fresh air, get yourself a coffee? Have you eaten anything?" My belly growls in response. "I'm here, I've got Nanna."

I've never seen her be so capable. If it's this latest medication that insulates her from grief and fear I've got half a mind to ask for some myself.

I can't face any of the yellow food at the hospital Costa, and only realize the error of my ways once I'm outside the main entrance with the smokers on drips and the worried relatives tapping their phones. The eels are back, and this time they're sliding all over the sky. Black coffee on an empty stomach after twenty-four hours with barely any sleep trips me into vertigo and paranoia, so when I first see Jesse I don't trust my brain. He's drinking tea from a flask with two other paramedics, their green overalls camouflaging them against the scrubby little roundabout. In the half-second before I remember how we left things, instinct jumps ahead and I want comfort from him; I want someone who knows me of old to tell me it's going to be all right, even though—*because*—I know it isn't.

When Jesse sees me, he hands his cup to his colleague and he's at my side. The eels clear from the sky. His green overalls are stained with God only knows what and there's a millimeter of white around his hairline.

"I'm sorry about your mum," he says, like she's already died.

"Thanks." There's an awkward silence. "Honor's in with her now."

He raises his eyebrows. He hasn't seen Honor for years.

"Jess, I can't stand this," I say. "On top of everything else going on, I can't stand this tension."

"Well, you asked for it," he says. "Laughing at me. Lying to me. Stringing me along."

Stringing me along! I've spent so many years indulging his delusions. Anger is a physical force in my chest. How dare he talk to me like this when my mother is *dying* in the block behind us? I turn away; I can have my coffee inside. "I've got enough on my plate without you adding to it. I haven't eaten or slept for days, you of all people should know what this feels like."

He catches my hand. "Ten grand's *nothing* to you." I try to read his face. Does he actually believe he has a claim to a share of what's mine, or is he trying to hurt me in the pocket because I have so long denied him the rest of me? How dare he feel entitled to *any* of me?

"You got your pound of flesh off Helen Greenlaw!" I explode. "Don't try for another one from me. *You* started all this up, playing us off against each other. All I did was tell a little white lie about my flat and you've gone mad."

The furrow in his brow flatlines. "What do you mean, I got my pound of flesh?"

The words are out before I can stop them. "I *saw* you fish it out of the fucking bin! I know she gave you the money."

I would give everything I have for a time machine that would take me back five seconds. He opens his mouth and closes it again. Open and shut. Open and shut. In terror, I watch him mentally flipping through the options. "Did you *follow* me?"

I'm not taking it back and he's not denying it. It's done, it's out. A man in a dressing gown and slippers starts vaping, a sick blueberry cloud that turns my stomach even more.

"I drove her from the station. She didn't want anyone to see her. Helen can't drive herself anymore, her eyesight's shit."

"Helen! It's *Helen* now, is it? How's she even got your number?"

"I had to get in touch!" I'm aware that I sound like a hysteric, my crazy pitch halfway to laughter. "To check whether she was going to go to the police. Jesus, Jesse, what did you expect me to do?" I'm shouting now: the blueberry vaper, sensing scandal, inches closer and I drop my voice in response, move in close enough to smell the stale booze coasting on Jesse's breath under the topnote of sugary tea. "If she'd gone to the police, Honor would've found out and you know what that would do. You *know* it."

His lips are white, like they've got bones in them. I have seen sides of Jesse that no one else has, but never fury like this. He almost can't get the words out.

"You're in cahoots with that . . . *monster*. I don't even know you. I can't believe I trusted you. You talk about respect for what we had—we might not be a couple anymore but I still thought we were *united*. I can't believe you'd do this to me. I can't—it's the worst thing you could have done."

"What about what you've done to me? You know what I'm going through. If you've *ever* loved me you wouldn't upset everything like this."

"You know what? Fuck you, Marianne." And if me using Helen's first name offends him, then him calling me anything other than "babe" makes my insides cave. Across the way, radios crackle into life and the paramedics spring into action. "I never thought you'd shift your loyalties so easily," he goes on. "You *are* just like her, only hiding behind Honor instead of your career or whatever! You know what, I'm going to tell your precious little girl the truth about you. I'll tell your daughter what a double-crossing bitch you are. What you're capable of. See how *you* like it."

"You wouldn't," I say. "She doesn't deserve that."

He nods toward the geriatric ward in reply. He could undo thirty years in as many seconds.

"*Jesse!*" His colleagues are bellowing his name across the roundabout. Jesse holds my gaze, resisting the siren until his driver has called his name three times.

"Fuck's sake, Jesse," she says, when he swings, scowling, into the passenger seat. "What is the matter with you lately? Man up, mate."

He doesn't break eye contact even when the door is shut.

"Mum?"

I whirl around. Honor is standing behind me, her face tear-stained, and for one sickening second I think she's heard everything.

"Mum, Nanna's awake!"

She takes my hand. I have time for one backward glance. Jesse's gaze, as the ambulance pulls away, is on me and my daughter and if looks could kill he would pierce both our hearts with a single arrow.

20

It's an iron-gray Sunday, the first in December. I'm nervous about going to Ipswich Hospital again in case I bump into Jesse. He's gone quiet since yesterday and I have no idea what that means. My skin is itching to get out of this flat, out of this shitty haunted building. I could do with a swim but he's poisoned the water in the pool. I'm seriously contemplating spending the rest of my mother's life in the Eye Hotel. It feels as though Jesse has exiled me from my home for a second time.

I'm ten miles away from Nusstead when Radio 2 cuts out for the ringtone and Jesse's name lights up the dashboard.

"I'll be there soon." I recognize his drunk voice even though it's just gone lunchtime.

"Be where?" I can't make out the background noise over the hum of my own engine. Hubbub and static, a hiss. A distant rhythmic clanking.

"Honor's place." He names her road, then her building. I drive straight past a yield sign without slowing, just missing a white van, and there's a Doppler effect of the horn as it shoots out a belated warning. "I've been following her." What's he talking about? He was on shift when she caught her train back to London yesterday, there's no way he could have trailed her home. Heart hammering, I scan the verges for a layby. "She puts it all out there, doesn't she?

Here's my morning run, here's my bus stop, here's my college, blah blah blah, I live in a bubble—"

I pull over, two wheels on a grass verge. Now I can hear him properly. "Jesse, what are you doing?" There's a patronizing parental note in my voice but the alternative is a scream of terror. "Stay where you are, I'll come and get you, we'll talk this through."

The beginning of his answer is lost in a screech of feedback I recognize as train wheels braking. I only catch its tail: "I've given you every chance. Actions speak louder than words."

There's the chhh of a tin opening, a fizz and a gurgle. Distorted announcements in the background tell me his train is at a station. It's too busy to be one of the branch lines. If he's in Ipswich I might be able to catch him up.

"I'll get the money. Get off the train, Jesse." We know I can't. It's a Sunday afternoon. Cash machines have withdrawal limits even if I *did* have the money sitting in my account. "I'll get some money, anyway."

"It was never about the money. It's about payback. You sided with Greenlaw. The one person in the world . . . You couldn't have done a worse thing."

"Come home now." Desperation makes me inventive. "Get off at the next station, I'll pick you up at Diss or Darsham, I'll come into Ipswich if you like. Come back to the flat. Come to bed with me. Is that what you want? You can come back now, you can do whatever you want to me, just please don't tell Honor. Don't make her a pawn in this."

His heavy breathing tells me he's thinking about it but he doesn't answer. Instead there's a bing and a woman's voice announces that this station is Stratford International.

I pull up the mental Tube map that all Londoners carry. Red line then blue, vein and artery, Central to Victoria. Maybe fifteen minutes from Stratford, a three-minute change at Oxford Circus and from there, Green Park, Victoria, Pimlico, Vauxhall. With good connections he'll be there in thirty minutes. I scream into my phone. "Jesse. Jesse, talk to me, don't do this, please, come back!"

There's a suck and a whoosh as his train goes under and then only the hum of my speakers.

I sit there in a layby 200 miles away from south London, flanked by balding dark green hedgerows, fingers skidding on the keypad as I pull up Honor's number. Her phone is off. Of course it is. Fuck her 4 p.m. rule and fuck Sam for encouraging it, I think wildly, and wonder how the hell I can reach her before Jesse does.

I leave a message. "Honor, it's Mum. If you get this, can you leave the flat? I can't explain, I don't want you to panic, but it's just—go out for a coffee or something. I'll meet you and explain everything. Text me when you're safe."

I leave a message on Jesse's phone. "Don't do this. You're better than this. Please call me. Please. You can have whatever you want." My voice breaks on the last word.

Another three minutes have gone by; I picture Jesse's train passing through Mile End station, then Bethnal Green.

I don't know anyone in London who will be able to get to Honor before him. A brainwave crashes: I can go through her social media, message a couple of Goldsmiths friends, tell them to rush to her side and take her out. I'll start with Facebook.

She doesn't exist.

It's the same story on Instagram and Twitter. She's finally made good on her promise to deactivate the lot.

I bring my head down onto the steering wheel then pull it back up when the horn sounds. I brought this on myself.

I scroll blindly up and down my phone, searching for someone, anyone, who could help me and screech to a halt at *S. Sofia*. They met in the Larches; we swapped numbers when Honor's phone was briefly confiscated by staff. I'm *sure* Sofia was living near Brixton Tube. I call her, hardly daring to hope. It takes a few seconds to connect and the tone is the dull beep that tells you the phone is outside the UK.

There is no one else I can trust. No one else I can think of.

My satnav shows me a two-mile tailback going into Ipswich. I can't afford to lose an hour. My train app says there's a fast train leaving Diss in twenty minutes. If I drive fast, I can get to Honor. Not in time, but I can be there to pick up the pieces. I do a three-point turn in the road and head toward Diss.

My last chance occurs to me as I drive the narrow Hoxne Road at 70 miles an hour. Of course I know someone who lives near Vauxhall. I keep both hands on the wheel while I say her name. This time the ringtone is familiar and so is the cold, clipped voice.

"Yes?"

"I'm sorry to call like this but I don't know anyone else who can get to her in time. She's just around the corner from you, she's five minutes in a car."

I know it sounds like nonsense. My panic and emotion arouse the opposite in Helen. "You'll have to be clearer."

"Jesse just rang, he's on a train to her flat, he's going to tell her everything. She lives on top of the newsagent on Kennington Lane, near the Royal Vauxhall Tavern. Just off the Vauxhall Cross round-about. I know you can't drive there but you could get an Uber. Or you could walk it, Helen. On foot even *you* could be there in twenty minutes. Please help me."

"Why?" She is giving me slightly more attention than I imagine she would a cold caller. My hatred of her, at that point, is a match for Jesse's. I must look mad, bombing through the country lanes shouting at my windscreen.

"I don't bloody know why! And it's not even the point. I need you to stop him. Just—do whatever it takes to get her out of there. Her phone's off, I can't get through to her, there's no one else I can trust in London, no one else close enough. He'll be there in twenty minutes. Please can you go to Honor's flat and stop Jesse from talking to her!"

She sighs at the inconvenience. "Is he a *physical* threat to her?"

"I don't know but he doesn't even need to be, she's her own threat."

"Marianne, I'm sure that your daughter won't tell the police, or the press."

Does she *ever* stop thinking about her own reputation? "It's not about the police, it's about my daughter knowing and what this might do to her! You don't know her history." I take a deep breath: it never gets easier to say, even in panic. "She tried to kill herself once when she thought I'd lied to her about—a tiny thing, comparatively. If you ever cared about any of these patients whose lives you destroyed—"

Does she interrupt me there deliberately? "Even if I could get there, which I can't—"

"You can, she's half a mile away from you." I take the blind hill of a hump-backed bridge too fast and blind, leaving my stomach trailing two seconds behind the car. If the level crossing is red, that'll be it, no hope of getting to Honor for at least three hours.

"Why should your daughter trust me? And what if he's already there? I am eighty years old. How do you expect me to overpower an angry man thirty years my junior?"

"I don't know, Helen."

Fuck. The crossing is closing. The three lights flash in their dizzying amber triangle but there are no cars queueing on either side so it must *just* have started. "Just do *something*," I beg as my foot reluctantly finds the brake. "If you won't do it for Honor, do it for yourself. Once he tells one person, what's to stop *them* telling the world?"

She actually tuts at me, a nasty little kiss distorted through my speakers. "Marianne. This resurrection of the unpleasantness is *not my fault*. You brought this on yourselves. You may keep it to your own little tangled scene. I do not deserve this."

She cuts the call and with it, my last chance of preventing the end of the world. The landscape through my windscreen reflects my abject isolation. The sky is wide and white. Black paper cut-out birds wheel and swoop over black paper cut-out trees. There is no train approaching. I remember the time I sat here for twenty minutes for no reason and inch toward the track. Look left, look right. It's clear. I can get to my girl. Pushing from first to second, I grind the gears and stall halfway across the tracks.

The vibration comes not from within the car but through the wheels.

The next second blows wide as eternity.
The noise.
Back into first gear.
The shadow.
Biting point.
The train driver's face.

nazareth hospital
1988

21

"Next week we'll talk about how Chairman Mao used artwork as propaganda. Actually we've just got time, if you turn to page—"

The hometime bell shrilled over the thunder of chairs across floors. I lip-read the homework instructions and copied them into my journal while Ms. Harker stacked books on her desk. History was my favorite subject. I was always bemused by the debate over whether flight or invisibility was the most desirable superpower: it was obvious to me that time travel was the thing. Ms. Harker sounded like something from a history book, or at least an old-fashioned novel; her accent was the Chalet School, Trebizon, Malory Towers, the fictional boarding schools, half-castles, which I longed to attend myself. As it was, I had the weight of expectation—top stream for everything—without the resources. The ambition they tried to instill could never be fulfilled in Waveney Secondary.

When I stood, a button popped off my waistband and rolled across the room to Ms. Harker's feet. She bent to pick it up, saw the straining zip it had left behind.

"Oh, Mari*anne*." Pity from the person I respected most set my cheeks on fire. The skirt I'd been wearing, the skirt that my mum said she couldn't afford to replace this term, was too short and bursting at the seams. In the last few months I'd got height, hips and tits virtually overnight. My shirts pinched my elbows and strained at the bust. I wore my school tie unfashionably thick to cover the string of gaping ovals down the button line. For years I'd lived in the contented disregard of the early-blooming girls from Nusstead, with their hairsprayed fringes and blue mascara, but in the last term their neutral cold shoulders had become catty comments made too low to catch. I felt it keenly, even if I was too proud to show it.

Ms. Harker beckoned me to her desk. "Come to lost property in five minutes. There's another pupil needs extras too. The clothes need washing and pressing but half the stuff's like new." She winked, which made it worse. "No one'll know."

Lost property was in the PE block, bare yellow brick and wire-mesh glass, a pet-shop smell of socks and sweat. I dragged my feet along tatty square corridors I knew backward and hated forward, knowing no one would tell the school bus driver to wait for me. Kicked-in lockers banked the walls. I counted seven cock-and-balls graffiti, up two from the beginning of the week.

Two more years, I thought, tugging my skirt down. I've survived five years being called a swot and a virgin and a snob. I can do two more, if it's my passport to university. The previous term I'd sat a handful of scholarship exams for independent schools and found out that the top stream at Waveney Secondary didn't count for a lot when you were up against grammar-school girls who'd been tutored since they were three. I'd failed the lot. Ms. Harker had tried to comfort me, saying private school wasn't all it was cracked up to be, but that was easy for her to say, in her plum-round vowels and perfect *l*s.

She wasn't at lost property but Jesse Brame was, leaning against the wall like something from an Athena poster, blue-black hair Brylcreemed into a pompadour, leather jacket dangling from his hand. This time my blush was a full-body one. Jesse was so unlike the studious chess-club boys who usually caught my attention that a crush had started to develop while my guard was down. I'd known Jesse my whole life—you couldn't not know everyone in Nusstead, and our parents had been at Waveney together when it was a brand-new secondary modern—but I'd barely spoken to him since we were children, or rather since we stopped being children. Occasionally we'd nod an acknowledgment to each other in the free school meals queue but he wasn't in my class—Waveney had a policy of scattering the Nusstead kids throughout the year, as if to dilute the poison—and he didn't get the school bus anymore. A few years ago, while the other boys were still playing Star Wars, Jesse's life had been put on fast-forward (I was still waiting for mine to start). He'd had a string of older girlfriends; rumor had it that he was currently seeing a married woman on the other side of Ipswich.

When he saw me, he did a double take.

"*You* waiting for Harker an' all?"

I was flattered by his surprise. "Yeah, well," I said. "My mum's got me and Colette on her own, in't she?"

"At least she's in work," he said. "Six months, my dad's been on the dole." I knew from my mother that Mark Brame hated claiming benefits. He had been head charge nurse at Nazareth and a union man. Proud and moral, he was one of the first to be cleared in the embezzlement scandal.

"That's shit," was all I could think of to say. Jesse had a shadow on his jaw at half past three in the afternoon. The last boy I had kissed had barely started shaving. I noticed how close we were standing and took a step back. He dropped the rebel pose and stood straight. His trousers were three inches too short but he wore them with a confidence that suggested that wide hems fluttering at the calf were a bold new fashion, and made fools of the boys whose trousers reached their shoes.

"It's unjust. *Fucking* Greenlaw." I nodded my automaton sympathy. Helen Greenlaw was to Nusstead what her boss, Margaret Thatcher, was to the miners. You grew up hating her by default. In our house she inspired a kind of passive antipathy, but I knew the Brames gathered round their loathing of her like other families might a fire.

Jesse kicked at the skirting, trousers flapping. "If my dad can't find work by summer I won't be able to stay on here and do my

BTEC." It was clearly a source of pride, and for good reason: Jesse's surviving brothers, Wyatt and Clay, had both left school at sixteen, Wyatt to sing jukebox classics to pensioners on Mediterranean cruises and Clay straight to work as a porter at Nazareth, an appointment that had ended in disgrace before the hospital's closure. His baby brother, Butch, born between me and Colette, had died of meningitis at seven.

"I'm sure he'll find something," I said, but I knew how many Nusstead parents were out of work.

"Yeah." We examined our shoes until the jangle of keys told us Ms. Harker was on her way.

"Thanks for waiting, guys," she said, plunging the key into the lock. "I always forget what a hike it is to this part of the school. Now, I know it's not ideal, but it's end of term soon and they'll only get thrown out at the end of the year. Marianne, what are you, 26-inch waist?"

When she opened the cupboard all three of us wrinkled our noses. I held up the skirt she gave me to inspect it for stains or holes but there were none.

"Thanks."

"That's in good nick, that," said Jesse. "You'd never know it was secondhand."

"I know there are only a few weeks of term left," said Ms. Harker, "but I thought you should sit your exams looking the part, with a bit of dignity. The clothes maketh the woman."

"Thank you."

The clothes she found Jesse were more worn. "If you end up not coming back, you can always return them." It was said without side, but the implication was clear. She meant, if he messed up his GCSEs and went straight into a job or on the dole, as Nusstead kids were expected to do. I was mortified for Jesse but his mouth was set: to respond to the insult would be to acknowledge it.

The minute hand jumped on my fake Swatch. If I ran, I could still make the bus. "Well, thanks again, Ms. Harker. I'd better go."

I threw my goodbyes over my shoulder, footsteps echoing in the corridor. Long legs didn't make me an elegant runner, with my skirt riding up and my bag whacking against my thighs. The hated exercise was all for nothing: I made the car park just as the bus pulled out. I resigned myself to the forty-minute wait for the public bus, and the ensuing walk along a winding B-road to get to Nusstead. I tried to see the good side: Mum was at home today, so Colette was looked after. This was respite from the school bus dog-whistle bullying, there was light to read by and—the clincher—the weather was dry. The puddle that appeared opposite the bus shelter when it rained always churned into four-foot waves and for every driver who slowed down there were two who sped up for a laugh. I had time to turn over Ms. Harker's words. I was torn between being flattered at the respect and, I dared hope, recognition that she showed me, and discomfort at the way she'd dismissed Jesse, only just able to grasp that it was about something more subtle than grades.

Jesse must have walked his bike through the car park because I didn't hear him until he was in front of me. He saw me take in the red moped, its paintwork striated with rust, and misread my mind. "I ride a *proper* bike when I'm out and about," he said. "This is just for school." He opened and closed his mouth a couple of times, a goldfish pop that would've been funny if his eyes weren't so serious. "Please don't tell anyone about me being a charity case. None of this is my dad's fault, all right?"

"'Course not." There was an awkward silence in the wake of Jesse's unexpected vulnerability. I paraphrased something I'd overheard Mark say at the last of the futile demonstrations, not because it was a belief I held particularly deeply but because I wanted to see Jesse's lip curl again. "None of us can help it, can we? No one in *Nusstead* caused the hospital to shut down." It was the right thing to say: he nodded, considered for a second, then handed me the crash helmet he was carrying.

"Put this on. I'll give you a lift home." I knew it was calculated, a quid pro quo; a ride on the cool boy's scooter to buy my silence. I also knew I might never get the opportunity again.

"What about you?" I said, gesturing to his head.

"Ah, I'll be all right." He raked his hands through his hair. "Been riding since I was twelve, haven't I? Come on."

The inside of the helmet smelled of Lynx deodorant. I tried to grip the sides of the seat. "Don't be shy," he said, taking my arms and wrapping them firmly around his waist.

I didn't want that ride to end. Pressed against Jesse's shoulder blades, the wind in my clothes, the familiar Suffolk countryside seemed to have all the glamour of a foreign country, of a Roman summer or a Parisian spring. We sailed through Stradbroke and rumbled over the level crossing at Hoxne. Jesse took the back roads the bus couldn't manage. The old hospital seemed to follow us, the clocktower a spike that the whole horizon seemed to revolve around. When we overtook the school bus, I hoped the girls saw the bulky bag on my back and recognized it as the one they made fun of every day. Nusstead and the Crown car park loomed up all too fast. My head, when I took off the crash helmet, felt light as helium and my thighs shook. Delighted laughter rose and bubbled from my throat before I could stop it.

"That was *brilliant*," I said, when I'd caught my breath. My utter lack of cool was apparently infectious: Jesse mirrored it.

"You look like a different person."

I felt like one, but I wasn't going to tell him that. I nodded to my front door, twenty yards across the street. "I can probably walk myself home. Thanks so much for the lift."

"Thanks for—you know." He mimed zipping shut his mouth. It was our first conspiracy and the trust cost him eye contact.

"Don't mention it." I hauled my backpack over one shoulder and tugged my skirt down, pretending to check the road for traffic when really I was wondering how I could stretch the moment until the school bus passed us and everyone saw me.

Jesse cleared his throat. "Wanna go out later?"

Shock made me throw the invitation back in his face. "Where, around here? Anywhere worth going costs money."

It was the first time that smile was turned full-beam on me. "I can show you somewhere to go that's free."

22

At seven that evening, Jesse was at the war memorial not on a moped but a bashed-up Suzuki I recognized as Mark's; Jesse wasn't legally old enough to ride it. His spare crash helmet smelled different: floral, feminine. I tried not to think about who else had worn it.

"Where are you taking me?" I asked, but my words were just steam on the visor. He took the chicane on Asylum Road so fast that my leg skimmed the ground. We slalomed along the old cedar avenue, swerving craters and rocks. A tingle rose inside me. The night had suddenly taken on the feel of a horror movie: haunted houses, initiation rites, ouija boards and conjured spirits. None of these held anything like the excitement and terror of an evening alone with Jesse Brame. I had decided not to push my luck, but to receive whatever he had to give me. Hoping had never got me anywhere, so I girded myself not for his kiss but for the moment it didn't come.

"Whoa," I said when we dismounted. The hospital was invisible behind a corrugated fence. Seven feet high, it was wider than the hospital, wider probably than Nusstead itself; the hospital grounds had always dwarfed the village that served it. Signs nailed at intervals warned that DOGS PATROL THESE GROUNDS and THESE PREMISES ARE GUARDED 24/7.

"We can't go here," I said, as Jesse hid the bike and helmets in chest-high scrub, and pulled an old army holdall from the pannier.

"There in't any dogs. Never have been. Those signs are just for show. I've never even seen a security guard here. They had security before the murder but not after it, which is typical of their logic. Dad reckons Larry Lawrence, the bloke who bought it, he's deliberately letting the place fall down. He's surprised they haven't torched it for the insurance yet." He tapped his nose. "They'll be playing the long game."

The fence appeared impenetrable, but Jesse knew better: a kick in the right place and a breach was revealed, a whole panel swinging like a cat flap.

"Bloody *hell*." Only the hospital's outline was familiar from my childhood memories. The biggest ground-floor windows were boarded up but on the top floor, ivy had punched out windowpanes and buddleia tufted in the guttering and chimney pots. Roof tiles collected in little piles, exposing struts and rafters, and the clock hands sagged at half past six. The setting sun glowed peach through a lacework of iron and steel. The great storm of the previous year, which had made matchwood of vast ancient trees and revealed the landscape's true flatness, had clearly done its work here, too.

"I know," said Jesse. "I mean it was more or less derelict anyway, but they reckon the storm did fifty years of damage in a single day. It's gonna take millions to restore. After it shut, Clay used to take me up here a lot. This was the one place that ever appreciated him, you know?" I nodded, even though it wasn't strictly true. Clay had been an orderly—a job he'd got through Mark—and he'd been caught selling on half the contents of the hospital pharmacy. These days, you'd know he was out of prison if you saw his bloodred Harley-Davidson parked outside the Crown or the Social.

We stopped outside huge double-height doors. The wood was warped, so that they no longer fit the pointed stone arch. The top peeled inward, revealing the stump of a rusting bolt. Jesse reached into his jeans and took out two huge keys on a ring. "Clay copied me a key but he obviously got it done by a mate. You can hardly take it to your local locksmith, can you? Anyway, I'm just showing you this to impress you, really. Clay's one works but this one's shit, you have to fiddle with it for ages. It's easier to go round the side."

The thrill of riding pillion on Jesse's bike was nothing to him taking my hand. Every few paces he'd turn around and smile at me, to check I was OK and I was, I was more than OK, I was leaping inside. I even felt a sick little buzz to know I was walking where Julia Solomon had taken her last steps.

"We never go in there," he said, gesturing to the low-rise villas dotted about the place, windows shuttered with steel screens. "They're riddled with asbestos. But then, we don't need them when we've got *this*."

At the very end of the building, Jesse pushed open a side door that gave instantly and we stepped into a corridor so long it had a vanishing point. Dim light came through tiny windows, too high to see out of. Striplights arrowed down the centerline of a concave ceiling and instinctively I put my hand to the switch, immediately feeling foolish for expecting the flicker and buzz. Jesse laughed and reached up to the lintel above the door, thick enough to act as a shelf, to retrieve a little yellow torch.

"This was the service corridor," he said. "But the patients were put to work too so it wasn't just for the porters and nurses. If you were on laundry duty you'd wheel great big trolleys of linen up and down all day. The next floor up's where the proper wards are, that's where your mum would've worked, and your nan. And my grandparents. Whole generations, until Greenlaw got her fucking way." I followed him past old key-code fire doors hooked flush against the wall and peered into dim rooms with strange switches and dials built into the walls. The corridor was eerily repetitive, like one of those cartoon backgrounds that loops around and around in a chase scene; dirty window, dead light, metal door, repeat. Occasionally a fire extinguisher would break the pattern.

It took three minutes to walk it. Eventually we were in the entrance hall. Even in the half-darkness and filth it took my breath away. In Suffolk you get used to space around you but only outdoors. For the first time I understood how beautiful, how inspiring, a generous interior space could be. Huge rectangular scars evoked long-gone paintings. A sweeping double staircase was a folded wing. All of the balustrades were gone and in some places the balcony itself had fallen away, so the doors seemed set in mid-air, like a giant advent calendar.

I was almost shaking with the effort of feigned nonchalance.

Jesse knew what lay behind every door. "That's the old offices and that up there," he said, pointing. "We can get into them through the back ways. Actually most of these doors down here are out of bounds. The view from the clocktower's brilliant but the stairs are fucked and the banisters are going. Even I wouldn't go up there. That one next to it leads through a little corridor to the chapel, which was so dodgy they shut it up even before the hospital was closed. Come on, let's go upstairs."

We pushed through the door marked WOMEN and climbed a narrow stone staircase. Here were the wards proper: barred windows, beds with plastic-covered mattresses still at their stations. In one ward a pair of lilac Stead & Simpson bedroom slippers rested in first position under the bed, and in another a pair of glasses, opaque with dust, lay on a bedside table next to a Catherine Cookson novel with the bookmark still in. Ragged yellow privacy screens billowed in the breezes that wound through broken windows. The place had the air of somewhere abandoned in a hurry, after the four-minute warning. Jesse had all but handed me a time machine. My excitement at being here overtook my nerves about being with him.

"I in't been anywhere like this before," I said. In a teetering wall unit we found a box containing what looked like a giant test tube with a kink in it. I unfolded the instructions, got as far as the words "portable douche enema" and dropped it, carpeting the room with glass.

"Sorry!" I grimaced.

"S'OK," said Jesse. "It's only equipment and they'll want to replace it all when it reopens." This made no sense—the new mental health unit in Ipswich was state of the art—but I shrugged it off.

According to my mum, by the time Colette left school, this would be the poshest hotel in Suffolk, rich ladies who lunched paying a fortune to have their cellulite beaten away with twigs, and jobs here would be the most sought after in the area. I hoped they would save a corner of the hotel for its history; build a miniature museum for the curious guests. Perhaps I could even look after it. *That* would be the kind of job to keep me in Nusstead, a way to stay and do something I loved without leaving the people I loved.

"Are you thirsty?" he asked, when he saw me licking dust from my lips. "Here." From his army bag he took a pewter Thermos flask and carefully poured me a tiny cup of tea. Any nerves I'd ever had around Jesse Brame evaporated. It didn't get less rock 'n' roll than a Thermos.

We passed a thick steel door signposted OCCUPATIONAL THERAPY. The bow of a key protruded from a door. "That shouldn't be there." Jesse frowned and pocketed it. "It's not like me to leave something like that."

In the ballroom an ornate molded ceiling overhung sports-hall markings on parquet. Midsummer evening light poured through the windows. I tried to calculate how many times you could fit my house in here and gave up at thirty. An old wheelchair was parked by a bricked-up fireplace, its leather seat cracked and sagging. Standing on the rusted footplate, I scooted around the room, one pointed leg out behind me like a ballerina, the wheels tracing circles in the dust.

"So what do you think?" said Jesse. I didn't know that I was about to pass the test that the other girls had failed at the first trespass, revolted by the stench of the corridors, or too freaked out by the Julia Solomon connection even to get off the bike.

"It's *beautiful*," I said. I made my arms wide and spun around, embarrassment at my childish abandon settling on me by the first rotation, then flying away when I saw that Jesse's smile was sincere, not mocking.

"You," he said, "are a lot cooler than I thought you were."

I watched him jangling his keys like a janitor, and thought how different he was to the housewife's-bit-on-the-side image he projected. "You're a lot *less* cool than I thought you were." I tasted my own daring like salt on my tongue.

"Yeah, don't tell anyone." He put his finger to his smiling lips.

We climbed onto the stage, where the boards were snowed under with pigeon shit. I stroked the gray velvet curtain and left blue trails in the dust. Half a dozen pigeons came flapping out of the folds. Jesse screamed and grabbed my hand tight.

"Sorry," he said, his palm pulsing fast. "I fucking hate pigeons."

"They're idiots," I said, as one bird flung itself repeatedly at an intact window, ignoring the gaping hole beside it.

"They're idiots with beady eyes who shit in your hair given half the chance. God, that one's only got one *foot*. Let's go and see if the art students are around."

"Students?" There had been no sign of anyone else. I was surprised at the stab of possessiveness I already felt for the place. He doesn't want to be alone with me, I thought. Only as hope sank did I realize I hadn't been able to suppress it.

"I know, students are knobs, but better to have someone here, keeping an eye on the place."

Back in the atrium Jesse pushed gently on the door to the men's wing. It fell flat from its jamb like a drawbridge, the thwack and reverberation announcing our presence.

"Jesse?" Round male vowels came bouncing down the corridor. "All right?"

This wing was the women's wing reflected but here the walls had been primed and painted. A huge griffin, gold wings wide, stretched the length of a ward. A side room had been painted in thick yellow and black stripes and branded with the sign for toxic waste. In a bathroom, a row of shop mannequins, all shiny bald heads and cheekbones underscored in shimmering russet blush, were trussed in straitjackets and a bath was brimful of elegant plastic arms. The students were in a little seclusion room next door, papering the walls with silver foil. There were three of them, two young men in overalls and a girl with spiky pink hair who swept her eyes over me with such contempt that I had to look down to check I wasn't still wearing my school uniform.

"Hi Alex," said Jesse to the tallest of them.

"How's it going, Jesse, man?"

"Can't stop," said Jesse. "I'm showing Marianne around."

"Don't worry, we'll keep to our side tonight," said Alex, raising an eyebrow.

We retraced our steps along that echoing corridor. I didn't want the evening to end and yet I was keen for it to be over so I could begin the serious, lonely business of evaluating it.

Our tour ended back where we'd started. The hospital was in darkness save for a dim light from the men's wing. Above us, the wide Suffolk sky was paint-splashed with stars; Jesse took my chin and tilted it to show me Orion's Belt, then lowered his head to mine. His kiss was a secret and a promise.

I drew away first. "My mum says I have to be home by ten on a school night." I waited for Jesse to lose patience, to decide he'd go back to his married woman who probably knew how to do all the things I'd only read about in *Cosmopolitan*.

"Don't want to get on Debbie Smy's bad side," he said, mock cowering. "Don't worry about it. We've got forever. I'll bring you back after your exams, all right?"

I was almost disappointed by how easy it was to become his girlfriend. I never got the school bus home again; within a week, Jesse's spare crash helmet smelled of my shampoo but that was as far as it went. The rumors that trailed me through the school corridors outstripped what we actually got up to.

He was true to his word. The afternoon I sat my last exam, Jesse came to pick me up, his duffel bag stuffed with an old but clean duvet that Trish would never miss from the back of the airing cupboard. I wasn't nervous anymore. I was thrilled to have discovered a soft secret side to him, not the angry outsider of local lore but quiet, respectful, as interested as he was interesting, the kind of boy who says *forever* on a first date.

23

That summer, Colette went to holiday club and my days were my own for the first time since she was born. Jesse and I both had part-time jobs—his sought-after shelf-stacking work at the little co-op, and my babysitting—but all our free time belonged to Nazareth. The art students packed up and went inter-railing, leaving us the square mile of the hospital and its grounds to ourselves. The occasional camper or bum spent one or two nights there but they never bothered us. We spread the duvet on the grass outside; Jesse got a very nice tan on his back and I got one on my shins. I put into practice all the moves I'd learned from *Cosmopolitan* magazine but I must have missed something because most of the results seemed to be for Jesse. Sometimes we hauled the Suzuki through the gap in the fence and rode it along the half-mile corridor, heads bare, hair flying, screaming as we went. He taught me to ride his bike and although I was terrified to go over thirty, after a few hours of his patient tutelage I could close the throttle, press the gear shifter and complete a wobbly length of the cedar drive.

Jesse only spoke of the other women he'd taken here in the abstract. "You're the only girl who really gets this place," he said and because I knew it was true, because I had come to love the mysterious wreckage of it as much as he did, the old jealousies died. If the Ipswich housewife had ever existed, she was long gone now. Jesse didn't have time to be with anyone else. If I was jealous of anything it was the attention he paid to the place itself. I wouldn't have been surprised to hear him refer to Nazareth as "she," like Clay referred to his huge red motorbike. Jesse was paranoid about vandalism and decay, and would patrol the place every day, noting out loud the faults as they appeared. When beds weren't left the way he thought he remembered them, he taped one of my long hairs across the door to see if anyone was coming in (they weren't). He measured a crack in the wall at the base of the clocktower to see if it really was widening by the day (it was).

I didn't mind trailing in his wake. The display of competent, adult masculinity was so clearly for my benefit that I was only flattered, and besides, my fascination equaled his, eclipsed it in some ways. There was always something new to inventory. In an unexplored side room we found a bed with leather straps on it, a rusty trolley and a cream enamel tub, about the same size and shape as the spin-dryer we had in our kitchen, covered in switches and dials.

"Dental equipment?" said Jesse. He fiddled with some of the dials and put the tube to his teeth.

"No it in't," I said. *The Bell Jar* had been a set text in English. "It's an ECT machine."

"A what now?"

"Electro-convulsive therapy. They did it with the suicidal patients, when medication had failed. They fried your brain, and it sort of shocked you out of your depression." I rummaged behind it and brought out a huge pair of metal callipers, pads on either side. "This is what they put on your head. Sylvia Plath had it done."

"I knew that," said Jesse with a confidence that told me he'd never heard of her.

There was a blank electroshock treatment record on the trolley, columns labeled *Date, Time, No. of shocks, Glissando*—this lovely Latinate word, combined with the bars and bullet points, felt more like sheet music than a medical record—*Resistance, Voltage, Duration (secs), Type of response, Grand mals to date, Medication* and *Clinical notes*. I folded it up and slid it into my pocket.

"Babe, why're you taking that?" If Jesse's smile lit up his face, his frown could darken a room. "I had enough of this sort of thing with Clay trying to rip out the fireplaces and that."

I laughed at him. "I'm just interested in old things, that's all."

"Yeah, but . . ." He put his hand in my pocket and slid it out, placed it back on the metal tray and patted it. "Best to leave it there. In case they need it. To work the equipment."

I still didn't get it. "They're never going to sell this stuff now," I said, gesturing to the ECT machine, the trolley, the filthy beds. "It's years out of date for a start, and anyway who'd come and get it?"

I could tell he was trying to stay patient with me. "Not for *selling*. For when the place reopens. You never know what they might need."

I searched his face for signs he was joking but he was more serious than I'd ever seen him. A soft weight seemed to descend inside me as I realized that he really did hope—no, *believe*—that one day this rotting, obsolete building would be a working hospital again. "That's what my dad's campaigning for, isn't it?" he said, with the forced patience of someone talking to an idiot. "Get Greenlaw's decision overturned. Reinstate all the jobs." I hadn't known Mark's campaign went beyond whingeing in the Social.

"But Jesse," I said, not knowing how to begin. "All the old patients, they're all settled now."

He shook his head. "You don't understand, babe." I could tell he enjoyed the rare moment of superiority. "We need to get Nusstead back to how it used to be when we were kids." He gestured out of the window to the village over the fen. "Everyone in work, weekends down the club, you knew you had a job waiting when you came out of school. A proper community, not half the men on the dole and the rest of them scattered all over the place. Not your mum freezing her arse off taking two buses halfway across Suffolk."

I didn't put Jesse straight. I would hardly be telling him anything he hadn't heard before and besides, I didn't want my pity to make a fool of him. Jesse's misguided convictions revealed a vulnerability behind the front of machismo that he still kept up even for me. A part of him that was only mine.

If Jesse was Nazareth's caretaker, I became its curator, scouring cupboards and shelves for what I secretly called my "clues" while he fretted over rotting window frames. The hospital was seething with stories: they were in the graffiti (most of which proved the locker hall at school was part of a longstanding folk art tradition) and in the scratch marks on the walls of the seclusion rooms. In the old Occupational Therapy room, where Jesse was concerned by warping floorboards, I was moved by the brittle fading pictures kept in flat drawers like at the art room in school. One patient had repeated the same incredibly detailed sketch of the clocktower over and over. In a drawer near a typewriter with a dead ribbon were sheaves of shorthand and typescript. Someone had typed the phrase "a lad had a salad" across pages and pages, which I thought was a symptom of madness itself until I realized that they must be typing exercises. On the third page, halfway down the rows of perfect text it said *typing this sentence in the middle to see if the thick bitch even reads it ten bob says she doesn't*. The typist had then resumed the exercise: a lad had a salad, a lad had a salad, a lad had a salad.

I sneaked my clues past Jesse, sure that if I could just gather enough fragments, the human stories I craved would reveal themselves. There should have been rich pickings in the records room, an echoing hangar on the top floor behind the old admin offices, but this maze of floor-to-ceiling shelves had been cleared out during closure. The odd folder or page had survived the cull and been left flat on the stacks. My hands would tremble to hold them. Mostly my finds were disappointing. Endless pages of figures, financial documents, meaningless numbers filled in by hand in fading cursive script on sheets of paper softened to beige chamois. Sometimes the form itself would have survived but the ink would have faded away, handwriting becoming its author's ghost, typescript blurring, absorbing into paper. A 1963 book from the hospital pharmacy listed drugs that meant nothing to me: Largactil, somnifane, paraldehyde, phenobarbitone.

The shelves at the back of the room were packed tightly and could only be accessed by turning a wheel set in the wall. I steered it to the left, feeling like a ship's captain, and the stacks drew apart to reveal yards of empty shelves with a few fallen leaves of paper. Here at last were snippets of notes, maddeningly unconnected to names:

> *The patient persists in her grandiose delusion that she is Anastasia Romanov, escaped daughter of the last Russian tsar. That she is a twenty-five-year-old seamstress who has never left Suffolk cannot be made to penetrate.*

Another read:

> *She insists that she is already dead, and sleeps with pennies on her eyes to pay the ferryman for her journey into the next world. Her fellow patient saw the pennies in the night and ate them.*

An old admissions register had at some stage got wet down one side of the page, obliterating most of the forenames. Only a very long first name would show up: the "ine" of Josephine or a Christine, I supposed. The "tte" of a demented Charlotte, the "dra" of a tortured Alexandra. Otherwise there were surnames: Lummis, a Morris and a Matthews, half a dozen Smiths. No Brames but a smattering of Smys. The same names you saw on the war memorial in Nusstead. The staff here were looking after their own.

These clues, these snapshots of madness became the main exhibits of what I had come to call my archive. I had only two feet of privacy in the world, a shelf above the bed I shared with Colette, too high for little sisters to reach. Here I kept my textbooks and notes. I squirreled my scraps away in a plain box file which I labeled *James I: Foreign Policy*. I told myself I was reading with a historian's mature detachment but the truth is I was a bored child looking for stories. The women in these notes were jigsaw pieces, crossword clues, barely human at all.

24

August, and the hottest either of us could remember. There was no breeze but the air around the hospital seemed in perpetual motion, thick with flitting bees.

"Look." Jesse had a dead butterfly in his hands, the lilac tissue of its wings torn at the edges. "She'll love this." He'd bought Colette a kids' microscope in a charity shop—a plastic magnifying glass set on top of an acrylic pyramid—and he delighted in finding things for her.

"Pretty," I said, twisting my hair into a knot on top of my head; it felt like removing a layer of clothing. "God, I need to get out of the sun."

Jesse ineffectually fanned the back of my neck with his hand. "There's only one place cool enough."

"I thought I knew everywhere," I said, as he led me down sunken steps in the north face of the hospital. I hadn't known there was a level below ground. "Where is this?" He nodded upward at the sign saying MORTUARY. "Are you serious?" I asked, but every step cooled the air by a degree. The light was filtered through ivy and dirty glass, giving our skin a green, alien tinge that countered the heatwave's flush.

"What are these?" I asked Jesse. The units recessed in the white-tiled walls looked, at first glance, like bakers' ovens with their huge trays on trolleys. He folded his arms, waited for the penny to drop.

"Oh, Jesus," I said, and sprang away.

Today, Jesse's bag contained a scouring pad and cream cleaner, which he used to scrub the limestone slab. I'd assumed it was one of the caretaking rituals, but instead he rolled out the blanket.

"Oh Jesse, we *can't.*"

He smiled a wolfish smile. "We can."

I gave the performance I had learned to put on in place of the elusive abandon. Still I didn't hear the footsteps in the corridor and when the door slammed shut we both froze. The key turned, the video-nasty sound of it prelude to the screaming girl in a thousand straight-to-VHS horror films.

"Who could it be?" I turned to Jesse for reassurance. "Alex, having a laugh?"

"They're all traveling. And anyway they wouldn't." I reached for his hand but he was on his feet, dressing, clumsily rucking his cut-offs over his hips. My thoughts were pulled in the obvious direction as I scrambled into my dress. Darius Cunniffe was locked up for life but there were hundreds more like him. "Stay there," said Jesse. The floor was littered with old pipes, torn from the walls: he picked one out of the dust before approaching the door and pulling down the wicket.

"Who's there?" His voice echoed.

"You little *perv.*" The voice was high, the accent thick. "You dirty sod." Jesse's shoulders lowered and he set the pipe against the wall.

"Oh for fuck's sake, Michelle." He threw me a look of terrified apology, his initial panic replaced by a different kind of fear. He was scared of my reaction. "Open the door, babe."

My endearment thrown *her* way. I knew he had taken her here. The jealousy I thought I'd mastered reared its head.

"Bollocks I will." Whoever Michelle was, she was furious. I

scanned the space; that huge door I'd taken for more cold storage might be another staircase. Surely even the Victorians designed emergency exits? I tried to keep my breathing even.

"Meesh," he said. "Come back here. Put the key back. Come on, babe."

Over his shoulder, I saw the girl—the woman—in the murky corridor: one hand on a hip, oversized key dangling from the other. She had long red stringy hair and wore denim hotpants, a pink bikini top, chipped gold nail varnish. A rash of spots circled a full, wide mouth. Jealousy gave way to indignation. Was *this* my competition?

Michelle stepped up to the wicket, looked me up and down as I had her. "This is her, is it?" She was going for contempt but couldn't quite get there.

"Come on, babe, let me out," Jesse wheedled. "This in't going to solve anything. I can't talk to you properly through this window, can I? Come on, it's all water under the bridge, in't it? We said, din't we, no hard feelings. Come on, you don't want to do this, I haven't done anything wrong. Good girl, good girl." The rest of their conversation was inaudible to me, Jesse's voice was lowering by the sentence, almost as though he were trying to calm an animal or a very young child. Whatever he said to her worked, because the key was posted through the wicket and he turned it with a screech of metal on metal. Jesse put it in his pocket then comforted Michelle in the corridor, stroking her hair and muttering into the top of her head. At one point she tried to kiss him: when he pulled away, and nodded in my direction, she slapped his face and screamed, "Up yours, Jesse Brame!"

We watched her reddened heels disappear up the steps and both flinched at the postscript of her temper tantrum, the slamming of a door, somewhere far away. We stayed still and wordless until a faint, faint throttle and roar of an engine told us she had gone. I waited for Jesse to fill the silence. He pressed his palms into his eyes before speaking.

"An old flame that didn't get the message," he said. "She lives out in Diss. Babe, she din't mean anything to me, all right? I just shagged her. I *love* you."

"Oh, that's every girl's dream, that is. How old is she, anyway?"

Did he look ashamed or did I only want him to? "She was in Wyatt's class at school." I wasn't sure how old Wyatt was but knew he'd left Waveney Secondary before we started there, making Michelle at least twenty-two. "I only went with her because she had a car—it was before the bike—and it was the only way we could get here. It only happened a couple of times, she din't like it here. She's a nutter, I din't realize till it was too late. She drinks too much, she's jealous, she has these meltdowns. I don't think she can help it, she's not very well in the head. This is the best place for her, ironically." I looked at the slab in alarm and Jesse shuddered. "No, the mental hospital, I mean, not the morgue."

"I can't believe that was your famous older woman."

Jesse mistook my scorn for jealousy, and shook his head violently. "You know what she makes me realize? All that time I was getting off with my brothers' mates and stuff, I was off in the wrong direction. I have to *admire* a woman, d'you know what I mean, and I just thought—girls my age, you know, I thought you'd have to go older for that, find someone with a bit of experience under her belt but that's not it at all, is it? It's—what you've got, it comes from *inside* you. You're clever, you've got class, you're beautiful." While he was talking, he had cupped his hands around my jaw, searching my face. "I love you, babe, I *adore* you, and one day I'm going to get this place reopened and it'll be like it was before Greenlaw ruined everything. We can have the life our parents should've had."

I shivered despite the heat. Only now, in the explicit stating of Jesse's dreams, did I realize how vastly they differed from my own. Why did he have to spoil it by talking about the future? Wasn't here and now enough? I couldn't divide Jesse from Nazareth. It was where we went, it was who we were. I couldn't imagine us existing outside the bubble of it. I met his eyes, shining with sincerity and hope, and realized that the only thing harder to imagine than staying with him was hurting him.

25

"Speech!" The cry went up at about 9 p.m., and Mark was delighted to gather his family on the stage of the old Social club. The glittery curtain was up and Trish had made a banner: she'd painted "Happy 50th Birthday Mark!" on an old hospital sheet that said "Save Nazareth from Closure" on the other side.

Mark took off his ten-gallon hat and slurred, "First time all five of us have been together in two years." He was in full cowboy outfit, his arms around his boys. Jesse suddenly seemed very young next to Wyatt, who'd had his mullet frosted with highlights, and Clay, who was only in his mid-twenties but looked as though he had lived twice the life of the rest of them. "I'd like to thank you all so much for coming. Dedicate this to my Trish, my gorgeous girl"—Trish raised her glass and stabbed herself in the eye with a little turquoise cocktail umbrella—"and my fine boys, all grown up into men now, although we still miss Butch, we still miss him every day, don't we Trish?" Trish aged two decades in a second, and buried her head in Wyatt's shoulder. Mark, sensing the drop in mood, changed tack. "All I need now is for one of them to give me a grandchild, eh, boys?" Mark was looking at Clay when he said this but Jesse winked at me across the dancefloor. "And now, I want you all up on your feet. No excuses."

Wyatt took the mic and launched into "Come on Eileen."

"Babe," said Jesse. "What're you having to drink? I love you."
I'd never seen him properly drunk before: he was just the right side
of charming. He waved a twenty at the barman. When the Brames
had money, they liked you to know about it. To my astonishment,
Clay had persuaded Jesse into an act of desecration. To pay for the
party—the band, the dance caller, the bar staff—the three brothers had spent a backbreaking day cantilevering the Victorian fireplaces out of some of the rooms in Nazareth it was still safe to enter
and a few that it wasn't, and selling them to antique dealers down
in Essex. They'd told Mark it was Wyatt's tip money and he had
believed them, or pretended to.

"You're beautiful," he said, handing me my Babycham. "You
look about twenty-one." I was dressed to kill for the first time in
my life, in a bandeau dress and red stilettos from the Littlewoods
catalog that had cost me a week's babysitting cash. I couldn't walk
properly or eat anything. You have to learn how to be looked at,
and it was a skill I accrued readily, giddily. "I'm so bloody proud."
His words were a reminder that I was not on display in my own
right, but paraded as his girlfriend. Our relationship had been con-
ducted entirely in a state of trespass but everyone is famous in a
small town and now we had gone public to much congratulation;
we couldn't have received warmer wishes if it had been our wedding day. I no longer felt like an alien: Jesse had naturalized me.

"What was that wink for, then?"

"Don't worry, we've got long enough for that. You've got to
finish your A levels first. I don't want our kids having a thick mum
as well as a thick dad." His respectable set of GCSEs was something he constantly downplayed, knowing that any day his family's
need might outweigh their pride, and Jesse would have to leave
school for full-time work. "You'd probably even get into college in
Ipswich."

I bit my lip. A stash of university prospectuses had replaced the
boarding-school pamphlets, stashed next to my archive from the
hospital. I saw, if I wanted to progress, what I would have to leave
behind and wondered if I had the requisite hardness in my heart.

"Yeah." I let my gaze travel the length of the bar. Next to the optics, packets of dry-roasted peanuts were attached to a picture of a glamour model, another inch of flesh revealed every time someone bought one.

"We can have our wedding reception here," said Jesse. "Handy for the church."

"I din't know you were into church. I've never seen you anywhere near it." It came out stronger than I'd expected: I suppose it was easier to call him out on his hypocrisy than to set him straight about marriage.

"Oh yeah," he said, clearly hurt. "Heaven and hell, good and evil. I believe in all that. You don't have to go to church to try and be a good person."

Clay appeared at my side, waving an empty pint glass at the barman. He was taller and thicker than Jesse, with close-cropped hair and a broken nose to Jesse's straight one but the resemblance was there in the high coloring and the broad brow and the same essential hair-and-skin smell, overlaid with engine oil and leather. Clay buzzed with a threatening energy, like the pylons that spiked the sunset outside. He followed my gaze to the peanuts and said, "I'll take the lot," and roared with beery laughter at his own joke. I smiled weakly back, and turned to face the room. There was a working dartboard in one corner. Someone had skewered a picture of Helen Greenlaw, dart through the vitreous bullseye of her right pupil, so that it looked as if the tip itself had pulled the blackness from her iris. On the wall someone had written in marker pen "Lest we forget." If only, I thought with a wave of frustration. I didn't like Helen Greenlaw any more than the next Nussteader but the Brames were *obsessed*.

"You heard they had camera crews up at the old place?" Clay asked. "They're making a documentary on it."

This was news to me. We hadn't seen anyone. "About the murder?"

"Nah. About institutions in general. Private schools. Prisons." The lip curl he gave was pure Jesse. "Greenlaw's son's behind it.

He reckons his posh school fucked him up. Doesn't talk to his mum. Well, would you?"

I was concluding that it might not be a great idea to tell Clay that I had tried and failed to be fucked up by a posh school when a screech of feedback turned all heads toward the stage.

"Whoops-a-daisy, sorry about that," said Wyatt, then switched to a cod American accent. "Let's slow things down with a song for all you lovers out there." When he sang "Always on My Mind," the dancefloor broke into couples who held each other and circled in pairs. Mark and Trish Brame moved fluidly together. When Jesse steered me into the middle of the dancefloor, Michelle snagged in my peripheral vision, the specter under the disco ball. It was the form, when you were dancing cheek to cheek, to keep your eyes closed, but whenever I lifted mine, she was in front of me, as though she was gliding around after us on wheels. When Wyatt finished, everyone broke apart to clap. Michelle was gone, but my mother was staring at us.

After Wyatt's set a DJ took over, chart music flooding the dance-floor in a way that the live band hadn't managed. Jesse let Colette tutor him in the actions of the YMCA. Look how good he is with children, I thought, and then seconds later: where did *that* come from?

I caught Wyatt at the bar. "You sang beautifully."

He raised a plucked eyebrow. "This isn't really me, it's just as a favor to my dad. I'm more of a belter, really. Torch songs, show tunes." Wyatt was the first camp man I ever met, as effeminate as Clay was bruisingly macho. "But my dad wants country on his birthday, he can have country."

"How long are you back for?" I asked.

"I'll be on the road again as soon as I can without causing offense to the old boy," he said. "I find I can never stay here for too long. I hardly need to explain to you. You've got it too."

"Got what?"

Wyatt waved his hands theatrically. "Wanderlust, ambition, call it what you want. Five minutes after I get back here I want to be traveling again. What, you want to live in Nusstead your whole life?"

I felt sick. Wyatt had recognized in seconds what I knew his brother never would. "Vegas is the goal for me," said Wyatt. "Clay's the same, can't stay in one place. Ironic really, given that he lives half his life in captivity. Jesse, though, he's like my dad, he's a homebody. He's got everything he wants right here." He must have understood the implications of what he was saying, but left them unsaid. Disco-ball diamonds skidded across the dancefloor and floated up the walls. Jesse, Trish and Clay were arm in arm singing the chorus to "Hi Ho Silver Lining" and in Jesse's face I saw Mark's, clear as a photograph, nights like this as good as it ever got. I willed myself to want it as much as he did.

I didn't go home with Jesse that night. We still hadn't stayed at each other's houses. Why would we, when we had Nazareth? Autumn, though, was starting to bite and I wondered what the winter would bring.

Colette, jacked up on Coke and party food, ran ahead of us back to Main Street. Mum's nurse's calves made her sure-footed even three sheets to the wind and in high heels. "Are you taking precautions?" she asked unprompted.

I hadn't known a blush could sting. "Yes. I've got myself on the pill."

"Good girl. Should've had this conversation earlier, really, but I didn't realize how serious it had got till tonight."

"Everyone my age is doing it."

"Oh, Marianne, I don't mean sex. I don't know if you've noticed but this is the big one as far as Jesse's concerned. Same face on him that Mark had when he met Trish. You could really hurt him."

"Hang on, isn't this supposed to be the other way around?"

"All I'm saying is, I can see which way the wind's blowing. Once you go off to college that'll be it. Where's the jobs round here, for a girl like you? I'm not stupid." Mum's voice carried over her shoulder and I could tell that she couldn't bear to face me, that this was not a conversation but a practiced speech. "Where d'you go with him anyway? Trish says you're never there, and you're certainly never here. I know ideally you'd have your own room, but you're welcome to bring him home."

"We just go out," I said. "Around."

"Well, they invented sex before they invented beds. When I was your age, we used to wait until the fields were full of haystacks and—"

"Jesus, Mum, that's *enough*!"

She laughed, fishing in her coat pocket for her keys. "Well, if you do get yourself in trouble or anything, come to me, first sign of it—we'll catch it in time."

"All *right*. Can we please change the subject?"

Inside, Mum kicked off her shoes and was half a head shorter than me. "Bed, munchkin," she said to Colette, who vanished upstairs with uncharacteristic obedience. "Just let me say my piece then I'll drop it. Babies and nursing's all I ever wanted but I want you to do better than me. That's the difference between me and Mark. He wants his boys to stay and be the same. Whereas I want more for you than I had. I want more for you than I can give you. You've got clever blood in you, and I don't mean mine." She pulled off her hoop earrings and set them on the mantelpiece as though referring to my father was something she did all the time. "Make us a cup of tea, will you, love?"

I could have challenged her on it but the shock froze my brain. Instead, I asked: "Do you want sugar?"

"Oh yes." She closed her eyes. I waited for the kettle to boil working up the nerve to go and ask her more questions. When I carried the mug into the front room she was out cold on the sofa, mouth lolling open, and I was relieved. I tucked her under an old hospital-issue blanket.

I drank her tea, feeling hours away from sleep. I had been seen for the second time that evening and my denial about mine and Jesse's future was impossible to sustain. I went downstairs for water, tiptoeing past my gently snoring mother. As I drew the living room curtains, I saw two figures writhing against the war memorial, illuminated by a flickering streetlamp. Not teenagers, but a man and a woman: Clay Brame, stocky and blue in jeans and a denim waistcoat. There was one long white leg hooked around his back and his hand raked through thin red hair.

26

Late that year, Jesse grew out of his leathers, gave them to me, and inherited an old set of Clay's. We were still getting taller but we had no meat on our bones. There's an old Suffolk cliché that there's not a single hill between us and Siberia and that's why the wind blows so chill. That winter, I believed it.

Freezing rain fell constantly. The fen froze and black ice on Asylum Road islanded the hospital. We began to spend time in our homes, which were barely more hospitable than the old wreck. The Brames' pipes burst and their boiler failed. My house was only bearable because Jesse had lagged our Victorian single-pane windows with bubble wrap. Trish's arthritis took hold fast as frost and she had to give up her Saturdays in the launderette. I took over her job. When we saw her and Mark, walking hand in hand like they always did, she looked more like his mother than his wife. They were adamant that Jesse would stay in school but he had to work stacking shelves in the little co-op through the nights. Our wages were swallowed by our respective household budgets. My mum had all her overtime cut and the reality of raising two children on a nurse's wage bit hard. We lived off on-the-turn food that Jesse foraged from the bin outside the co-op and he would have lost his job if the manager, Nazareth's former site manager, a father of four, hadn't been doing it too.

It was the end of November before we could return to Nazareth. It was late afternoon and a weak sun shone on land that just would not dry out. Jesse had brought Clay's old toolbag in case anything needed fixing.

"Won't he miss it?" I'd asked, as he'd hauled it from a hook in the Brames' lock-up. You didn't want to get on the wrong side of Clay.

"He's in the nick again, in't he?" said Jesse, nodding at the red Harley-Davidson in the corner, as though its presence not only accounted for Clay's absence but explained it. "Handling stolen goods." He colored in shame. One brother dead, one forever at sea and the other in almost permanent disgrace. No wonder Jesse felt he had to single-handedly continue his father's doomed campaign. "I don't kid myself I'm a professional," he said, slinging his bag over the back of the bike, "but I can patch things up."

It was a pipe dream. I understood that now, even if he didn't, and pretense was a price I was willing to pay for our return to our playground. But my shy awe had gone: I found myself snapping at him. I didn't know that the journey from grudging tolerance to contempt only goes one way.

The fence had been flattened and vandals had been in, almost as though they had known the building's unofficial curator was on enforced leave. A battered Ford Escort, license plates ripped off, had been abandoned near the chapel. "Joyriders," said Jesse. "No respect." The place had changed almost beyond recognition, the advancement of dereliction human rather than organic. Everything Jesse had worked to maintain had been ripped out. He caressed holes in the plaster and tried to see the positive side. "The whole place would've needed rewiring anyway." I told myself that passion was always attractive, even when it was misdirected, and believed myself. I was seventeen.

The supporting wall at the base of the clocktower had been knocked through with a huge hammer that they'd left in the rubble. A fire had burned out the whole of the men's service staircase, and black soot obscured the art students' murals. It broke my heart that such a beautiful building seemed to me beyond restoration, too far gone for my own little fantasy of a place that was part hotel, part museum.

"Why the hell isn't the owner on to this?" I asked Jesse.

"I wouldn't be surprised if Lawrence was *behind* this. I'm condemning this whole wing." He opened the clocktower: the stairs ran wet like little mossy weirs. The stairwell should have dropped to the mortuary level but the black water was five feet deep, mirroring the criss-cross of the suicide-proof iron bars that now seemed to be the only thing holding the structure upright. Jesse plucked two fallen balustrades and arranged them in an X across the door.

There was a lake in the ballroom, the grand ceiling rose reflected perfectly in the floor. When Jesse stirred the glassy surface with a curtain pole, the foul water revealed itself. He closed the door behind us. "There'll be nothing left for us by summer."

My beloved building was dying, stone by stone.

We finished our day in the records room, wringing visibility from the dusk. As if to honor the special occasion, Jesse used the Brames' most powerful torch with the prohibitively expensive batteries, hooking it from an old light fitting. He wanted to check whether the damage below had worsened a crack in the wall. When he started mixing spackle to stuff it, I couldn't bear to look anymore.

I walked around the room until I'd stripped the place of all its remaining paperwork, brushed dust and rubble from empty shelves and furniture in a tactile goodbye. One of the steel filing cabinets supposedly fixed to the wall wobbled under my hand. It had shifted a full two inches to the left. I pulled it gently to one side and heard a swish of falling paper. Squinting into the crack, I saw a pale rectangle. I could picture the chaotic closure, a furious member of staff hurriedly boxing up old files, watching one loose folder slipping from the top of the pile and thinking, *fuck it*. I grazed my knuckles retrieving a beige folder, its grubby white ribbon loose. I stepped into the pool of Jesse's light to read.

Instead of the usual incomprehensible figures were extensive notes. Paragraphs, not columns. Looping doctor's handwriting, so unlike my modern ballpoint scrawl. Addresses. Dates. Names! A P. Preston, a C. Wilson, an H. Morris. My heart tripped over itself in excitement and I let the whole cache slip from my hands. *Photographs!* I was left with a dozen-odd detached sheets of paper in no order, and three postcard-sized black-and-white portraits, not named but with case numbers blurred to illegibility on the rear. I saw a girl with long dark plaits; a plump woman with frizzy hair, and another whose glossy portrait could have been an actress's head-shot. As with all non-contemporary photographs, the lack of color and the clothes and hairstyles I associated with "old women" made it almost impossible to guess their ages. The girl with the plaits was clearly younger than the other two, who could have been anything from twenty to fifty. I had found Nazareth's daughters, the patients whose stories would bring the past back to life.

"Jesse, you won't *believe* this."

He didn't even glance up. "Later." He began to smooth over the crack, which snaked halfway up the wall, describing an imaginary coastline. "I want to get this done."

I stuck two fingers up at his back, and read to myself. It was impossible to know whether these notes all referred to the same patient, or different women, and whether these were the women whose names and addresses I had.

The patient is of the better class but presented in a very aggressive state, pouring forth a torrent of foul language. Following a violent outburst upon admission this patient spent six days out of the last seven in seclusion after repeated violence against female nursing staff. We will recommend that she is given a pre-frontal leucotomy to release her from these violent impulses and have written to the neurosurgeon at Ipswich with a view to the procedure being carried out as a matter of urgency. Without this treatment the patient must be transferred to a secure hospital. With it, she has every hope of resuming normal life.

What did "the better class" mean? Was it the frizzy-haired woman, the girl or the glamourpuss? In my experience, posh people were much scruffier than the women I knew. Ms. Harker, for example, never wore makeup.

The next page had a different number for a different patient.

This is her seventh admission to Nazareth and one of the most debilitating cases of this nature we have seen. It must be noted that past responses to insulin therapy have been very poor. However with the newer treatments prognosis is excellent and her spirits are relatively high, and her moods stable.

I turned the page and found an entry dated the followed day: *PATIENT DECEASED.*

The loss took my breath away.

"Marianne, I'm trying to *concentrate*," said Jesse.

I shoved the notes into the breast of my leathers. What if there were others where they came from? Greedy for more treasure, I took Jesse's big hammer and gave the steel cabinet a whack. The first impact woke up muscles in my arms I hadn't known about, but it only dented the side.

"Whoah!" said Jesse, but I was already swinging the hammer again. This blow did part the cabinet from the wall, with a bang as loud as a firework. A long metal bracket and half the bricks in the wall came with it. The coastline in the plaster became a cliff face, the pale blue sea of the wall sending up white horses of filler. At first, I thought the sensation of the floor lurching under my feet was the shock but a second later I understood it was some deep structural shift in the building as the shelving units began to tilt our way. Jesse was ashen, as though already filmed in dust.

"Shit, Marianne. What've you *done*?"

He unhooked the torch without stopping to turn it off and grabbed me by the wrist, pulling me out of the records room and down the stairs so quickly it felt like falling. In the atrium, the double doors loomed in front of us.

"You could try your key?" I said.

"I wouldn't risk it. Come on."

We ran the half-mile corridor, not stopping till we were back on the bike. Jesse scooted to the top of the cedar drive as though the hospital itself might come after us and only then did we pause to recover our breath. I didn't know whether he was shaking through anger or exertion.

"We could've *died* in there," he said. "What were you thinking?"

"I'm sorry, I was just curious. I din't think one little whack could do so much damage. Where does that wall back onto, anyway? The chapel?"

Jesse squinted as he consulted his internal blueprints. "No, it's over the ballroom so the wall you cracked backs onto the tower. Like, right behind it is where the staircase is. Fuck's sake, Marianne! You've made the whole place out of bounds now."

"What? We can still go back."

"Not into the main bit, we can't."

But that was where everything *was*. I wanted to howl.

The moon came out from behind a cloud and briefly lit the building in silver.

"I think the clocktower's at a weird angle," I said. "The fire escape looks like it's come loose." It was true: the little ladder seemed to swing from the brickwork.

Jesse shook his head. "No. That's just the way the clouds are moving." It didn't look like an optical illusion to me. He turned the handle on his bike, revved the engine and sent bats flying from the trees. "Jesus, babe. For a clever bird, you can be a right idiot sometimes."

It was the first time since getting close to Jesse that I'd felt inferior to him and there was comfort in his anger: pleasure in the unaccustomed feeling of respect.

27

The day after our disastrous final visit to Nazareth, Mum's shift patterns changed without warning. Suddenly I had no time, between school, homework, looking after Colette and my shifts at the launderette to see Jesse, let alone indulge my little museum. It was ten days before I had an afternoon to myself. I parked Colette in front of *Neighbors* with half a Twix and promised her my share too if she left me upstairs to do my "revision."

I smoothed the double counterpane and laid out my archive in what I had to accept was its entirety. The booklets, the chipped bowls and glasses, the typescript, the ECT records, the watercolors and the patient photographs with their half-familiar faces. I arranged them as though for display in a case. Lastly, reverently, I unfolded the psychiatrist's notes. I had read and reread them but the idea tonight was to get them into some kind of order, to tally the clinician's words with the names on the list. Their arrangement was as arbitrary as shuffled playing cards; unnumbered pages leaped back and forth between treatment and diagnosis. There were the names, first: H. Morris, 19, of Sizewell, P. Preston, 32, of Wangford, C. Wilson, 40, of Lowestoft.

Who had died, and how, and why? Was it the violent woman they'd wanted to operate on, and had she died on the operating table? Was it the patient who'd been in half a dozen times before?

There was no reason it was either of them: I knew my assumption that the three names I had were necessarily related to the notes was baseless. The whole find was arbitrary, evidence of nothing so much as Nazareth's notoriously and chronically poor administration. Much had been made of the lax data security during the closure.

Using Colette's bug-viewer I studied the smudged numbers on the back of the photographs. Different patients or just different sessions? I laid the black notes in order as best I could. If those oval blurs at the end of the case numbers were sixes, then I was as sure as I could be that these were Morris's notes.

She has naturally injured herself and will remain on the admissions ward awaiting classification until Dr. Bures is here on Wednesday. However, my initial assessment, based on the crime committed, tonight's interview and history supplied by her father and doctor, is that this is a psychopathic disorder. This is the first known example of criminal behavior but is part of a longstanding pattern of defiance and unfeminine behavior starting in puberty and which has recently come to include persistent lying and cunning, exhibitionism and speaking in tongues.

It wasn't as good as the pennies-on-the-eyes episode, but speaking in tongues was pretty out there.

Such consistently unnatural behavior suggests a psychopathic disorder rather than a single episode of mania, and thus our treatment must be management rather than "cure" of which there is of course none. Her supportive parents are at their wits' end and it is as a last resort, and partly to avoid criminal charges, that they have agreed to admit her to Nazareth. One would expect to see this patient admitted under certificate but the family are keen to avoid a scandal and she has agreed to be admitted as a voluntary patient. She has shown cunning throughout her

*time here, exploiting other patients to her own ends.
Others do not appear to be human to her: and indeed she
exhibits the kind of inhumanity, an almost complete lack
of empathy, common in such disorders.*

What had she *done*? I flicked backward to the point of admission, but those pages were missing and the subsequent notes presupposed knowledge of the crime.

*It is clear even from our early observations that she is
not suitable for the "career" that so obsesses her. For
this young woman to hold any position of responsibility
would be a grave error, and would only put others in
danger. Any kind of professional stress would trigger
another outburst. She is very insane, as we can see by the
devastating pursuit of her ambition. She shows no remorse.*

The next page was missing. I wanted to scream in frustration. The others had sounded mad, but this one sounded evil, the doctor's warning the starkest yet: beyond cure, beyond empathy. I wondered what kind of crime was punishable not by prison but by hospital and how I might find out. It would be easier, surely, to go through death certificates, but I had no idea where one would begin. It was the kind of thing Ms. Harker would know but I couldn't ask her without telling her exactly where I'd been and what I'd done. Trespass was against the law: my removing the papers theft. What if it went on my record? Would any university let me in?

I ran my finger over the date: 1958. The younger women might still be alive. Nazareth had been full of old women when they'd closed it: a whole ward of them shipped out to sheltered housing in Framlingham. Harmless enough by then, although that was what they thought about Darius Cunniffe.

"Mariaaanne?" Colette's voice carried over the closing credits of *Neighbors*.

"Coming." I went to pack away my little archive. Colette's bug-viewer rested on the photograph of the girl with the long dark plaits. The lens was poised over her eye, highlighting what the original resolution had lost: a zig-zag smudge in her right iris.

I leaped back across the bed like I'd been electrocuted.

H. Morris.

Helen.

Already it didn't feel like new information, more the confirmation of something I'd known for ages. I double-checked, pointlessly: once you knew it was there, it was all you could see. Even with long dark plaits in place of the platinum bubble of hair, this was the face I was used to seeing as a chalk drawing on the news, on the front of the papers, on a dartboard, skewered through one distinctive eye.

Helen Morris, the girl so unlike a normal human that a psychiatrist had recommended she never leave hospital, never work, had been a patient here, and was clearly criminally insane. Somehow, she had got herself out, she had become Helen Greenlaw and then—using that self-serving impulse the doctors described—decades later, she had come back, closed it down and devastated a community. They should have thrown away the key. Nazareth had missed its chance to contain the monster.

28

"Do you reckon the hot water tank's full yet?" asked Jesse.

The bathroom in Main Street was downstairs at the back of the house. Jesse had a ragged hospital-issue towel over his arm and his eye on my mum's bath gel. He'd been washing at our house for weeks; it was February but the Brames' boiler still wasn't fixed. He had forgiven me for making Nazareth out of bounds to us far quicker than I had forgiven myself.

"I dunno. I turned the immersion on an hour ago."

"I'll start the bath anyway. I don't want to miss it."

"It" was the documentary Damian Greenlaw had filmed in Nazareth's grounds. I'd kept my discovery quiet, biding my time until I had done my homework. I had wanted to present the whole story to Jesse as a fait accompli but frustratingly, the marriage certificate proving that Helen Morris was indeed Helen Greenlaw was the only document I could find that backed it all up. I'd sat in Ipswich Central Library and scanned through microfiche files of thirty-year-old copies of the *East Anglian Daily Times* until my eyeballs felt bruised. I read myself ragged, trying to find evidence, before understanding that if she had been hospitalized to cover the crime up then of course there would be no paper trail. Now it had been so long since the original discovery that my declaration seemed tainted by the fact I'd kept it a secret all this time. Jesse hated us to have secrets, and the one guarantee about things concerning Helen Greenlaw was that he would overreact to it. Some days I wondered if I needed to tell him at all.

He emerged after half an hour, steam rising off his body, skin bright pink against the grubby white of his towel. "Did I tell you, they've just told my parents it's another fucking two months' wait to get our hot water back? I'd like to invite Helen Greenlaw round to tea at ours." He let his towel fall open and started to dry his back.

"Would you put that back *on*," I said.

"No one can see in." He nodded at the bubble-wrap window.

"Colette could come down any second. I don't want her being traumatized by your willy."

He clicked his tongue but edged away from the stairs to dress. "Greenlaw should come here, see how normal people live, see what happens when you take a man's job away. No, better than that, I'd like her to live like this herself, I'd take away all her fucking expense accounts and luxuries and see how she fucking likes living hand to mouth like this." His voice was temporarily muffled as he pulled his sweater on, then clear again as his head emerged, wet hair flopping in his eyes. "I mean you can tell by looking at her that she's completely divorced from reality, never known a day's discomfort."

"Have you finished?" I said. "Because you'll be talking over it at this rate."

"Sorry." He kissed me on the mouth. "It's just—knowing it's going to be on telly, it's stirred it all up again." He sat down, put his feet on the coffee table and threw his arm around my shoulder in one fluid movement.

"Up next, a personal and provocative exploration of the English institution," announced the television.

"You know this isn't *all* about Nazareth, don't you?" I said, as the Channel 4 logo shattered into primary-colored chunks.

"Of course," he snapped. I knew why Jesse was nervous. He wanted this to be a love song to the old hospital, a call to reopen it, and even though I'd been telling him for weeks that Nazareth would be a footnote and not the focus, part of him still held out hope. I nurtured a similar tiny spark that perhaps Helen would even "out" herself on this program, and I wouldn't be keeping a secret anymore. He pulled me close. I still loved the smell of him and the way his arms seemed built just for me. When I was curled against his chest, his heartbeat on my cheek, I thought, with a sad little squeeze of my heart, how easy it would be to stay this way for another fifty years.

"Here we go," said Jesse as the camera panned, not across flat Suffolk fields to Nazareth, but up, up, up the Royal Courts from the famous front steps to the rooftop statue of the scales of justice. And so began a polemic against the English system whereby small boys were torn from their families and sent to boarding schools, encouraging them, in Damian Greenlaw's bitter opinion, to transfer all the affection and dependence they should have had for and on their mothers to institutions, which they then went on to prioritize over humans once they were in government. It was a persuasive film, beautiful shots of stunning buildings at odds with the brutalities they enshrined. I wasn't surprised when he later won a BAFTA for it.

Nazareth featured for a few minutes toward the end. Jesse leaned forward but the hospital was only a blurred gray monolith in the background as Damian Greenlaw and Adam Solomon walked the perimeter, two middle-class men in sensitive conversation.

"I suppose it was too much to ask that *she* justified it. Fucking coward," said Jesse.

"Shh."

The men discussed what might replace the old asylums and whether the individual was truly being served by community care. Both were vehemently opposed to the old Victorian-built asylums; their views were the opposite of what Jesse wanted to hear. Adam Solomon was a vocal campaigner but he was very attuned to the rights of the mentally ill; his magnanimity toward Cunniffe had been one of the reasons why his campaign was so respected. He had never held him responsible; it was the system and its operators he blamed for what had happened to his family. The final shot, of a doughy little woman who'd been in Nazareth for twenty years, contentedly preparing her own food in a gleaming one-bed flat, told a happy story.

We started the film with Jesse holding me. At the end I was holding him, his head in the hollow of my neck. I muted the TV. We sat in silence for a long time afterward bathed in the flickering rays of the *News at Ten*.

"You OK, Jess?"

He was tearing up. "They're never gonna reopen it, are they?"

To punch the air at the death of his dream would have been a cruelty. In that moment, I wondered how I'd ever had anything but tenderness for Jesse. "They couldn't, not safely," I whispered. "It needs millions of pounds, years of work. It's not fair to ask the NHS for all that when the new clinic's already cost so much."

It was nothing I hadn't tried to tell him before, but he was finally ready to hear it.

"I just can't bear the thought of Helen Greenlaw getting away with doing this to Nusstead, d'you know what I mean? My dad's been out of work for two years." His voice cracked and he started to cry. These were the first male tears I'd seen since primary school and I was tipped into fight-or-flight panic. Growing up without men warps your expectations of them, puts impossible standards in your head.

I wrecked four lives because I couldn't stand to see my boyfriend cry.

"Stay there," I said, as though there was anywhere else he might be going. "I've got something that might cheer you up."

He grunted, and I could tell that even that had been an effort. In my bedroom, I stood on the edge of the double bed and reached above Colette's head. She tried to cuddle my ankle. Half a story was surely better than none. It wasn't as though I would ever show anyone but Jesse, anyway. My intentions already ran beyond the short-term goal of changing his mood. I thought that diminishing the woman he felt had so much power over his family would help him to let go.

I ought to have remembered, when moved by his tears, the delusion that had triggered them.

Jesse had turned over to the snooker. His eyes were red but not wet. My file was clean but I blew imaginary dust off it for effect.

"What's that?" he said, brow puckering. "Did you steal that from Nazareth?" He straightened up as though to lecture me, then remembered that everything had changed, and slumped deep into the cushions. "I suppose it don't matter no more. Last thing I want to think about is Nazareth."

I was indignant that he didn't want to see the fruit of my efforts. "It'll cheer you up," I said. "Read them."

His eyes skidded over the page: now he was humoring me.

"Read the name."

"H. Morris. So?"

I slid the photograph across. "OK, I found a picture of her. Study her face."

"It's just some poor cow, innit? God, talk about rubbing salt in the wound. Can I not just watch the snooker?"

"Trust me, Jesse. You know this person." At last, I had sparked his curiosity and I was thrilled that I had built this little game for him. I could see Jesse's mind processing it, probably running along the same lines mine had: working out her current age, searching for family resemblances.

"Nope," he said.

"Look into her eyes."

"Why, is she gonna hypnotize me?"

"Just do it." I placed Colette's toy microscope over the photograph and kept talking as Jesse bent his head. "Helen Morris was locked up for having a psychopathic disorder in 1958. She did something so bad that they put her in hospital because it was either that or prison." My words ran fast over my failure to find the full facts. "She's a psychopath. It was recommended she should never be let out. She had ECT to try to cure her. It didn't work, but somehow she got out and got married." It was all I could do not to beat a drum roll on my knees. "To a man called Robin Greenlaw."

Jesse raised his head in stunned slow motion. I'm mortified to recall the glee I felt as I watched comprehension dawn.

"Helen . . . Greenlaw?"

He stood up. The expression on his face now terrified me: he was twenty years older, he was a middle-aged man. I suppose I had thought he would tell me I was clever. Instead, I watched anger surging up through incomprehension. "She . . ." He was actually spluttering. "So you're telling me that some mental case was in charge of the whole . . . some insane bitch made all these decisions?"

"Don't scrunch them up!" I took the papers from his fist but his fingers stayed curved.

"This is a . . . this is a fucking scandal. It must be illegal. I can't believe they gave her the job, knowing what they did."

As far as we were concerned once you were "mental" you were always a liability.

"I think it's more likely that they don't know," I said.

"Jesus Christ, I need to get this into my head." He paced around the tiny room, then stopped to face me. "I've got to ask you something, and I need you to be honest with me." For a white-hot moment of panic I thought he was going to ask me if I wanted to marry him. "Babe, are these real?" It was so far from what I had been expecting that I didn't know what to say. "It's just that it's a bit of a coincidence that these are the notes you found. That show up my worst enemy as a psycho. And you're so clever, you know so much about history and that, I'm wondering—if you made it up, to make me feel better. I know how much you love me. I mean if you did, I'd understand."

"I wouldn't do that." I didn't add, because that would be an act of insanity worthy of my own committal.

"Then if it's not a forgery, it's fate." A gust of wind from outside made the bubble wrap on the window bulge like a sail. "If only we'd known before it was shut, though. We could have stopped it, that's what I can't stop thinking about."

"If it hadn't been abandoned we'd never have found her records in the first place."

He was too far gone to let a crucial detail like this break his stride. He lay back and closed his eyes but I could tell by the twitching of his mouth that the machinery of his mind was in furious motion.

"I can't believe you kept this from me until winter's nearly over. We could have had the heating on at Christmas."

The non sequitur floored me for a second. "Babe." He opened his eyes. "This isn't just about Nusstead anymore. We can turn this to our advantage. We can get our public apology and solve our money worries. We can make *thousands* off her."

29

"*News of the World,*" he said out of the corner of his mouth. We were in the free dinner queue, inching toward a shepherd's pie with our vouchers in our hands. We'd been living off beans on toast for a week at home, and my navel shrank closer to my spine every day. "Sunday papers, they're the ones with the money. She shouldn't even be in work! People *died* because of her!"

Jesse did not share my view that my archive was for our eyes only, and my assumption that he would had been staggeringly naive. The get-rich-quick scheme everyone in Nusstead dreamed of was there, tied up with revenge for the most hated figure in the community.

"I *know* that," I snapped at him. The food, a bright yellow slab of starch with a thin line of meaty glop at the base, came into focus. My mouth watered against my better judgment.

"Then why are you dragging your feet?"

The truth was, I was tempted. Life had descended into humdrum, premature domesticity—double-dating with Mark and Trish down the Social on a Saturday night—even faster than I'd anticipated. Selling the story might be a way of reclaiming that sense of shared adventure that we'd lost when I had expelled us from Nazareth. If it was a game, it felt justified, because that was how Greenlaw had treated others; as chess pieces in the game of her own career. It seemed so outlandish, so unlike anything I would do, that it almost took on the safety of play. Or it did until I thought about the real-world consequences, the law-breaking. Jesse kept talking about newspapers protecting their sources but he was just as clueless as I was and operating without the speedbumps of caution. "She's still making decisions that affect people's lives," Jesse pressed, as the food was slopped onto our trays. "It's our *public duty.*" Jesse saw her exposure as righteous and I had some sympathy with this, but there was an element of humiliation in his plan that I couldn't revel in.

"A journalist might dig up the *actual* crime. No offense, but you don't really know what you're doing, do you, babe? We could a hundred percent bring her to justice."

This spoke to a different reservation; I was jealous of my archive. I didn't want some tabloid hack butchering what I saw as *my* story, handing my precious evidence over to a man with red braces and a word processor. I wish I could say that I wanted to preserve the project's scholarly intensity, but it was childish possessiveness.

"It just doesn't feel right," I said, over a burble of stomach acid. I'd cleared half of the food in thirty seconds and Jesse had noticed.

"Don't tell me you couldn't do with the money."

"Of course I could," I said. I might have grown out of my boarding-school dream but I would still have loved to, in order: buy my mum a car; have myself fitted for a proper bra in a department store; wear makeup because it suited me, not because it was end-of-range in the bargain bin from the co-op. The lesser sin I proposed seemed guaranteed to satisfy Jesse without the attention and risk.

"What if we made a private approach," I said. "Went straight to Greenlaw?" I was running the idea past him as you might toss a coin in a well to test its depth. Jesse's quiff quivered like it had picked up an important signal.

"*Blackmail?*" It's a horrible word, said aloud. It's ugly in the mouth, and I put it there.

"She's got the money," I said. "She might even have more money than a newspaper."

Jesse shook his head. "If we go to the papers, we take her down *and* we get the cash."

"But we only get it once. My way, we could have a bit for years."

"No! Then justice won't be done."

I said, "We could even do both. Money first, story second. She's only just become an MP. If she becomes even more powerful, like if she gets a high-profile job, then we'd really clean up."

Did I mean it? I don't know. I would have said anything to talk him down from the ledge of publicity. I saw the decision rise up in him. "We'll do it together," he said. Of course. Once you were a proper couple, you did everything together.

Colette was in bed and I had an evening to myself for the first time in weeks. My eyes skimmed blindly over Nancy Mitford's *The Sun King*. I couldn't take in a single detail of Louis XIV's relationship with his mother; my thoughts were consumed by our lunchtime conversation. I closed the book and opened it again, as though that would reset my brain. If my powers of concentration were so diminished I couldn't even read a good book on a subject that interested me, how would I possibly manage at university? I slipped into a new daydream, picturing myself walking through an imagined quad, its architecture a bastardized blend of the Oxford I knew from *Brideshead Revisited* and the Versailles courtyard of Mitford's description. In my vision, I wore a cap and gown and carried a stack of books under my arm. The picture was so pure, so easy, so right, that I understood with a sudden, icy clarity what I had known for months in the opaque.

I was going to leave Jesse.

It wasn't about loving him or not. It was about the life I was meant for and the absolute impossibility of sharing it with him. I was going to shatter his heart.

I understood then why I had suggested blackmail. Without knowing it, I had been offering him a consolation prize. Not the money—if it even worked—so much as the secrecy, the trust, the joint enterprise; I hoped that, one day in the far-off future, Jesse would understand that I had done this because even though I had to go, I would always love him.

30

The Waveney Secondary secretarial room was state of the art, rows of electric typewriters under pristine covers. Mechanical typewriters were edging their way into retirement on a desk at the back of the room. In the third year, boys did woodwork and girls did typing as a matter of course, and my WPM was around 50.

"I still think that cut-up letters from a newspaper would have been better," said Jesse. We were not supposed to be here, so we'd kept the lights off and had our ears tuned to footsteps in the corridor. We were of course practiced in trespass.

"This will be more professional." I fed a blank sheet of A4 into the roller and typed, without forethought: *a lad had a salad a lad had a salad a lad had a salad*. I tapped out the alphabet in lower case then upper, studying the text for flaws in the characters—an E with a missing central stroke, or a distinctive blip in the tail of a g—because that was how people came undone in the TV dramas we seemed to be basing this on.

"Fair dos," said Jesse, pulling some handwritten notes out of his pocket. "Let me go over these one more time."

Everyone knew that the House of Commons postbag was checked for letterbombs, meaning our demand would be intercepted. Mark's doomed campaign meant we knew the finer machinations of government. Jesse had been dragged regularly to the local MP's weekly constituents' surgeries. Helen Greenlaw's seat, Dunwich Heath, cradled the coastline and was on the other side of the county. We'd decided that we'd ride out to Dunwich and deliver our letter by hand.

Footsteps in the corridor approached and retreated. We froze; for a second I thought we'd got away with it, then Ms. Harker's face appeared round the door.

"What d'you think you're—oh, Marianne, it's *you*." She looked from me to Jesse in surprise and horror.

"Just getting a bit of practice in," I said, and mimed a bit of touch-typing.

She frowned. "I hope your aspirations go a bit beyond the typing pool." Subtext: I hope your aspirations go a bit beyond Jesse Brame. Ms. Harker's reaction shifted something inside me; where once I had been proud to be seen with him, I felt a flare of shame, although I was ashamed of the shame. "Listen, twenty more minutes, then the cleaners are in."

"Stuck-up bitch," said Jesse when she'd left the room. He spread his crumpled paper out in front of me. "This is what I came up with so far."

To Helen Greenlaw or should I say Morris
    We are two residents of Nusstead village and we have uncovered your dirty little secret. It's time your crime was truly punished and brung to light. It's disgusting that someone with your track record was ever allowed in to power in the first place. Nazareth would still be a working hospital if it wasn't for you and if the papers knew what you done and what your really like it would be curtains for your precious career. If you want us to stay quiet then leave the money in a paper bag.

"What do you think?" he asked. "It took me like five goes to get it perfect."

"It's very—confident. I'm going to tone it down a little bit, if that's OK."

"No, yeah, this is your department." He sat beside me, his right hand resting on my inner thigh.

Dear Mrs. Greenlaw,
*   We are two concerned residents of Nusstead. Recently some documents came into our possession which have been of great interest to us.*

"How'd you learn to *write* like that?" said Jesse, as though I were Nabokov.

They refer to your time as a patient at Nazareth.

"How comes you haven't put all the details and that? You don't mention about her dodging prison."

"If someone else reads this we don't want to give too much away. We want to have her wondering what we know as well."

"Yeah, that's good," he said. "That's clever."

*   It isn't important how we got them, but your hypocrisy needs to be exposed. How would your prime minister feel, or your family, if they knew about your criminal past?*
*   I'm sure you can appreciate that like so many other residents of Nusstead, the fallout from the hospital's closure has left our families very badly off, more so since the tragedy that followed.*

I was pleased with that last line. "It makes us sound like we're adults with families to support."

"We *are*," said Jesse.

*   We live with the consequences of the hospital closure every day and think it only fair that in return for our continued silence you give us*

"How much are we going to ask for?" I asked, fingers poised over the keys.

"A million pounds."

I counted to three in my head. "Jess, no—less, a *lot* less."

"Half a mill. She's *rolling* in it."

"Let's ask for something she wouldn't notice, shall we? Something like . . ." I had no idea. A hundred pounds was a fortune to me then.

"Forty thousand?" I said, tentatively.

"We'll call it a hundred. This is her life."

It seemed too big. "What if we're going to ask for it time and again, though? Let's ask for sixty—that's thirty each, Jesse! That's life-changing money."

"We could buy a house with that." He nodded his assent. "And still have some left over to look after Mum and Dad, and Debbie."

I typed on, trying not to picture bricks stacking up around me.

£60,000 as fair compensation. It is, after all, a small price for the two families we have to support as a direct consequence of the closure of Nazareth.

We will give you ample time to cash in this money.

Please meet us at

"When and where?" I asked Jesse. "Got to make it seven days from when she gets the letter."

"Make it a week Saturday, then," he said. "At night, so no one's around."

"Makes sense," I replied. "Where, though? It needs to be somewhere quiet and private. Gotta be able to count out the cash properly, and she'll want to see what we've got, too."

"Nazareth, obviously." My gut reaction was thrill: that we would go back, before I remembered why we'd had to leave. "We could wait outside, or just inside if it was raining. We wouldn't have to go in the dodgy bit."

In the swoop of disappointment that followed, my conscience finally asserted itself. "Is that not a bit much, making her go back?"

"Why not? She should see what's happened to the place since she fucked it over."

"What if she flips out? I mean, she might do a Cunniffe on us."

Jesse hesitated. "Nah, she won't do that. Anyway there's two of us, one of her. I lift boxes that weigh more than she does every day." He drummed his fingers on my thigh. "Just put: come toward the light. That way we can set up wherever we can get access."

"Come toward the light? That makes it sound like she's dead and there's angels coming for her."

"In't no angels coming for Helen Greenlaw."

"All right then. How 'bout this?"

Nazareth Hospital is derelict now and we won't be overlooked there. Please meet us at the site at 11:30 P.M. on 20 February. Ignore the security signs, there is never anyone there. Look for the torch's beam. We will be waiting.

I had a thought, so obvious it should have been my first. "What if she's not on her own?"

Jesse snorted. "Who's she gonna bring with her?"

"Coppers. Blackmail's against the law."

"Nah." Jesse chewed his lip, then said, "But write it down, just in case."

Do not bring anyone with you. Otherwise the next step is writting to the News of the World.
Yours sincerely,
M and J of Nusstead

I read it back, noticed the typo in "writing." The cupboard with the correction fluid was locked, so I had to pull the sheet from the rollers and retype the whole thing. This time I spaced out my paragraphs and shifted the margins to tidy it up. Jesse crumpled up the spoiled paper and threw it across the room into the wastepaper bin, where it landed without touching the sides. "Goal," he said.

"You plum. Anyone could find it there. What if Ms. Harker comes back and finds it? She'll know it was us. Get rid of it somewhere no one's gonna find it." He blushed, took the paper and stuffed it into his back pocket.

31

The Suffolk coast isn't like Cornwall or Devon, where the sea tantalizes you through dips in the hillsides for miles on the approach. For such a flat county, the sightlines are poor, coastlines banked in defense, and you can't see the water until you're almost on top of it.

Jesse guessed two hours for the journey to Sizewell but we did it in just over half that. With fifty minutes to kill before Helen Greenlaw's surgery opened, we headed to the beach. The nuclear power station with its huge golf-ball roof throbbed beside us, pylons racing away from it in all directions. "Her mansion's somewhere round here," said Jesse. "You'll notice she didn't shit on her own doorstep."

There hadn't been a mental hospital to close on her doorstep, but I knew better than to point this out.

The cafe was shut for winter but Jesse had a flask of tea and a KitKat in his pannier. We sat on the shingle and passed the mug between us while he went over his plan.

"So. I'll go in, you wait by the bike and when I run out we'll be on it and away like *that*." He tried to snap his fingers but his leather gloves dulled the sound. I had no need to be there; if anything, I was a liability. I wondered if he sensed where this was going, if my growing detachment was manifesting in my moods or in bed and this was his way not only of strengthening our bond but of putting me somehow in his debt.

The surgery was a mile inland, in Leiston, in the Quaker Meeting House. There was a man on the door wearing a suit and tie, a coffee pot at his side, and a sleek navy Jaguar was parked outside.

"That's her car," said Jesse. "She was in it that time my brother kicked off." Clay's part in the first protest was the stuff of Brame family legend. "I wonder how much that set her back. How many working men's years' wages." He bounced on the balls of his feet. "OK, here we go. Be ready to leg it, yeah?"

My breath was loud and misted my visor. The man on the door had folded arms and stood with his feet apart, clearly telling Jesse he couldn't come in unless he removed his helmet. Our local MP Paul Lawshall's surgery had been held in Nusstead church hall, with no security, just some local volunteer behind a trestle table, but then we'd never seen anyone try to enter wearing a crash helmet. Jesse flexed the letter in his hands then turned and ran to me so fast that I thought he must have done it, even though he still held the envelope. I jumped on behind him and held tight while we roared out of the car park. A block away, Jesse parked up near a little parade of shops and threw his helmet on the ground.

"I fucking bottled it, didn't I?" He kicked at the front tire.

I flipped up my visor. "What do we do now?"

"I dunno, all right? I din't know she'd have a fucking *bouncer*. He's seen me now, looking dodgy in my leathers and that. I'm a dickhead. I've fucked it all up." He kicked again, so hard the bike nearly fell over.

I could have put an end to it so many times. I think of those chances now as door after door along an endless corridor, and I slammed them all behind me rather than face Jesse's feelings.

"That guy on the desk had a pot of coffee on the go," I said. "He can't stay outside forever. Go back, wait; put it under the windscreen wiper, even. It's a shame we can't leave it on her front seat."

He turned to me, ecstatic. "You're a genius, babe."

"What did I say?" I asked, but he was already sprinting toward a little newsagent and a bundle of yesterday's *East Anglian Daily Times* propped against the outside wall. Jesse took the box-cutter he always carried to the plastic tape that bound them. "Why d'you need a paper?" I asked, but it was the tape he was after.

"Sometimes having Clay for a brother is brilliant," he said.

We resumed our stakeout of the hall. It was an hour before the front door was left unguarded. Jesse made a hook of the stiff plastic, slid it in the gap between the car door and body, and wiggled it until the lock clunked open. On the passenger seat was a newspaper, Salman Rushdie and his fatwa on the front page. I placed our letter on top of his face, where it couldn't be missed.

We rode home with the airstream in our favor. Jesse never went over 60 miles an hour but the alignment with the wind made it feel like the bike was going too fast, like it was out of our control.

The walls were thin in Nusstead's new houses, and the TV rumbled through Jesse's bedroom floor. Mark and Trish, who were watching *Bullseye* under an electric blanket, occasionally laughed loudly and in perfect unison. In Jesse's bedroom all three bars of the plug-in fire glowed orange. His few clothes hung on a rail, all the Jesses I knew: the lumberjack shirt and jeans he wore with me, the secondhand school uniform, the co-op shelf-stacker overalls and the leather he showed to the world.

It was five days since we had sent our letter to Helen Greenlaw and our elation had been short-lived. It didn't feel like a game anymore. Now, Jesse flicked nervously through facsimiles of Helen's notes, and her photograph. I'd had to copy my archive to convince him that we would still go to the papers even if she showed up. Doing it myself meant there would only be one set of duplicates to destroy. It wasn't that I thought Jesse would double-cross me as an insurance policy—his trust in me was suffocatingly absolute—but that I couldn't trust him to contain his enthusiasm. All the energy and emotion he had previously invested in reopening the hospital now poured into this new vendetta. It had the ingrained feel of a years-long obsession.

"She *could* have the police on us." When he paced in his room, the wire coathangers jangled and I knew the light fitting would be shaking downstairs. "Just because we're morally in the right, doesn't mean it's technically legal, what we're doing. She *could* come after us, but that risks it coming out."

"What will we do if no one shows up?" I pulled him onto the bed, more to stop the pacing than a need for closeness. "Will we really go to the papers?"

"Of course," he said, astonished—*hurt*—that I was even questioning this part of the plan.

"We should allow for the possibility that she didn't see it, that's all. She might have chucked her briefcase over the top of it, or thrown it away without reading it."

Jesse frowned. "Well, going to the papers was always plan A so it's basically just a return to that."

I flopped back onto the bed, as though supine I would think of the magic sentence that would change his mind, that would release us both from my stupid plan. Jesse, as ever, took it as an invitation; he was on top of me, his face eager and shining.

"There's a house for sale two doors down from your mum," he said. "Needs tarting up, but we could have our own place, babe."

The opportunity to be truly honest only seemed to come at the moments when it would hurt him most. "Yeah," I said miserably. "It's something to think about."

32

We were there at noon, circling the exterior under heavy gray clouds.

"If there are coppers," said Jesse, "I mean there *won't* be, but if there are, they don't know the terrain like we do. We've got that advantage. If we comb the site then at least we'll know that no one's gonna be lying in wait for us."

"And what about when we get nicked for breaking and entering?"

"Babe, don't be stupid. I wouldn't let you go down for it, I'd take full responsibility."

"That would finish your parents off. Two out of three sons with a criminal record?"

"Four." His chin wobbled. "Two out of *four* sons."

I nodded miserably. I had lost so much weight in the last few days that I was even starting to walk differently; vanishing thighs shifting my center of gravity to my hipbones. Showing Jesse those records had been the stupidest thing anyone had ever done and suggesting blackmail was the worst idea anyone had ever had. At last, I was scared enough to find the courage to leave him. I vowed that on my next visit to Jesse's bedroom, I would destroy his wretched backup copies while he slept, and it would be my last time there.

We went over every inch of the site on foot, including the old villas and the gardens, until Jesse was satisfied there were no trespassers (we didn't count). We'd intended to wait for Greenlaw at the entrance but the rain set in at dusk. The first few drops sat like marbles on Jesse's black leather but within a minute it was a pressure-jet in the drive, canceling our tire tracks.

"We'll wait it out at the women's entrance." Jesse had bought us each a head torch: the bobbing spotlight picked out new debris; glass and roof tiles crazed the rubble. Inside, he took the big torch from Clay's toolbag. The service corridor lit up and we both lost our breath. "Oh, look what's happened." Jesse touched the damp wall like it was my cheek. The floor was thick with filth, the terrazzo obscured by slime and tiny corpses, pigeons—Jesse shrank away from them—and rats in various stages of decay. We pulled our T-shirts up and into masks. How had I ever taken my clothes off and laid down in this place? I imagined how vile the basement must be now, black eels from the fen colonizing the old mortuary.

We set the torch at the door, where it turned the rain into platinum sparks. Anyone approaching couldn't miss it. "Right, let's save all our batteries for now," he said, cutting the beam and feeling along the lintel for the little yellow torch. "I'm sure I left it there."

"I last saw it in the records room," I said.

He flinched at the memory of what I'd done up there as he stretched to the lintel. "OK, old school it is. *Fuck!*" A bundle of candles fell into a black puddle. I rescued those I could, singed the ends and stuck them onto the windowsill.

There were still hours before Greenlaw was due. In the old laundry, we sat cross-legged on top of the giant tubs and listened to the music of the storm.

"Remember the first night I brought you here, babe?" he said. I smiled, wishing I could take a magic pill to recapture the way I'd felt about him back then. Whatever happened next, Jesse had given me this place: he had shown me what I wanted to do with my life. "The way you lit up when you came in. I fell in love with you that night, only it took me so long to say it. Whatever happens to this place, it'll always be special for us. I'm coming around to the idea of getting a job on the build. You'd *walk* into a job in a posh hotel." His words were handcuffs clicking around my wrists; I would have spat out the magic pill.

"If she pays up," I said, to change the subject, "what are we going to do with the money? I mean, short term. How would we store it? You can't just go around spending great wodges of cash."

He shrugged. I couldn't tell whether he hadn't dared think that far ahead or if it simply hadn't occurred to him. "Pay it into the bank bit by bit, I suppose. Say you're saving up your wages. Are you worried about the taxman?"

"God, Jess, the taxman's the *least* of our worries." I laughed, and instantly regretted how nasty it sounded. "I mean, living with a load of cash under the mattress. Your mum changing your sheets—she'll think you're on the rob or something." This sobered him; I knew he took pride in being the "good" brother.

"Look, can you not tempt fate, anyway?" He'd never snapped at me before.

"Sorry." I examined my nails, already dirty and ragged after a few hours back in Nazareth. There was one more thing I needed to say before midnight.

"What if she calls our bluff in return? We don't actually know what she did, or have you forgotten that?"

His eyes flashed. "Could you stop being so bloody negative?"

I decided to stop talking.

We took up sentry at the door from 11:30, head torches in place. Jesse tried to kiss me, tried to make it some big romantic adventure, but the crunch of plastic on our foreheads made it impossible and I was relieved.

We first saw the light on Asylum Road at 11:55.

"Just one set of headlamps," Jesse squinted into the rain.

"Anyone in the car with her?"

"Can't see from here." He blew on his hands, then turned on the light as the navy Jaguar bumped over the ground. "Shit. Shit shit shit, this is *it*."

Helen Greenlaw's trim figure was topped by an umbrella. Rain was deflected in sheets as she picked her way through the rubble.

Chic little peacoat, pale gray tapered trousers, flat shoes. I had expected her to be somehow swollen with everything she had done but she was *tiny*.

She wrinkled her nose at the light. "Please turn that away from my face so that I can see you." The voice expected obedience and to my surprise, Jesse angled the torch inside without protest.

"Come out of the rain," he said, in a voice I had to strain to hear standing next to him.

She shook her umbrella off and placed it neatly in a corner. Her posture was perfect. Those hands that had held the pen that signed off the closure that destroyed so many lives; those hands that had done God knows what to get her in here; they were not the bloodstained claws of my imagination but dainty, pale pink, manicured and ringed. Dirty water had splashed like black oil around her ankles. I wondered what it must be like to be able to ruin a pair of shoes and know you could replace them.

She didn't need amplification, the refraction of a screen or the height of a lectern, for her authority to carry. I saw that Jesse recognized this and hated himself for it. A new squall blew in a horizontal torrent that forced us further into the corridor. She barely seemed to blink. She doesn't care, I thought. The fact of her being here suggests she's scared, but she's completely emotionless. The vice of guilt loosened just a little. I had never found myself face to face with someone I knew was a psychopath and I couldn't suppress a little sick buzz.

"Now," she said in a tone that told us that Helen Greenlaw was going to take charge of her own extortion. Jesse kept looking over his shoulder nervously, for policemen I supposed, for headlights or torches to tell us that we weren't alone. Her arrival didn't mean she meant to pay us. His paranoia was infectious: I too fancied that I heard footsteps all around, doors slamming, keys turning and even at one point the hum of an ECT machine being switched on—a sound I'd never even heard. My imagination had cut loose. It was as though my conscience was a fourth figure, prowling around outside, cracking fallen tiles underfoot.

"I'll see the paperwork first," she said, in the familiar monotone.

"Not until I've seen the cash." Jesse's swagger was more like an Elvis impersonation than the hardened racketeer he was aiming for, and even in my fear there was room for a sharp dart of shame.

Greenlaw opened her handbag; a purse, car keys, gloves, a matchbox, a slim torch and six compact sheaves of cash. Even big money packs up small in the right denomination. It was only the second or third time I'd seen a fifty-pound note. For no good reason, I had pictured twenties. A lone fifty in the house would be cause for suspicion.

Greenlaw peeled a note from midway through a wad and gave it to Jesse, who held it up to the light to reveal a watermark Queen. He tore into the silver strip. Helen, from the bored, contemptuous expression on her face, might have been getting it checked by a cashier at the co-op.

"I should like to see my records before the exchange is made." I had the originals in my inside pocket, still in the folder. Something scuttled outside: I shrank from the sound but it was nothing to Helen.

She merely glanced at the photograph, and read through her records with all the emotion of someone reading—I thought of a gas bill, but they weren't read without emotion, not in our house.

"Who gave you this?"

Jesse tilted his chin in pride. "No one. We done it with our . . . investigative powers. It was left behind, up in the records room. That's what happens when you do things by halves. Well, it's not the *worst* thing, obviously."

His sneer was so unnecessary, so unconvincing. There was nothing Bonnie and Clyde about this. We were cheap little crooks from the middle of nowhere.

I waited for the blue lights. When was the point of exchange, when would the crime be committed? Did it become blackmail once the deed was done, once we'd taken the money or once we had handed the documents over? Or had we crossed the line days ago, with a length of plastic tape and a car door?

"All there in black and white, in't it?" said Jesse. "Proof of what you are. What you *done*."

I could tell what he was doing: trying to elicit a confession. I held my breath.

"Yes," she said. "I can't contradict you there." Now my blood charged at the arrogance of the woman. Even now, the evidence in her hands, she couldn't admit or apologize. She looked up. "How do I know you haven't made copies?"

"You'll just have to trust us," said Jesse.

I wondered whether her disorder made her good at reading people, the better to exploit them, or if her lack of empathy was a barrier. There was nothing on her face to tell me either way.

Helen slid her history into her handbag, then gave the notes not to Jesse but to me. He made a fish mouth but I glared a warning at him: let's just get this over with. I stashed what I could inside my leathers and offered the rest to Jesse, who threw his share into Clay's toolbag, then hoisted it over his shoulder.

"You won't hear from us again." I looked at Helen but aimed the words at Jesse.

The next squall was different: a pull as well as a push, more vacuum than wind, as though somewhere else in the hospital a deep chimney had been unbricked. The backdraft slammed shut the back door; the loose lintel finally came free, bringing half the brick-work down under it with a gunshot crack.

"Shit," said Jesse.

There was a landslide of tiles, bricks, waterlogged plasterwork sluiced down by gallons of filthy water. Within thirty seconds the rubble was waist-high, and our only exit blocked.

"Fuck," said Jesse, switching on his head torch and inching toward the mess. A beam fell from the roof and missed his head by inches. Something outside shifted—a roof tile, another brick—and thudded dully onto the ground.

"*Jesse!*" I screamed. He whipped around and glared at me. I couldn't see his expression behind the dazzle of his torch, but I could picture his fury: I'd said his name.

"We'll have to leave through the front," he said.

"Did you bring your key?" I asked. Even a key that took twenty minutes' jiggling to tumble the main lock was better than nothing. He patted down his body, then his face fell. "It's in the bike. I can jemmy one of the panels off the windows and we can climb through." He took in Helen. "*I'll* climb through then let youse two out. Somehow."

It was descending into farce and he knew it. His pride was bruised in front of me as much as Helen, who had been following our conversation without expression. Even in a crisis, I sensed her contempt for our inefficiency. This is not how I would have carried out blackmail, her eyes seemed to say.

Our head torches gave us only a few feet of visibility and we kept our strides short. "Puddle!" shouted Jesse, his boots ankle-deep in an unseen hole. I could vault it with effort but I was two generations younger than Helen. It was clear that she would only get past it with help. Some inner chivalry made Jesse offer his hand. She took it, to steady herself to cross the puddle, but then she wiped her hand on her coat, as if he were dirty, contaminated. I caught his face, pooled in the light of the torch, contorted with the effort of not saying what he thought. I knew I'd hear about it, at length, later.

I wondered how much Helen remembered of her time here and how much of it had changed. In the brief moments her face was illuminated she was blank as a bedsheet. I focused on the end of the corridor, a point of glitter, a cat's-eye twinkle where our torches had caught on a window or a puddle. As we drew close, the light grew brighter but less precise. I understood it was a source, not a reflection, the moment we turned into the atrium. Clay Brame sat open-legged on an old chair, our little yellow torch like a buttercup under his chin.

33

Behind Clay, the atrium walls wept and leaves whirlpooled in dark corners. I couldn't tell whether the huge key that dangled from his belt was the original, or the rough copy from Jesse's bike. I looked to the double doors; Clay followed my eyes, then patted his key.

"Don't even think about it," he said.

I turned to Jesse but his face was in shadow. Had he broken ranks, brought his big brother in for backup? The thought was interrupted before it could fully form.

"What the *fuck*?" Jesse's surprise was as genuine as his anger.

"You've made a right bollocks of that door round the back."

I locked eyes with Jesse; Clay had heard everything. He *knew* everything.

"I'm out on good behavior," said Clay, which explained his liberty but not his presence. "Been in Diss at a bird's for a couple of days. Had to drain my balls." He put his hand on his crotch. Helen's shudder expressed the revulsion I felt.

"Fuck's sake." In his shock, Jesse had dropped all posturing. "Do Mum and Dad know?"

"Don't think so. They weren't in when I went home."

"But what are you doing *here*?"

"I was hunting down the back of the sofa for some loose change," said Clay. "And when I couldn't find any there, I went through your pockets. You really want to empty them out more."

He produced from his own pocket a bundle of paper, the topmost of which was our first draft of the threatening letter, the one with the typo. Jesse staggered, bouncing torchlight off the walls. "Started up quite a treasure hunt," said Clay, fanning out Jesse's little stash of blurry photocopies. I swallowed a furious curse. They would have been meaningless to Clay if Jesse had properly disposed of that letter. They made liars of us to Greenlaw.

She stepped forward. "What have you got there?" For the first time, there was emotion in her voice. I'd read about this; how the only person the psychopath truly loves and feels protective about is herself.

Clay trained his little beam on her. "An audience with the Right Honorable Helen Greenlaw. Our old man would've killed for a face-to-face with you in the old days, but you didn't want to know, did you? Still, I'm glad some good's come of it, in the long run." Now Jesse was in the spotlight. "I'm guessing by the fact that she's here she paid up?" Jesse's eyes went to the toolbag before he could stop them. "Good. In full?" Jesse nodded. Clay held out his hand. "Then I'll take my cut. Call it backpay."

Jesse realized what Clay was asking for a blink before I did.

"But you din't do anything to earn it. This is *ours*. Mine and—hers."

The air seemed to vibrate between the brothers, both convinced of their moral right to this filthy money. If Helen and I had both walked away, if we had been able to, neither of them would have noticed.

Clay was fast for such a big man, up off the chair and bowling into his brother's chest. I winced as Jesse's coccyx hit the tiles. Clay used his brother's growl of pain to snatch the bag. The little torch clattered to the floor. By the light of the big torch, Clay threw the photocopies in along with the rattling tools and the bundled fifties.

Helen was in on it now, reaching for them. "Oh no you don't," said Clay, snatching the bag away. "I in't got backup for these yet."

She reverted to her earlier stillness; I wondered what calculations were going on in that freak brain.

Jesse staggered to his feet and stood in front of the double doors, pulling me roughly in front of him like a hostage. In the spotlight, I was conscious of the blocky padding of the rest of the money under my leather, and crossed my arms over my chest.

"You'll have to get past us first."

"Don't be a prick," replied Clay. "Who showed you this place? Who worked here? I know it better'n you do." He turned to the clocktower door and I saw his escape plan: up to the clock, down the fire escape, a route made impossible by the storm and the vandals.

"No!" we shouted together, as he smashed through Jesse's make-shift barrier and the white light disappeared.

"Mate, it's not like it was in there, you'll break your neck."

We followed him, heedless of our own warnings. Inside the clocktower, rainwater poured through the holes in the roof. In the flooded basement of the stairwell, concentric circles crashed and shattered. I saw Clay's light dancing through the iron crosses that braced the tower.

A third light joined my beam and Jesse's: Helen was behind us, her little pen torch a dead star between two suns and Clay's rising white light picking out rotting spindles, broken windows, the rusting cogs of the clockwork itself.

"I'm going after him," said Jesse.

"Are you insane?" I put my hand over both our torches so we could see each other's faces. The light glowed blood-orange through my hand, picking out veins and bones.

"He's got everything we've worked for," said Jesse. "And I haven't got a key, have I? Apart from anything else, he's the only one who can get us all out of here—oh, bloody hell."

There was a new figure in front of us now, a little pale ghost winding skywards. While we were arguing, Greenlaw had slipped past us and begun the ascent herself. In the rain, her hair collapsed like a souffle.

"The money is something to discuss between you but I insist that you give me that paperwork," she called up the shaft.

"Jesus *Christ*." There was no safe way to climb that staircase even in daylight, even in the dry. Moss on the concrete steps threw off our footholds and when I grabbed the iron handrail it came away from the crumbling wall.

I found myself on the first floor where going down seemed as risky as climbing higher. Cold air scraped at my lungs as we gained on Greenlaw. Clay stopped abruptly at a landing, where the clockwork proper began, and the stone staircase gave way to rickety wooden steps and the huge rusting guillotines of cogs and levers. His light vanished as he punched out the door and, in a shower of splinters, edged onto the exterior fire escape.

"It'll never hold your weight!" shouted Jesse. Even if it did, I wasn't setting foot on it. Clay could be out of the county before we had even worked out an escape plan. The clockwork hung over us, dripping water onto our faces. A shard of opaque glass from the clock face, hinged between six and seven on the iron that had once held it fast, teetered in the wind. There was a nerve-grazing screech, like the disused hinge of a giant door being opened. The impact of the fire escape crashing to the ground outside shook the tower like an earthquake and another sheet of glass slid from its ironwork. All three of us closed our eyes against its shattering and opened them when the crunch of glass underfoot told us that Clay was back on the landing. Relief that he was alive was swiftly chased away by the rage on his face.

"Did you set me up for this, you little shit?"

I couldn't believe his nerve. "*You* followed *us* here!" I protested. "And he tried to warn you."

Jesse grasped at the threads of control. "Let's get back down the stairs in one piece and have it out there. OK?" He kicked the worst of the shards down the central well. "There's literally nowhere else to go."

We stood there for a moment, each with our back to a shattered clock face in the closest thing to silence I had experienced that evening. We might have stayed like that for a second; it might have been ten. I only know that my hand reached for the bag at the same time as movement exploded from every direction. All four of us were tussling in the dark, the darting spotlights picking out only the missing bricks, sliding tiles, wrought-iron numbers and the occasional terrified face, like stills from a horror film. In one frame I saw my own hands grabbing at dark leather just before skinning my knuckles on rough stone. In another, Greenlaw's tiny hands fought Jesse—or was it Clay?—for the bag. I felt the keyring on Clay's belt and pulled hard. There was a clang as metal hit stone. When I bent to retrieve it someone stamped down on my right hand with the force of a dropped cannonball and the pain took my breath away but the fingers of my left hand closed in on cold metal and it was mine.

In the next frame, Clay had Jesse by the collar and held him over the edge of the banister. Helen was on Clay's back—to save Jesse or to push him I couldn't tell.

"Leave him alone!" I screamed. I lunged forward as Clay reared up, throwing Helen off. An elbow was in my ribs, a knee in my thigh.

The wood cracked as it gave way.

All resistance vanished instantly and Greenlaw, Jesse and I were fighting black air. Jesse and I whipped our heads to the void of the stairwell. Two beams collided and a fuzzy spotlight traced Clay's descent. There were three separate impacts: the first, a crack and a splash of red on the white tiles, the uncanny angle of the neck. The second, a spine against an iron strut on the way down, the great broken body hung for a second in its impossible backbend. The third, the splash.

After that, nothing but our breathing and the snare-drum rolling of the rain.

34

"No!" Jesse shouted into the stairwell. The tiled walls concentrated the light: all we could see of Clay's broken body was a pale face, paper in ink, suspended for a few seconds and then sinking without bubbles. "I'll go down to the basement, see if I can get in that way."

I tried to take his hand but his skin was as wet and cold as mine and my fingers slithered on his wrist. "Jesse, it's flooded. You'll kill yourself."

"He's my *brother*," said Jesse. He'd lost the color in his cheeks; his eyes and lips had gone silent-movie-star dark.

Greenlaw stepped in front of him, her small hand on his chest. He flinched at her touch but the only way past would have been to throw her down the stairs.

"He's gone." Her clinical tone made it all the more final.

Jesse slid down the wall, leaving a vertical smear on the dirty tiles. I opened my hand to show him Clay's keys—the huge Nazareth door key, a Yale and a Harley-Davidson key on a leather and metal fob—and gave them to Jesse. He twisted them in his hands, black eyes staring blankly up at the clockwork as though he wished it would fall on us.

"What do we do?" I asked Greenlaw. I was a child desperate for a grown-up to help me.

She steepled her fingers and pressed them to her forehead. "It's clear that our immediate concern must be to retreat to a place of safety," she said.

"What?"

She could barely conceal her impatience at my idiocy. "We need to go down the stairs."

I squatted level with Jesse. "Did you hear that? We'll go back down now, and then we'll find a way to make it all right. OK? Come on." This time he did take my hand. He carried the bag; I took the big torch. Greenlaw carried herself upright as a ballerina. We used our hands on the old brickwork for balance. It was a miracle we had all climbed the tower at all: the stairs were steep, deeper than they were wide. The descent took us twice, three times as long as it had to climb up. One false footing and we would all go down. To stop myself from screaming I counted the steps. Ten, eleven, past the spray of blood flowers where Clay's head had hit the tiles. Twenty, twenty-one, past the bar that had cracked his spine. Thirty-two, thirty-three, every tread bringing us closer to the moment where she would tell us we must call the police. She probably had a car phone in that Jaguar. Thirty-nine, forty. I replayed the moments before Clay had fallen. It seemed to me that after the initial grab, everyone was reacting to Clay and his whirling rage. I remembered my hands on his collar, trying to wrench him off Jesse. Every time I had seen Greenlaw she had been either cowering or reaching for the bag. Forty-seven, forty-eight, forty-nine, and we were back in the atrium.

We faced each other, three sides of a square. My hands and Jesse's were ingrained with dirt, black outlines on our knuckles and nails. Greenlaw's remained immaculate.

"Which of us—" asked Greenlaw. Her cut-off question was an answer in itself, her guard lowered but not dropped. People lie to cover their tracks all the time but in the aftermath of true horror, there is a window—minutes, even seconds long—where shock drives out dissemblance and there is only room for a kind of devastated honesty.

"I don't think—" I could no more finish my sentence than she could. "Who—" I tried again. I had to know, even if I found out that it was me who'd done it.

"I don't know," confessed Jesse. "I was just lashing out. You were both in there, too. I don't know if it was me."

"Me neither," I confessed. "But that means it could've been me as much as *not* me, do you know what I mean?"

We bounced our horror off each other in darting stares we were afraid to hold. I believe, in that moment, we would all have been as happy to take blame as to assign it. What was the difference? We were all in each other's debt.

Freezing water from my hair dripped down the back of my leathers. Jesse's hair was matted with rubble and dust. Greenlaw put her hands to her own collapsed hairstyle and slicked it back with rainwater, slimy lowlights swooping from her temples. The little action returned her composure. "It's an extraordinary situation," she conceded. "I would guess that it was his own bodyweight against the wood; he was a substantial man. But I couldn't swear to it. It might have been any of us. It could well have been me." She shrugged, like she was saying yes, perhaps it was me who used the last of the milk. It wasn't that she was lying: it was that she didn't care who was responsible. It didn't matter. Clay had already become a problem to be solved.

Her hard heart was our only hope.

"So what do we do now?" I addressed them both, but it was her response I awaited. "Seriously. What do we *do*?" My teeth began to chatter on the last word, snapping into five syllables. Greenlaw pressed her fingertips between her closed eyes. I steeled myself for her to tell us that we were all innocent in a way, that the police would understand and the law would support us. Whoever had caused Clay's death, Jesse and I were still liable for blackmail. She could sell us down the river and she knew it.

Then I saw her face and it all changed. She had become her own chalk drawing, ashy white skin, lines etched in charcoal and it struck me that the only time apart from Parliament that you saw those drawings was when someone was in court. My mind's eye sketched Jesse and me in the dock.

"How soon before he's missed?" she said.

It was so far from what I expected that I mistook her meaning. Jesse leaned forward, as though he were about to throw up, then dropped to all fours and stared at a dark corner. I wondered if he even knew we were there.

"I think Jesse's missing him already," I said. Helen remained impassive while my understanding caught up. The chill on my skin reached the bone. I saw now the composure she must have needed to secure her release, and after Julia Solomon died. Here was the inhumanity we had exploited serving us. If we went along with this, we were no better than she was. We were worse, because we had set this night in motion.

I lowered my voice and turned to her. "He might not be missed for a while," I said. "He comes and goes. It can be months. His parents don't know he's out."

That brought Jesse back to the moment. "But we can't just *leave* him here," he said. I beckoned for him to stand; with a foal's stagger he was back on his feet.

"I don't know how one would possibly retrieve him," said Greenlaw. "I'm afraid that unless you want your little plot exposed, we need to pass this off as misadventure." She could not have delivered her threat more plainly but Jesse's spaced-out face told me I still needed to parse it for him.

"You mean we make it look like he did this on his own?" I asked.

Jesse shook his head slowly; Greenlaw nodded hers at the same pace. With sickening certainty, I knew she was right. Was that agreement the moment I truly staked my flag in the same ground as her? The alternative was one, two, *all* of us convicted of manslaughter, of trespass and two of us of blackmail. We had tried to wield power over Greenlaw; now we had as much to lose as she did. I had been mad to think she would want us to go to court.

My earlier scream had scraped the honey out of my voice but it had released something too that let me talk without crying. "OK,

Jess, listen to me now." I took his face in my hands. "It's awful, it's horrible and I'm so sorry, but I think we have to do what she says. OK?" This time when he shook his head I clamped it still, tiny muscles in my arms and wrists flexing against the force of his jaw. "Look at me. No one else comes here. You *told* him not to go up those stairs and he did it anyway. It's just the kind of thing he would've done on his own. In't it?" Jesse's tears—the tears I had gone to so much trouble to avoid—washed white deltas in the grime on his face.

"He's my *brother*."

Grief I would allow, and guilt, but brotherly loyalty I would not. Without Clay's interruption we would, about now, be turning left into Nusstead. "Don't forget why he was here in the first place."

"He might lie undiscovered until such time as the building is developed, and that's likely to be years." I was almost impressed by Greenlaw's cynicism, the way there was no situation in which she would not exploit insider knowledge. "You say yourselves that this kind of misadventure was not out of character."

Jesse put his head in his hands and gave himself a moment of hell before throwing his toolbag at Helen's feet. The money was still there, although the notes were wet and wavy now, not the crisp bricks of earlier.

"Take what you have to, do what you want," he said. Helen didn't touch the money but took out her records and added them to her handbag. We made no attempt to stop her. Our insurance policy was something we could never now cash.

"You are young. You have your whole lives ahead of you." It was said without wistfulness, only as a statement of fact. "Everything about this has been regrettable. A terrible thing has happened here but the fall at least was nobody's fault." For a second, her pale eyes shone. "I have *worked* to get where I am today." The potential assault on her career seemed to move her far more than Clay's death. She composed herself so quickly I wondered if I'd glimpsed vulnerability at all. "There is no reason why your interference should cause any more upset. We shall have no more contact. Is that understood? We all have a very great deal to lose."

"Yes," I said miserably. Helen tilted her chin toward Jesse, a strict teacher with her unruliest pupil. He looked to me for guidance: I gave the tiniest nod.

"Yeah," he said through tears. "Yeah, we—yeah."

I handed him Clay's keyring. When Jesse placed his gloved fingertips on the lock surround, the door creaked open at the pressure of his touch alone. Clay had been bluffing. It had been open all along.

Helen's back, as she picked through the mud and debris to her car, was plumb-line straight. Her composure was an insult to everything that had just happened. I felt broken, as though I would never hold my head up again.

Red lights retreated along the cedar avenue.

"What if I can still save him?" said Jesse suddenly. "He might be trying to get out and he can't." He began to strip off, as though he were going back to the basement to dive in.

"Jesse." I caught his arm, smoothed out the gooseflesh with my thumb. "Jesse. I'm sorry. He's dead. You *saw* him."

He was off before I could stop him, torch around his neck. He didn't go down at all but up, up, up to the top of the tower.

"Come down, Jess," I shouted. "Fucking stop it!"

I stood in the doorway, shielding my eyes while he used a length of something to knock between the rafters, dislodging the remaining roof tiles and leaving only a frayed felt lining in place. Water collected in pools and then burst through into a steady fall, straight down the hole and onto Clay. "That's enough!" My scream was shrill enough to get through to him. He came down the stairs in the dark: his face by the light of my torch was too much.

"What are you doing?" I asked.

"Burying him," he said.

We stood side by side in the doorway. Greenlaw had reached the end of the cedar drive and the Jaguar was out on the sweep of

Asylum Road. With nothing else to see for miles around, the Jaguar's taillights were intermittent streaks of red in the rain. Greenlaw would be at home by four in the morning, she would beat the dawn to London by hours. I pictured her in a bath with gold taps, washing the night off her, rinsing debris out of her hair with expensive shampoo. How would she explain the spoiled clothes to whoever did her washing for her?

Just as the red lights were fading to pinpricks, the car seemed to stall. Then it reversed.

"Jesse!" I nudged him and pointed. "What's she doing? Is she coming back, do you think she's changed her mind?"

"Fuck knows," said Jesse. "A phone box?" He knew as well as I did that there was no public telephone between here and Nusstead. The red lights died, replaced by a tiny dancing yellow glow. Jesse shielded his eyes. "Is that fire?"

"I don't *get* it. How could anything burn in this rain?"

"She's at the bus stop, in't she," said Jesse. Of course. Greenlaw had reversed because she had caught sight of the abandoned bus shelter. At the first dry ground, she had set her records on fire.

35

We made a half-hearted attempt to rub away the worst of our foot-prints from the corridor. What was the point when our fingerprints were all over this place?

When we had done everything we could, it was our turn to pass through the double doors. Using the huge formal entrance for the first time made the expulsion complete.

Jesse's bike was parked where we'd left it, helmets damp and cold.

"I'm going to hell," said Jesse. "That's it, in't it? I'm going to hell. Fucking—fire, eagles pecking my eyes out." I was scared how fast the narrative had skewed from "it was no one's fault" to "we killed him" even if they were both, in their way, true.

"Jesse, you need to calm down. This isn't helping. We agreed with Greenlaw, it was a horrible accident."

"But he's still dead." The last word collapsed into sobbing. "My mum," was all he could manage. The thought of Trish's face brought home Clay's death to me, made the bile rise in a way that seeing his body hadn't. Everyone's expectations that Clay wouldn't make old bones was no consolation. "I can't tell a lie that big every day for the rest of my life. I can't do it, babe. I mean, I know you'll have to do it to your mum and everything but you won't be lying about someone she *loves*."

"I know." The cells of my guilt were dividing and swelling and I knew that it had not even begun to achieve its final mass. "Jesse, come on. Let's go home. Let's clean up and go to sleep. It's not going to do us any good staying here."

On the cedar drive, Jesse's headlights caught Clay's bike, scarlet and chrome, tipped against the black gorse. He braked hard.

"What the hell are we supposed do about his *this*?" His voice was cracking again. We both slid up our visors.

"We'll have to just leave it parked here," I said, thinking out loud. "The more natural it is, the more it'll seem like an accident."

I realized the flaw as soon as I'd spoken; we didn't *want* him to be found.

"But if Dad sees it gone from the garage, he'll know Clay's out, and then they'll know he's missing. And if someone finds it—it's like, where's the rider? You don't just forget where you parked a Harley." He pushed his soaking hair off his brow. "It's 1690cc, it's too bottom-heavy for you. But you could ride mine?"

"I can't." I'd never ridden Jesse's bike on a proper road, let alone in the dark, in the rain.

"It's either that or I walk back here to pick it up later, and it'd take me all night, and I can't . . . I can't do this on my own, babe."

My grip on the bars was so tight that muscles I didn't even know were related—my shoulder blades, my sides—fired up in support as I followed Jesse slowly back to Nusstead, his taillights red streamers across my visor. He set the pace, not too fast, and I followed his lead round the back of the new houses to the lock-up garages. Clay's key opened the door, which screeched open on its coasters at an unearthly pitch. I waited for a window to glow, for a blind to flick open, but there was nothing. The torch's batteries were dying now but in its faltering light we rubbed the bikes down with a chamois. When they gleamed like new, we hung our helmets on hooks.

Jesse's face had caved in on itself. "How can I go in there and act like nothing's wrong?" I was too saturated with my own pain and fear to absorb a drop more of his, and I knew that if I didn't keep it together, both of us would fall apart. Right then, freezing and dirty, sore, soaked and scared, I wished to feel nothing, and drew on the actions of the one person I knew who would be—who clearly was—unscathed by this. I straightened my spine, focused on facts and put everything I had left into keeping my voice under control. "Because to them nothing will be." I needed to head off the invitation to stay with him before it came. The honesty of touch would have killed me. "Jess, I need to be in my own bed, I need to wash in hot water in my own bathroom. All my clothes are disgusting."

He dropped to his knees and wrapped his arms around my waist. "I won't be able to sleep without you."

I felt like kicking him off. "I'll see you tomorrow." I had my hands in his filthy hair as he cried at my feet.

"Oh, thank God I've got you, babe, thank God I've got you, and we'll always have this to keep us together, won't we?" His eyelashes were spiky with tears. How did he think we could possibly go on?

I was grateful that night for poky little cottages with downstairs bathrooms. I shampooed my hair three times and stayed under the hot water until it ran lukewarm. Hair still in a towel, limbs and lungs screaming, I put on my old flannel pajamas and crept into the bed I shared with Colette. I turned to my little sister for warmth as she turned to me for comfort. "Love you, Marianne," she murmured in her sleep, and the dam broke. I cried until her hair was as damp as mine.

Mum woke me up what felt like thirty seconds later. Jesse, Greenlaw, Clay: every image from the night before was a blow upon a bruise. Actually it was eleven o'clock in the morning; the heating had gone off, and my breath steamed indoors. I ached all over, knots of muscle holding trauma close.

"Trouble in paradise?" she asked.

I made a sound that came out, "Wuh?"

"Jesse knocked for you just now, looked very sorry for himself.

I heard you come in late last night, you must have been in a right strop." She pulled the duvet off, an old trick she used when I wouldn't get up for school. My legs cramped in protest.

"Mum!"

"Lovers' tiffs, it's all part of the drama, part of the appeal at your age. Prince Charming's going to wait outside." She threw the curtains wide. The clouds had gone: cold yellow sun filled the room but didn't warm it.

"Anyway, never mind Jesse Brame." Mum peeled a corner of bubble wrap away from the windowpane. "Get a load of this, you won't bloody believe it."

I got to my feet and saw nothing; the rain had stopped and the clouds had gone. Just a load of blue sky, an unbroken Suffolk horizon, nothing taller than a tree and—

Christ.

I realized what was different right as Colette burst in and said, "The clocktower fell down in the night!"

It was true. The brickwork was intact but only then did I realize how much of it had been ironwork and glass. Mum tiptoed to get a better view. "It's been on the news. *National,* not local. We had a month's worth of rain in three hours last night, apparently, and that was the last straw. The whole building's been condemned. They're having it roped off and everything, proper security fencing, not that crap they had before. I saw Mark when I was getting the milk in, he's got a day's work helping put the new fences up around it. He reckons Larry Lawrence put someone up to it, insurance job. They should knock the whole rotten place down, you ask me."

I dressed in a soft old tracksuit that rubbed like armor. Jesse was waiting at the war memorial, his own bike at his side.

"Did you sleep?" His eyes were the answer, pink at the rims and set in deep gray bowls. "I can't believe it fell down the night we were there," I said. "Could've been us."

"It was me, going at it with the bar. I should've left it. This has only drawn attention to it. Anyway, let's go."

I blinked in disbelief. "Back to Nazareth?"

"I can't stand not knowing what they're gonna find."

Dozens of cars spilled out of the forecourt and along the cedar drive. Police vehicles, a digger and a truck. Their tire tracks had gouged up the earth around where we'd ridden but there was no crime-scene cordon. Men, including Mark Brame, formed a queue in front of a woman with a hard hat and a clipboard. Mark seemed to sense Jesse behind him, and turned to give his son the thumbs-up at the prospect of cash in his pocket tonight.

Jesse couldn't keep his hands off me; they were on my shoulders, around my waist, catching at my sleeve. I clenched my fists to stop myself from swatting him away.

"Why the coppers?" I asked someone I knew by sight. "Was it vandals?"

"Criminal negligence, more like," he said. "This is what they *want*, for it to fall down. I know the developer, Larry Lawrence—he's going to leave the whole place to rot."

"Not if English Heritage have anything to do with it," said a woman in a Barbour gilet.

A lorry carrying slabs of fencing on its pallet parted the crowd. I couldn't look at Jesse: these would be the walls of Clay's tomb and his own father would be among those to lay them.

36

The conspiracists were right about one thing. In 1991, Larry Lawrence sold up at a loss of three million pounds and was taken to court for allowing dereliction of a Grade II listed building. The buyers' surveyors were thorough, no brick unturned. Clay had spent seven seasons shedding his flesh in damp and debris and the find was reported in terms of human remains rather than a body. He was identified by his prison dental records.

It was assumed from the start that the verdict would be misadventure. The Essex antiques dealer came forward and it was thought Clay had been after the numbers from the clock face or even the hands for scrap. Normally a death like that would have gone unreported but since Darius Cunniffe had turned the place into a haunted house, the tabloids talked about the Curse of Nazareth. Adam Solomon was on BBC *Look East* saying the whole place should be knocked down and that the site should be made a wildlife sanctuary, blending into the fen.

After Clay's death, I'd lasted another six weeks with Jesse, squirming under his desperate touch, before I'd escaped to Cromer Hall, a genteelly dilapidated East Sussex sixth-form crammer, down on their luck enough to take cash. I told Mum that one of the scholarships I'd applied for had come good when their first choice dropped out in the middle of term, and in her ignorance and pride she believed me. Cromer Hall was not the Malory Towers of my fantasies, and no hotbed of excellence—it was, essentially, a place for thick posh birds to save academic face and self-made men's daughters to iron out their vowels—but it was far from Nusstead.

I'd forbidden my mother from telling Jesse where I was going.

"Mari*anne*." I was unused to seeing my mother ashamed of me, and it hurt more than I had known it could. "You owe him a good-bye. Please. I brought you up better than that."

"A clean break," I said. "It's the only way. I'm being cruel to be kind."

Kind to her, perhaps: protecting her from the truth about her daughter. But I did Jesse no kindness. I was being cruel to survive. I couldn't look him in the eye. I couldn't bear the sick intimacy of what we had done. I could not bear knowing him and, worse still, being known.

I made it clear, during my phone calls with Mum and Colette, that the clean break was a two-way thing. Talk to me about Jesse, keep telling me he's started drinking or that he's dropped out of school, or that he smashed up the Social last week and did a night in the cells, and I will hang up on you now and I will never come home again.

"How did you get so cold?" she crackled down the line.

"You told me to better myself," I said, hating myself for using her own ambition against her. "Isn't this what you wanted?"

"Not like this, Marianne," she said. But that hurt protected her from a greater one. Better she put her head in her hands and say that this was not what she meant, that she couldn't believe she had raised such a little snob, than she understand the awful truth.

Weeks turned into terms and still I didn't come home, paying my holiday board by working every shift they would give me in McDonald's in the A23 services. I was a novelty in a school where at half term some pupils would be picked up by helicopter from the playing field. I got good marks and I ironed out my vowels until by the end of the first year I might have been saying all the wrong things but at least I was saying them in the right sort of accent. I got a place at Glasgow University—full grant, because of my parental circumstances—to read History of Art. I had three stars on my badge at McDonald's: transferring to the Jamaica Street branch by Glasgow Central Station was easy. By day, I lost myself in Hunter, Whistler and Mackintosh; by night I managed a team, occasionally wiping down the tables or serving the fries myself, then washed the vegetable oil out of my hair in time for lectures the next morning. There was little time for making friends or socializing: I was Scarlett O'Hara in a brown nylon uniform, determined never to be poor or hungry again.

Nusstead caught up with me, as I had always known it must. I was working the tea-time shift in the restaurant and found a copy of the *Daily Mirror* spread under the detritus of a Happy Meal, the headline *Local Man Found After Two Years* stark above two black and white photographs: a face; a building. I recognized Nazareth before I recognized Clay.

I called Jesse that night, a five-pound phonecard in the slot. Trish answered the first time, and Wyatt the second. I let the receiver drop. On the third try, I got him.

"It's me." I used my old voice.

There was a shuffling while he took the phone from the living room out into the hall. I was braced for the hail of accusations. "You've got a fucking nerve," he said, almost under his breath.

"I know. I'm sorry. I shouldn't've called, I'll go."

"Don't you *dare* hang up on me." I could picture his face, the twist of his mouth. "You can face the music for once in your selfish life, you don't just get to disappear when I've had to keep it together down here. The funeral's on Thursday. Show your face, it's the least you can do."

Was it a threat or did my paranoia turn it into one?

"Why do you even *want* me there?" I asked.

"I don't." His voice was muffled. "But you owe me."

37

My connecting train was late, so I missed the service and had the taxi bring me straight to the Social. The place had deteriorated further in the thirty-two months I'd been away, the felted roof curling alarmingly away from the outer walls. It was already busy inside; I searched the faces for the one I knew best but I couldn't see him and my stomach plunged at the thought of the grand entrance I'd have to make.

Wyatt saved me in the end, emerging from a car with a bag of ice. Mutual recognition took a couple of seconds. He'd had his hair cut into a step and the black suit was the most sober thing I'd ever seen him wear. I was suddenly conscious of my Sloaney blonde streaks, the preppy mini-kilt, black trench and penny loafers. Wyatt's face showed shock, then so much anger that for a fleeting second I felt sure he must know everything.

"Wait there," he said without smiling. "I'll get him." He vanished into the smoky throng. I stood outside, shredding a tissue in my pocket.

Jesse emerged from the Social and guilt flooded my guts. The top button of his collar was already undone, black tie hanging loose around his neck. I could smell the lager on his breath from five paces away.

"Couldn't face the coffin, huh?"

"The train got stuck," I said pathetically.

He shook his head and laughed cynically. "You told your mum you got a *scholarship*. Couldn't you have come up with something a bit less fucking Enid Blyton?"

His legs buckled through drink, or perhaps the weight of grief. Instinctively, I rushed forward to catch him, but his palms were up and he caught his balance again.

"I said I'd won the pools. Want to know what I done with it?" He nodded backward to the party. "This is almost the last of it. I set money aside for it, I knew this would happen and it was obviously pretty quickly I'd be footing the bill on my own. There should still be a couple of grand left after tonight. God knows I'll be needing it." From nowhere, his fist punched through the soft wood of the club's prefab exterior. The wall buckled but didn't break. Splinters porcupined his knuckles: he gazed down, apparently unable to feel pain.

"Here," I said. He let me take his hand and pull out the spikes one by one. The familiarity of his skin on mine had worn off, replaced by the old charge.

"I couldn't stay. How could we be together, with that hanging over us every day?"

Feathery grass grew through a crack in the drainpipe. Jesse picked a long stalk and started to strip the chaff.

"Well, we could have, because that's what couples do. They help each other when times are tough, they don't fuck off into the sunset on their own."

"We're not talking about a bit of boredom here or a late rent check."

"I know that. Don't talk down to me. You think my mum and dad fell apart when they lost Butch? You think they're at each other's throats now? No. They *pull together*."

Telling him I'd been going to leave him anyway would have been pointless and cruel, like dumping him in retrospect. Better for him to think it was because of Clay, even if it did perpetuate his belief that we'd been cut down in our prime.

"I had to deal with so much shit and the one person I could've—I couldn't even *phone* you. Your mum said you didn't want to talk to me. How d'you think that made me feel? Just waiting till you lowered yourself to ring home?" He balled the stripped blade of grass and threw it down, where it sprang back into shape. "I think about what it means to die *all the time*. Like, one minute you exist and then you just . . . don't. Like, if there's an afterlife, where did he end up? If you do as much stupid shit as Clay did, but then you die like that, does it cancel it all out? I keep wondering if he knew—" His legs went again and this time I rushed to break his fall. I staggered under the familiar weight of him, twirled him around to the side of the building, the blind spot of the corner. We leaned side by side against the outside wall, which throbbed against our spines as Wyatt's "Danny Boy" rattled the windows. "That's not even the worst part. The worst part of it all was missing you. When you went away, I was *gutted*. I'll never have anyone like you again, I know that, but . . ." His hand was on my cheek. "Ride with me now," he said. "For old times' sake?"

I knew what he was asking. He had been drinking, and he was angry, guilty and grieving. I should have said no but a strange detachment settled on me: if I took this one risk and died then I deserved it. Muscle memory swung my right leg over his saddle; it was all so familiar, right down to the length of my skirt.

We rode bare-headed, not toward Asylum Road and the fen but out to the nothing of the fields, my arms around his waist and my nose buried in his neck and when Nusstead and Nazareth were out of sight we found some dry ground and lay down. It was two years since we'd touched—since I'd been touched by anyone other than a hairdresser—and his skin on mine was a detonation. Here at last, with grief and guilt as aphrodisiacs, sex lived up to the promise of our first kiss. It was the last thing I would ever do as my old self, and when I got up I almost expected to see my body lying in the flattened grass.

We came back in separately, of course. The edge was gone now, the charge spent.

I went first. Someone had tried to make a photo montage of Clay's life but for most of it the Brames hadn't had much money for photographs and so there were the same five or six pictures dotted on repeat around the room. The food, though, was plentiful; pyramids of sausage rolls, a cheese and pineapple hedgehog, and the bar—oh, Jesse—was free. He'd even hired someone to go around with a tray full of glasses; I took two glasses of white and had already dispatched one when Colette charged me.

"Marianne!" Her arms were tight around my waist. She was eleven now and Mum had evidently given in at last to her demands for a perm. Her long hair was wound into crisp curls that looked like they would shatter like glass if you grabbed them in your fist. She was hair mousse and Impulse, her little-girl smell gone forever. "Where's Mum?" I asked. Colette nodded across the dancefloor. Mum was crouching down to hug Trish Brame, who was now in a wheelchair, wizened and broken in black lace.

I picked my sister up as if she were still a little girl. "I'm sorry, Colette. I'm never leaving it so long again."

"What's that in your hair?" she asked. I put my hand to my head and a tangle of long grass came away. Jesse walked in, flushed and disheveled, mud on one knee. If Colette noticed, she didn't make the connection, but the sight of him did something to her. She cast her eyes about the room as though checking for spies, then lowered her voice. "Mum said we weren't allowed to tell you," she began, "but you should probably—"

"*Clay!*" The name pulled a cord; silence fell on the room. I'd heard that harsh voice once before. I'd completely forgotten about Michelle and Clay. Her long red hair was piled up and her face was puffy: they'd been seeing each other when he went missing but I hadn't known they were close enough for her to be screaming his name at his wake. The murmuring started up again, mourners turning away embarrassed. "Clay!" Michelle said again, this time addressing the floor. "Clay, God's *sake*."

Jesse shot through the crowd, ducked abruptly out of my view and reappeared seconds later with a toddler in his arms. A little boy in a blue sailor suit, black hands and knees, nappy bulging, dummy pulsing. I didn't know the first thing about babies, he could have been anything between six months and three years old. He handed the child to Michelle, who didn't thank Jesse but barked at him: "Fuck a you been?"

"Sorry, babe," said Jesse. "Let's go and get him changed, yeah?" Only when Michelle shifted the child onto her hip did I notice that she was very heavily pregnant. I tipped up my glass even though it was empty, and cast around for a refill. "Sorry, babe," he said again, and this time he was apologizing to me, looking back over his shoulder even as he steered her away. Dates flurried in my mind like pages torn from a calendar. Why hadn't I paid more attention to babies, so I could tell at a glance when a kid might have been conceived? I was surprised how much it mattered.

"I think this wine's got your name on it, Marianne," said Mum, at my elbow, fresh glass in hand. I held the drink away from my body and pressed her into a hug. "Are you staying?" I heard the plea in her voice.

"I am," I decided. "Jesse and Michelle, eh?" My voice rang with forced cheer. "I didn't see *that* one coming."

"We tried to tell you." Colette wedged herself in between us. "But every time anyone mentioned Jesse you went mental and Mum said not to."

"Something that big, though," I said, forgetting how patient they'd been with me.

"You said you'd cut us off." Mum's hurt came brimming to the surface. "Have you any idea—" She held up her hands. "I'm not going to do this here, Marianne. It's not as if you want him back, so what's the difference?" I stared into my glass. What *was* the difference? Was it that it undermined what we'd had, and only now did I see how much Jesse's adoration had meant to me? Was it that I still wanted him to want me, even if he couldn't have me? Was it that I wouldn't have fucked him in a field just now if I'd known? I couldn't swear to that.

"I know. I'm sorry," I said. "Tell me now."

Mum bit her lip. "I'm ever so thirsty. Colette, can you be a poppet and get me a glass of water?" When she was out of earshot, Mum said under her breath, "Trish swore me to secrecy."

"Mum!"

"I'm only telling you because you're you. OK? Baby Clay is Big Clay's son," said Mum. A knot of muscle in my neck came undone; my shoulders dropped by inches. "Michelle went to the Brames, must have been a couple of months after you went, for child support. And Jesse must have felt sorry for her or responsible or, I dunno, maybe he was on the rebound, but they're bringing up Baby Clay together and not telling him who his real dad is. Seriously, don't breathe a word. Trish'll have my *guts*. And for God's sake don't tell your sister, she already knows too much for someone her age." I'd forgotten about the special double-time voice Mum used for imparting gossip, delivering the maximum information in the minimum time to leave more space afterward for discussion and analysis. It always took a few seconds to process what she'd said.

"How do the dates work out?" I was thinking about dates myself: wondering how I'd get out of Nusstead in time for the morning-after pill. My hand went to my own belly.

"She's due in about six weeks."

"Not the bump." I couldn't bring myself to say Baby Clay. It sounded ridiculous. "The kid. How old is he? If everyone thinks he's Jesse's, will they think he was cheating on me?"

Mum did the sums in her head. "I mean, it doesn't look like he let the bed get cold, but it just about convinces as a rebound—oh, hello sweetheart."

Colette was there, carrying a glass of water in both hands and looking at the hand that still rested on my abdomen.

"Were *you* pregnant?" Colette ignored my mother's warning glance. "It's not fair on me, not knowing. I couldn't sleep without you for ages. I lay awake and I wondered if you'd got pregnant and gone off to have it adopted like they did in the olden days." For all the perm and the deodorant she was still a little girl, not understanding that an unwanted pregnancy in 1989 was not the stuff of a Catherine Cookson novel but an inconvenience that any good doctor could treat. Another layer of guilt to pack down hard into rock with the rest. "I would have helped you out with a baby. You didn't have to go off."

I bent to Colette's level. "Sweetheart. No, I was never pregnant. I just split up with him, that was all. I got a chance of a good education and I took it. It was nothing to do with you. I hated leaving you, I missed you every day." Tears came and I didn't fight them. "I'm not going to have a baby for a long time, but when I do, you can babysit anytime you like."

Colette narrowed her eyes, then crooked her little finger. I hooked mine through hers and shook.

Baby Clay had been cleaned up. Jesse was feeding his "son" a bottle while Michelle put her feet up on a chair, puffy ankles the only extra weight on her frame. Over her shoulder, he gave his head the tiniest of shakes. I nodded in return to show him I wouldn't tell her about the bike ride and the field and the way I could still feel his hands on my skin. Forgiveness flowed between us, private and absolute.

Michelle followed my gaze and looked not triumphant or proprietary but terrified. I wondered again how long she'd watched us through the door that time and wondered if she'd recognized my performance for what it was. Her face told me she hadn't. I hoped the smile I tossed her conveyed that I was no longer a threat. She reflected it nervously, almost pretty when she smiled. But Jesse wasn't all hers, and never would be. Michelle might be bound to him in new life but he and I were tangled in death. When I checked Jesse, the old longing was in his eyes. I had to get away.

Someone had left a bottle of Chardonnay unattended. I took it outside and pressed it to my lips, feeling the acid scour away my emotions. I leaned against the Social and gazed across the shimmering fen to the Nazareth, the wide, low, broken sweep of the place. Helen Greenlaw must know that Clay had been found and laid to rest. Once again, crime had slid off her while others paid the price. I wondered if she was marking the occasion in her own way. I wondered whether she felt remorse or relief or this relentless churning blend of the two. I doubted she was capable of feeling anything at all.

nazareth mental hospital
1958

38

Helen Morris knew two things about what her parents called her "daily constitutional." The first was they must never know that instead of the sedate walk of their imaginations, she was running, as fast as her feet and heart would allow, two long plaits like whips on her back. Running, for girls, was something one left behind after cross-country. Helen ran in plimsolls, hiding her old school PE knickers under a dirndl skirt, which would be taken off and carefully folded into a little hollow she'd made in a hedgerow. The part of the world they had dumped her in this time, on the wild, shingled coast between Aldeburgh and Southwold, was criss-crossed with wide, flat, deserted back lanes and byways that invited the slap of her feet.

The second thing about her daily constitutional was that without it, the already tiny box of her life would shrink to nothing. It made the difference between a cell and a coffin. Helen had a theory—kept from her parents—that if only everyone could be made to run once a day, there would be fewer illnesses, an evenness of temper that might in time affect the whole country. When foul weather kept her indoors, her mind began to itch. She argued with her mother on rainy days. Eugenie had married Peter Morris late in life, and never made a secret of her disappointment that her "miracle" only child—at forty-five, she had already thought motherhood beyond her—was so willful, so unwilling to conform. It was almost, Eugenie despaired, as if Helen didn't *want* a quiet life.

And now there was a third thing to know about her daily constitutional; or rather, a consequence of it. Helen's body had understood long before she did. The sudden ineffectiveness of a perfectly serviceable brassiere: the taste of pennies on her tongue, muddled thinking and lungs that lost a little more capacity each day. Today it had been all she could do to drag herself the three miles inland to Greenlaw Hall. She had given up long before its chimneys were properly in focus, and turned to drag herself homeward to Sizewell Cottage.

Misery turned to panic when she saw the hedgerow. Her skirt was not where she had left it.

Fear temporarily restored her old energy and clarity. Robin was in London, and anyway this was not his idea of a joke. There was no wind to blow the skirt away. Could someone have stolen it? Hardly. The whole point of Helen's route was that (almost) no one knew about it. This bridle path was unused, too overgrown and potholed for horses and neglected by walkers in favor of the newly laid coastal footpath. It was the route's seclusion that had begun it all in the first place.

Energy and clarity did not produce the skirt, however, and there was nothing for it but to return home in her running clothes. If Helen could sneak upstairs then all might yet be well; the blue was not one of her best skirts, and before Eugenie had a chance to miss it, all of Helen's clothes would be gone and she with them.

She leaned against the postbox at the end of the garden path. Habit drew her hand inside, feeling for a letter or package from Rochelle, but of course there was nothing. It was impossible to see, from the gate, whether her parents were inside. The deep-set windows' little diamond panes threw back green and gold harlequins and reflected a hundred half-dressed Helens. She opened the gate quietly, conscious of the sun on her thighs. Peter would be at work, managing the land earmarked for a huge nuclear power station to be built a mile along the coast. If she was in, Eugenie was likely to be in the kitchen, which meant the front door—honeysuckle cloying in curls around a thatched porch—offered the best chance of going unnoticed. She put her hand to the doorknob and twisted. The blow to her head came with such force that when Helen turned she half expected to see Eugenie brandishing a plank of wood, not a palm.

"Get in." Eugenie seized Helen by the collar. "What in heaven's name is *wrong* with you?"

It was dark in the hallway, and by the time Helen's eyes adapted, she saw that Eugenie had the skirt between her hands, holding it so tightly she seemed to be wringing it out.

"I can—" she began, but Eugenie wasn't listening.

"This is the last straw, Helen. I *defended* you. Mrs. Johnson said she had seen you in your underwear in public, and I said to her of course Helen wouldn't do that." Even the hair in her bun seemed to coil tighter. "These people are—this community . . . we're just starting to settle in Suffolk and already you're making a fool of me. Worse, you're making a liar of me."

"It's not underwear. It's my old gym kit."

"I don't know what to do with you," said Eugenie. "It's worse than the hieroglyphics."

"You know perfectly well that was Pitman shorthand," said Helen.

Eugenie threw her hands in the air at the resurgence of this old trauma.

"*Please* don't start that again. Taking a salary away from a man who'll need it for his family. If supporting you, and your father, and making sure a house runs shipshape isn't a life's work then I don't know what is."

Helen had learned to swallow the fireballs of her opinions on this matter. Eugenie was so deep in the trap she couldn't see her life for what it was. She dictated Peter's letters and decided whom he should hire. He was little more than her mouthpiece and yet his name was on the deeds of the house, on the checkbook. She no longer even had the petty queendoms of Helen's childhood, family allowance and the ration book. She had to go cap in hand to her husband whenever she wanted anything.

"Don't look at me like that, Helen. You've got to get over these ridiculous ideas. They'll only lead to disappointment." This, Helen thought, was the reason that, though frustrated by her own life, Eugenie nevertheless insisted on the same for Helen. It wasn't jealousy, which could be challenged and pitied; it was protection, which was harder to oppose. "It's for your benefit." Her despair poured water on Helen's anger until it fizzled into sadness. That Eugenie's refusal to acknowledge who she was came from a place of love made it even worse.

"I'm going upstairs," said Helen. In the bathroom, she wetted her hair and in her bedroom she hung up her skirt, torn at the waistband where Eugenie had twisted it. She made a quick inventory of her room, checking her suitcase. The pill-bottle was still safe under a pile of sanitary napkins and tucked into a tear in the lining was a train ticket for next Thursday's 08:40 from Saxmundham to Liverpool Street. Five shillings and six, one way. Rochelle was, along with three hard-won A levels, the only legacy of Helen's time at school. Her sixth-form conspirator had shrugged off their shared bluestocking image and moved to London, defiant and glorious in trousers meant for a much slimmer girl. Her parents had let her—*encouraged* her to—go straight into a job: the two friends had been plotting by letter in a pidgin of boarding-school slang and Pitman shorthand ever since. Rochelle had "pulled some strings I shouldn't even be able to reach, dear," and found Helen a little job in her office and put a deposit on a new room, big enough for them to share and within walking distance of Regent's Park.

The sea dragged back and forth outside the window. Greenlaw Hall lay across miles of swishing fields and its heir had started in her belly.

The worry was not that her parents would not approve. They would hate the scandal, of course, and lie about the dates, but when they found out Robin was a Greenlaw, son of the local MP and in line for a hereditary peerage, they would quickly come around. Nor was the worry that Robin would abandon her. The true horror was that they would give the couple their blessing. The true horror was that Robin would stand by her.

39

Their first meeting had been almost a collision. Rounding a blind corner, Helen had dug her heels in to stop barreling into the chest of a blond man in shirtsleeves rolled to the elbow, and with a wheelbarrow of saplings at his feet. He held her blue skirt between his hands, loose as a hammock.

"Well, that answers my question," he said, handing it back. Helen climbed into it, cheeks on fire, but if he wasn't going to mention her bare legs, neither was she. "I've been noticing various items of women's clothing appearing over the last few days. It appears, it disappears. Thought I was going quite mad. A rather strange haunting. And yet here you are, very much in the flesh. Robin Greenlaw." He wiped a dusty hand on flannel trousers and held it out to her.

"Greenlaw," she said, picking at a twig that had snagged the cotton. "Like the house."

That seemed to amuse him: a dimple flashed in his cheek. "Like the house. We're on Greenlaw land now."

"Goodness." She couldn't help but be impressed at the reach of the estate. She'd left the house behind nearly half an hour ago.

"Where did you spring from, then?"

"We've not long moved to Suffolk. We move around a lot."

"Army brat?" It was a tease, not an insult.

"Technically we're nearly all army brats since the war," she said, thinking that life on a barracks would surely have been preferable to the Morrises' succession of oversized, isolated houses. "But no. My father's a forester."

He gestured toward the wheelbarrow. "Not much call for forestry at this precise moment in time, but do you know much about hedgerows? I'm supposed to be filling in the gaps in this one and it's backbreaking work." A single skein of lean muscle flexed in his forearm as he leaned on his shovel.

"If you fill *all* the gaps I'll have nowhere to put my things."

"Well, we can't have that, can we?"

It was as though there was a piece of string, one end connected to somewhere low in Helen's pelvis, the other to the dimple in his cheek: when he smiled, there was an internal tugging sensation. It was as thrilling and unexpected as finding a new room in one's childhood home.

"Your voice doesn't match the work you're doing."

"There's the feeling up at HQ," he nodded at the horizon, "that it would be good for me to get a bit of manual labor under my belt before I finish at LSE and spend the rest of my life pushing paper. One of my father's men could do this in a day. I'll be here till bloody September at this rate." He ran his fingers through his hair. "Still, if I want to represent those men one day I ought to be able to look them in the eye."

"Represent them?"

"Well, I'll probably end up taking over my father's seat. Dunwich Heath has returned a Greenlaw to Parliament since the Great War." He said it casually, as someone else might discuss inheriting a secondhand car, or a watch. "I'm not complaining, it does a body good. I think this would be a good substitute for National Service, don't you?"

He was there every day after that. Helen would stop on the other side of the hedge, take five minutes to touch her toes and let her runner's flush fade to a flattering rose. Robin would help her into her skirt, then, seemingly unsusceptible to the little electric connections firing off inside her, give her a lecture parsing whatever he'd heard on the wireless that morning. He was rather like a wireless himself, set to broadcast but not receive, but Helen let his words wash over her, watching instead the dusting of stubble on his chin and envying his razor. It was impossible to reconcile his droning with the effect he had on her body but the pull itself, which might in any case be a figment of her imagination, was enough for Helen. She had grown used to her own company, to being alone even when with others. She was happy simply to drink in the sight of him, store it up inside and enjoy the restlessness that flared in her at night, tangling the bedclothes.

"The new life peer rules came into force today," he said one day, leaning glumly on his shovel. "There could be women in the Lords by *August,* they reckon." This grave injustice propelled him along to others, and she soon had a list of things women shouldn't do, which included wearing trousers, playing tennis or cards, drinking anything that wasn't a snowball. At last, he was talking about something she could grasp: at last, she could argue with him.

"You don't seem to judge me nearly as harshly as you judge the world," she said. "You don't seem bothered by women who take their skirts off and run along country lanes."

Robin's face changed, as though he were in sudden discomfort. "Oh, I'm bothered all right," he said to the shovel under his boot. "Very hot under the collar, truth be told."

She took the first step. That would be important later. That invisible string suddenly, urgently, reeled itself in and the answer of his flesh told her that of course it was attached to him too, she had been a fool to doubt it.

"You really shouldn't," he said, but his hand was on her waist and he was guiding her off the path.

The mechanics of it were innate, like steps to a dance she'd been born knowing. Sixth-form rumors about bed had all been wildly divergent except on one point; the man would know what to do, he would take care of it. Helen had paused, hand on Robin's chest: "What if there's a baby?" He'd laughed and told her he wasn't stupid, he would be counting, he knew how to stop it and then in the next breath he'd said, "Good lord, it's like a knife through butter," and then he lost his language.

It was nothing like the dormitory whispers of gritted teeth and bloodied sheets. This great mystery that was supposed to be bound up in love and morality, Helen found uncoupled to either. She thought herself lucky to have found a man who was experienced enough to make up for the shortfall in her own knowledge, who knew how to do it without consequence. Either it was like this for everyone, and there was a conspiracy of silence for good reason—surely if everyone was walking around like an unexploded bomb the whole country would come to a halt—or she was different, abnormal, in her desires because Robin seemed to think so. "You're not like other girls. Do you know what a find you are, always ready for me?" There was something like horror in his voice when he said, "I want to have you whenever I want you." The next day, he had raised the possibility of meeting her parents and for the first time she had frozen on him. He never asked again, and the arrangement returned to its delicious convenience, beautifully impermanent.

But then he had gone away and left her counting not until his return but waiting for the curse that never came. Robin had been wrong. Or had he? *I want to have you whenever I want you.* What better way to enslave her than this? Robin was either far more, or far less, intelligent than Helen had supposed, and she did not know which made her angrier.

The choral society was performing *Spem in Alium* at the Quaker Meeting House in Leiston. Peter and Eugenie were not Quakers, but Eugenie, conscious that this was the community in which they would spend their retirement, was throwing herself into local "society" and attending everything. They had decided to walk into town, two miles each way. They would, Helen reckoned, be gone for at least four hours.

She sat cross-legged on her bed, the little brown pill-bottle in the apron of her skirt. Rochelle had posed as a girl in trouble to get Helen the prescription that would make her regular again from a doctor in Wimpole Street, and signed off her last letter: "if you let me down, I'll never speak to you again."

Helen didn't quite see how she would be the one letting Rochelle down if it didn't work, but apparently it was a moot point: success was guaranteed. This was a gray area, legally and morally, which Helen was uncomfortable about, but Rochelle had assured her time and again that pills didn't count and that it took *months* for a baby properly to start. Rochelle had promised her that and she was a legal secretary and must know what she was talking about. Thank God there was someone who knew how to help her without breaking the law. It was only when one got further along and needed what Rochelle called the "razor on a stick brigade" that it became illegal. This was just what they called family planning, and even the Church backed that now. Rochelle's doctor had told her simply to expect "all her missed periods to come at once" and since Helen had missed only two, and her periods had never broken her stride, how bad could that be?

She rolled the bottle between her palms, then tipped it out onto the blanket. Two white chalky pills, big as pebbles on a beach. Helen put the empty bottle back in her wardrobe, behind the pile of unused sanitary napkins; then removed a napkin and hooked it onto a belt.

So.

Something else Rochelle had said in her letter: if you were already showing, it was too late. *Then* it was a crime, *then* you were guilty. Helen rummaged in her desk drawer for her old wooden kings and queens ruler, lay back and rested it across her hipbones. If her belly made a fulcrum for it she could not go ahead. She closed her eyes and prayed: it wasn't my fault, I didn't *know*, she told God. But the swell beneath was gentle, the ruler level.

Outside, a young moon climbed. The sea was a gray monster with a million arching, feathered backs. Helen swallowed the pills with a glass of milk and felt her gorge rise. She fought her body to keep them down, reminding herself that her only chance of survival waited on the other side of the night.

40

She had collapsed halfway to the bathroom, skidding in her own mess. Her nightgown was soaked through with sweat and vomit, urine and feces and the one bright merciful streak of blood. There was a roaring noise inside her head, as though her ear were pressed against a thousand seashells. By the time Eugenie and Peter came home, her screams had dwindled to a wordless lowing, not because the pain had subsided but because her energy had. Eugenie took the stairs two at a time, shoes and coat still on.

"Helen!" Her knees clicked as she knelt down. "What's the matter?"

Helen threw up the last of her lunch on her mother's feet: tiny boats of lettuce floated on a pool of yellow bile. Eugenie pressed her hand to Helen's forehead, then bellowed down the stairs.

"Peter! Peter! Helen's been taken ill. Get Doctor Ransome. Take the car. *Now!*"

The door slammed. Eugenie dragged Helen back to bed, propped her on clean pillows.

"Let me sponge you down, see what's what." She was back with a pink sponge and a bowl of water, lifting Helen's nightgown before she could stop her. "Oh, dear God, you're *bleeding*. Let me get your napkins."

Helen realized, too late, what this would mean. Eugenie's head was already in the wardrobe.

"No!" she said, but it came out the wrong shape. She watched Eugenie's shoulders hitch, then her back straighten with devastating slowness. She seemed to turn without using her feet, like a figure on a cuckoo clock. In her arms were napkins piled two months high, the little brown pill-bottle balanced on top. Whatever Helen had expected to see on her mother's face, this was worse.

"You're—" Eugenie couldn't make herself say it. "What have you done to yourself? What will we tell the doctor? Who *did* this to you?"

It was unclear to Helen whether Eugenie meant Robin or Rochelle. She would not name either. She wanted rid of Robin, and Eugenie's expression suggested that she would need Rochelle more than ever. The questioning continued, the repetition acquiring the soothing monotony of a sermon, as Helen slipped into darkness.

A knock on the door brought her abruptly back to consciousness. Peter hovered a few paces behind the GP. Helen had seen Dr. Ransome only once before, when they had registered at the practice. His wide-set eyes and long top lip had made her think of a hare and she had taken against him instantly, even before he had slid the stethoscope an inch lower than it had needed to go.

"How much did you tell him?" Eugenie asked Peter of the doctor, as though even now, at the point of intervention, saving face were an option.

Dr. Ransome answered. "I have the gist." He gently placed himself between Eugenie and the bed. "If I could have some space around my patient." He set his black leather bag on the bed and undid the clasp, revealing the orange hose of a blood-pressure cuff. Eugenie began to tear at the bookshelves, opening novels and shaking them, looking for—what? Helen didn't know and she wasn't sure Eugenie did either. In any case, there was nothing to find. Rochelle's letters had all been burned in the grate.

"First things first." Dr. Ransome drew a thermometer from its case. Helen opened her mouth, felt the glass between tongue and teeth, and gagged. Peter watched his wife's increasingly frantic pillaging of the bookshelves through his fingers. Another spasm tore its way through Helen. She dry-heaved and the thermometer smashed on the floor. Everyone paused to watch the mercury worm its way across the floorboards.

"What was in here, then?" Dr. Ransome held the pill-bottle up to the light, as if a label might suddenly appear. "No way of telling without your help."

Helen shook her head, felt her bowels turn to liquid again. The sheet underneath her was soaked before she could think about moving.

Dr. Ransome shifted to the foot of the bed, and addressed Peter. "There's no way of telling what she's taken. Since she won't co-operate we need to get her to hospital, get her a purgative." A purgative! What was this, if not a purgative? Ransome assumed an expression of professional gravity. "Naturally my priority is pres-ervation of life. I can't ignore the fact that she has broken the law but we can talk about whether to report her for procuring an abor-tifacient after she has been to hospital."

A new sickness, one that stemmed from the heart rather than the belly, rose inside her. She hadn't heard the word before but she knew what it meant. Rochelle would not have done that to her, would she? She said so: it didn't count. She had trusted Rochelle. Then again, she had trusted Robin. It was her parents' fault for keeping her ignorant, forcing her to rely on others. It was her fault for not realizing this and educating herself.

Peter at last raised his head from his hands. "She cannot—you can't mean to call the police."

"Not in the first instance, but after recovery . . ." Ransome's eager look was at odds with his regretful tone.

Eugenie squatted at Helen's bedside and stroked her hair, smooth-ing the damp, filthy strands along the hairline. Comfort was so un-expected, and so welcome, that Helen felt the tears begin. Eugenie's smile was one Helen hadn't seen for the best part of a decade: it was the soothing smile for a grazed knee, a reward for a poem memorized or a prayer read aloud.

"Helen," she whispered, her voice trembling and her eyes wide with hope. "Did he force himself on you?"

Robin force himself! Helen had literally wrung the life from him. When she shook her head, Eugenie's cheeks seemed to lose mass, her eyes to hollow out. She was *disappointed*. She would have preferred Helen's violation to her pleasure. Motherhood was still only on Helen's horizon: orphanhood settled on her then.

"He must be married." Eugenie closed her eyes against the shame of it. Helen was still too stunned to correct the assumption. *She would rather I had hated it. She would rather I had been forced.*

Dr. Ransome held Helen's wrist in the air, counted her pulse. "You're very weak." He set the dead weight of her hand back on the bed.

"Has it worked, though?" Helen needed to know.

"It's not *natural*," Eugenie breathed. What wasn't natural? The wanting of the man or the ridding of the child?

"Hard to say, without you telling me where you got the pills," Dr. Ransome said. "Most of the time when these things work they do so by killing the child and taking the mother with it. Do you know what's in them? Mercury, turpentine, laburnum, quinine; I've even known them to include *gunpowder*."

Boom, Helen thought. Send me off like a firework, raining stars over the fields. A sparkler in the back garden. Remember, remember. She started to laugh: a dark, sick dislocated laughter that hurt muscles sore from vomiting.

"There's something wrong with her," said Eugenie. "This is the last straw, but since she was a child she's been cold. Unnatural. I've made excuses for her for years, but this . . ."

Helen expected Dr. Ransome to somehow recognize and dismiss the well-worn whinge but instead he nodded to himself and, after half a minute of apparent deep thought, raised his head to her parents. "Are you able to give me any examples of strange or destructive behavior?"

The glance Eugenie and Peter exchanged told her they hadn't expected this either.

"A few days ago, she was . . ." Eugenie lowered her eyes and her voice. "Helen was seen running about the countryside in her underwear. She came home half-naked. I should have locked her in her room. I had no idea, Doctor, what she was up to. She can be very cunning." Peter had begun to creep about behind Eugenie, picking up the books and replacing them gently on the shelf. "And then there's her involvement with that Rochelle. Sits with her legs apart, like a man. Of all the girls in that school she had to take up with her. They speak in their own language, cover paper in these strange symbols."

"It's Pitman." Helen would have spoken through gritted teeth if her chattering jaw had allowed it. "You know what it is. It's for work. And it's got nothing to do with Rochelle. I was sixteen before I had a friend, so please don't ruin it."

Ransome licked his lips. "So your childhood friendships were difficult?"

It was true, if irrelevant. At first the mothers would say that she was *her own person* and then that *she had some bold ideas* and finally that she was a *cold fish* and then they would stop bringing their children around altogether. "She was never interested in the same games, never picked up a doll. She—Peter, do you remember? She *cried* when the war ended. Why would anyone . . . it's not . . . it was the strangest thing."

"That's not fair. I was a child, I didn't understand. I just cried because the Wrens were leaving." The demobbing of the local WRNS unit, the loss of them in the town in their glamorous uniforms and little felt hats, had devastated Helen. They had always looked so smart, so *important*. "What does any of this have to do with . . ." How could she describe what she had done without naming it? She had the notion that if she didn't say the word police or mention the law then Ransome might forget his duty to turn her in. "With tonight?"

Ransome spoke over Helen's head. "There is a way around this that I think will help Helen and also avoid the worst kind of scandal. We could send her, now, to Nazareth."

Helen wondered if it was a euphemism, like being sent to Coventry, or whether it was some kind of religious order. Nuns were the *last* people she needed. Eugenie clearly knew what Nazareth meant. She stepped backward, cracking the spine of a splayed book.

"Are you sure that's possible? Aren't there . . . systems you have to go through? We don't want to involve the magistrate."

The doctor leaned back. "No, no. It's not like it used to be. I trained with one of the clinicians. Martin Bures? He's made quite a name for himself in recent years. Been after a chance to work with him for some time." His voice climbed in pitch before he caught himself and returned to his usual register. "Yes, he's the best in his field. If anyone can help Helen, Martin Bures can." There was a creep of pride in Dr. Ransome's voice, which shifted into annoyance when the name clearly rang no layman bells. "Anyway, I'd appreciate the chance to refer a patient to him. The hemorrhaging seems to have stemmed rather. I wouldn't call her critical now. If you—actually, perhaps we should take this outside."

During the murmured conference on the landing, Helen fought her heavy eyelids and lost. When she came to, her mother, still in her coat, was folding the last of her clothes into her suitcase. A fresh jolt of panic shot Helen up from the pillows but Eugenie tucked balled stockings into a corner and if she heard the telltale crackle of paper, it didn't occur to her to investigate it.

The only mercy, on the freezing drive to this Nazareth place, was that as they passed Greenlaw Hall, Helen's face was in darkness and her expression could not give her away. She slumped in the back, her suitcase sliding around in the boot. Eugenie sat beside her, vibrating with shame and fury. Peter drove in silence. Ransome, in the passenger seat, gave occasional directions. Periodically, signposts would flare into view. Saxmundham. Rendelsham. Strad-broke. Hoxne. Diss. They were virtually in Norfolk.

"Slow down, next left," said Ransome when they had been driving for so long that Helen could no longer feel her thighs. Peter drove slowly through a village centered around a war memorial, where men-at-work signs and the ersatz Punch-and-Judy stripes of workmen's tents edged a building site. It was gone as soon as glimpsed, but a short while later they slowed to a crawl approaching what must be Nazareth. As they rounded the bend, clouds briefly parted to bathe the place in moonlight. It was extraordinary: wider than she could take in, dull orange lights behind vast windows. A single tower soared in its center. Helen's vision went woozy, the lines bending like a trick photograph, before righting themselves. Her pulse danced rapid and light. She'd lost blood. How did one get over anemia? Steak, pressed against the temple. No—that was a black eye. Or was that oranges? Why did one eat oranges again?

She had to be helped out of the car, her father taking one arm and her GP another. Eugenie brought up the rear. Stone glowed white above huge double doors, capital letters chiseled between carved scrolls. Not Nazareth or anything like it, but The East Anglia Pauper Lunatic Asylum.

41

"What kind of place is this?" Not to panic. Old Victorian hospitals changed function all the time, everyone knew that, especially since the war; near their old place in Northamptonshire, a chest hospital had become a spinal injuries center and never reverted. This must be a women's hospital now, or even a general hospital; certainly it was big enough. Sure enough, a high-pitched cry carried from some unseen ward. Great double doors were opened by unseen hands and Helen was hit by a smell: thick, sickly, at once chemical and putrid, it robbed her, for a few vital seconds, of breath and sight, of thought and voice. She inhaled to speak and found that even in her horror she would have to breathe through her mouth. "What is this place?" She experienced her voice as being both nasal and raspy, but quickly began to doubt she was audible at all.

Dr. Ransome's free hand was already outstretched to the man—white coat, round face, half-moon specs—emerging from behind the broad mahogany desk. "Medical Superintendent Kersey, thanks for taking my call. It's good to see you again. Ah, is Martin here today? I understood that he worked here for the latter part of the week."

"Changed his rota. Cambridge on the weekends now, I'm afraid," replied Kersey.

Dr. Ransome actually made a fist. "I had hoped to catch up with him."

His affronted tone was lost on Kersey, who said, "Bad luck. He's only ours Wednesday to Friday these days. He wouldn't necessarily be the one to admit her anyway." He lowered his glasses. "I'm afraid you'll have to make do with me."

Ransome recovered himself. "No disrespect intended, sir."

Helen felt a reflex of self-concern; Ransome had made it sound as though her care was entirely dependent on this Dr. Bures. Kersey didn't seem worried, though, replying to Ransome with a breezy, "Well, good psychiatrists need to be shared."

Psychiatrist. No. No no no. "Is this—you can't put me in a bloody asylum! What's wrong with you all?" It was the first time Helen had ever sworn in front of her parents; she observed Eugenie's wince.

Superintendent Kersey slowed his voice and stooped slightly, as though addressing a small child. "We haven't called them asylums for thirty years now!" His lips were purple and his breath thick, evoking the bottle of claret he'd clearly been called away from. A crease above his eyebrows assumed the "m" shape of a child's drawing of a bird in flight. "The modern term is *mental hospital*."

There was nothing modern about the place. The walls were dirty green and hung with nineteenth-century portraits. The floor tiles, all leaves and dragonflies, were the kind of squirming Victoriana that made one instantly dizzy and the stout woman pushing a wheelchair toward Helen wore a starched, winged cap from a history textbook. Old gaslight fittings were still in the walls: only the electrics, snaking squarely through piping, gave away that it was 1958.

At the nurse's nod, Peter and Dr. Ransome let Helen go: she collapsed into the wheelchair, pins and needles bringing her legs back to life.

"Matron," said Ransome. "This is Helen Morris, she's nineteen."

"Can anyone even *hear* me?" pleaded Helen. "Mental hospital, asylum, it's all the same thing! I haven't—whatever you think of tonight, I'm not *mad*." Her voice reached a pitch it hadn't since childhood. She sounded mad: she must look mad, vomit embedded in her plaits, filth hardened to a crust on her legs.

"Never mind that," said Matron. "Let the doctors talk."

Dr. Ransome took back the reins, speaking only to Dr. Kersey. "Further to our earlier conversation, this is Peter Morris of Sizewell, whose daughter Helen is presenting with—well, she has taken some kind of abortifacient, the latest episode in a long history of unnatural behavior. She needs medical attention in the first instance." Kersey was scratching something onto paper with a fountain pen. "I can't ascertain what she's taken and she won't say how far along the pregnancy is but if it has held, clearly she is still in her first trimester."

All eyes went to Helen's belly, her own included. Only then did she notice that the wheelchair had leather restraints at the waist, the wrists, the ankles and—she glanced in a panic over each shoulder—the neck. She tried to push herself up and out but Matron was onto her, a cold hand on each shoulder.

"Let's not get off on the wrong foot, shall we?" Even if Helen had not been weak, her struggle would have been pathetic. This woman had bigger arms than Robin. "You sit tight while the paperwork's done."

"Please can someone tell me what's happening?" Helen's voice cracked on the question. "Are you having me committed?"

"The Morrises wanted to avoid a scene with police and so forth," said Dr. Ransome, "and as I mentioned, this incident is just the culmination of months"—he turned to Peter and Eugenie and suggested, "years?" They nodded, Peter wearily but Eugenie enthusiastically. "Years of obsessive, manic study, of public nudity, speaking in tongues . . ." He was all but rubbing his hands together.

"This is *nonsense*," said Helen. "Tell him, Daddy, you can't 'speak' Pitman, I had my knickers on." It was coming out wrong: jumbled and ridiculous. Eugenie was temporarily cowed by the size and might of the institution. Helen forced herself to speak evenly.

"Please, Mummy. I'm sorry, I'll stop running." Here, her tingling legs twitched at the betrayal. "I don't need to be here."

Eugenie looked closer to deference than Helen had ever seen her. "They'll be able to talk sense into you, Helen. God knows I've tried, but this . . . It's not my fault, is it, Dr. Ransome? She can't help the way she is?"

Helen remembered Robin's words so clearly she almost felt his breath warm her cheek: *you're not like other girls.*

"There is nothing wrong with me!" screamed Helen, realizing on seeing Matron's passive expression that of course they must all say that.

"Miss Morris, calm down," said Kersey, the twinkle in his eye turning to a twitch. "We need to admit you, but since the 1930 Mental Treatment Act, we *can* do that on a voluntary basis. You don't strike me as a case for certification. You are your parents' dependant, but you are of age. We'll keep you in for observation, get your strength up, and after seventy-two hours you'll be free to discharge yourself."

"Can they really do this?" She twisted to ask Matron.

The reply came almost before Helen had finished her question. "Dr. Kersey does things properly. Sit straight."

Helen thought as fast as her sapped brain would allow. Seventy-two hours. Long enough to get the worst of this stuff out of her and still make her train. The thought of a clean bed made her slack with longing. Whatever lay on the other side of the door marked WOMEN could not be worse than a mother who wished she had been violated and a father who didn't have the courage to stand up to his wife, let alone other men. "Yes," she said. "I'll do it."

The register was filled in, Helen piecing together the questions from their answers. Nineteen. Sizewell Cottage. Spinster. Methodist. Peter Morris.

"What d'you call it? What's wrong with her?" said Eugenie.

"Nothing, at this point," replied Kersey. "She hasn't been assessed. But I expect it's psychopathic disorder or schizophrenia. What used to be known as dementia praecox."

Again, Helen's parents understood what she did not; they took a collective step away from her. "But look, it's really for Dr. Bures to worry about."

At the mention of Dr. Bures, Ransome grew misty. "What a shame that I've missed Martin. I've been following him in the *Lancet* but it's not the same as catching up in person."

He had mentioned Bures's name more often than hers, she noticed.

"Yes, well." Helen didn't know whether Kersey's impatience was with Ransome's toadying or because he wanted to get back to his wine. "Matron, do the necessary, will you?"

Matron began to wheel Helen backward, away from the desk, toward the women's wing. The last thing she heard her mother say was to Superintendent Kersey. "You will get it out of her, won't you?"

Helen's heart leaped, then crashed. She didn't mean the child. She meant Robin's name.

The door was locked noisily behind her. The corridor Helen found herself in was endless: striplights like road markings on the ceiling produced an unsettling, topsy-turvy effect as they wheeled her past door after door after door. She raised her hand and tried to breathe through her sleeve. If the smell in the atrium had been a gas, here the same odor was solid, like a grease that slathered itself over her skin, seeped into her pores. The underlying odors of disinfectant and urine were mild, welcome even, by comparison. The only sounds were the wheel that squeaked on every rotation, Matron's heavy breathing and, from somewhere far away, crying in a dozen different registers.

In a dingy bathroom, taps gushed into a sunken bath, a cross between a sheep dip and a baptism tank. While it filled, Helen was stripped and nurses puffed coarse powder in her face, her hair, between her legs. Her kneecaps jutted and even the fan of metatarsal bones on the tops of her feet seemed more pronounced than they had been that morning. She had lost weight from everywhere but her belly.

42

Thin gray light struggled through filthy windows. Helen's bed had sides like a cot, which someone had raised in the night: into the rusty metal was stamped *Property of East Anglia Pauper Lunatic Asylum.* Six leather belts ran its width. A nurse in the corner of the room was flicking through *Reveille,* feet in a steaming basin, chatting to a friend perched on the edge of her desk.

"I've had my shifts changed." The girl on the desk was pretty in a beaky sort of way, dark hair pulled tight under a scrunchy white cap. "*Three weeks* before I'm on with Dr. Bures again."

"As if he'd look twice at you." Her friend wiggled her toes in the water. "He works in London one day a week. Who'd have a Nusstead girl when they could have some girl in high fashion?"

"You never know. He's all rugged, like Richard Burton. I wouldn't kick him out of bed for eating crisps."

"*Marian!*"

The stark wards threw the nurses' cackles from wall to wall in sinister echoes.

Rails but no curtains divided the grid of lumpy beds. Half were occupied by geriatrics, sexless under the blankets, wiry gray hair in identical pudding-bowl crops. Corpses with their chests heaving, noses whistling when they breathed. One scratched her head in her sleep. Even from here Helen could smell that awful distinctive rank scent on their breath; meat on the turn. To her right a big woman slept soundly, only a frizz of blonde hair visible above dozens of blankets.

Helen tested her belly. Was the baby still there? She had stopped bleeding.

Sixty-eight hours, now, to get to the station at Saxmundham, even if it meant hitchhiking from the hospital gates and traveling in her nightie. What had they done with her suitcase? She would work forever, she would pay Rochelle back. A surge of heat reminded her how furious she was with Rochelle for misleading her. Had it been naivety or something worse? She was as bad as Robin. Did *anyone* know how these things worked? When Helen got out of here, she would find out what was what, she would teach herself about family planning, and when she knew she would stop young girls in the street and tell them that a delicious trap was nevertheless a trap.

The woman in the next bed lifted her head and shoulders; she wore a quilted nightgown. Her fair hair was in a growing-out perm; feathery wrinkles but high plump cheeks made it impossible to guess her age.

"Hello!" she said, casually and unembarrassed as though they were in a queue at the post office. "I'm Pauline."

"Helen." The ward door clanked open and a squeaking of wheels took the form of a trolley with dull steel cloches over dinner plates. Helen salivated despite herself. As the old ladies were propped up in bed, Pauline said to Helen, "What've they brung you in for, then?"

She didn't have the energy to make up a story. "I tried to get rid of a baby."

Pauline was sympathetic. "How many you got at home?"

"What? None."

Pauline nodded wisely. "Married, is he?"

"No."

"Skint?"

Helen thought of Greenlaw Hall, of the estate's huge perimeter. Of the way even Robin's voice wore a coat of arms. "No. He's got money. He's rich, actually."

Now Pauline was puzzled. "Then why can't he look after you?"

"He probably would, if he knew."

Although she didn't know Robin well enough to know whether he had trapped her deliberately or not, she knew she could count on him marrying her. His pompous decency would see to that.

"You're jokin' me!" Pauline's eyes were perfect circles. How could Helen explain that if she had to bring up a baby, if she didn't get out into the world, she would die? That the thought of ending up like her mother made her heart turn to ash?

"I've got a job waiting for me in London," covered all of it and none of it.

Pauline blinked in affable incomprehension. "But if he's got money, you wouldn't have to work. God, no wonder you're in the nuthouse. Open and shut case! Me?" she said, although Helen hadn't asked. "Here for the baby blues. Baby came yesterday. Little girl. We're calling her Sandra. My milk hasn't even come in yet. I get down in the dumps like you wouldn't *believe*. God, the places my mind goes. I'm all right now but give it a couple of days. When it hits, you won't recognize me. I've got seven at home and it's getting worse every time. They put me in after every baby now. I used to fight it but I actually signed myself in this time. Early, as a precaution against me doing myself a mischief again." The nurse had put her stockings and shoes back on and was making her way along the beds, arranging trays on bed-tables and dishing out medicine in little paper cups. Pauline dropped her voice. "Where'd you go for it? Somewhere local?"

"I didn't go anywhere," said Helen. "A friend in London gave me something to take."

Pauline tutted. "That's a mug's game, that is. You should've gone to London if you've got connections there. You can get it done properly, proper doctors, safe as you like. You poor love, din't you have no one to set you straight? Din't your mum tell you about the birds and the bees?"

Helen laughed. "You clearly haven't met my mother."

"Shame on her." Helen was touched by Pauline's anger. "I've got a daughter not much younger than you at home, I sat her down as soon as she starting budding and told her what's what." The thought of Eugenie doing the same was laughable, but when Helen opened her mouth it was to cry. "Oh, darlin'." Come here. I din't mean to upset you. Come here." Pauline released the sides of her cot with one expert touch and swung her legs over the side of the bed. A sweet metallic smell enveloped Helen as Pauline held her close. This stranger had shown more concern, interest and understanding in a two-minute conversation than Eugenie had for years and the tenderness was almost more than Helen could bear. She gave in to the fizzing in her sinuses and the shaking lower lip. "Oh, darlin'," said Pauline again. "Shhh. It'll all come right."

The nurse Marian, the one with the crush on Dr. Bures, rattled the dinner trolley their way. Helen now saw that along with the silver cloches were little paper cups filled with colored pills.

"Naughty Pauline! You're supposed to be on bedrest!"

Pauline kissed the top of Helen's head, then saluted the nurse. "Yes, Sergeant Major, yes sir!" she said, before returning to her own bay.

"She's a one, that Pauline," said Nurse Marian. "She cracks me right up." She checked the notes at the end of Helen's bed. "No paraldehyde for *you*, mum. You want to build yourself up, get yourself back on the ward."

A plate was uncovered under Helen's nose: something beige, something brown, something green and stringy. "Ooh," said Pauline, when it was her turn. "Nothing tastes better than a meal someone else has cooked for you, does it?"

Helen smiled weakly, plowed her own food around with blunt cutlery.

One of the old women across the way soiled herself; the nurses didn't seem to see the problem with cleaning her up while people were eating. How were people who were genuinely sick supposed to heal?

43

They stood in the corridor, awaiting transfer from the infirmary to the ward proper. Two figures approached from the far end, peg-doll tiny: Helen could cover both of them with one thumb.

"What you got in there, anyway?" asked Pauline.

Helen's fingers tightened around the suitcase handle. "Nothing much."

The ticket was still in there. Two days to go and no time to lose. A buttery smell was rising from the spreading patches of milk on Pauline's breasts. Any foodstuff, any strong smell before noon made Helen's mouth swill with bile. That coppery taste was still on her tongue: her breasts were still tender. They had taken blood so they would know too. She was resigned to the birth in a numb sort of way. She would have to give the poor child away, because Rochelle wouldn't want a baby in their London flat any more than she did. One thing was certain: there was no way she was risking her health again.

On one side of the corridor, long windows gave out onto land-scaped gardens that dipped into some sort of bog. The other was lined with ward after ward, each 100 feet long, ceilings supported by thick iron pillars and beds packed tight as patchwork. The walls were bare and the windows barred. If the people who ran this place had their wits about them they could use this corridor as some kind of exercise gallery, rather than a depository for trolleys and cleaning equipment.

"How long does this usually take?" she asked Pauline. "I mean, I'm hoping I can see a doctor after this."

"That's anyone's guess. They won't do nothin' till Matron gets here."

"Right." The constant percussion of hospital life was amplified in the corridor. The slide of iron on steel as locks tumbled, the shuffle of slippered feet and the rumble and squeak of endless wheels; trolleys, beds, wheelchairs. The sound of high heels was alien when it came. The patient on Matron's arm was now in focus: red hair in a bob, circle skirt, a short-sleeved sweater and white slingbacks. Lipstick.

"Celeste Wilson," she said to the nurse on the door, as though she were introducing herself at a job interview. It was the first educated voice, other than her own, that Helen had heard since entering the women's wing. "Not to be a nuisance, but I think there's been a mistake. I really oughtn't to be in this place. I've certainly done nothing wrong."

Hope quickened Helen's heart. Perhaps she was not as alone as she had thought.

"Back of the queue, Celeste," said Matron.

"Actually," said Celeste, "if I could just talk to your superior?"

Helen realized, as Celeste tried to struggle, that her sweater was torn, completely, at one shoulder, the sleeve a knitted amulet sliding toward her elbow.

"I *have* no superior in this wing," said Matron. "Back of the queue, Celeste, unless you want to find yourself back in the Fives."

Without warning Celeste swung her head around and smashed it, hard, temple crashing against the dirty tiles with more force than Helen would have believed a woman capable of. Celeste repeated the movement; this time her jaw connected with the doorframe with such force that one expected the wood, not the bone, to yield, yet a sickening crack and a popping of flesh released a geyser of blood that clogged Helen's eyelashes and washed the ward red.

She spat a cold white chip of something that could have been tooth or tile from her mouth. Two beefy nurses caught Celeste by the elbows. Her lower lip was torn in two.

"*Beds!*" shouted Matron. About half the patients obeyed. The rest of them began screaming, a sound that seemed to pass through Helen's skin and into her bloodstream. So much noise, it was impossible not to absorb it: it was like driving a car without a windscreen.

A whistle was blown, a dozen nurses materialized and Helen was shoved roughly to one side as Celeste was pinned to the floor.

"Straight to the Fives," Matron ordered. It took three nurses to drag Celeste away from the ward. Her white high heels dragged wavy lines in the floor then fell off. A minute or so after the crisis had begun it was over, two runaway bride shoes the only proof it had happened.

"What are the Fives?" Helen whispered to Pauline, who shuddered theatrically.

"Ward Five. Disturbed ward." She pointed down the corridor. The repetition of doors and windows stretched so far into the distance it seemed unreal, a trompe l'oeil. "Locked the whole time. Even I've never been on the Fives. You tend not to come back."

Staff Nurse was brisk capability itself as she cleaned Helen's face with a flannel. "You're not going to give us any trouble, are you, Hannah?"

"It's Helen," she said, but the nurse was already sponging down the next patient.

They had given her a bed next to Pauline. Across the tiny gangway, a woman brushed the same ragged skein of long, yellow-gray hair: "Eighty-six, eighty-seven, eighty-eight." The brush was dragged over the same patch again and again, scraping the gloss of an exposed pink scalp into dull raw red. She counted fast, even talking on the in-breath. When Helen said hello to Pauline—who still seemed fine—the woman with the hairbrush turned and growled like a dog. "You've made me lose count!" she said.

"Susan, love," soothed Pauline. "You were on eighty-eight."

"I've only got your word for it," said Susan. "One, two, three . . ."

"Who's this, then?" Helen traced the new voice a knight's move across the beds, where a wizened old woman sat with her knees drawn up to her chest.

"This is Helen, Norma," said Pauline, and then to Helen: "Norma's an institution within an institution. She's been in here since she was your age."

If Norma was fifty—which Helen thought was a generous guess—that meant she had been in here for *thirty years*. "Why?" asked Helen, appalled. "What do you have to do to end up living here?"

"God only knows! It's lost in the mists of time!" Norma waved knotty fingers as if to conjure this temporal miasma.

"She lost two brothers and a sweetheart in the Great War," said Pauline quietly.

"But how is she—will she ever get out?"

"In a wooden overcoat, I should think," whispered Pauline. Helen was blank. "In a coffin, dear. She in't going nowhere. Eventually they'll put her in geriatrics and that'll be that." Helen's blood chilled. "Look at your face! It's all she's ever known, she'll be all right. Does she look unhappy to you?"

Norma didn't look unhappy but she didn't look healthy and Helen gagged to realize that what she had taken for a line of trim on the breast of the old woman's nightgown was actually a tiny parade of silverfish, running like stitching across a seam. It didn't seem to bother Norma. Helen took heart from her own revulsion: it proved she wasn't one of them. Yet. If one wasn't mad upon admission to Nazareth, one certainly would be within days. If Helen had to stay here a second longer than her allotted seventy-two hours she would lose her mind and then Mental Treatment Act or no Mental Treatment Act, voluntary patient or not, she would be committed, she would belong here. The thought made her clammy all over.

"One hundred and twenty-four," said Susan. "One hundred and

twenty-five." She pulled a cumulus of hair from the bristles and let it float to the ground.

"What about her?" Helen asked Pauline.

"Susan's been here at least two years 'cause she was here when I came in after having Raymond. Not sure what her story is. She's under certificate, that much I do know. There's a husband some-where, but he won't come for her."

Pauline spoke with the offhandedness of one who presumes knowledge, and at Helen's, "Oh?" softened her voice. "If you're under certificate then it's not really up to the doctors. Your family have the say-so. Whoever put you in can get you out. Has to be next of kin. I'm a voluntary this time, like I said, but I've been certified all the other times, we're doing it this way partly to save on the paperwork."

Helen choked on air. "Weren't you ever worried that your hus-band would leave you in here?"

Pauline cackled. "That's not happening, is it? As bad as it is with me at home, there always comes a stage where it's worse without me, and they come and get me out, so . . . either way I'll be back home within a couple of months."

Helen thought about Peter and Eugenie. If she were not free to leave, if she was dependent upon them for her release, would they come to get her out?

She knew the answer. It had been carved in her mother's face.

Helen stuck to Pauline all morning, like a new girl at school, trail-ing her from the ward to the day room, to the airing court, through into Occupational Therapy with its badly woven baskets and na-ive paintings. When the lunch bell rang, she followed Pauline into the refectory where food trolleys buckled under great tureens. Hel-en's mouth watered: when the morning's nausea receded, appetite always rushed in.

"Can't wait to see what today's chef's specials are," said Pauline, as they slid onto their forms. "Caviar? Fine wines? Oh, marvelous, it's gray soup." Despite herself, Helen laughed, her throat not quite knowing what to do with the sound. Laughter, a rare occurrence even before Nazareth, took on an alien quality here.

"How do you keep your spirits up?" Helen wanted to know. "I want to cry."

"By keeping *your* spirits up," replied Pauline. "You've gotta have someone to look after, haven't you? It raises you up." She hugged Helen without stiffness or self-consciousness: comfort passed from one body to another, sure as desire and much less trouble.

The soup was allegedly lamb and broad bean. The cafe that Rochelle went to for lunch served toasted Italian sandwiches and frothy coffee.

Susan, the hair-brusher from the dormitory, was struggling to eat. Her spoon might as well have been flat for all the liquid she could hold in it. It slopped down the front of her peach woolen cardigan, catching on the little bobbles, and her hair trailed in the mess. A nurse walking past wiped her mouth with a dirty cloth.

"What's happened to her?"

"I reckon the fryer din't agree with her today," volunteered Norma.

"The fryer?"

"Electroplexy." Norma's abrupt switch to received pronunciation was a jolt in itself. "Electro Convulsive Therapy. Ee Cee Tee." She smiled, proud of her vowels.

"That's right," said Pauline absently then turned back to Helen. "They're mad on it here, pun intended. They plug you into a machine, shock you out of yourself."

Norma nodded. "Lights *actually come on* in your eyeballs." She had fallen back into her own voice.

"Bloody *hell* Norma, no they don't," said Pauline.

"They use it to make you give up your secrets," said Norma.

Helen turned to Pauline in alarm. Robin's name felt like the only thing she had left. "Is that true?"

"It gives you a little fit, that's all, for a minute or two, it shakes you up and out of your bad mood. I'll have a course of it if I get in the doldrums again." Helen still could not believe that Pauline was capable of anything more profound or disturbing than mild irritation. "She must be fresh out to be in that state. She'll be right as rain in a couple of hours, you won't recognize her."

"So what's the downside?"

"It can leave your memory full of holes. Great big swathes of your life that you can't get back. Never had that effect on me; I forget words for an hour or two afterward but that's about it. Sometimes it's just what you had for your supper the night before they took you in." Helen's horror at this idea which sounded both medieval and futuristic at the same time must have shown, because Pauline put her hand over hers. "If you're lucky, though, you forget the worst thing that ever happened to you." Her words were for Helen, but her eyes were on Susan. "If you're lucky."

44

Helen and Pauline sat in the day room. The black-and-white film they were watching had been clumsily edited to remove any references to sex, madness or violence. It made no sense.

"Helen Morris." It was Marian, the giggly nurse with the crush on Dr. Bures. "You're to come with me."

Her seventy-two hours were nearly up. She was going to the office for the formality of being declared sane and signing her way out of the asylum. She re-trod the length of the corridor they had wheeled her along upon her admission. To reach the famous Dr. Bures's office, Helen had to walk, escorted by a nurse, past the admissions desk. The atrium was different in the daylight; the tiles were pretty rather than sinister and the moustachioed Victorian men in the oil paintings were avuncular rather than disapproving. Here, you could see that at some point, someone had had good intentions. Where had it all gone so wrong? She had that morning pictured herself in Matron's shoes, keys jangling at her belt, clipboard in hand stacked with lists and budgets, marshaling the staff into competence. The only problem with this daydream was that of course in order to rise to the rank of matron, first one had to serve as a nurse. Helen knew she cared about people, but not at close quarters. In fact, she couldn't think of a better way to sum up the reason she was in here.

Compared to the wards, the air in the administration block was as fresh as on Sizewell beach. A grandfather clock ticked toward her deadline. She would refuse to be released back into her parents' charge. Would the hospital staff drive her all the way across the county to Saxmundham or would she be expected to make her own way to the station? Where was Saxmundham from here, anyway? How would she get across London? Could one walk from Liverpool Street to Regent's Park? She had no idea. London was a picture postcard, a paperback A–Z. She might, at a push, have been able to find the Thames from Trafalgar Square but that was about it.

The door to Bures's study was closed.

"Looks like he's running over." Nurse Marian glanced down at the watch on her breast. "You have a seat, love." Helen didn't want a seat. From up here she could see across the grounds. Two dozen men trudged loose laps around the airing courts. Surely their time would be better spent engaging in some kind of purposeful exercise? Anyone could see that the airing courts wanted weeding, that the wall needed whitewashing. She started as from inside Bures's rooms came a thump, and a woman's anguished voice: "Do you think I enjoy being this way? Christ, if I could help it, I would!"

When the door handle turned, Nurse Marian checked her reflection in the polished bronze of the light switch, licked her palm and smoothed her hair into place. The patient who left the room—or rather was shoved from it, by a thunder-faced charge nurse—was not a woman after all but a man, slender and elegant even in threadbare, ill-fitting clothes.

"Thank you, Nurse," said Bures, and he ushered Helen through the doorway and into another country. In here, it was all potted ferns, Turkish rugs and leather-bound books. Helen couldn't fault Nurse Marian's taste in men. It was hard to believe the man standing in front of her was a doctor at all, let alone a contemporary of Dr. Ransome. He wore slacks and a fisherman's sweater over an open-necked shirt, and his brown hair was the longest she'd ever seen on a man, curling almost to his collar. There was no white coat, not even one hanging on the back of the door.

"Miss Morris, welcome. Do sit." Helen perched on the edge of a high-backed chair while Bures read through her notes, making faces. "I see you were referred here by Andrew Ransome." There was scorn in his chuckle but Helen couldn't tell for whom. She focused on the baize noticeboard on the back wall. It was pinned with black-and-white photographs, pages of text apparently cut from magazines and reams of handwritten notes in which only the odd oversized exclamation mark was legible. They had been grouped loosely into headings: *Sodomites. Pederasts. Deviants. Reproductive Control. Behavioral Correction.*

"When I leave here, I don't want my parents to collect me," she blurted. Bures's strange smile held fast. "And, also, while I'm here, before I go, I've got so many ideas about how the place could be improved. Do you have any such thing as a patient council?"

Bures held up his hand. "Let's not run before we can walk. First I'd like to ask you once again whether you were violated or if the baby's father is married."

So he wasn't interested in her ideas. Helen's image of herself as Matron turned to vapor. "No to both questions." She felt that she had done a good job of keeping the sulk out of her voice.

Bures dipped his fountain pen in the inkwell and squeezed. He was left-handed, and his letters smeared comet trails behind them. Helen had been left-handed as a child but forced to write with her right. Eugenie had tied her left hand behind her back, smacked her on the back of the legs with a rubber spatula if she tried to revert. Bures used firm pressure to scratch an impression onto the carbon paper below his notepad, then set down his pen and smiled. "And are you willing, now, to name him?"

"No!" Bures's smile disappeared and Helen reminded herself that she must turn down her fury, keep it under control.

Bures lit a cigarette. Nurse Marian conjured up a clean ashtray from somewhere. "Well, Miss Morris. It looks as though, in much the same way even a stopped clock gives the right time twice a day, Andrew Ransome has actually referred a genuine case to me. I can see that I've got myself a bright button here, and there's no point talking down to you. If I let you know a little more about my work, then I think you'll come round." Come round to what? Suspicion cranked into gear inside Helen: a spiked wheel revolving in her belly. "Behavioral correction is an *incredibly* exciting new field. The patient before you was a sodomite, for example. He is a persistent law-breaker, a constant clog in the judiciary system, but I've made great progress already. Some people have what we call isolated incidents, single psychotic episodes, but others are—well, their brains are set permanently in disorder. They can't help it. But from my point of view it's the difference between cure and containment, do you see?"

The churning feeling intensified. What was he talking about? "Now . . ." He dipped his head to her admission notes again. "It appears that your most recent act follows a long history of rejecting healthy female traits, as well as the public exhibitionism—and of course speaking in tongues has long been a flag. The good news is that these days we don't think of illness as having a moral dimension but rather as an imbalance in the brain, something we can manage with the new treatments."

"Hold on, hold on—treatments? I'm not here to be *treated*. The arrangement was that I would stay here for three days while the dust settled and then I'd discharge myself. My time's nearly up."

Bures looked to the nurse, who fluttered an apology. Ash fell on Helen's notes as he pressed on. "I'm sorry you haven't had it better explained to you. I'm afraid that refusing treatment is not going to be an option. What patients so often fail to understand is that they resist treatment *because* they're ill. That's the point. Your . . . rebellion here is a symptom of your disorder."

"But I'm not ill! I just . . ." *I just what?* she thought. I'm just stupid? I'm just a slut? I'm just naive, I just trusted the wrong people?

Bures ground out his cigarette and picked up his pen. "Even a short course of electro-convulsive therapy will let me see if we can't break you down, so that we can build you up in the correct way." Helen remembered Susan, after her treatment, brought low and confused; a sob scraped its way up the sides of her throat. "I can see that's alarmed you. Perhaps demolition wasn't the best analogy. Think of it rather as rewiring a house where the lighting is faulty. Wouldn't you rather live somewhere the bulbs don't flicker, somewhere you can trust the flick of the switch?"

"I've seen what the fryer can do to you," said Helen. "It turns you into an invalid and a fool. It's a way of killing me and keeping me alive at the same time. I won't let you. I'm not ill."

"Miss Morris." Bures's voice was heavy with regret. "You are unwell and have been for some time, perhaps your whole life. You need treatment. If you don't cooperate, I'll have no choice but to put you under certificate—in fact, it's easier for us to do it here than it is on the outside."

It was a trick, it was a witch trial.

"So you *are* having me committed."

"No. You may remain as a voluntary patient . . ."

"But if I agree I'm mad, you have to keep me here? And if I disagree, then you have to keep me here because I'm delusional?" She had meant it sarcastically: Bures looked delighted that at last she had grasped it.

"You must see that it will be much easier to treat you with your cooperation, Miss Morris. There is still the chance of you harming the child, and that's not a risk I can take. My dear, you were lucky to get Andrew Ransome. He's the reason you're here and not in a cell somewhere. The man's been after an excuse to work with me for years." Here, Bures gave a little unconscious toss of his head. Helen felt a little voltage in her fingertips. It was true, then. She had been sent here in the hope she might further some rural GP's career. "But if you went on to break the law again, and you didn't have a protector to recommend that we treat your illness rather than criminalize you, well . . ." His words were iron bars, staking themselves into the floor around her. "I know that you think of this hospital in terms of a prison but with the right treatment you can achieve a kind of liberation; freedom from all the behavior that's currently making your life such a misery. Miss Morris—I wish you could appreciate how thrilling these advances have been for us. It's unnatural for a woman not to want children. You will want to have this man's child and to tell us his name by the time we've finished. It'll be a release. Please don't cry. Even five or six years ago, you'd have been dosed up on Largactil and, to all intents and purposes, left to rot. You're actually *lucky* to be ill in this day and age."

45

Ten bays, ten beds with ten turned-down blankets. Helen waited in this unfamiliar ward with nine other patients, among them Celeste Wilson, barely recognizable from the fashion plate of a few days before, in soiled nightclothes, her hair sticking up in peaks. Helen held Pauline's slack hand, unsure whether her friend even knew she was there. The jokes and advice had dried up; now Pauline morosely haunted her own nightie. Her face had gone from prettily plump to gaunt almost overnight and the milky smell had turned rancid. The "curtain had come down," as Norma put it, and the consensus among the long-term patients, those who knew Pauline well, was that the sooner she went into the fryer the better. She was retreating further into hell by the minute. Helen had begun to grasp that something as violent as electrotherapy might be the only way to bring someone back from these depths. Concern for Pauline had all but eclipsed Helen's own nerves about the treatment. In the last few days she had been mothered for the first time and this living loss of Pauline hurt.

The ward sister who had been supervising disappeared through a door. Stomach acid burbled in Helen's belly. She had hidden in the lavatory during breakfast—her morning sickness was getting worse as the days wore on—and the nurses hadn't come after her. Helen hoped that they were finally coming around to the idea that she was capable of regulating her own appetite. Norma, concerned by Helen's absence at the breakfast table, had smuggled her a dry bread roll, dropped it into her pocket with a wink. Now, Helen coaxed a few morsels of bread down Pauline's throat.

Sister reappeared with a tray full of empty glasses. "Teeth!" she commanded. A handful of the older patients hooked out their dentures. As their mouths imploded they dropped them into the waiting tumblers.

"Can Pauline go to the front of the queue?" she asked, as Sister marked names on the glasses with a pen.

"You're a nurse now, are you?"

Helen knew better than to come up with a smart remark. "I just think she needs it more than me."

"Oh you're a *doctor*. I beg your pardon."

"Look at her." She gestured to Pauline; her eyes were open but the shutters were down, the darkness on the inside.

The nurse narrowed her eyes. "Dressing it up in false concern for your friend—I call that a low blow."

"It's not false concern. If it wasn't for me she'd have had nothing to eat today, for goodness' sake."

Now Sister's eyes protruded. "What do you mean?"

Helen wasn't going to apologize for taking responsibility. "She hasn't eaten anything for two days and no one on the ward gives a fig. I gave her a bit of bread roll this morning, I—what are you doing?"

Sister had Pauline by the arm, guiding her back out into the corridor. Another nurse came from behind a floral screen to take her place. When one nurse vacated a post in Nazareth, another appeared within seconds.

"Where's she taking Pauline?"

"It's nil by mouth before treatment," said the new nurse. "They can't treat her if she's just eaten. She'll have to go in tomorrow's session."

That was why they'd left Helen to her own devices this morning. Not out of respect, but because she'd been doing their job for them. Why hadn't they told her? Why did no one ever tell the patients anything? It was fury, not guilt, that swelled inside her. Simple communication with patients would have prevented this. A word of explanation the night before, that's all it would have taken. Why didn't Matron better equip her nurses to inform her patients? The problem, and the irony, was that in the absence of help from the staff, Helen had been relying on Pauline for everything.

"You're first," said the nurse, and nodded at a door behind the screen. "There's some medical students in with him today. Just so you know."

The ward contained a flat bed and something resembling a newfangled washing machine; sleek, cream-painted, switches and meters and lights. The trainee doctors—several men and, to Helen's envy and astonishment, one woman—stood in a horseshoe around Dr. Bures, his casual clothes giving him more, not less, authority in the bank of white coats.

"Take a seat, Miss Morris," he said. Helen stood. Bures's irritation crackled like static. "As we discussed and you can see from the notes, Miss Morris is a complex case: very bright but very entrenched in her behavior, anti-social, obsessive ideas about working. I'm hoping that a short course of ECT will enable her to cooperate with us in her treatment. It will let us feminize her, if you like."

As they were talking, another nurse—light brown hair, freckly arms—entered carrying two small chipped enamel bowls. Helen caught a waft of methylated spirits. "Sit down, dear," she said softly. "Just going to rub you up so the shock takes—ah, I'm out of cotton wool. Sorry, Doctor, back in a minute."

"Is it safe?" asked the female student. She wasn't much older than Helen herself and Helen wondered if she were studying medicine with her parents' blessing or even encouragement, and if so, whether she knew to treasure the privilege. She had blonde hair teased and set in a perfect circle around her face. That hairstyle said freedom, independence, money and time. If—when—I get out of here, I'll cut my hair off and have it done like that, Helen thought.

"Absolutely." Bures's tone was bordering now on the evangelical. "Not only is it safe but it opens up the possibility of treatment where before it would have been dangerous; Largactil, insulin therapy and so on would obviously have been too risky for the fetus." The female student nodded, began to make notes on her pad, and Helen felt foolish for having considered her an ally. "I think we're really only just beginning to uncover the applications of this treatment. The implications are not just for individual mental health. We can create positive ripples through the whole of society."

The nurse was back with a bowl of swabs. "Hello, love. If you'll just hop on the bed, here."

She dipped them in one solution as Dr. Bures flexed a pair of little round pads on wires. Helen could not bring herself to sit near the assortment of ugly tubes and boxes, the needles and the switches.

"Close your eyes," said Dr. Bures.

Dr. Frankenstein, thought Helen. He's going to take the *me* out of me and when I wake up I'll be a monster.

"No." Withholding her consent gave them permission; there were hands on her shoulders, her knees, her wrists. Shapes and bodies were around her, the skin on her temples was scoured and then darkness exploded inside her as she was fired into a night without stars.

Helen came to in a side ward, lips loose and dribbling, limbs feeling as though they had been wrenched from their sockets and popped back in. She had limited access to her own mind; some doors gaped upon well-lit memories, others were locked tight. Dr. Bures and his followers were in a line at the foot of her bed, the grubby god and his Persil angels.

"Who's the Prime Minister?" Bures's pen was poised over his pad.

Helen's head swam. She wanted to say Eden but then Churchill kept boomeranging back into power, didn't he?

"I don't know," she said. The emotional reflex to cry started up inside her but without the accompanying physical symptoms.

"What are the names of the Queen's children?"

She let her heavy eyelids fall. If she pictured them first, the words came easier. "Charles and Anne."

"Let's try something closer to home." The word *home* was a hook in her heart. "What's your address?"

She saw the interior first: the stained bedsheets, the swiped-clean bookshelves and the gaping wardrobe, before she could picture the outside.

"Sizewell Cottage," she said.

"And your boyfriend's name?"

There he was, golden hair falling in his eyes, shirtsleeves rolled to the elbow to reveal a ripple of muscle that even in the middle of all this plucked at that invisible string. Her teeth were on her lip for the roll of the R, but another image came to her: stuck in a kitchen, surrounded by babies, someone's *wife,* and she caught herself just before she fell.

"No."

Bures's pen tore through the paper.

"Back to the drawing board," he said to his students. "Some personality disorders are unusually resistant to treatment. It's a more profound case than I thought. Treatment is a matter of months in these cases. Sometimes even years."

46

Helen mounted the staircase, the only sound her own footsteps and Matron's nasal whistle.

"What's this about?" she asked Matron.

"I don't know." The admission was clearly uncomfortable. All bucks stopped with the medical superintendent. Perhaps they were finally going to apologize to Helen for not explaining the nature of her treatment. Kersey actually opened the door himself and beckoned Helen in. "Have you had your breakfast?" His smile was kind. "It never does to start off on an empty stomach." There was, Helen noticed, a shiny egg stain on his tie.

"Is this about Pauline? Is she having treatment now? She wasn't at lunch, so maybe they're keeping her hungry for the next round?"

"Never mind Pauline." Kersey's voice dropped a pitch: the M above his brows deepened from curved lower case to jagged capital. "I'm here to tell you about a change in your legal position. Your parents telephoned me late yesterday. They found and . . ." he pushed his half-moon glasses up his nose, the better to read the scribbled notes in front of him, "and decoded a letter from a friend of yours, expressing fury that you hadn't taken up a job in London. Well, we have your motive, at least, for wanting rid of the baby, and it's consistent with your parents' statement about your history."

Decoded was the operative word. Helen pictured Eugenie with

the Pitman Guide in front of her, pencil in her claw. She would never have risked the shame of asking anyone to help her. And Rochelle may have expressed fury but she was still writing in Pitman. That must mean that part of her was still on Helen's side. And she hadn't, unless Kersey was keeping it to himself, mentioned obtaining the pills. Was that loyalty or self-preservation?

"Now that your parents understand the extent of your deception it has confirmed for them our diagnosis of psychopathic disorder. They feel that it's best if we treat you from now on but that if you want to be supported outside the hospital it must be by the man who got you into trouble."

The words made sense individually, but Helen couldn't extract any real meaning from them. "How does this affect my position? I don't understand."

"Your parents have gone away," he said, his voice rich with tenderness and regret. "They have disowned you, for want of a better word." Helen's first instinct was anger. They had taken control of the situation: *she* had wanted to be the one to leave *them*. Hurt was hot on anger's heels. Their love had always been conditional, and, Helen never having met those conditions, essentially withheld; but they were still her parents and she could not help but need them.

"I'm sorry, Miss Morris." Superintendent Kersey slid a box of paper handkerchiefs her way. Helen dug her fingernails into her palm, determined not to let excess emotion mark her out as unstable, but there were no tears to hold back.

"So where do I go now?"

"No—it . . . Miss Morris, it doesn't change the fact that we must treat you, and that if you resist treatment you will be put under certificate."

"But if I want to get out?"

"You would have to appeal to the Board of Control, the government department to whom I answer. Two independent visiting inspectors."

"And they'd take my word over yours?"

Discomfort sailed briefly across his face. "They would take my opinion and Dr. Bures's into account."

Then the Board of Control were as good as toothless.

"My friend in London," she said. "She'll sign me out."

"It's not a question of signing you out."

"Vouch for me, whatever the correct term is. Could she?"

Rochelle was a flimsy lifeline but the only one Helen could bear to grab on to.

"We can only release you into the care of your nearest relative. You have no siblings, and as we all know," he leaned heavily into his words for emphasis, "you have no spouse."

"So who's my next of kin now?" Helen wondered aloud.

Kersey set down his spectacles. Whatever he was about to say, he didn't relish it. "Unless you tell us who got you pregnant, Miss Morris, and we can appeal to his charity, then to all intents and purposes, *I* am."

She was dry-eyed and blind with rage. She had fallen for their voluntary patient trick, she had let them electrocute her and still she could not win. She wanted Pauline, to lean in close, even if she had to drape her leaden arm around her own shoulders. But Pauline wasn't in the ward, the airing court or the library, she wasn't in Occupational Therapy or the bathroom or the day room. Norma was in Pauline's usual seat, letting Susan brush her hair into a wire-wool dandelion.

"Has anyone seen Pauline? Norma? Has she gone off for ECT?"

"No, they're doing the men today," said Susan.

"Pauline!" Shrill as Helen was, only half the heads turned.

"She's down the laundry, in't she?" said a mousy patient Helen didn't recognize. "Saw her taking her sheets down there a bit ago."

Pauline didn't work in the laundry and even if she had, even the strictest nurses at Nazareth wouldn't have put to work a patient who could barely support her own head.

A bone-deep instinct made Helen turn and run. She knew the

laundry was on the ground floor, off the spooky service corridor that ran the length of the hospital. She descended stone steps and burst through double doors into a half-buried tunnel, intermittently lit with fritzing fluorescent lights. There were no signposts but steam and the smell of borax drew her to one end of the corridor. There were three different laundry rooms, two filled with shuddering, billowing machines, porters and patients barely distracted from their work when Helen screamed Pauline's name. Only one patient, stirring a giant copper, looked up and pointed, her mouth a perfect O.

The very last door stood ajar, a smell like soiled bedlinen emanating from the dark. Helen shouldered the door and in the echo chamber heard the drip-drip-drip of a leaking pipe. She took a step forward. The smell intensified. Not stale bedsheets but fresh urine. Not the drip of a leaking pipe. Helen fumbled behind her for the switch, bashed it with the heel of her hand and in the white dazzle saw bedsheets knotted around a thick pipe that ran the width of the ceiling. At eye level swung two dirty bare feet, a clear droplet fattening on each toe.

She did not have time to call out: the room was full of men in white overalls, shouting, righting the chair that Pauline had kicked over, unwinding her, lifting her and setting her down, roughly pumping her arms and chest. Screams echoed in the corridor as Matron yelled for calm. Helen pressed herself against the tiles. She thought of Pauline's children and included herself. She would not survive Nazareth without her friend. She would end up like her if she did not get out. It was a fact, like the body on the floor.

Kersey came bowling in, white coattails flapping as he dropped to his knees and placed his fingers on Pauline's wrists in a way that must have been just for show. "Well done, boys," he said to the charge nurses. "You did your best. Please return to your patients." One of the nurses made the sign of the cross. Kersey slid his hand down her face, closing her eyes without appearing to touch them.

"Time of death, three fifteen," he said to Matron, who stood in the doorway, face red and shining.

"Oh, dear me, no," said Matron, in someone else's voice. "Oh, *Pauline.*"

A decision was forming in Helen, a little moth beating its wings in her chest. She knew how to honor Pauline and save herself. She had always known, but only now was the urgency clear, her own fate laid out in her friend's wretched form. It was upstairs too in Susan's raw scalp and the seclusion room of Norma's mind. Nothing was worse than Nazareth and there was no one it could not kill.

She opened her mouth and the moth flew out.

"Robin!" The word rebounded off the tiles, as if to reassure the astonished Matron and Kersey that they'd heard her correctly. "Robin Greenlaw. Like the house."

47

Helen climbed the staircase to the minstrel gallery for the second time in as many days, slippered feet knowing now which of the steps would creak at her tread. An itching crawled across the nape of her neck and behind her ears.

They had telephoned Robin within two minutes of learning his name, and he had taken the next train out of London. Whether he had come in rescue or rage she wouldn't know until she saw his face. He could choose to believe the truth of her actions: she had showed that she did not love him, that she found the idea of marriage to him so horrific that she had risked her life trying to abort his baby. Or he could choose to believe that she was ill, that it was nothing personal, that she couldn't help it. He wouldn't come all the way to Suffolk just to tell her off, or to gloat in abandoning her. Robin didn't have the imagination for cruelty. She stopped outside Kersey's door. Who was she fooling? She barely knew him in any meaningful way.

She dared not imagine the best-case outcome: that Robin would recognize that she wasn't ill, that this whole thing had been a grave injustice.

The men—Kersey, Bures and Robin—sat in a row like magistrates behind Kersey's wooden desk. Only Robin got to his feet when she entered.

"*Helen!*" Robin couldn't hide his horror. It was days since Helen had seen a mirror but she knew that her hair was lousy, her clothes had gone gray in the wash and doubtless she had absorbed the paraldehyde stench of the asylum. The double-breasted suit and gold tie-pin made a stranger of the man she knew every inch of. Seeing him reminded her, with the force of new news but the momentum of the old rage, that all this was Robin's fault in the first place. She clamped her lips against the accusation: not helpful, not now. She concentrated instead on the tickling sensation in her hair, shrinking her focus to not scratching.

Robin raised his eyebrows at the doctors for permission and at Kersey's nod, stepped around the desk to take her hands in his. Helen felt the current between them before she could insulate herself against it. "You should have told me," he said. "I would have done the right thing by you. I mean, I *will* do the right thing by you. I had no idea, Helen, I would never have let them send you here."

Did that mean that he understood? That he knew she wasn't ill, that it had been a misunderstanding that had spiraled out of control? She tried to telegraph the truth to him, but their connection had never been mental. Robin addressed the doctors without letting go of her hands.

"How ill *is* she? I mean, what's the prognosis for recovery?"

Hope sank before it had had a chance to soar.

Bures didn't give Kersey a chance to answer. "Most of what there is to know about Helen's illness you've already read in her notes. With the right care, she can live a normal life. It's important that you understand this is a lifelong condition and that relapse is always on the horizon."

Robin had been told more about Helen's "condition" than she had in her almost two weeks' residency.

"I naturally don't want a scandal," said Robin. "It's out of the question that my child—my *heir*, Helen!—be illegitimate." He dropped her hands and began to stroke his chin in a classic thinkers' pose. "And then there is the secondary scandal of . . ." He gestured broadly around him. "I'm concerned that we marry sooner rather than later, and that we present it to my parents as a fait accompli."

Kersey shifted forward in his seat. "Mr. Greenlaw. We don't presently feel that Miss Morris has the capacity to marry, but another few weeks on our behavioral correction program should stabilize her."

Helen's rescue chute telescoped up on itself. Another few *weeks* here? The superintendent looked to his star psychiatrist for confirmation. Bures nodded eagerly. "We didn't get off to the best start with Helen, but the fact that you're here tells us it's working."

Robin put his hands behind his back—had he always had such a repertoire of ridiculous patrician gestures?—and walked to the window overlooking the airing courts.

"If we marry, I assume legal responsibility for Helen. If she relapses . . ."

Bures smiled. "The irony, given the nature of her crime, is that Helen will be well suited to a domestic sphere where she won't be overstretched. But if there's another crisis, we'll always be happy to treat her."

Here, then, was her choice: marry a man who believed her to be mentally ill, or stay and go mentally ill, permanently or even fatally so, in Nazareth.

"What do you think, Helen?" Kersey's question was clearly moot.

"Yes." She saw they were expecting more, and forced out what they wanted. "Thank you."

Robin smiled and caught her wrist. *I want to have you whenever I want you.* Helen felt an internal tumble and slide, the barrel of a lock falling into place, as her sentence was commuted to marriage.

48

1960

Mrs. Helen Greenlaw stood in the en-suite bathroom of her London home, left foot on the linoleum, right foot against the basin, rubber diaphragm flexed between the thumb and forefinger of her left hand.

Outside in the stucco horseshoe of St. George's Square, the birches bent to the will of the wind that carried the chimes of Big Ben into her bedroom. Two hundred yards south, the low-tide Thames gurgled brown between bridges. Downstairs, Robin began to lock up the house for the evening. Helen inserted the diaphragm, washed her hands and was in bed while Robin was still checking the area door.

Helen tried very hard to focus on the advantages of marriage and this was perhaps the greatest: that wives were given family planning as a matter of course. She could not risk a daughter. The relief of having a son had been comparable with that of physical delivery. A son would move through the world with ease. She thought she could manage not to envy him that. But a girl? Too complicated, another rusty link in a female chain she was all too glad to see dissolve.

The doctors preferred to withhold contraception until one had produced at least two children. Her own GP had protested at first, but then progressed through her notes to the letter from Nazareth and said that in her case, it was advisable to stop at one. That letter from Dr. Kersey, those carbon copies of her discharge notes were there to stay, her false past given truth by the little brown envelopes and her own acquiescence: she had to fight the urge, every time, to reach across the desk and grab them from their little brown folder, claw them to shreds, but that was just the kind of behavior that would see her back in hospital.

"Thanks for warming the bed," said Robin, sliding his braces off his shoulders. Helen's eyes rolled of their own accord but by the time he was in bed, by the time his hands were under her nightgown, she had begun to stir. She had made a choice, early in her marriage, not to set the magnet to repel. She would not give this up, and if her fury escaped between the sheets he had, in his own words, "No complaints in that department, no complaints at all."

When he was safely snoring, Helen tiptoed to the bathroom where she carefully removed the diaphragm—she could do this now without it pinging across the room—and replaced it in its case, hidden inside an old Max Factor box where Robin would never think to look. They had achieved a kind of peace and that would do in place of being known, or understood. He believed she was ill and he still wanted her. What was that if not love?

In the sitting room, there was a faint talcum smell in the air and a little blue matinee jacket drying over the clotheshorse. This was her stolen time, the hours of the night that made the day bearable. She took down from the shelf the legal textbook she had hidden inside the dust jacket of a Truby King child-rearing handbook. The coffee-morning mothers who fancied themselves progressive were against Truby King's rigid routines but Helen needed the discipline just as much as Damian. Here was a thing that taught her how to mother him; to measure out care in ounces of formula and minutes napped.

Damian yelled out and a fist of frustration clenched inside her. King was very clear that a hand between the shoulder blades was all it took to settle a baby and after a few sleepless weeks, Damian had come begrudgingly to agree. Now, Helen could settle him in under a minute. In the soft glow of the night-light she noticed again that his several chins and his hair, coming in tufts around his ears, made him look just like Sir Ralph. Damian only had one set of grandparents—Peter and Eugenie had no more tried to contact her than she them—but what grandparents they were, devoted to their little heir, redecorating Robin's old nursery in Greenlaw Hall with a Peter Rabbit frieze and proclaiming the boy's genius when he gummed at his silver rattle.

Helen, for her part, kept Damian warm and fed, would care for and educate the boy. She could do everything except want him. She thought often about the mother he might have had if she'd been allowed to give him up. Someone like Pauline, perhaps, poor but blessed with the instinct for caregiving. But look where Pauline's devotion to maternity had got her.

She would stay with Robin for Damian's sake: to offer stability when everything else ran dry. Wasn't that level of sacrifice a kind of love?

Helen pulled the cord on the table-lamp and spread her text-books before her. She had sailed through correspondence courses in secretarial skills and progressed to bookkeeping, office admin-istration and was now on employment law; in lieu of the experi-ence she craved, she crammed herself with theory.

She rarely drank but tonight she poured two fingers of whiskey into a crystal tumbler. At one minute to midnight, she opened the sash window onto the square, the better to hear Big Ben strike. A fox nosing in the gutter disappeared into the thick of the gardens. The strokes tonight would have greater than usual significance, although few outside knew about the change that would occur.

One of the things Helen had studied while Damian was napping, while Damian was playing in the park, while Damian had his arms looped around her ankles, was English lunacy law, past and pres-ent. That blasted 1930 Mental Treatment Act they were all so fond of quoting had come to personify the injustices of her treatment almost as much as the hospital itself. What Helen hadn't known was that even as the act had been used to trap her, it had been a dying thing. While she had been in Nazareth, Parliament was debating it. While she had been forcing out her marriage vows in the hospital chapel, Kersey and Bures blotting their names on the register, Parliament had been drafting a Mental Health Act to stop patients being dumped in asylums by their families like something from a Victorian novel. The act aimed to bring psychiatric care into line with the rest of medicine: patient-led and unshackled by outdated laws. The Board of Control was to be abolished. Had she been sent to Nazareth under these new laws, she would never have had to marry her way out.

Big Ben began to chime. Helen leaned out of the window and raised a glass to the young Helens, the Normas and the Paulines and the Susans, whose lives might now be their own. The twelfth peal reverberated up and down the river, and the act became law.

49

1965

Robin was blotchy on the threshold of Damian's bedroom. The carpet bore the imprints of the trunk and the train set; the pillow had a dent in the shape of Bobble the teddy bear, which Robin had packed and unpacked a dozen times before he had reasoned that the trauma of Damian's sleeping without the bear would be worse than the ribbing he'd receive for bringing it.

"It's got to be done," he sniffed. If Helen could have been conditioned to feel the way Robin did about their son, would she have done? "But he does seem so very *little*. I don't remember being that young. I remember feeling like a man about it, that sense of—Christ, I don't know." He put his hands in his pockets, strode to the window and gazed onto the square, where the birches were still lush and green, obscuring the houses opposite. "He won't be the same when he comes home, you know." She was equal parts ashamed and thrilled by the stirring in her breast. She joined Robin by the window. "What will you do with your days, now?" he asked. It was a rhetorical question but Helen's heart leaped. He had just given her an opportunity she had thought she would need to create herself.

"Wait here, and I'll show you."

She was back a minute later: Robin was waiting with his back to the window, arms crossed, faint amusement turning into puzzlement when she returned with a sheaf of paper. Perhaps he had been expecting her to be wearing a new dress or necklace.

"Here." She handed him the letter, dated three days ago, offering her the position of administrator at the ear, nose and throat department of University College Hospital. "*Here's* what I'll be doing with my days." Robin read it once with his glasses on, and then again with them off, both times as though he were reading hieroglyphics, or indeed Pitman shorthand. Then he held the paper in one hand and his glasses in the other.

"They said that they wouldn't normally offer the job to a married woman but for me they would make an exception. They said"—Helen could not keep the pride out of her voice—"They said I was an outstanding candidate."

"Helen, my love." Robin's mustache twitched with the effort of biting down on his smile. "How did you bluff your way into this? You aren't qualified for this job."

She cleared her throat, then showed him the rest of the certificates in her hand. "Actually, I am."

She laid out the certificates she'd earned on Damian's bed: made a quilt of her qualifications. Robin was no longer amused. His face seemed to drain of blood with every page she produced.

"When did you do this?" There was an unfamiliar edge to his voice. "What was happening to Damian while all this was going on? Why weren't you *mothering* him?"

He would hardly be mothered at boarding school either, but Helen knew better than to raise this. "He was at pre-prep five days a week. And I worked at night."

"I need a moment." Robin returned to the window, knuckles on the sill, shoulders up around his ears. Helen sat on the bed, put the certificates back in a pile.

"What is it you need?" He addressed the windowpane. "Would you like your own car? I earn enough money for two, surely?"

A pair of Woolworths paste earrings earned with her own money would be worth more to Helen than anything he could ever buy, but she could see how thin the ice was.

"You're a wonderful provider. But I need more, Robin. I've always wanted to work." No one knew that more than Robin.

He turned back to the room. "They warned me you might relapse, but after seven years, I thought we were safe."

I could tell him now, she thought: he has known me for seven years and I have never, ever given him cause to think I was insane. She took a deep breath. "It's not a relapse. Robin, I was never ill in the first place. It was a mistake putting me in there. You *know* me. You must see that, now."

It was finally out there. Helen looked for understanding but saw only concern, in the way his mouth followed the downturn of his mustache, and she knew she had failed. It was too big and hurtful a thing. It was easier for him to believe she had acted through illness than to accept the truth: that she had not wanted his child, that she did not love him, that her life was only ever supposed to be hers. He sat next to her on Damian's bed but kept the distance of a doctor on ward rounds.

"But Helen, you would say that. This is a sign that you're ill." It was like having Dr. Bures back. The seven-year-old scream ballooned again in Helen's lungs. "You working goes against medical advice, the best medical advice in the country. The doctors said that too much excitement is just asking for another breakdown." He began to gather her papers, stack them face down on top of each other. When he had squared the blank pages off, he finally met her eyes. "They would never employ you if they knew about your past."

Was this a threat disguised as concern or concern coming out as a threat? Helen searched Robin's face for malice and found only dumb trust in the establishment. She spoke very slowly, as though this would give her a chance to reel in any wrong words.

"But my past is a secret, Robin," she said. "I was in Nazareth for less than a month. Those nurses hardly knew my name when I was there, they wouldn't remember me now, and they're hardly going to examine the staff lists for a London hospital, are they?" It occurred to her that a leak, if there was one, was far more likely to come from, say, a secretary at her GP, but they paid Harley Street money for Harley Street service. "The only person likely to remember me is Martin Bures, and for all his faults it's more than his reputation is worth to break confidentiality—he'd be struck off. Outside the medical profession the only people who really know are you and me."

She was serving his own threat but stripped of its garnish. If he was going to counter it, he had better do it now and in plain English. As a girl she had watched other children challenge each other not to blink; she knew, now, how it felt to play, and as Robin dropped his gaze, had a taste of what winning might be like.

"What if I begged you not to do it?" he said.

"Robin, I've made up my mind."

"What if I *forbade* you?" he asked, but he couldn't put air into the words, let alone conviction.

"Your choice is to take the tiniest chance on it coming out that your wife spent some time in a madhouse, or I don't work and I go there again," she said.

"Then I really have no choice at all, do I?" He smoothed the counterpane of Damian's bed, once to get rid of the dents, a second time to get rid of the creases and then over and over again, like Susan with her hairbrush, until Helen couldn't stand it anymore and took his hands.

"You'll never have to say, 'I told you so,'" she said. "If that's what you're worried about."

"Oh, God, Helen, I do hope not, because if this backfires . . ." He shook himself out of her grip, straightened and plumped the pillow. "I realized something about you when I was packing away the train set," he said. "In all these years—not even when your parents died, for heaven's sake—I've never seen you cry." It was true. Nazareth had cauterized her tear ducts. She couldn't tell from Robin's tone whether he was admiring a strength or naming a weakness.

50

1983

Helen's tracksuit—pale pink and gray marl, matching headband and legwarmers—hung in the wardrobe of her corner office. The headquarters of the newly established East Anglian Regional Health Authority looked like a geometry kit, all set-square gables and pro-tractor windows in glass and chrome. The whole of the Ipswich docklands was being developed. Soon the brownfield site of Helen's morning run would be built up into what the papers called yuppie flats. So what if it wasn't picturesque? Sentimentality about Victorian architecture was one of the reasons hellholes like Nazareth endured.

The telephone on Helen's desk buzzed. "Paul Lummis is here," said Coralie. "That makes everyone."

Helen leaned into the speaker. "Thanks, Coralie. Show them in."

The boardroom table was a throwback, a long mahogany oval. Ostensibly the rounded edges meant there could be no head but Helen would not relinquish her seat at the prow. Michael Stein, the Minister for Health, was the most senior attendee but Helen, as Chair of the Authority, had been waiting her whole career for this meeting and wanted there to be no doubt about who was steering it.

The delegates filed in: Michael Stein first, a parade of faceless civil servants, then Davina Deben, the Health Authority press officer. Davina had, in the last two years, taught Helen how to speak, how to breathe from her core to override the shallow feminine breath of panic and emotion. Next to Davina, Paul Lummis, local MP, left-wing bruiser and proud Nusstead boy, sat with his legs at twenty past eight.

But today was only ever going to be a two-hander.

At Helen's right hand, in a shiny blue skirt suit and with her shaggy blonde hair caught in a Fergie bow, sat Jenny Bishop, the new general manager charged with the impossible task of managing the decline of Nazareth. Jenny was a qualified psychiatrist, a bleeding-heart liberal, a do-gooder, and all wrong for the job. The press might be up in arms that people like Helen, with business rather than clinical backgrounds, were coming in to manage the hospitals but Jenny Bishop was too close to be efficient. What was the point of knowing your patients' names if you couldn't afford to feed them?

"Thanks for coming in today, everyone." Helen's voice held steady. "As you know, we're here to discuss the future of Nazareth Hospital. As with all mental hospitals, closure has been slated for decades but the new plan is to accelerate the process. We have run it down to just under nine hundred patients, but with the old men's wing now closed, overcrowding is still a huge problem."

Jenny cleared her throat. "I know we're on borrowed time, but you're trying to fast-track something that needs to be managed over a much longer period."

"Jenny, I have great sympathy for you," replied Helen. "But it's worth reiterating, even for those of you who have recently visited the site, how rapidly dereliction has progressed. Nazareth cost us £4 million last year. That's ten percent of the Health Authority's budget. The cost of maintaining the buildings alone is astronomical. It is absolutely unjust that public money should be spent on the upkeep of an outdated Victorian building. And that's just to stop the roof falling in and to bring the wiring up to date. It doesn't begin to cover modernization." Helen checked in with Davina; was she holding herself right, was her voice controlled enough? Davina flashed a toothy smile, a prompt to lighten her tone.

"So you're happy to turf patients who've been institutionalized for decades into bedsits?"

Helen felt her heart quicken at the thought of granting even the oldest patients a few years' liberty. Modern flats, their own little kitchens; who wouldn't prefer that to the cold brick and tile of the hospital? How could anyone, in all conscience, with modern psychiatric services, with new miracle drugs approved every month, perpetuate this outdated care model?

"I'm running the place on agency staff at twice the price and a handful of locals who've been there since the year dot," continued Jenny, unwittingly doing Helen a favor.

"I know you've done your best," said Helen, her voice back under control. "But the culture of petty corruption is just too deeply embedded. If you could just remind the board what happened at your last stocktake?"

Jenny colored. "Unfortunately there hadn't actually *been* a stocktake at Nazareth for well over fifteen years before I took up my position, but we've managed to turn that around and—"

"I'm sorry, but you're still not in control," said Helen. She spoke over Jenny's head, addressed the men. "The deficit from the pharmacy alone was half a million pounds. A hospital porter was arrested just last week for selling prescription medicine." Davina had placed the story in the local press: Coralie had made Xerox copies, which Helen now circulated. Heads bent over the article. The young man had had a string of convictions to his name and should never have been allowed to work with vulnerable people; his father had got him the job through the back door.

"You don't need reminding of the pressure from the Department of Health. We can work together to make the closure of Nazareth a flagship for the rest of the country. The race is on to be the first authority to make a success of care in the community."

"And where is it?" snorted Jenny. "Where is this marvelous,

tolerant, enlightened *community,* full of compassionate residents who will welcome group accommodation for large numbers of the mentally ill? Many of whom don't actually want to leave what has for years—decades, in some cases—been a place of genuine healing? Where is it? I'd love to know."

Paul Lummis stirred in his seat. "We can't do this without talking jobs." His accent was broad Suffolk and above his collar and tie was the ruddy weathered face of the farmer he had once been. "You say, Jenny, that you're running the place on a skeleton staff but Nazareth still employs over four hundred workers from Nusstead alone. That's a huge proportion in a town of five thousand. Many families have both parents employed by the hospital." He spread his empty palms. "There are no other jobs in the area. This will devastate the local economy."

"Well, the black market for Valium will dry up overnight," said Michael Stein. Helen chose to let that go.

"In the short term, jobs will go but don't forget the level of redundancy pay many of the long-term staff will be entitled to." Her voice caught in her throat for a moment. This was the one place Helen's confidence faltered; job losses, however necessary, were always horrible. Robin had reassured her time and again that the market would provide where the state no longer could, and he had found, through a contact in the City, the perfect developer. "We presently have an offer from the hotelier Larry Lawrence, well over market value as a mark of how fast he wants to move." She was on firm ground again. There would be better-paid jobs in construction for the unskilled men, no more clearing up dirty protests and dodging blows. Nurses who'd been on their feet for twenty years could relax into customer service. "By his reckoning there will be more than enough jobs firstly in construction, and then in the resort, to offset the losses. But we have to move fast, too. The money won't stay on the table for long. The brutal truth is that if we keep throwing good money after bad, and we don't make a profit on the site, we can't afford the new unit."

"That unit is still a year away from completion. Where do my patients go till then?"

"They'll be in halfway houses."

"We're talking about some of the most vulnerable human beings in society!" Jenny shouted while the teacups trembled. "Mrs. Greenlaw. My chronic patients consider Nazareth their home. They're not just institutionalized; they are tormented, daily, by frightening auditory hallucinations. They cannot cope without high levels of support. I don't believe you have that support here yet. With respect, you do not have a clinical background and this is the very human consequence of applying business-school management to mental illness. It's unconscionable."

A rage rose in Helen, a full-body fury that had her gripping the arms of her chair in an effort to stay seated. The words *you weren't there* threatened to burst out of her mouth. If Jenny—if anyone around this table—knew how it felt to be trapped in that monstrous place they would empty it tonight. The building itself was sick, the institution madder and more inhumane than its inmates. If Helen had her way she would drive the wrecking ball herself, she would—

"Helen?" Davina Deben's voice had the stress of someone repeating a name for the second, third, fourth time. Ten faces angled toward her with a kind of nervous curiosity. Had she spoken? Had she given herself away? Davina tilted her head in a private warning Helen couldn't translate. Was she expected to speak? Had she missed a question? The second hand on the clock slow-clapped her performance until Michael stepped into the breach.

"If we could just return to policy for a moment," he said.

Paul Lummis grunted in response. "If by policy you mean ideological warfare on the welfare state . . ." he began. The ensuing twenty-minute slanging match let Helen gather herself in time to rejoin the meeting and, eventually, call it to a close. Jenny and Paul Lummis left the boardroom together, heads bowed. In the end only Helen, Davina and Michael were left.

"What happened there?" asked Davina. "Are you all right?"

"Fine," said Helen, but Davina made a note on her pad: *further media training*. At least she shielded it from Michael.

"You held your own," said Michael. "We're in stalemate now, but we didn't make any concessions." Clearly, her panic had only been perceptible to Davina; she still had Michael's respect. She drew in her breath and got back down to business.

"We have two options," she said. "We can hold scores more meetings, wasting money and time, and set up an investigation into best practice and admin."

"You're not selling it to me," said Michael. "What's plan B?"

"We go after the building itself. Somewhere in that hospital there will be such a grave contravention of health and safety regulations that we could, effectively, close it overnight." Helen rubbed her finger over a scratch in the mahogany. "I'll call the chief surveyor this morning. We can be in by the end of the week."

51

Helen watched the surveyors file in to Nazareth, a parade of shiny beetles in their hard hats. They would do their job independently. She need not be here, but she had to look the old place in the eye: square up to it. As a girl, she had been tricked into entering. Now, she was doing so deliberately, and on her own terms. It was important. Admittedly, she had nearly driven into a verge upon seeing the sign for Asylum Road, and after parking, it had taken her ten minutes to open her eyes. But after that first glance, it hadn't been too bad. It helped that the building was weak, already well on the road to dereliction. The roof over the old men's wing sagged and half the pearly panels on the clocktower had blown out, giving the face a jack-o-lantern leer.

Helen blew her nose, patted her hair, refreshed her lipstick in the rear-view mirror and tried to put herself in the position of someone driving up to this place for the first time. Even transformed into a hotel, with its windows curtained and gleaming, stonework sandblasted and little potted trees either side of the doors, this place would surely always look like the prison it was. What did Larry Lawrence want it for? The views, perhaps, over the two miles of fenland at the rear, impossible to build on.

Jenny Bishop stood in front of the double doors, one hand on the arm of a man in a cowboy hat. His placard was hand-painted with the insignia of COHSE, the hospital workers' union, and the slogan read 125 YEARS OF CARING SACRIFICED TO PROFIT.

"Is this a publicity stunt?" she asked, suddenly wishing she had brought Davina with her.

"You don't need me to tell you how fast the jungle drums beat in the trades unions," said Jenny. "My staff are concerned for their jobs. They have the right to protest—Mark, keep it peaceful. Mrs. Greenlaw, please, come inside."

The double doors creaked open. The atrium had been painted sky blue at some time in the last quarter-century, and the gas-lamp fittings were gone. Something more fundamental had changed too, something that went deeper than a coat of paint. Helen looked at the portraits, the banisters, the doors, wondering what huge architectural detail she had missed before understanding that it was the smell. That sickening paraldehyde reek had gone, replaced with the synthetic alpine tang of air freshener. She wondered if present patients appreciated that one of the many wonders of modern pharmacology was the loss of the stench? A glance into the day room did not suggest these patients appreciated much. They were shapeless in tracksuits, slumped in front of daytime television. Most of them were women and the average age was, at a guess, around sixty. Helen made a mental note to ensure that the community accommodation was centrally heated. Old bricks and old bones were a grim combination.

"You're free to interview any one of them," offered Jenny.

"I'm interested in your bookkeeping, not the patients' records," said Helen. She pushed a door to PHYSIOTHERAPY without asking. The room was empty, foam bursting through the pads on worn-out equipment. Half the windows were boarded up. They'd even got this wrong. Who would want to ride an exercise bicycle in this dungeon? Helen would ensure that in the new unit, the gymnasium was flooded with light.

"If I could see the administration block?" She was on the stairs before she realized that Jenny had yet to direct her that way. A voice carried from the clocktower. "Jesus *Christ*. Steve, come and see this."

Jenny winced.

The same old steps creaked underfoot. Jenny's office was a crude sub-division of Dr. Bures's old room; where Bures's rogues' gallery had been were health and safety posters and a calendar that had expired two years ago. The esteemed Bures had been discredited, or rather had discredited himself. He had come out as gay in the early seventies and before his recent death had published a memoir about how barbaric his practices had been. Helen placed her briefcase and coat on the hat stand and asked to see the hospital's books.

Empty-handed, she followed Jenny through a door in the paneling she hadn't noticed as a girl. Jenny's keys jangled on her belt. Helen thought that they might be over the ballroom.

"Step into the inner sanctum." Jenny opened another door into a huge library; no, not library. The yards and yards of shelves here stored not books but boxes and files. One window was broken and boarded over, but light shone through a gap and the chants of the mob drifted through it. Jenny gestured to a table stacked with perforated computer printouts, along with a tower of brown envelopes.

"Are these your accounts?"

"No." Jenny flushed. "They're patient notes. I'm begging you, Helen, before you start number-crunching, take a look at the human side of all this." Helen stared down the length of the shelves, her conscious mind running a few seconds behind the warning tug in her belly.

"But this is an extraordinary amount of paperwork for a few hundred patients."

"Try ten thousand patients," said Jenny. "You're looking at the history of everyone who's ever been treated here. Some of these records date to the beginning of the NHS itself. They're filed by year, according to discharge. I'm afraid that records stored in the darkest days of the Kersey administration have been a little slapdash, but I assure you that since my tenure everything is in order. It's obviously current patients who matter today."

Helen fought nausea at the thought that she might be only yards away from the information that, in the wrong hands, could undo everything she had worked for. "I had assumed that records would have been centralized," she said.

"They have. We *are* centralization. Have been since the sixties." Jenny was talking as though she could not hear the drilling of Helen's heart. "Anyway, back to these long-term patients." She peeled the topmost dozen pages from her doorstep of paper. "I've picked out a couple of case studies here who I hope will change your mind. I really think it would influence your decision if you just saw that . . ."

Her voice became a burble, a teacher droning Latin. Helen was seized by the conviction that her own notes, ignored for years, would suddenly leap from their file, flutter out of the open window and into the hands of the little crowd on the forecourt. When the hospital was decommissioned all these records would have to be moved to some other archive, and who knew what might slip out? Her world shrank to the need to destroy her records before her history came roaring up into the present. Logic abandoned her and floated away, as though it was only a balloon she had been holding all these years.

"Why aren't the records locked?" She hardly cared that she was interrupting Jenny. "They're loose on the shelves. Surely these are confidential; this is a huge privacy issue."

Jenny held up her keys. "No one gets this without my permission."

Both women flinched as, somewhere outside, glass smashed and a cheer went up. "Oh, hell," said Jenny. Helen saw her chance to be alone in here; cunning returned, even if reason was gone.

"Never mind," said Helen. "I'm sure your second-in-command

will bring this under control soon." Jenny didn't take the bait, but her left eyelid was flickering. Technically, she had nothing to lose but pride. Nazareth would not pass or fail an inspection on her display of authority. Helen was depending on Jenny's professional pride being as strong as her own. The cheer turned into a chant.

"Gosh, it's like a football match out there. Your staff can certainly think for themselves," said Helen. "I suppose it's a relic of Kersey's time. Never mind the lunatics taking over the asylum, the staff ruled the roost then. I would have thought that you—"

Jenny's chair scraped back along the floor. "I'll be five minutes." She pushed the topmost printout Helen's way. "Time enough for you to read this." She dangled her keys apologetically. "I'm going to have to lock you in, for security."

Whether it was Helen's security or that of the records, she didn't say: she was gone, the sound of the key as familiar as if it were yesterday. Helen was on her feet before Jenny's footsteps died, steering the shelves apart. The stacks were labeled by year. 1985, 1979, 1970, 1965, 1960. The century rewound itself around Helen as she walked back through her life, London and Robin in the house and Damian at home and London before that, early motherhood, then back to Suffolk.

If Jenny caught her, her career was over. Worse, the whole campaign to shut Nazareth was fatally compromised. The irony was not lost on Helen that it was difficult to maintain indignation about a false accusation of insanity when one felt this close to madness. All the symptoms were there: the sweating palms, the pounding heart, the feeling that adrenaline might actually levitate her off the floor. She was sane enough to recognize the madness of risking everything but powerless to control herself. It was this place: the building was the opposite of a hospital. There was something in its stones, a poison gas that sent the sane mad and made the insane worse. How else could she explain why she was halfway up a seven-foot bookshelf, scrabbling for finger-holds like a child climbing a tree?

1958 was seven shelves deep, everything in brown archive boxes with a reassuring inch of gray dust on top. The labels were faded but legible. Only three women had left Nazareth in September 1958. Here, then, were the madnesses, false and true, of Helen Morris, Pauline Preston and Celeste Wilson.

52

Helen could not bring herself to read Pauline's notes. Celeste's fate she absorbed in the beat between two blinks: transferred to Rampton Secure Hospital with the recommendation that she have a prefrontal leucotomy if her violence didn't subside, although there was no indication of whether that was carried out. Her own notes were neatly filed, beginning, as one would expect, with admission. As she read, the physical symptoms of that night seemed temporarily to return: a lightness, a biting cold, legs filmed with her own filth.

> *Admission: The patient was referred to us by her GP and parents after attempting to procure an abortion. She refuses to divulge the source of the abortifacient or to name the young man in question, and must be kept here for the safety of her unborn child as well as for her own treatment.*

Helen dragged her fingernail across the words *procure an abortion,* making a little concertina of the soft paper. It was easy, like peeling a label off a wet bottle. The next few pages were in Dr. Bures's hand, the left-handed drag and smudge sending her back to his study; she found herself scratching the back of her scalp. It was worse than she had thought: she saw that the diagnosis itself was that her condition was permanent: *a psychopathic disorder rather than a single episode of mania.* They said she would never get better. *For this young woman to hold any position of responsibility would be a grave error.*

She breathed deeply, tried to get some perspective. One didn't need to be a clinician to see that the notes were outdated, the diagnoses old-fashioned, the treatment wholly inappropriate. But Helen knew that public attitudes had not caught up with medical understanding and this would be a gift to the rabble outside who wanted nothing more than to undermine not only Nazareth's closure but the process of deinstitutionalization itself. She lost sight of the difference between her knowing what was written here and the public knowing. In that moment, it was one and the same thing.

A new noise outside made her start: Jenny's voice, plaintive even through the fuzz of a bullhorn. "Come on guys, let's show our best side today." The noise of the crowd died down just a little. It wasn't as if the local workers had true nursing vocations. In two years' time they would be working in a beautiful hotel, earning more in tips than they made in a week at Nazareth. Helen spread the rest of her notes across the top of two filing cabinets, Celeste's and Pauline's records scattered underneath.

Psychiatrist's Report After ECT

This patient appeared at first to be an excellent candidate for ECT. Behavioral Conditioning is not working for this patient. Her response to Convulsive Therapy has been disappointing. Her behavior remains hostile and unfeminine, with no guilt over the attempted termination. The uppermost problem now is what to do about the child upon delivery. The patient still refuses to divulge paternity. Adoption looks likely, with the mother to remain at Nazareth under certification. Since her father's abandonment there is no one to petition for the patient's release and she has no visible means of support.

This must have been written directly after she had embarrassed Bures in front of his medical students. His spite rose off the page. She flicked forward, one ear cocked for Jenny's return.

Medical Superintendent's Report Upon Discharge

She was slow to respond to Convulsive Treatment but since the breakthrough great progress has been made. There is no damage observed to memory or cognitive function following ECT; however in this case it would not be a problem, given that housewives' livelihoods are not dependent upon intellect or memory.

The patient understands the nature of the vows she is being asked to make. She is discharged into the care of her new spouse on the understanding that this is a trial period, and that any further transgressions will result in her readmission. I am satisfied that Behavioral Conditioning has been a success in this case. She no longer means to harm the child and has come to terms with impending motherhood. She will thrive within the stability of marriage.

Heavy footsteps sounded in the corridor outside and Helen's heart, already beating at double its resting rate, spiked again. She gathered up her notes, tipping the pages in panic: Pauline's records and at least one page of Celeste's slid in slow motion into a tiny gap between the filing cabinets and the wall they were bolted to. Helen gathered up her notes, her admission details on the top. She flipped to the back page and saw Kersey's discharge report, with the meat of her diagnosis and treatment in the middle.

There was the unmistakable sound of a key in the lock; *Jenny*. Helen was stranded in the stacks, her possession of the twenty faded pages an act of gross misconduct. It struck her then that of *course* she could have replaced them, that the chances of them somehow leaping out during the archival process, let alone the connection being made, were almost nonexistent. Reason's return was too late. Her briefcase was in Jenny's office. Her slim-fitting dress had no pockets.

"Are you in there, Helen?" It was a male voice, one she recognized. Helen ventured out from her hiding place, the notes at arm's length behind the shelves. Surveyor Steve Price's steel-toed boots and hard hat were incongruous with his suit and tie.

"Jenny said I'd find you up here."

"How did you get those?" She gestured to Jenny's keys in his hand.

"Oh, that. Yeah, she would've had me sign the Official Secrets Act if she could have. No, she's talking down a yobbo outside and I overruled her on knight-in-shining-armor grounds." Helen gently lowered her hand, so that the file rested against her thigh. Steve's eyes traveled over it without changing expression, although it seemed to her as though it must glow. "I've come to get you out of here. Serious structural issues with the main staircase so I'm evacuating the whole admin block until we've had a chance to give it the all-clear. It'll only take an hour or so. Patients are mostly on the wards so no need to worry about them."

Helen thought fast. If she could get to her bag before Jenny, she could drop these notes into it and destroy them at home. She turned into the corridor, but Steve's hand was on the small of her back.

"Sorry, the whole zone's out of bounds. One of my team's already picked up your stuff. I need you to come out the back way." He nodded at the service staircase, and mistook Helen's horror as a reaction to the state of the building. "Oh, trust me, the staircase is the least of it. Come on, let's get you out."

She had last descended this stone staircase on the day Pauline had died. Her notes throbbed in her hand. Perhaps she could tear them and flush them away. Anything was better than marching out into the crowd clutching them.

"Might I use the lavatory?" she asked, but the door to the first floor was padlocked from the other side.

"This is supposed to be an emergency exit!" said Steve, as they descended. "I think you'll have to come out and go in again. Here we are." He held open the door and they were back in that long, echoing half-mile corridor. Sweat sprang from Helen's palms, soaking through the soft paper.

"Not a single fire door shut," tutted Steve. "And who left *that* there?"

A yellow refuse bag was slumped like a drunk in a doorway, the words Medical Waste For Incineration stamped on the plastic. While Steve made a note on his clipboard, Helen tugged at the bag's mouth, gagging as the smell escaped. She dropped her notes in among the soiled adult nappies. Words seemed to light up: child, paternity, housewives, discharged. She closed the bag and shook it so that the loose pages slipped between the filthy dressings.

A giddy rising euphoria was soon punctured by the realization that Steve was leading her toward the old laundry rooms. Sweat drenched her back. She tried to concentrate on what Steve was saying.

"I thought I'd seen some hovels, but that . . . it's like something from Dickens." He pushed his hard hat an inch away from his brow. "Never mind closure, we've got grounds for evacuation. More breaches than I can count, I found three separate ligature points out of staff sightlines—the piping down there is almost a scaffold." Helen's feet stopped of their own accord. Her hand on the tiled wall was all that kept her upright. That pipe should have been boxed in within hours of Pauline's death, yet years later vulnerable patients still had access to a private gallows. "There's dry rot in the floorboards, mold spores in every bathroom . . . it's worse than slum housing; it's not fit for anyone, let alone vulnerable patients. I'm condemning the whole building—are you all right?"

"I'm fine," said Helen. "I just—bit claustrophobic down here."

"Sorry, yeah," said Steve. "Tell you what, we can go out this way." He pushed at a fire exit; the noise of the crowd shoved him back. "First though, we've got to get past this lot."

53

The lawn was thronged; cars were parked at angles on the lawn and the bicycles leaned against the cedars. Where had they all come from, so fast? Someone had written SAVE OUR HOSPITAL on a perfectly good bedsheet. A few of the patients, recognizable by their tracksuits and slippers, were cheering and nurses had wheeled out the geriatrics.

"This is them!" came a disembodied voice. "This is the ones who want to sell us off to the highest bidder!"

The crowd turned to Helen and Steve like starlings in a flock. Where the hell was Jenny? The answer came from directly behind her, buzzing through the bullhorn.

"All staff and patients, inside now," she said, to a wall of booing and jeering.

Most of the nurses and patients shuffled inside, but the protesters drew closer together, and began to chant: "Save Our Jobs! Save Nazareth! Save Our Patients!"

The cowboy who'd been first on the scene jostled to the front of the rabble. "My family have worked here for a hundred years!"

Helen thought that he couldn't have better expressed the problem but said, "This is a routine inspection. No decision has been made," in a voice that, even to her, sounded flat and mechanical, and faltered when she found herself nose to nose with a round face wearing a pair of half-moon glasses. Former Medical Superintendent Kersey, five years retired, had decided to lend his voice to the place that had been his responsibility—his home—for over two decades. Helen waited for remembrance, for the accusations of hypocrisy to fly.

"What you don't seem to understand is that this isn't a hospital," he said. For a moment Helen wondered if he were quite well himself; he was the age for dementia. "It's a community, of staff, patients and the town. I would think very carefully about disrupting it."

Kersey spoke with passion but without a flicker of recognition. Helen's surge of relief was instantly buried in anger. *He doesn't have a clue who I am. He ruined my life and he doesn't even remember me.* Jenny Bishop redoubled her efforts on the bullhorn. "All staff and patients back to your wards now or face disciplinary action or loss of privileges."

"What disciplinary action?" shouted the cowboy. "We're going to lose our jobs anyway if she flogs it off to the highest bidder."

Jenny lowered her bullhorn. "Mark, you do more to harm our cause than help it when you get like this."

He dropped his placard. The other protestors set theirs down in a ripple and the crowd began slowly to disperse.

"Where are you parked?" Steve asked Helen. She nodded to the forecourt, where the Jaguar fell under the shadow of the clocktower. "Let's get you to your car in one piece, then," he said. "This lot are out for blood." He shielded her with his arm.

The rabble had blocked the cedar drive, but Jenny beckoned Helen across the lawn. She bumped over the grass, testing the Jaguar's suspension. Jenny's shortcut backfired as a youth in a denim waistcoat sat down in Helen's path.

An elderly woman had been parked in a wheelchair and apparently forgotten about. There was something familiar about the little body in its pastel twinset, pop socks wrinkled around spindly ankles. The gray hair was white now and sparse. *Norma.* Helen mouthed the name before she could stop herself and recognition was mutual. Norma was suddenly animated, gesturing at the car. "Helen! She's my friend! She's my friend, she's come back!"

A flustered nurse materialized behind Norma and trod on the wheelchair's brake. "She's no one's friend," she said, struggling with the mechanism.

"That's what you reckon. I knew her in the old days!"

"That's nice," said the nurse. "This bloody footbrake's jammed solid."

"Why won't you listen to me?" said Norma.

"Hold tight!" The nurse dragged Norma roughly back across the lawn until the force released the wheels. Norma started to scream; the nurse's patience snapped.

"For fuck's sake, Norma! Give it a rest, will you?" Helen could still hear Norma's crying after she had disappeared back into the building.

Jenny had finally persuaded the youth to give Helen passage. Helen drove calmly, not letting her narrow escape find its way into her nervous system. Hands, feet, eyes, all were engaged in the meditation of driving. Mirror-signal-maneuver, first-gear-second-gear-third-gear as the hospital shrank in her rear-view mirror. A thin spire of smoke rose in parallel with the clocktower. The conviction that she would somehow be uncovered was now exposed for the lapse of judgment it had been, but there was satisfaction to be had in watching the death of Helen Morris as the records burned to ash.

54

1986

Two phones on Helen's desk and Coralie was instructed not to put calls through to either of them. Coralie had gutted the relevant pages from the newspapers: there would be no other story today. For Adam Solomon and his son there would be no other story again and Julia Solomon's story was over. The photograph repeated in various sizes, the overblown snapshot of the pretty, dark-eyed woman, the back of a toddler's head. Headlines and snatches of text leaped like fish from the newsprint.

In front of her three-year-old son

Cunniffe struggled to adjust to independent living

Early closure of Nazareth to blame

lost so much blood that she

missed last three outpatient appointments

Lawrence skimped on security for derelict site

Julia's hour-long ordeal

Bang Him Up In Broadmoor

Hotel complex axed in a further blow to local job market

The child was found half a mile away in the undergrowth, clinging to the dog's body. He was physically unharmed but witnessed the worst of

Hospital workers: "We told you so"

Coralie backed in with coffee and tea on a tray. Helen surveyed its contents as though playing Kim's Game: the scalloped tea set, the plate laid out with Bourbons and custard creams that nobody would eat.

"Show them in," said Helen.

"Don't judge us by Cunniffe's atrocity" plead patient groups

Jenny Bishop and Davina Deben's watery eyes emphasized Helen's dry ones. Even Michael Stein looked puffy about the face.

"Press conference is in an hour," said Davina Deben. "We'll announce the inquiry then but let's do what we can for damage limitation now . . ." She fanned the air in front of her face, as if she could wave away the tears on her cheeks. It was the first time her professionalism had cracked since Helen had known her. "God, what a tragedy. What an awful bloody waste."

Nazareth had had its revenge on Helen, punished her for her defiance. She had played God and in retaliation the institution had taken another life, one last soul for its collection, and an innocent one too. It was clever, it had come up with something far more devastating than the loss of a career or a reputation.

Darius Cunniffe weighed sixteen stone to Julia Solomon's eight. She didn't stand a

Jenny cleared her throat. "If I could just start off with my two pence worth. This could have been avoided if the hospital had been wound down over a different timescale."

Larry Lawrence leaves locals in the lurch

Michael Stein shook his head. "The place was unfit for purpose. I'm sorry, Jenny, but I'm surprised you didn't have more deaths on your hands. And whose decision was it ultimately to discharge the patient into the community?"

Jenny shook her head. "Darius had been a model patient. His relapse could not have been foreseen. You read his notes, Helen, you were in there for ages." Helen didn't trust herself to speak. "Fifteen years without incident," continued Jenny. "But because *you* couldn't wait till the new unit was ready, I had to house him in the community. I warned you that such abrupt closure could turn a model patient volatile. It gives me no pleasure whatsoever to say I told you so."

bound her by the

Helen cleared her throat. "I am so very devastated by this, and profoundly sorry." Such stupid, inadequate words, but what could one say? I can't eat, I can't sleep, I would gladly give my own life for hers? "It's clearly a terrible tragedy, and I can't get the woman's ordeal—or her son's—out of my head." Her voice was going: she took a deep breath. "That said, I closed that hospital down in good faith and on expert advice. I know that you did your best, Jenny, but you weren't able to turn around a culture of neglect and laziness. It's an uncomfortable truth. I don't think there is anything to be achieved by pointing fingers."

Widower: she was a wonderful wife, a wonderful mother

Michael Stein turned to Helen. She knew what he was going to say. "Helen, this tragedy was a one-off and it can't be seen to undermine deinstitutionalization. You have been one of our greatest champions and the department appreciates your work more than I can express. But . . ." Michael shifted in his seat. Davina stared out of the window. "As you know, part of your role is to absorb the impact of tragedies like this." She had known the axe was coming but that didn't blunt the pain. "It was, ultimately, your choice and your responsibility. The payoff will be modest, for appearances' sake, but sufficient to reflect the fact that you may struggle, for a few months, to find work in the sector."

Davina coached her on the steps. "Best face on, Helen. Just deliver the statement, don't rise to their bait. You can do this. You did nothing wrong."

Health Authority "rushed closure of mental hospital"

She followed Davina and Michael through the revolving door: they were at her side on the front steps. An angry mob roared from behind a police cordon but the press pack were up close. Helen saw herself reflected in a score of lenses, a tiny doll against a grid of steel and glass. Shouted questions rolled over her in a tide. "How do you feel about leaving a three-year-old boy without a mother?"

Time to reopen the asylums?

"Isn't it *you* who ought to be decommissioned, Helen?"

Pressure groups warn that this is the first of many such

No. She pictured the headlines shrinking, the words whirling away. She could not afford the distraction. On the in-breath, she imagined forging her spine into steel. "I was absolutely devastated to hear of the murder on the old Nazareth Hospital site. Our profound sympathies are with Adam and Jacob Solomon. I cannot imagine the scale of their loss. My heart goes out to them. I made the decision to close Nazareth in good faith and am personally devastated that the system has failed not just this patient but an innocent family. The authority is in close contact with the senior investigating officer and all the right questions will be asked. An inquest has already been opened." She heard her voice, disconnected from the words' meaning, like a reluctant schoolchild reading in class. I'm losing them, she thought, as she ended her speech with the words: ". . . that they have accepted my resignation with immediate effect."

"You don't look that bothered," said a female journalist in the front row.

Oh, to be able to summon the tears for once. Helen had worked so hard to control herself, she had completely internalized the process. But the journalists needed facts, process, fairness, not soundbites or platitudes. Helen responded against Davina's instructions. "I closed the place in good faith," she repeated. "As chair of a public authority, I have a duty to the public purse."

She knew she had misspoken even before the gasp went up. The reporters who weren't shocked smiled into their notepads, knowing they had their soundbite. Davina was moving through the crowd toward her, damage limitation personified.

"D'you think Adam Solomon cares about the public purse?" came a voice from the scrum of the press pack.

"We won't be taking questions today," said Davina. Helen froze on the steps. The mania rushed through her again. I could confess now, she thought wildly. I could tell them exactly what kind of place their beloved institution was, the rottenness of it, I could tell them first hand, I could be on every front page of every newspaper for weeks if I went public. She parted her lips to speak.

"Helen?" Davina's warning look brought her back to her senses. Spilling her history wouldn't bring Julia Solomon back, nor would it comfort her widower. What would it achieve, other than having her own story hijack Julia's, and turn the clock back to the bad old days?

Robin, the husband on whom she was once again financially dependent, was waiting for her in the Jaguar. Helen turned off the radio rather than risk hearing her own voice on a news bulletin. They stayed silent as the city gave way to countryside. It was late August and the fields were as they had been the summer they met, acres of wheat a rippling golden sea on either side of the road.

"That could've gone better," said Robin eventually.

Helen pressed her head against the window, letting her skull absorb the vibration. "No one will ever employ me again." Her words bloomed in little steam flowers on the glass.

Robin took his hand off the gearstick for a moment to pat her on the knee.

"Would that be such a bad thing, hmm? Some enforced leave, to let you recuperate?" She knew what was coming next. "I'm so sorry it took a tragedy to make you see it, but the doctors were right all along, darling. You should *never* have stretched yourself so far. Let me be a husband to you. Let me take care of you now, before anyone else gets hurt."

55

1987

"In the midst of life, we are in death."

There was no wind to carry the vicar's words. The hurricane had barely blown itself out when they started to call it the Great Storm. Of course by other countries' standards it was a stiff breeze but England had known nothing like it in living memory. The whole county was razed, its skyline pulled sharp, its vast flatness laid bare so it felt as though only the curvature of the earth stopped one seeing all the way to London. The wind had skittled down centuries-old trees; the largest oak on the estate had fallen across the drive of Greenlaw Hall, blocking the ambulance while Robin's arteries shrank to pinpricks.

Sir Ralph Greenlaw stood unevenly before the family plot that had expected him next. Damian had made an effort; haircut, shave, suit. To Helen's surprise he wore Robin's signet ring, a bourgeois gewgaw he had always professed to despise, on his little finger. It was the first time since school she'd seen him out of jeans. The suit did a lot for him, smoothing over his nebulous "career" in the "media." At twenty-eight, Damian had Robin's build and his golden coloring but had grown into Eugenie's features, that Helen now saw clearly had always been meant for a man: the right angle in the jaw, the strong straight brow. Peter Morris's genes were evidently too sheepish to assert themselves even in legacy.

The new girlfriend, Michiko, was nervously toeing the plastic grass that lined the graveside. Something in publishing, long shiny hair. Damian hadn't formally introduced her yet. They would have beautiful children. Helen was as surprised by the thought itself as she was astonished by the pang that accompanied it, a low deep twang somewhere that might have been an ovary past its use-by date.

The vicar, who had only come to Sizewell last year, had rhapsodized at the pulpit about how well loved Robin had been by his constituents, how devoted he had been to the region, how passionately he had defended his seat in June. Now, as the coffin descended, Helen mulled over the words and thought: *I did that. He is being buried with a reputation I sealed. I increased his majority, translating what Robin wanted to say into what voters needed to hear so subtly that even he had not seen the difference.* Bored halfway to true insanity, she had canvassed with him, tentatively at first, until she realized that Nusstead and Sizewell might have been on opposite poles for all the constituents had in common. They knew about Julia Solomon in Sizewell, of course they did, but here on the coast it was not personal. Watching him deliver the acceptance speech that she had written, she recognized the bitterness inside her as her mother's and understood that she must divorce him within the year and strike out at last on her own.

Then Robin had died. He was no longer here to stop her, and he had taken the knowledge of her background to his grave.

Maids in white aprons carried silver platters between gray men. A house like Greenlaw Hall came alive on an afternoon like this; it was made for parties, for the traipsing caterers and pockets of mourners. There was far too much food. Local women had taken it upon themselves to bring plates of sandwiches, sausage rolls, cakes. They were all the same on the doorstep, gently weeping over taut cling-film. They had a uniform look about them, the eager, dumpy Anglo-Saxon church wardens and Sunday School teachers, the Women's Institute members, the Brown Owls and the Akelas. The days since Robin's death had given Helen a profound appreciation for a notion she had previously resisted: England runs on Tory women. Anyone who thought the party cruel, that compassionate conservatism was an oxymoron, overlooked the bustling housewives at its regional roots.

Of course she would rather die than be one of them. She nearly had.

Her gaze halted on Damian and Michiko. Michiko caught her staring and nudged Damian. He didn't bother to hide his reluctance, but over he came.

"I didn't get a chance to introduce Michiko properly earlier," he said. "So. Mum, Michiko. Michi, this is my mum."

Michiko smiled, everything she'd been told about Helen running behind across her face, then it was gone and the mask of sympathy was there.

"I'm so sorry to meet you on such a sad day," she said, taking Helen's hand.

"It's good of you to come."

"Oh God, I couldn't have let him do it on his own," said Michiko. The implication was clear: to be with Helen was to be alone. "Anyway. Damian. Let me refill your glass. I'll drive home. And your plate, actually—you need to eat properly."

Helen had never seen Damian look at her—at anyone—with the tenderness he bestowed on Michiko.

"How's work?" she asked him.

His shoulders dropped an inch. "It's going really well, actually. I've just landed a job as an assistant producer on a documentary series."

Helen was stunned that the endless internships and stalled "projects" had come to fruition. "But Damian, that's marvelous!"

"Well, it feels weird. I mean, I took the call straight after I found out about Dad, so . . . doesn't feel like a celebration. But yeah, it's the obvious next step for the film I really want to make."

"Oh yes? What's it about."

His chin jutted defensively. "It's a history of the English institution. I'll be mainly talking about boarding schools and the damage they do to young children." The barb pierced Helen's skin if not her heart. Boarding school had been at Robin's insistence, but she had never resisted it. "But also prisons. The judiciary. Like, what would replace it, is our society ready, what's the alternative?" Suddenly nervous, Damian put his empty glass to his lips. "Asylums, too."

"Well, you know I think those places were barbaric," said Helen.

"Oh, I think the whole country knows your view on mental healthcare," he said. It was the most direct reference he had ever made to the Cunniffe case. "But you're right. Those places are barbaric." It was clear he wasn't talking about asylums anymore. The air between them seemed to thicken and set.

Michiko returned with a glass of red for Damian and a sparkling water for herself. "You know, if you want a drink, you can have one," said Helen, appealing to Michiko. "I made up a room for you. There's more food than I can ever eat."

"No thanks," said Damian. "It doesn't feel like home with Dad gone."

His eyes, Robin's eyes, suddenly began to shine. He turned tail, Michiko mouthing apologies to Helen as though *she* were his mother. A grief greater than any she would ever feel for Robin engulfed Helen. He knows, she realized. All the trouble she had gone to, all the risks she had taken to ensure that he never found out he was unwanted but of course he knows. He might not know the details, but he knows.

Michael Stein, Party Chairman now, emerged from a throng of adoring matrons, vol-au-vents piled high on a china plate.

"I'm so sorry, Helen," he said, kissing her on each cheek. "He was a great man."

They both knew it was flannel; had Robin been great, his career would have mirrored Michael's. Robin had had greatness thrust upon him, and worn it like an old cardigan.

"It was good of you to come," she said. "You must be terribly busy."

"Better busy than idle," he said. They passed the time talking about the problems in the Gulf, and presently steered the conversation around to the problem of Robin's successor, and the up-and-comers the party had in mind. Someone who'd been a management consultant. A former columnist for the *Daily Telegraph*. "It almost doesn't matter," said Michael. "This is a safe seat for us; the people of Dunwich Heath are conservative with a small c as well as a large one. The only trauma will be in not electing a Greenlaw."

She could not have asked him to feed her a better line. "Then why inflict change upon them?"

Of course Michael's gaze went immediately to Damian and rested there for a few puzzled seconds before he grasped her meaning. He covered his shock by coughing into his napkin.

"There's nothing I don't know about Robin's work," she said. "I could do a better job than he did." Michael turned his frown into a smile with practiced speed but they both knew she had seen it. "You're worried about the fallout from Nazareth Hospital," she said.

He only faltered for a second. "I know you're capable," he said. "It's just the wider public."

"It's not the wider public. It's a dwindling pocket of resistance in one region. Even Adam Solomon doesn't blame me anymore. Look around you. People in the party respect me. People here love me. I'll regret Julia Solomon's death for the rest of my life but I promise you I have learned more from it than any other experience." The regret was true. She lowered her eyelashes and looked up slowly through them. Davina called this move the Princess Diana and Helen had resisted it until now. "An MP with a scandal in their past would hardly be an anomaly."

Michael placed his hand on Helen's shoulder. "Dear Helen," he said. "It's practically a *requirement*."

56

1989

Rain threw sheets of water at the windows. The clouds that had darkened the day had burst at dusk. The radio warned of a county under water. The River Alde had burst its banks at Snape: a month's rainfall was expected in the next two hours.

Helen sat at her dining table in Greenlaw Hall, bricks of money stacked before her. The house had grown dark around her while she had sat there, unfolding, rereading and refolding the letter. It had looked like nothing. At first she had taken the slip of paper for some correspondence left in the car by mistake. Then she had read it and her old fears about her diagnosis going public were immediately dwarfed by this new threat: exposure of the gross abuse of her position. They knew about her past, and worse, what she had done to cover it up.

Her mind had been a whirr ever since, questions breeding like maggots in old meat. J and M. Who were they? Nusstead residents, former employees. That narrowed it down to hundreds. And what records did they have? *Some documents came into our possession . . . they refer to your time as a patient at Nazareth.* How could they possibly have got them? She remembered seeing her admission notes slide into the incinerator bag. Some lurking nurse or porter must have watched her try to dispose of the records, read them and matched Helen Greenlaw to Helen Morris. It was the only explanation she could think of, although it didn't quite make sense. Why wait? Why not expose her in the immediate aftermath of the Cunniffe scandal? Perhaps they were longstanding members of staff who had been waiting until they had burned through their severance pay, or, more shrewdly, waiting for Helen's stock to rise. The letter had been literate, persuasive, cunning. She could not underestimate them. Had Adam Solomon's investigations or, God forbid, Damian's documentary uncovered some parallel paper trail that Helen was unaware of? Damian. If he found out this way, after all this time . . .

Were there other ways to access records? A good tabloid journalist could do anything, but again, where was the source? This set-up had all the hallmarks of a perfect tabloid sting: the loony-bin past, the present-day corruption, the immediate yielding to blackmail that must prove her guilt on both these counts.

They wanted to meet at Nazareth. This calculated cruelty frightened her more than the blackmail.

The pips on the radio told her it was nine o'clock. On a clear dry day, Sizewell to Nusstead was well over an hour's drive. If she was to get to the site in good time she should leave soon.

She looked down to find the notes in her handbag and her car keys in her hand. She had known from the minute she read the letter that she would pay them. And her blackmailers had, in crossing the line into crime, gambled their own freedom. They must have known too.

Even in a storm, driving remained the best antidote to panic, to thought itself. Watching the road through frantic wipers took all her focus. The radio provided constant, if fuzzy, updates. The Blyth had breached its defenses at Walberswick but there was no mention of the River Waveney flooding, nothing about the fenland becoming impassable. Few others were stupid enough to drive in these conditions; rain blurred signposts. Helen missed Nusstead the first time, only realizing her mistake when she reached an unfamiliar level crossing, and she almost drove past the turning for Asylum Road.

She killed the engine long before the headlamps, then looked, as per her instructions, to the light. The white glow came not from the double doors as one might have expected but from the far end, the old women's ward. Rain made a waterfall around the circumference of her umbrella; her feet were soaked within seconds. The light grew brighter and brighter, almost obscuring the two—only two—figures in the doorway.

J and M. M and J. It took a second for her to see how thin they were. It took her another to understand that they were babies.

57

J and M. The sum demanded, the wording of their letter and their access to her notes had led her to believe that they were adults well into middle age or even her own contemporaries. Were they acting on someone else's behalf? They were clearly fathoms out of their depth, all ticks and tells. Helen might have the negotiating skills but would there be any reasoning with these poor, nervous children? She hoped that the sweat breaking out on her face could still be passed off as rainwater. Had she known their ages she never would have matched their sum. How would they explain the money away? Did they even have bank accounts? Jenny had still been paying some of her staff in cash when the hospital closed.

Thinking of Jenny fortified Helen. If she could treat this humiliating rendezvous as a work problem—as a difficult surgery, going against the whip at PMQs, an awkward meeting with a local journalist—then she could do this. If only they were anywhere else, but of course that would be part of their plan. She channeled Davina and pulled on her "meeting face" as she passed into the hateful corridor. The length of it was mercifully in darkness but candlelight pooled on peeling, mouldering walls; it had deteriorated faster than Helen would have thought possible.

"I'll see the paperwork first," she said. Good: her voice sounded brisk and authoritative. It hid what was happening on the inside:

standing up had suddenly become very complicated, her head twice as heavy as usual.

"Not until I've seen the cash." He was like a bad actor in a police serial, making a show of examining the money, as if there were nothing he would love more than to be able to accuse her of counterfeiting.

"I should like to see my records before the exchange is made."

She knew they were the real thing before they were in her hands; she found herself fondling a remembered dog-ear in the top right-hand corner of the front page. It was too dark to see whether the stains on the pages were due to age or something worse. Her mind spooled rapidly, dizzyingly back. The words were still legible: *she is very insane*. She seized upon one thing: there was only half a story here. There was no mention of an illegal abortion. She hadn't imagined destroying those pages.

"Who gave you this?" Voices, like muscles, have memories, and Helen's was well trained. Her scream, filtered through years of media training, came out in words and with a Parliamentarian evenness.

The boy tilted his chin in pride. "No one. We done it with our . . . investigative powers. It was left behind, up in the records room. That's what happens when you do things by halves. Well, it's not the *worst* thing, obviously."

Helen thought back six years. The bang on the door—her blood skipped even to recall it—and the fumble of papers. She must have switched over the papers in her panic. Stupid, stupid woman. What then had she burned? She had pardoned Pauline, whose reputation was worth nothing. Celeste, too.

"All there in black and white, in't it?" said the boy. "Proof of what you are. What you *done*."

He still hadn't mentioned the botched abortion, and anyway, would kids this age judge her for that? What he had was presumably tantamount to proof of her "illness." It would be good enough for the tabloids. And the existence of these would uncover her interference. A journalist would demand to know their sources. Jenny Bishop would not have forgotten the time Helen spent alone in her archives. They were more incriminating than this boy knew.

"Yes," she said. "I can't contradict you there." It was true. Once something was committed officially to paper it became fact, whether it were true or not.

"How do I know you haven't made copies?" She asked merely to test their guile; of course there would be copies.

"You'll just have to trust us." The quiver in the girl's voice told Helen that she *wanted* to be telling the truth. When Helen handed her the money, she divided it into two bundles. It was an unconscious gesture but Helen understood: this front is not as united as the boy thinks it is.

"You won't hear from us again," said the girl. Again, she seemed sincere, but Helen knew that of course they would come after her again. That was how blackmail worked. You paid up, you gave in. If only something would give her leverage against them. She could afford it, but that was hardly the point. For now, she would concentrate on destroying the—

A sudden blast of wind almost knocked her off her feet. The bang of the door, metal on old stone, was loud as gunfire. A thunderclap of falling plaster and brickwork had them all leaping deeper into the corridor, away from the billowing dust.

"*Jesse!*" screamed the girl.

J for Jesse. The look he gave the girl turned Helen's hot sweat cold. Her tormentors talked in panicked whispers, discussing doomed exit strategies. The rubble was waist-high and the ceiling bowed.

"We'll have to leave through the front," Jesse said.

He was right; their only way out was at the other end of the half-mile corridor.

All Helen had to do was survive a three-minute walk in a straight line. How hard could it be? One foot in front of the other. Think not about the catacombs of memory but focus forward, on her own little pen torch and its feeble beam. Think not about swinging bare feet but the cold, dirty water in one's own shoes.

She could not do it.

She could not pass the room where Pauline had died. Each step was progressively harder, as though the act of treading doubled the weight of her shoes. She stopped two yards in front of the laundry door. She would have to beg them, there was nothing else for it. She would have to beg them, she would have to tell them and if she showed them weakness they might leap on it, decide to leave her here to teach her a lesson, or for fun. Helen's pulse kicked against the skin of her neck. Time was folding in on itself, she was nineteen again, running past the laundry door. I was mad to come here, she thought. Nazareth has done for me at last.

The young people had stopped too, but not because they had noticed her fear. There was a deep puddle across the laundry threshold. Well, that was that. They'd have to turn back and clear the rubble, even if they had to do it brick by brick. As if sensing her hope, the hospital threw another chunk of masonry onto the floor. It was this or nothing.

A pale hand was extended toward her. Jesse couldn't look her in the eye but he could do this for her. Taking his hand meant that she could walk past the laundry with her eyes closed, trusting him to guide her through the shallowest water. This clumsy, instinctive chivalry went straight to Helen's heart. She screwed her eyes tight, tortured by the insane notion that power would suddenly be restored to the old building and those fluorescent lights would buzz and blink on and Pauline would still be there, old bones hanging grotesquely, impossibly, from the pipe. Helen's face was under control but her hands were liquid with sweat. Ashamed of her body's betrayal of her fear, she wrestled her hand away from Jesse's as soon as she could and wiped her palm on her slacks. He saw it and misunderstood, thought she was wiping traces of him away.

After that, they let her trail two paces behind them and she was pathetically grateful for the chance to let her face fall into horrified repose. The darkness exerted an almost barometric pressure behind her. Their torches bobbed as they splashed toward the atrium and their only exit. The movement played tricks on one's perception, making it appear that there was a separate source of light at the end of the corridor.

58

They were brothers. It was obvious in their faces, the younger man's a refined, more handsome version of the bashed-about elder's.

"Started up quite a treasure hunt," he said, fanning out blurry photocopies. It was clear from the couple's wild expressions that they had known about these copies—made them, probably—but not known they were in this man's hands. "An audience with the Right Honorable Helen Greenlaw. Our old man would've killed for a face-to-face with you in the old days, but you didn't want to know, did you?" Helen did not rise to his bait, recognizing a truer danger here. This man was closer to her expected blackmailer.

"This is *ours*. Mine and—hers," said Jesse, still protective of the girl's name. When he reached for the bag, Helen found her hands following his, her fumbling for the papers telling the older brother all he needed to know.

"Oh no you don't," he said, snatching the bag away. "I in't got backup for these yet."

Helen's arms dropped limply to her sides. She tried to keep her face still as her mind whirred. The good: all the evidence against her was in this room. The bad: how could she possibly overcome three angry young people to destroy it?

The decision was taken out of her hands as the man disappeared through the clocktower door, followed by Jesse and M.

For the second time Helen Greenlaw's world shrank to the need to get her hands on her own medical records, whatever the cost. She gave in to the madness she had come here to deny as she chased the others through the door of the clocktower. Led by her own faltering torchlight, she slipped past them up the treacherous stairs. Inside, a secondary rainfall dripped from the patchy ceiling. Her foot dislodged some unseen debris into the stairwell, and the answering splosh suggested deep floodwater in the basement. Jesse and M were hot on her heels, their bouncing head torches creating a horrible effect, like blinking in reverse, split-second flashes of illumination in the murky dark.

As Helen climbed, she thought of the future in ten-second intervals, each little unit simply to be survived. Ten to get her breath back. Ten to make it through the tangle of limbs for the bag. She counted in her head with such precision even her heart rate seemed to assume a metronome tick. Ten to pry the bag from his hands and another ten to extricate herself. Ten seconds to clear each landing. And then what? Stone walls, a locked door, an impassable corridor.

They caught up with her on the balcony: the older man disappeared and then returned, angrier than ever but the bag still over his shoulder, close enough for Helen to reach out and touch. Her fingers twitched, then all of them moved as if obeying a starting pistol. In the push and pull, the swerving torchlight, Helen barely knew which way was up. Elbows, knees, leather and skin. She was shoved, by whose hands she could not tell, against the wall, setting her vertebrae on fire. A circle of light swooped to the floor, spotlit the notes in the toolbag. Helen plunged back into the slamming bodies, hand outstretched toward the bag, ready to grab and destroy. Her muscles were expecting pressure but the tension had suddenly gone, as though a string somewhere had been cut.

It did not take ten seconds. It took perhaps three from the crack of the balustrades to the final impact.

59

2018

"Ah, Helen!" Helen Greenlaw, Baroness Greenlaw of Sizewell, emerged from the Peers' Library to find Andrew Boswell, the Labor Party whip, waiting in the corridor. Beige teeth, beige hair: she couldn't stand the man at the best of times and had never wanted to see him less than she did now. "You weren't escaping the vote, were you?"

Her usual steadying deep breath did not come easily. Guilt had grown in Helen like a body part, a cord of gristle around the lungs, on the night of Clay Brame's death and it flexed now, stealing the depth from her breath.

"I'm giving someone tea," she replied. "I'll be in the Chamber for the vote." She could barely remember what they were voting on. Something to do with broadband in rural areas. Her thoughts were only of her guest. M. M for Marianne, not Michelle.

Jesse Brame—he had been easy to find, with a name like that, in a town that size—had married a Michelle shortly after his brother's funeral. She had died of sepsis a few months shy of her twenty-eighth birthday and then the secret was only split two ways. J kept his silence. The chokehold of Helen's guilt never loosened, but the fear, that bloodied thread that led back to that night, had frayed away almost to nothing. Until Marianne Thackeray's email had shattered her foolish assumption.

"I can always rely on you." Boswell's voice was pure vinegar. Helen had a reputation for voting with her conscience rather than the party line; the same conscience that had led her to cross the floor from Conservative to Labor. Neither side trusted her now. "We're few on the ground today. Hardly an emotive subject. Not that that's ever bothered you. We can always trust you to leave sentimentality out of it."

There it was again. That steel that a woman needed to get to the top was the very thing they were still trying to turn against her. Nothing had changed in sixty years.

"Thank you, Andrew." She nodded along the corridor. "I had better collect my guest."

Helen's even pace as she approached the Peers' Entrance was at odds with the darting of her thoughts. She had invited the girl who had the power to ruin her reputation to the very place where that reputation was cemented, because one couldn't make a scene here. Of course, she must think of her as a woman. Helen found that she was half expecting the underweight teenage girl in leathers instead of a distinguished History of Art lecturer. Helen stepped into the cloakroom and there she was. Marianne Thackeray, née Smy, smoothing down her dress and blinking nervously into the dusty sunlight. She wore middle age well, better than most people of her background. She'd kept her figure, more or less, and was glossy and blow-dried, like some old peer's third wife. She couldn't see Jesse having made the same climb. Were they still in touch? Whatever Marianne's important news, it must concern him, and it would doubtless be about money.

Rage loosened now inside her, a violent uncoiling of the tightly wound fury at the children whose sordid, stupid little scheme had ended in the loss of a man's life. Her life was littered with poor judgments made in good faith. The only time she had betrayed her principles was the rainy night she had driven to Nazareth, and that had been their doing. How dare they resurrect it now, so late in Helen's career, so late in her life?

"Dr. Thackeray." She couldn't bring herself to shake Marianne's hand. "Kind of you to come at such short notice." Helen fast-walked and small-talked her guest through the gilded corridors.

"I would never have recognized you," she said when they were seated. Marianne met her eyes and the ground fell away. Little black dots on her tear ducts told of mascara applied, cried off and reapplied, exposing the dark, desperate truth of their shared situation. Rage was abruptly, astonishingly, replaced by relief. The potential for release was closer than it had ever been. To share what had happened, would it strip the act of its power? Marianne, she wanted to say, as the silver cruet set was placed directly in the center of the white tablecloth, Marianne, you were *there,* you know, you understand what it felt like and what it has been like. She wanted to ask Marianne where she carried her shame, whether she too wore it like a cincture around her heart and lungs. Perhaps her locus of guilt was a stomach that pumped acid, or a headache that came on when it rained. She, too, must stagger under the weight of concealing a death. She knew about Helen's past and the relief of not pretending was so powerful that she almost didn't care if Marianne used it against her.

That thought checked Helen; of course she cared. She breathed in deeply and had grown businesslike by the end of the exhalation: "I suppose you're here for money."

Marianne withdrew an inch. As she protested, Helen noticed the Cartier watch on her wrist. She wore her gold like armor.

Marianne's defensiveness let Helen know that her estimation of her was still low. For all that she had taken a risk in contacting Helen, Marianne could not yield an inch of vulnerability. She clearly still believed in the sociopath on paper. And why wouldn't she? Nothing Helen had done in the intervening years would have changed Marianne's mind. The press caricatures—she had appeared in *The Times* as a robot in a wrap dress—had hardly softened her image.

What could she say to reassure the girl? They had skirted around the reason they were here but perhaps naming their complicity, their shared vulnerability, would show Marianne that Helen was—not on her side, for she could never forget the position they had put her in, but equally keen to stop this before it snowballed further. She would remind the girl how scant the evidence against them was, how safe they were if only they did nothing to upset it. She leaned in close to Marianne and said, "Detection has moved on, of course. In the unlikely event that anyone talks, it is as well for us that the body was cremated."

The fear in Marianne's eyes was momentarily replaced by something that cut deeper: distaste. Whatever she said, Marianne would take as confirmation of the doctors' verdict. The disappointment was more painful than Helen had anticipated. Marianne only thawed when Helen responded to the question, "What are you going to do?" with the assurance that she would pay Jesse off. Marianne sagged with relief. Of course, thought Helen, in the moment it took for Marianne to realign herself; that is all she came here to know. She is not interested in anything approaching support. We are too far gone for that. But what was this? Marianne was shifting, leaning forward as though she had something important to say. There was an opening in her face, a softening of the jaw. Helen did not dare imagine what form an alliance would take, but gripped the edge of her chair with bleached knuckles.

Marianne mentioned a child.

"Honor—my daughter—she has . . . look, I don't like the word disorder and all the judgment that comes with it, but just, she's ill and incredibly vulnerable." Unexpectedly, Marianne produced her mobile phone and showed Helen a picture of a young woman with pale pink hair and huge eyes that didn't—couldn't—quite meet the camera. Helen recognized the fragility instantly. That was Susan's expression, it was Celeste's. It was the kind of pain one needed to witness to believe it existed. It was the loudest echo of Pauline yet. "She's exactly the sort of person you say you care about. She's an extraordinary person, she lives life so deeply but everything hurts her, it's like—she's got splinters in all of her fingertips and glass in her feet. If this comes out, even by accident, if the police come for me and she finds out—she's been in hospital before, she's tried to . . ." Helen did not need to hear any more. All the details she needed were drips on a laundry-room floor. Something began in her, a rising pressure inevitable and unwanted as vomiting but centered on her head, in the sockets of her eyes. Surreptitiously she checked her reflection in her knife and was relieved to see her features were composed.

"It took a lot, you know, for me to come here today," Marianne was saying. "But I would do anything to protect Honor from this. As a mother, you know what that's like."

The pressure fanned out through Helen's sinuses. She didn't know. She knew how to be strong for her child's sake but it struck her now that to allow oneself to be weak out of love was beyond her experience, beyond her ability. Marianne Thackeray had overcome a wretched start to make a stable life for an unstable young woman. She had pulled her daughter close for protection where she, Helen, had pushed Damian away. What must it be like to love a child that way? The feeling intensified, strong enough now to be recognized despite its sixty-year absence. A squeeze in the throat, a heat in the nose, tiny muscles in the eyes prickling back into life.

The division bell was due to ring any minute. Why didn't it ring, why didn't the blasted thing give her an excuse to cut this meeting short? Marianne was trying to apologize now, appealing to Helen on the circumstances of her childhood. She had been hungry, she said, she had been cold. Helen felt her defenses falling.

The bell rang at last. Helen rose and Marianne followed. Say something, she screamed to herself, say anything that lets this woman know that you are on her side and you will work together to keep this secret. If you can let go in front of anyone in the world, surely it's her?

"Is it going to be all right?" said Marianne. Her mouth twisted, desperate for reassurance. But response was impossible; Helen knew that anything beyond stock phrases was beyond her.

"Thank you for your time, Dr. Thackeray." She recruited every muscle in her body to support her tear ducts.

When the bell rang for the second time, Helen ignored it. She could no more go into the Chamber than abseil down Big Ben. She staggered to the wood-and-chintz bathroom, slid the bolt behind her. In the cubicle the tears came, great ugly gulps masked by the clank and whoosh of the old plumbing and the rumble of the engineering work outside. She collapsed onto the seat, spine grinding against the cistern pipe. She cried for Marianne, who didn't want this mess any more than she did. She cried for Julia Solomon, for Adam and their son. She cried for Pauline, for Norma. Susan, Celeste. Into this parade of faces suddenly came Eugenie, head on one side, smoothing down Helen's hair and asking if the man had forced her into it. Helen gagged, heaved herself over the bowl as though she could throw up the memory, but there were only more tears, soaking her collar.

It was not only that she envied Marianne's capacity to love her child. It was Honor she envied too, despite her illness; the difficult, disappointing daughter, who was so clearly loved by her mother.

60

Helen usually relished Saturdays. There was enough correspondence and reading to keep her occupied, and usually someone to see in the afternoon or evening. Today, though, she had canceled her evening concert. If her past was catching up with her then so, finally, was her age. The past ten days' events seemed to have accelerated the body's great betrayal. Marianne's email had begun it. The encounter with Jesse on Parliament Square had propelled her into her ninth decade. She had become a little old lady scared to go anywhere on her own, inventing cataracts just so that she would have Marianne's company. In fact, she could barely remember a lonelier moment than when the salesgirl had mistaken Helen for Marianne's mother, and just for a second Marianne had smiled, not the forced upturn of her mouth Helen had come to expect but a softening that threw commas around her eyes as well as her lips and made an attractive woman beautiful. It had lasted less than a second, replaced by a hardening of the jaw that was all the worse for what had preceded it.

Helen's joints were hot and dry. She walked with a new slowness. The mirror showed the beginnings of a dowager's hump. Now, in her little flat, she trailed from room to room, straightening perfectly hung pictures and dusting clean shelves. How were they spending their weekends? Jesse would be frittering the money in

Nusstead, while Marianne would perhaps go shopping or have lunch with friends. Helen tried to think about something else, failed, and let out a little growl of frustration. Was this her life now? Worrying about where they were, what they were doing, where the next threat was coming from now that the thirty-year amnesty had expired? The texts from Marianne suggested that she was trying to talk him out of whatever act of colossal stupidity was next on his agenda.

She could not concentrate on the article she was supposed to be writing, 800 words for *Saga* magazine on the joy of computer literacy for the over-seventies. Being able to use the internet had brought little joy in the last few days. Out of curiosity, unable to forget Marianne's impassioned plea for her daughter's protection, she had typed the name Honor Thackeray into Google and lost herself for hours on Instagram, scrolling until the movement of the screen gave her vertigo. She found herself checking in every day to see how the girl was doing. The artwork wasn't Helen's idea of accomplished but she was drawn to the narrative of mental fragility explicit in the hashtags and implicit in the images themselves, in the weight suddenly lost and gained, in the long sleeves, and in the patterns of posting: months of nothing then dozens a day. Honor responded with grace to her occasional critics and had a network of fellow sufferers. God, if this had been available in my day, thought Helen, then realized she was thinking in terms of having been a true patient.

Fresh air; that would free her from her whirlpooling thoughts.

She tied a scarf around her hair, heard her knees crunch just like Eugenie's used to as she bent to fasten her hateful Velcro shoes, and stepped into the cobbled silence of the mews. These unambitious afternoon walks had long replaced her daily constitutionals but were just as necessary. Her mind cleared with every step as she walked through St. George's Square, past her old house and across the road to the bare spiky shrubbery and stone embankment of Pimlico Gardens. The tide was as low as it ever got, the river brown sludge under a colorless sky. On the south bank, luxury flats sprouted from the wasteland of Nine Elms. To her left, Vauxhall Bridge spanned the river in five broad arches; a barge dragged shipping containers underneath the central curve. Somewhere over that bridge, Honor Thackeray was making her art, taking her selfies and trying to stay alive.

Helen woke at five on Sunday morning, finished the article by half past seven and after the ten o'clock service at St. John's Smith Square lay back on the sofa to rest her eyes for ten minutes. Two hours later, her mobile phone broke into her sleep. She answered before her eyes were fully open but Marianne's voice was a shot of caffeine, pulling Helen up to sitting.

"I'm sorry to call like this but I don't know anyone else who can get to her in time." Marianne's voice was uneven, the words coming in gasps. "She's just around the corner from you, she's five minutes in a car."

Honor. She'd done something to herself. Helen's blood raced. She couldn't make out Marianne's next words through the distortion on the line.

"You'll have to be clearer," said Helen. In the background an engine revved. Marianne must be on speakerphone inside a car. She didn't get the chance to tell Marianne to pull over: the words were coming too fast for that, tumbling over each other like water.

"Jesse just rang, he's on a train to her flat, he's going to tell her everything. She lives on top of the newsagent on Kennington Lane, opposite the Royal Vauxhall Tavern." Honor's phone, said Marianne, was switched off, Jesse was almost on the doorstep and there was no one in London closer than Helen. Helen realized she'd been holding her breath, trying to make sense of what Marianne was saying. She let out a nervous sigh.

"Is he a *physical* threat to her?"

If violence was threatened then the first thing to do was call the police and hang the risk, but Marianne said no; his words were the weapons. Helen needed to calm Marianne down, find out what she needed, what she expected of her.

"Marianne, I'm sure that your daughter won't tell the police, or the press."

It backfired. Marianne told her about Honor's attempt to take her own life as if it was news. Even without Marianne's clumsy circling around the subject in the House, Helen would have understood that about the girl the first time she'd seen her photograph. She couldn't find an answer. Practicality, that was the way to deal with a crisis. Reflect Marianne's "facts" back at her so she might see the absurdity of what she was asking and then together they could arrive at a workable solution.

"Why should your daughter trust me? And what if he's already there? I am eighty years old. How do you expect me to overpower an angry man thirty years my junior?"

"I don't know, Helen. Just do *something*. If you won't do it for Honor, do it for yourself. Once he tells one person, what's to stop them telling the world?"

Helen forgot her sympathy for a second. "Marianne. This resurrection of the unpleasantness is *not my fault*. You brought this on yourselves. You may keep it to your own little tangled scene. I do not deserve this." But neither did Honor, and neither, really, did Marianne. She wanted to bury the past just as much as Helen did. "I'm sorry, I'm sorry. I know she doesn't know me and I'm limited in what I can actually do, but of course I'll help, within my means."

Only at the end of her speech did Helen realize she was talking into dead air. She held her phone at arm's length; her signal was strong. Marianne had driven into one of those reception black spots that Suffolk was full of. She would call back any minute.

61

Helen stood in her sitting room, one hand on the piano, the other gripping her phone. She had tried Marianne twice. It kept ringing out but some phones did that when the person was on another call. Marianne might have dropped their call to pick up one from Honor, or even Jesse. The whole thing might have blown over already. Perhaps one of Marianne's other friends had got in touch, and was even now on the way to knock on Honor's door and take her out for lunch. A godmother, perhaps, or a colleague. Someone Honor knew, and trusted. Someone younger than Helen and with no investment in this horror. Two, three, four minutes passed. She stared unseeing at the ersatz Constable landscape above the mantelpiece. Surely Marianne would call back either way?

She made a cup of tea to force down the knot of worry in her throat. Five minutes passed. Six, seven. Her mind drew a map of London, the modern kind one found on a screen. On it, Jesse Brame was a little blue dot gliding west across the city. Marianne had not been specific about his location but had insisted that time was of the essence. Helen refreshed her phone. Just one look at Honor's Instagram, to gauge the girl's whereabouts.

It was deactivated: user not found. It was as though Honor herself had been deleted. A foretaste of the worst-case scenario; the loss to the world if Marianne was right. Self-destruction might be alien to Helen's nature but she had seen it happen up too close to ignore. She tried Marianne again, telling herself that if she failed to answer this time, she would go to Honor and—do what? What, actually, had Marianne been asking of her apart from get there, be there, stop him? Wrestle Jesse to the ground? As for talking him out of it, she would be the last person to calm him down. She would do what she could, within the bonds of her frailty and her unfamiliarity.

Decision made, Helen moved with utter calm. She rinsed her teacup and set it on the draining board. The car key was in her hand, she was in the garage, she was easing her little car over the cobbles. She was turning left onto Grosvenor Road, driving parallel with the Thames, she was flicking the indicator right and waiting to turn onto Vauxhall Bridge Road, she was soaring over the bridge and across the rough silk of the river. She saw herself as another little blue dot, set to converge with Jesse or, if she could just beat this traffic light—yes!—perhaps arriving before him.

She circled Vauxhall Cross, the great concrete crab of its bus station, past the Starbucks and the little Sainsbury's, before she passed under the railway arches into Kennington Lane. She would leave the car on the curb or at the bus stop, she who had never even parked on a single yellow line before. She pulled up outside Honor's flat, two flights up from a newsagent. Relief came first: Honor was there, violet hair today, leaning out of the second-story window with some sort of bag tight between her hands and smiling across the street. Helen followed the girl's gaze. Jesse Brame, in leather again, approached from the Tube station. Honor's face was open, happy, trusting: if he got up there, he would shut that smile down, maybe forever. Marianne hadn't mentioned that they knew each other. All the more callous of Jesse to exploit their relationship to spite Marianne. His right foot was on the pedestrian crossing. Helen pulled down the sun visor so he wouldn't recognize her but he wasn't watching the car, he was staring up at Honor's window. Was it the sun that screwed his face into a frown or was it something more?

She put her foot to the floor.

Jesse Brame hit Helen Greenlaw's windscreen with such force that it seemed as though he had thrown himself at the car, that he was the moving object and she the point of impact, rather than the other way around.

the larches
2018

62

They could have named this place after any number of beautiful trees. Outside my window—the usual window, my old window—there's a gorgeous oak, hundreds of years old. Its generous branches are naked and acorns pile up at the base of its trunk. But no. They went for larches, the ugliest trees you can think of. Larches are the only deciduous fir tree and the one to the left of the oak has shed its needles. It looks cheap and scrubby, like a giant twig stuck in the ground. Every day my hatred of it grows. I am possibly projecting.

Dad's gone to the lounge to get me a proper coffee, decaf for me obviously although actually I have been feeling weirdly calm since what Dad is calling *the accidents* and the doctors are calling *the incidents* and the Brames are calling *the conspiracy* and the police are calling *the coincidence* but with heavy, threatening irony.

Everyone is concerned about how calm I have been (unless I'm talking about the fucking tree). You'd expect, given my form, for me to be giving it the full-on Bedlam lunatic by now, gnashing my teeth and rending my garments. I feel—actually, numb is a better word than calm. It's as though I've been drained of all feeling. I don't know if it's the need to keep things smoothed over for Dad or the sheer volume of what I've had to take in or selective serotonin reuptake inhibitors.

This is my first close encounter with death and I have not begun to absorb it. My mind is looking after itself in its own weird little way. I have always thought of my brain as a 3D labyrinth, ideas hurtling dangerously along the coiled neural pathways. Now it is as though safety mechanisms, almost like fire doors along a corridor, have been introduced, stopping the truth in its tracks until I am well enough to process it. The result is like being suspended in some kind of protective gel. And yet I am not psychotic: it has the quality of a lucid dream. I know what's coming for me when the fire doors are inevitably breached and it's going to make my life so far seem like a holiday camp.

Dad elbows his way into the room, a mug in each hand. "Full-fat milk, feed you up." His voice is hoarse. He hasn't cried in front of me and I'm grateful. I mean I am literally the last person on earth who would judge him for that, you should see the size of some of the men I've seen cry in this place, but he knows it's not the same and maybe that would be the thing that tipped me over the edge, seeing him break down. He has always been there for me but in the crises it's always really been just me and Mum, and clearly he feels he has to step into her shoes now.

"Thanks, Dad." He has this new habit of nodding his head and shaking it at the same time.

There's a fleecy blanket over the back of the sofa. Dad tucks it over my knees even though the heating is up so high that it makes waves in front of the picture window. The days have started to blur in a similar way. You always lose your grip on the calendar within minutes of setting foot in this place but because this time the trauma was external rather than something my brain generated it feels different: contained, somehow, the interval between tragedy and funeral weirdly like the week between Christmas and New Year.

"What time are the police coming again?" I ask Dad. The detectives Costello and Greene (which sounds to me like a luxury paint shop on Upper Street) ask me the same questions over and over. The forensic focus is on those last few seconds. Did Jesse definitely look before he crossed the road? Did he seem to recognize who was driving the car? What was the traffic like? It's like if they ask me often enough I'll suddenly be able to come up with a diagram or a photograph that tells them whatever it is they want to know.

Dad has never once asked me what they've said. I mean I'm not supposed to tell anyone anyway, but I think this goes beyond his natural inclination to do things by the book. He's giving me a break, after their interrogation. And I suspect that he plain and simple can't bear to know. Whatever his reasons, I'm grateful for that, too.

"As soon as morning therapy is over," he says. More waiting. I like it. When you're waiting you don't have to do anything. Dad hates it. When his phone rings, he tries to hide his relief behind a grimace of apology. "It's Neil, from Braxtons."

He's found a horrible shark of an estate agent—pink tie, sniffs a lot, chews gum on the phone, blatant coke habit—so he shouldn't make too much of a loss on the flat in Park Royal bloody sodding Manor. It's not about the money: he wants rid of it so much, he'd probably give it away for free. Under the oak, a therapist is leading two patients in a tai chi session, all three of them graceless in Puffa jackets and boots. In the corridor, I can hear Dad talking in his "work voice." Their conversation's over before I've got past the foam on my latte.

"Got a buyer," he says. "Cash. It could all be done in a month. Christ, I wish I'd never bought the bloody place. The Curse of Nazareth, indeed."

"Oh, Dad. You couldn't have known." He can't answer, because that would open up a conversation neither of us are ready for. I didn't realize their boring, stable marriage was so complicated, so interesting. Neither, it's clear, did he. Whatever was going on between Mum and Jesse, whatever the true nature of their connection with Helen Greenlaw, there was a huge dark core to her that we never guessed at. His heart is broken in ways that go beyond mere grief. Dad should have been Mum's partner and confidant, yet it looks like that role went to Jesse, and always had done. They were tied together in a knot that we, her mere family, will never be able to unpick.

63

Kids don't knock for each other these days. That's what Nanna always used to say when she came to stay with us in Noel Road, with a shake of her head at the pity of it all. As if we were going to kick a ball in the carbon monoxide, between double-parked cars and motorbike couriers cutting through the 20-mile-an-hour zone at 40 on their way through to Upper Street. She was right, though. We text each other and we arrange and we rearrange and more often than not we cancel but the excitement of a knock on the door, of someone unexpected asking you out to play in the street, was lost I guess with the advent of the mobile phone. I suppose it was that spontaneity I was trying to reclaim by turning my phone off, as much as creating the headspace to work without the constant distraction. Of course most of the time when the buzzer went it was an Amazon delivery for one of the neighbors, but word was already starting to get round that if my friends wanted me they could come and see me, they were forced to come and find me and I loved that. Nobody talks about Vauxhall as a place to live but once everyone found out how central it was and how often they'd passed through it—or, more likely, under it—without knowing, they were into it. I had more visitors in the ten days after I turned off my phone than I'd had in the preceding six months. So much for life off the grid calming me down. My mood started climbing. Does good work produce euphoria or vice versa? I still don't know, but that week energy and possibility soared inside me, powering me on without the need for food or sleep. Even visiting Nanna in hospital couldn't put a dent in it. I felt freer than I had in years.

I wasn't stupid. My open door policy had conditions. Rule Number One was obvious. Always check who it is. The buzzer works but the little camera thing is broken, and if you want to see who's on the pavement you have to lean out of the window. Rule Number Two, equally self-evident: don't let strange men into your house. Jesse Brame, though. He was a stranger and he wasn't. I'd spent the best part of a year thinking he was my father, for fuck's sake, and Mum and Colette had known him their whole lives. When I saw his upturned face two stories below I recognized him at once.

"Jesse?" This is interesting, I remember thinking: this has livened up a Sunday afternoon.

"You remember me?" He seemed surprised.

"Of course I do." I buzzed him in, glad of the distraction. I was four incommunicado hours into trying to tattoo a bolt of vegan leather, trying to make the ink sink in the way it does on the real thing, but nothing cuts like skin and the needle had been buzzing in my hand for so long that my whole arm was starting to tingle. Maybe I should have called Mum first but one of the things about mania is that it blinds you to all the little signals you would recognize in a more stable state, makes you plunge gleefully into situations you ought to flee. Plus, she was being a nightmare about the whole offline thing, and I was furious that she'd started sending her friends to check up on me. Probably if I turned my phone on, there would be half a dozen messages telling me to tidy up, put the kettle on. I'd been pinballing between guilt and defensiveness over this. I know she doesn't mean to smother and God knows I've given her enough cause to worry over the years but there had come a point where my privacy, my mental health, was more important than her peace of mind. I could hear it now: Jesse letting slip he was up in town to see a friend or a show or whatever and Mum pouncing: "I don't suppose, Jesse, while you're there, you could look in on Honor for me . . ."

There are only forty steps up to my flat and it was too much of a tip for me to get it into any kind of order, but I did make a space on the sofa, hastily load the dishwasher and wipe down the work surfaces. The kettle was halfway to boiling by the time Jesse got to the top of the stairs.

"Long time no see!" I said, when he swished through the beaded curtain. He could not be less like my dad and it's hard to believe there are only six years between them. Put bluntly, Jesse's *fit,* for an old bloke. Not that there was an atmosphere or anything between us, or if there was, it was an edginess, an arrangement of Jesse's features I've seen on other faces when I'm off on one, the face of the Not OK. I'd always had him down as a sad rocker throwback but basically salt-of-the-earth type. I gestured to the piles of skin and the needles laid out in descending order of size. "I'm not a serial killer! It's for a project. Cup of tea?"

"Yeah, be nice." He stepped over a pile of rags. It was only at close range that I caught the current of his breath, the sweet fresh beery smell undercut by something stale. He was making a weird shape with his mouth, like he was blowing out smoke rings. Even forty stairs do that to some people. I didn't want someone to have a heart attack on me.

"Have a seat." I nodded at the space I'd cleared on the sofa. "What are you doing in London, anyway?"

Jesse couldn't hear me under the rumble of the kettle. "Nice little place you've got here. Handy for the Tube, I suppose." Now I knew he'd been drinking, I heard the slur in his voice. While I waited for the teabags to brew, I watched his reflection in the kettle. He was muttering to himself as though rehearsing something. I'd seen this before, too, first time I was in the Larches: a bloke who cleared his throat as if for a big speech six or seven times a minute but never said a word. He drove me nuts. Well, more nuts. A little cold trickle of fear found its way into my veins. Even though it was just gone two o'clock, I went to text Mum, ask her why she'd sent him here, but I'd let the battery run down again and even after I plugged the phone in to charge, the little red icon told me it would be five minutes until it would be ready to use.

"Are you all right, Jesse?" I set the cup in front of him and his face fell.

"Have you got any tins in?"

"I'm sorry. I try not to keep booze in the house. There's an off-license downstairs?"

He nodded. "You're a good girl. You're so like your mum when she was your age. There's nothing of your dad in you. I mean, you do know your dad's your dad, don't you? You got over all that bollocks about DNA."

I smiled at the wall, silently raging that Mum had breached my privacy but glad that I didn't have to come out to him. "I did. We all got tested." I don't add that I did it again, privately and in secret, before I was convinced. I can't remember how many times. Ten? Twenty? I spent the best part of a grand on it, I do know that. I still don't know how Mum explained that credit card bill away to Dad.

"Your mum, she never done the dirty on your dad. Whatever her faults, she's been a good wife. Marianne Smy." His whole face twisted when he said her name but he couldn't sustain the attack in his voice as far as the third syllable and by the time he got to Smy it had broken. "I've always been so in love with her. I know she went off and made a life but everyone else—it was like—I've had a lot of women over the years but they were all leading up to her and then they were all leading away from her and this stupid fucking part of me always thought that somehow I'd have her again one day."

Tact is another casualty of mania. "Jesse, this is so not appropriate."

"No, it is. It is. It's got to be you. That's what I come here to tell you, it's all linked up." He wasn't making sense, but I wasn't really looking for it. He took a deep breath. "Me and your mum. When we were your age. No. When we were younger than you, but old enough, really, we done something really stupid and I came here because—I think it's time you knew."

My condition is not officially rapid-cycling but states can flip in a heartbeat. I was poised at the crest of the rollercoaster, the top of the death slide, my heart beating fast now for all the wrong reasons. I have this habit of scrabbling away from things I don't want to hear. I found myself pressing my back into the chair and scraping it across the floor.

"What do you mean, something stupid?" The possibilities went sailing past me: teenage pregnancy, drugs, bit of shoplifting? Mum was so studious, so straight, all scholarships and textbooks as a teenager by all accounts. I couldn't imagine her doing anything *like* the shit I'd put her through. But I believed Jesse. Why would he make it up? Also, you only had to look at him.

There was a sense of foreboding, a hammer striking a low note against my skull. My mother, who had always placed such a premium on candor, had lied to me. She had done something she didn't want me to know, the foundation stone of my life was about to crumble. Through family therapy we'd been trying to work out what came first, my illness or my mother's equally pathological desire to offer a world that is perfect and protective. Our level of entanglement is something most children outgrow by their teens but it is what it is, our dynamic, our imprint, our schema. My stability is tied up in my mother's; when she wavers, I collapse. My hand went to my arm as it sometimes does for comfort, tracing the crosshatching at the crease of my elbow, the raised white cat's cradle of years-old scarring and the pale lilac cross that's fading too slowly. It wasn't a tactic but it worked like one. Jesse seemed to sober up instantly. To stop him staring at my arms I pulled my sleeves down over my wrists. His eyes skittered in micro-movements like he was reading something invisible written on the jersey stretched over the heel of my hand and caught under my fingertips.

"It doesn't matter. You don't deserve this, you in't done noth-

ing. This is between me and Marianne, I dunno what I was thinking coming here." He stood up, peered around my little flat as
though he'd just unexpectedly been teleported there. "I can't even
get this right. Oh, Jesus, how has my life come to this?" When Jesse
started to cry, I found that I'd been expecting it. I know a breakdown when I see one. In the kitchenette behind me, my phone
flashed into life, but I knew the importance of what Dr. Adil calls
full-body listening when someone is trying to unburden. You take
your attention away at the wrong moment, you even mistime your
blinks, and the trust is gone. I couldn't risk him stopping. There
was, I realized, only one thing worse than hearing what my mother
had done that was so bad Jesse Brame felt the need to get tanked
up and doorstep me, and that was not hearing it. Jesse wiped his
nose with the back of his sleeve. It left a slug trail of snot and tears
across the leather. "That big bridge up the road, you ever climbed
it? Because right now it's pretty fucking inviting, let me tell you." I
didn't know whether this was the randomness of the drunk mind
or the disconnect of breakdown. The strategy was the same.
Humor Jesse, or rather show him the respect I had so often been
shown when my thoughts crashed into each other.

"What do you mean?"

"They're after me, ba— Honor. Fucking *sharks*."

"Sharks?" If he was having visions then someone should have
caught this weeks ago, but as he kept talking I realized they weren't
in his imagination. "I wanted to get Madison a proper pram, din't
I? One of those ones with big tires and it turns into a car seat."

My mind formed the picture, yummy mummies and their Bug-
aboos and their takeaway coffees walking three abreast along the
pavement, but, "What's that got to do with anything?"

"She was due same month as my son's birthday. Nicholas, the
one who lives in Spain, so I like to make the extra effort there. I
was only a few hundred short. A payday loan, and it was only supposed to *be* till payday but there was a school trip to pay for as well,
and it all . . . you take out another one, don't you, to cover that,

and before you know it three grand's turned into thirty and I don't know what to fucking do anymore. I've sold my car, pawned my bike." He was folding in on himself with shame.

I was horrified. I mean it was like something from a Ken Loach film. I felt suddenly, disgustingly spoiled. If I'd had the money in my account I would have transferred it to him there and then, but I could do the next best thing. "You should ask my parents!" My voice conjured the bubble I live in so vividly I could almost see the marbled oily shimmer of its surface. "They'll lend it to you—Mum would hate to see you in trouble like this."

Jesse looked like I'd stabbed him, then slumped further down the chair. "You know what? She might have, if I'd asked nicely."

"You mean you've asked her and she said no?"

I've never been any good at hiding my feelings: my horror would have been all over my face. "Nah, babe," he said. "I din't ask her. Don't worry about me."

I crouched at his feet. "You can't come here and tell me what you're up against and pour your heart out to me and then tell me not to worry! I have to help now. I can try and sell some art? It's not your fault, it's a shitty broken system, it's disgusting. We could set up a GoFundMe?"

Jesse gave a sad little laugh. "I din't come here to ask you for money. I shouldn't have brung you into this," he said, wiping his cheeks. "We barely know each other. I shouldn't have involved you, I'm sorry. I'll leave you to get on with it. I was just calling your mum's bluff. Not fair on you, this. I dunno what I'm doing anymore."

He got to his feet, and I rose too. "Jesse. You said you did something stupid when you were young."

He stood so close that for a moment I thought he was going to kiss me but before I could back away he chucked me under the chin, a fatherly gesture that was an inch the wrong side of creepy. "Ask your mum, babe," he said, and then he was gone, leaving me reeling in the rattle and swing of the beaded curtain.

Immediately I felt the call of the blade, as though carving a ravine in my own flesh would close the one threatening to open up underfoot. I summoned Dr. Adil's voice: *only you can take some responsibility for this part of your behavior.* But we're not there yet, I thought, as I eyed up the tattooist's needle. Karl Marx said that the only antidote to mental suffering is physical pain and I've never heard a better explanation of how I am.

There was another choice, of course. I could have called Mum then and asked her what was happening. Blade. Phone. Blade. Phone. The handset was lit up in my palm before I knew I'd made the decision and I congratulated the part of myself who wants to thrive; she doesn't always get there in time.

I unlocked the screen, not sure what I was going to ask Mum, only that I would start with Jesse's visit and see where she took it from there and I would deal with it. I'd been right; there were ten missed calls from Mum and as many increasingly desperate texts urging me to call her. The last one nearly made me drop the phone into the sink.

I CAN'T EXPLAIN BUT DON'T OPEN THE DOOR TO ANYONE.

I called but it rang out and out and out. I couldn't remember a time when Mum hadn't picked up the phone to me. She even kept it on vibrate at Nanna's bedside in hospital. What was left of the morning's euphoria switchbladed into paranoia. I bolted the front door behind me and ran to the window. Jesse was walking back up to Vauxhall Cross but had stopped outside the Pleasure Gardens and was frisking himself as though for a missing wallet. An unfamiliar ping drew my attention back to the sofa. Jesse's battered old Nokia had fallen out of his pocket. It stuck out like a tombstone from the gap between the cushions. A text from Madison glowed green on the dot-matrix screen.

Someone's changed the locks on the house, Dad. Bailiffs on the doorstep. WTF is going on? CALL ME.

I fumbled with the interface of the old-fashioned phone and worked out that he had spoken to my mother in the last couple of hours. I was with Madison. WTF was going on?

I knew that if I went back to the window Jesse would be heading back here, but the easy trust of earlier was gone. I wrapped the phone in two cloth shopping bags until I thought it had enough padding to survive a fall from my window to the pavement, then hugged it to myself for comfort. I set my face to "happy" and waved at him. He glanced both ways before crossing but when he was one stripe in, a little white car came from nowhere, mounting the pavement, catching Jesse and flipping him onto the windscreen. The glass shattered into sugar and showered down around him. Long after they took him away, it dusted the outline of his body on the tarmac.

64

I met Helen Greenlaw twelve days after it all went to shit, in the lobby of the Larches of all places. I was half blind after an hour avoiding eye contact with Dr. Adil but I recognized her instantly; that astronaut's helmet of white-blonde hair on top of her skinny frame, a caricaturist's dream.

There was no one on reception to ask how the hell she had got in, or, for that matter, "How come you're even allowed out?" I challenged her. "You've got a bloody nerve, showing your face after what you've done." My shock over her audacity temporarily breached the stupor of my denial. "A life is *over* because of you."

"I regret that, very deeply." She was formal but sincere: not as cold and robotic as everyone makes out. "You're right to be angry. And I'm desperately sorry about your mother." She didn't let that hang in the air for long, and I was grateful. "To answer your question: I've been what they call 'released under investigation.'" Someone being civil when you go in all guns blazing is disarming. You got the impression you could throw any level of emotion at her and she wouldn't freak out. I suddenly found that I didn't know what to do with my arms, so I folded them across my chest. "Aren't you taking a bit of a risk, coming here, talking to a witness?" I challenged her.

"Yes." Helen Greenlaw owned it, and I respected that. I was also grudgingly impressed that she didn't come right out and ask me if I wanted to talk to her: she made me offer.

"Well, we can go in here." I opened the door to the relatives' room. It's one of the saddest spaces in this place and that's saying something. Tasteful peach sofas face each other across a box of tissues on a coffee table. A little box of kids' toys is tucked in the corner. That poor anorexic actress in the Marigold Wing has her baby brought in to see her every day. Relatives' room is a bit of a misnomer really. It's where patients bring anyone they don't want coming into their room. It's where I talk to the police.

I sat on a sofa that was still unpleasantly warm from someone else's bottom. Someone had torn a tissue into tiny snowballs: a couple of them were still wedged between the cushions. I picked one up to flick it away and found it damp with snot or tears, which made me gag. I imagined someone soaking the tissue then shredding it, probably not even knowing they were doing it.

"Have you come here to give me some answers, then? No one's telling me anything and I can't stand it."

Helen placed dainty hands on skinny thighs. "What *do* you know?" Her voice is extraordinary. Like a really advanced artificial intelligence, or a phone-bot you find yourself talking back to before you realize it's a recording.

"Not a lot," I said. "You ran Jesse down for God knows what reason, probably to do with Nazareth because it's literally the only thing you could ever have in common." I willed her to say something that would preserve my memory of Mum the way I thought she was, an outcome at odds with the direction this conversation seemed to be taking.

"It's true that Jesse Brame's family believe I accelerated deliberately and that they are asking the police to charge me with murder. But they are mistaken."

"So what was it? The car's fault? Your fault?"

"It was my error. However, it's true that it wasn't a coincidence that I was in that place, at that time, and it is to do with the hospital closure."

I flinched like I'd heard a door slam.

"Honor, the police are aware that there is correspondence between your mother and I about Jesse, warning me of what she rightly believed were malicious intentions on his part."

A buzzing noise started up in my head. I think I might have swatted the air by my left ear before saying, "What's this got to do with *me*? Why was he at my flat?"

Helen tilted her head to one side in sympathy: it didn't suit her. "Because he was going to tell you something you would have found very difficult to hear, but which I believe you have a right to know." The buzzing got louder, a plague of locusts in my head, crawling around under my skin, stripping flesh from within. "Your mother was an extraordinary young woman, you know. She had a spirit and curiosity that exceeded her education or her background, and so when she came across something she believed implicated me in . . ." She flicked her eyes upward as though for divine inspiration. "She believed that there had been a criminal element to my past. Rather than approach me directly, she told Jesse Brame, and he inveigled her into a blackmail plot, to which I succumbed."

"Blackmail? My mum? What had you done that was so bad that they . . ." I'd been thinking a lot about the evening I spent on the beige sofa at Park Royal Manor, falling through my iPad into the past. "It was to do with that poor woman who died, wasn't it?"

"Jesse and your mother believed so."

Relief was knocking on the door but I couldn't let it in until I knew more. "They were kids when she died. It wasn't anything to do with . . ."

"Goodness, no. Your mother had nothing to do with Julia Solomon's death. As you say, she was a child. Rather, she thought I did."

The good memories started to reform, like a painting being restored.

"God, how unlucky are you? Is the grim reaper following you around or what?" Helen swayed a little at this. "I'm joking," I said. "So what did you do that was so wrong? I mean, you must have done it, or why did you pay up?"

"Contemporaneous evidence is regrettably always taken as credible and authoritative. Mistakes once committed to record will be received as truth and adhered to."

Jesus Christ. "Could you possibly stop talking like the House of Lords for a minute?"

Helen sighed. "Sometimes things aren't how they seem on paper, but the paper always wins. Your mother and Jesse Brame thought they had hit on a reason that the closure of the hospital was illegal."

"So they were basically social justice warriors." This I could get on board with.

Helen shook her head. "They were wrong." Her hands began to shake and instinctively, I took them in mine, stroking her palm with my thumb, like I did with Nanna after her stroke. To my astonishment, her eyes began to shine. "Thank you, Honor, for that," she whispered, even though I hadn't done anything, then gathered herself to finish her story while I steeled myself for what might follow. "The closure was not illegal, but there was a terrible misunderstanding. Your mother, I think, recognized that, but Jesse never accepted it and when your mother tried to make him see reason, he lashed out at her. Threatening you."

"What was the reason, though? How did they know?"

"A legal technicality. Your mother's research skills were quite something." Now this did sound like the Marianne Thackeray I knew: haring around Suffolk, going from library to library until she found the right book. This wasn't so bad. "Her greatest concern was not just that you would find out but that her actions from years ago would be made public, and that the police would have prosecuted her." I almost wanted to laugh at this, a dizzy lightness corkscrewing up inside me: Mum, scared because she'd done a little illicit research! Maybe she'd gone really mad and used someone else's library card. But Helen Greenlaw wasn't smiling. "The irony being that for a charge of blackmail to stick, I personally would have had to press charges and that was never going to happen."

"Jesse, though. He didn't feel threatening when he was in my flat. A bit of a sad case. But basically harmless."

"He was, as you know, under tremendous financial stress. I'm no psychiatrist, as has been well documented, but I believe he was on the verge of a psychotic episode."

"Did you think he meant to harm me?"

She answers the question I was really asking. "The accident occurred because I was driving too fast on my way to warn you. Not that I had any idea what I was going to do. The Brames are pushing for a murder charge and the police are taking that seriously. They have a team of specially trained crash investigators re-creating the incident today, I believe. They've tested the car for mechanical faults, and there were none."

"Right. So what do you do now?"

"I wait."

"Will you be sacked from the House of Lords?"

"One doesn't get sacked, as such, but if I were to be found guilty of murder then yes, I should no longer be able to sit."

"I suppose it's full of crooks anyway."

Helen smiled. "Any institution has its share of crooks," she said. "But many of us in the House have dedicated their lives to improving society and protecting the vulnerable." She got up, smoothed her skirt, looked out of the window to show me that our time was up. "You know, Honor, I have more experience with young women like you than you realize."

I could picture her, opening a new hospital wing or whatever it is they wheel the politicians out to do. "Yeah, well. Shaking a few hands for the local paper isn't the same as living it."

I held the door for her; she looked at me levelly before turning away. "I don't suppose for a moment that it is."

I walked back along the corridor wondering if this would be the thing that brought it all crashing down. My super-straight mother involved in a blackmail plot: I didn't like it but it was nothing like the scandal of my imagining. I hadn't asked Helen how old Mum had been but I knew that she left home halfway through her A levels so she must have been a child.

And Jesse. Helen Greenlaw didn't seem capable of the levels of passion needed to commit murder: but then neither did she seem like the kind of person able to lose control of *anything,* let alone a car. Old people, though. Their judgment goes. Colette had to stop Nanna driving.

I didn't know what to think.

It hit me then, and I stopped in my tracks. How did Helen Greenlaw know to come here? Patients at the Larches pay through the nose for privacy and discretion as much as treatment. I was about to tear after her into the car park but Dad was coming toward me, staring distraught at his phone. I thought it was to do with the flat, that his buyer had fallen through.

"What *now*?"

"Oh, Honor, love. I'm so sorry, on top of everything else. It's Nanna."

65

I was the only Thackeray to make Nanna's funeral. Dad bottled it but gave me what he called "day release" on the condition Colette and Bryan didn't let me out of their sight. Jack drove all the way to London to pick me up, with the enthusiasm unique to those who have just passed their driving test. My baby cousin, six foot tall now, cried twice on the way but didn't mention the accidents/incidents/coincidence the whole time except to say, "Nanna didn't know, you know. About everything that's happened with Auntie Marianne. So. At least she was spared that."

We are a small family, but the church was standing room only. The whole of Nusstead seemed to be crammed into the pews. Nanna's old colleagues and a handful of patients traveled from as far away as Wales. It had been naive of me not to expect the Brames there and I knew as soon as I saw them why Dad had not been able to show his face. There's a sense of community in Nusstead that the Noel Road Heritage Society could only dream of. You show your face, that's what I love about it. Mum escaped Nusstead as soon as she could yet there's nowhere I feel more at home.

It was wonderful, after the last few wretched years, to be reminded that Nanna had once been a respected, beloved, senior nurse. The burial was a brief interlude of relative privacy when me, Colette, Bryan, Jack and Maisie were the only people at the graveside, all of us crying for our own reasons. We were all equally glad, I think, of the opportunity to put our public faces back on at the party.

"Welcome back to the anti-Social," said Jack, ushering me across the threshold. It was the first time I had been back since I was little, and Nanna used to take me there when I stayed with her at the weekends. I was surprised it was still standing.

Jesse's absence and my mother's absence were the biggest presences in the room, overshadowing even Nanna's memory. Jesse's mum was in a wheelchair, wearing her pain on the outside on her ravaged face and in her giant hands and feet, her swollen red knuckles. "Three out of four sons," I heard someone say. "She's like some poor mother from the First World War."

It made me wonder whether any of the children were Jesse's. None of them were crying, but I knew by then that meant nothing. I couldn't remember how many children he had, how many kids Greenlaw had robbed of a father. Five? Six? I felt guilty and sick, our conversation recast now as a grubby collusion. It almost didn't matter what her intentions had been. The fact remained that she had taken a life, and I had given her my time.

"You all right, poppet?" Colette squeezed my arm. "You know why they're looking at you funny?"

Of course I did. Nanna had hated my green hair so I'd put a brown rinse on it out of respect. It was the first time I'd worn it natural in years and even I'd been shocked to see my mother's face in the mirror. I could tell who was from Nusstead and who were the colleagues who'd never really known my mother by the way they treated me. The locals shrank back, not knowing what to say so I piled my plate high with satay chicken skewers and made small-talk with the colleagues. For all that I hated my school, it did train me to excel in situations like this, instilling the kind of social graces that can put others at their ease when you're wondering if you can make it through the next five minutes without beating your fists on the floor.

Don't ask me what fucked-up impulse drew me toward Clay

Brame. Funerals are like that and I'm like that and I suppose it was inevitable. Because I wasn't the only doppelganger there. Jesse was present after all in his oldest son, or a version of him: gym-bunny body and long messy hair that said he didn't have an office job despite the suit. Over the course of an hour the room gently brought us together, the press of bodies bearing us into the center like one of those winding folk dances that leave the May Queen opposite her king. We recognized each other; we didn't need to introduce ourselves. I was ready for his proxy fury and was ready, too, to dump everything I now knew about Jesse on him.

"You were the last one he spoke to," Clay said. "I'm sorry you had to see it happen, I'm sorry he dragged you into it all. Are you all right?" My anger melted and my heart went out to this man; why was he apologizing to me?

I didn't know what to say apart from, "I'm so sorry."

"Me too, for you."

"Thanks. I'm waiting for it all to hit me. It's like there's this tsunami of shit on the horizon and I can't be arsed to get out of the way, if that makes sense."

"Yeah, no, I know exactly what you mean." Clay nodded. "Listen, can I get you a glass of wine or something?"

"Thanks, but I can't drink. I'm already ripped to the tits on antipsychotics." These days I come right out and say it. Saves people theorizing about alcoholism and I can tell by their reaction whether they're worth bothering with.

"Oh yeah?" said Clay. "What've they got you on?" It was the first time I'd had that response outside the Larches.

"20mg citalopram, diazepam as and when."

"I didn't get on with citalopram," he said. It was like we were wine buffs discussing the merits of two different Chablis from neighboring vineyards. "I'm down to 10mg Prozac."

"How nineties."

He laughed. "It is, in't it? Ten's nothing really, but I'm scared to come off it, know what I mean? I reckon it's the training that's made the real difference. You should see what I was on before I got healthy. You should come to my gym, I'll give you an exercise prescription, you'll halve your dose within a month."

"I already run."

"Then you'll know what I mean. Weights, though, it's a whole different discipline. This'll sound really weird but it's like—it keeps me at the right level of gravity. Like, on a bad day I can't even lift my arm up, it's like my brain's pinning my body to the ground. On a different kind of bad day it's like I should be wearing metal boots or something to keep me on the planet."

I stared at him, barely able to believe it. "God. You're basically me, with muscles."

"Well, some other vital anatomical differences as well, I hope." My body seemed to make an extra three liters of blood in one second; it flooded my skin. Clay blushed in return. "I'm sorry, I can't believe I'm trying to flirt with you at your nan's funeral. It's beyond wrong. Me and my big gob."

"No, it's fine," I said. "I can relate." The elephant in the room nudged me with its trunk. "So—can I ask—what next, for you lot?"

Clay winced but didn't dodge the question. "We're turning off the machines tomorrow. I'm next of kin but Madison wasn't ready to let him go and I had to respect that. They didn't part on the best of terms so she's got to process some stuff. I mean we all have." He started to work at the label of his beer bottle with his thumb. "Do *you* think she did it on purpose?"

He was asking me as a witness but my answer was shaped by my conversation with Helen Greenlaw, the visit I still hadn't told anyone about.

"No," I said, because why hurt him when I wasn't sure? His directness enabled me to ask the next question, the kind I'd been brought up to avoid. "Did you inherit his debt?"

"*She* paid it off. Least she could fucking do, in't it?"

There it was again, Greenlaw's puzzling streak of compassion, the flaw in the rock. I wondered if she would visit Clay eventually, make a little grand tour of the wreckage. I knew better than to warn him.

"Right." I didn't insult him by saying it must take the sting out of death or anything like that. A middle-aged man with close-cropped gray hair and the neatest beard I had ever seen came over. I could tell by his expression that he had known my mother. Clay went to introduce us.

"All right, Wyatt. This is—"

"Bloody hell, Clay, I knew who it was the second she walked in," he said. "I'm sorry for your loss, love. For all of it. None of us had any idea." He turned to Clay. "I know you can't help it but the two of you together, you look like—well, you must know how it seems. It's like going back thirty years and not in a good way. Do me a favor, don't let my mum see you together, it'd tip her over the edge."

"Let's get some fresh air," I said. Outside, it was almost too fresh. The tips of the grass were still frosted where the ground was in shadow. My breath left my body and mingled with Clay's. We walked around to the side of the Social where long grass grew between broken paving stones. A patch of plywood nailed to the outside wall had come loose at one corner, revealing a splintering in the cladding beneath. Looking at him was suddenly too intense, too intimate and I could tell he felt the same because we slowly turned toward the horizon, toward Park Royal Manor and its spike in the sky.

"I hate that bloody place," I said.

"They used to talk about the Curse of Nazareth when I was a kid," said Clay. "Dad was obsessed with it. I had an uncle died there, before I was born."

"As a patient?"

Clay smiled ruefully. "No, as a thief. He was trying to nick lead off a roof or something." We stayed there talking until our fingers were blue. The difference between his adolescence and mine was stark: not just in material terms but the support, the understanding we had from our parents. Living in the shadow of an asylum seemed to have done little to enlighten Jesse: it sounded like he'd been waiting for Clay to snap out of it for the best part of fifteen years. I was getting a picture of a man whose default state was denial. We inched closer as the light faded but while I was weighing up the need to close the gap between us versus the etiquette of hooking up at my grandmother's funeral, Jack appeared, tossing and catching Bryan's car keys, and I knew that nothing was worth missing my curfew for.

"I'd better go," I said to Clay. "Or I'll turn into a pumpkin."

He caught my wrist. "Will you come back for the funeral? I know him and your mum were in a weird place, but you *were* the last person to see him alive. And the wake will be in these illustrious surroundings." He waved his hand around the Social. "Surely that on its own will tempt you."

"I don't think that'd be fair on your grandmother, would it?"

He knew I was right but he held my gaze long and hard.

"Can I see you again, though? After—you know."

It was the last thing my parents would have wanted. I asked myself what I was doing, whether I was trying to reenact my mother's youth, get it right this time. There were layers and layers here. I felt easier in Clay's straightforward, non-judgmental company than I could remember being in anyone else's since childhood. Plus, who doesn't want to have a go on a personal trainer?

"It's a terrible idea." I handed him my phone for him to enter his number. "Let's do it."

66

The tai chi session comes to an end and the participants disperse from under the oak tree, their backs straighter now than ten minutes ago. Dad stares through them. I wonder if he's even noticed they're there. He notices the door handle turn behind us, though. It makes him jump in his seat. We turn away from the plate-glass window to watch it open, the nurse leading with her hip, dragging the wheelchair backward then spinning it round to face us, turntable-smooth.

"Hello darling," says Dad. "How'd it go?"

I'd know that look anywhere: post-therapy face. Mum's eyes are dry, but her cheeks are blotchy. Any minute now she'll surprise herself with a huge, shuddering inhalation. Tonight, it'll hurt when she blinks. She motions to the nurse to wheel her over to where we are. Her remaining leg is bare. I've been trying very hard to hide my revulsion but I can't stand to see it, the Spanish Inquisition torture instrument of the encircling metal cage and the spikes that drive directly into her swollen, purpling flesh.

"Let's get you warm," I say, shrugging off my blanket and throwing it over her leg. If I keep talking we can at least gallop past the moment.

"How'd you get on with Dr. Adil?"

"I never knew how physically draining it would all be," she says in that new shaky voice of hers, like it was her lungs and not her legs that had taken the brunt of it. "I knew you'd struggled but it never occurred to me until now how *tiring* it must have been." The sentence seems to have exhausted her.

"Please," I say. "I'm out of your league and you know it." In the hierarchy of the Larches her nervous breakdown is entry-level stuff. "You haven't even been sectioned, for fuck's sake. You're the virgin at the orgy. You—"

Dad explodes, rising from his chair. "Honor, for Christ's sake! Can you stop being glib, just for five minutes?"

"Sorry," I say. But there's a ghost of a smile on Mum's face. She knows it's when I stop joking that she really needs to be worried. She understands that this is a defense mechanism; knows that the minute I actually acknowledge what's going on I'll be on twenty-four-hour watch. I can't picture the crash, not because I don't have the imagination—if only—but because I can't extrapolate her experience from Jesse's. She reversed at the last second; the train only glanced her car but that was enough to slice off the bonnet like a lid from a tin, and spin the wreckage across two fields. The lower half of her left leg was found nearly half a mile away. I know that crossing, I know that car, I know my mother and yet when the film plays in my mind the Suffolk landscape suddenly has a London bus stop, traffic lights, grotty pavements and it's Jesse they stretcher out, in a zippered shroud.

Dad stands up, hands in pockets, crosses the room in five paces then repeats the action. "I thought I might take you both out for lunch today," he says. He's got a new voice too; forced jollity that's somehow more heartbreaking than if he wore his grief on his sleeve. "Give you a break from institutional food. There's a gastropub up the road that's got four stars for accessibility." He holds up his phone, shows me the TripAdvisor review.

"I've already ordered lunch in the room for all of us," Mum says. "Maybe tomorrow?"

"Sure!" says Dad brightly.

The two of us—experts, now, at this maneuver—lift Mum out of her chair and onto the sofa.

When the next knock shakes the door, it isn't a trolley full of food but Costello and Greene in their skirt suits. The police are always a surprise even when you're expecting them.

"Afternoon, Marianne, Sam, Honor," says Costello, the older of the two but the least formal. "Been a major development."

Mum goes rigid. "Can you tell me on my own?" she says. Dad and I glance at each other in alarm. What can she possibly have left to hide? Jesse's voice starts up its loop again in my head. *Me and your mum, we done something really stupid.* There's more to it than she's letting on; I knew it. There is something big, something so huge that Helen Greenlaw thought it was worth knocking Jesse into his grave to keep it quiet. Oh God. Oh God. My pulse starts to hammer again. This is catastrophizing or anticipatory anxiety. Isn't it? Dad and I move out into the corridor and I put my palms against the wall, as though I can push what's coming away.

"What do you think they're saying?" I ask Dad.

"I don't know, love," he says. I examine his face, the dark circles, the scoring around his mouth that wasn't there a month ago, the fuzz of hair that's nearly as big as Helen Greenlaw's. Mum could do anything and he would absorb it: it's the fact that Jesse still has—had—this hold on her, this bond with her, that's killing him. This is guesswork on my part, of course. He won't say it and despite begging him to open up to me I'm grateful, in this moment, for the way men repress their emotions. Mine, and Mum's, are all I can handle right now.

The door opens almost instantly. It's Greene. "Actually," she says, "please can you come in?"

I swear to God Mum's had a facelift or something in the last minute. Obviously she still doesn't look *happy* as such, but that puckered, agonized expression she's been wearing since she came round, since she learned what happened to Jesse, has gone. "Can you do it?" she asks Costello like a child to a mother.

"In a nutshell, we won't be bringing charges against anyone for

Jesse Brame's death. We don't have enough evidence to charge Helen Greenlaw with anything more serious than death by careless driving, which she's already pleaded guilty to, no custodial sentence. No more interviews for you to worry about, Honor. As far as your involvement goes, it's over."

That's why Mum's so relieved. Helen's words float back to me: *for a charge of blackmail to stick, I personally would have had to press charges.* When they turned off Jesse's life support, he took their secret with him.

I study Mum while her eyes are on Costello: she's not relieved, she's destroyed.

"Have you told his family?" I ask and Dad flinches but I need to know.

"I personally went to Nusstead yesterday and told Madison Brame that the CPS would never bring the case to trial. There's still some resistance there. Do let us know if they bother you."

My phone, my connection to Clay, feels hot in my pocket.

The police leave the room and seem to take all the air with them. We don't know what to say to each other: it's as though Jesse himself was in here with his feet up on the coffee table. Dad clearly feels it too. During lunch, the only sound is of cutlery on plates and the occasional click of his jaw. We watch the window like it's a TV and the gray squirrels jumping from branch to branch are performing a gripping drama.

"Anyone mind if I stretch my legs?" asks Dad. "There's probably only half an hour of daylight left and I'm starting to feel a bit like a mole." His hand is on the doorknob before he's finished speaking.

"Go for it. I've got Mum." We sit in front of the window and watch Dad walk past the ugly larch and the oak tree. A full circuit of the grounds takes about twenty minutes at a brisk pace and Dad's dragging his feet. I rest my head on Mum's shoulder. Gratitude for still having her at all mists my eyes.

"Are you going to meet up with Helen Greenlaw, now it's all over?" I feel her body tense and lean out in case I've crushed a nerve or something. "I mean, I know you couldn't before, what with her being released under investigation and that, but you *could,* now, couldn't you? Would you want to talk to her?" Her reply is a kind of gargle but I know what it's like to be so burned out that forming words is just beyond you so I don't push it. "Since we're having an awkward conversation," I shift in my seat, "I need to talk to you about Clay Brame."

It's like my words have unpicked the stitch that was keeping her face up. Her pupils blast open and she leans forward. "What do you know about him?"

I'm in no position to judge overreactions but this isn't what I was expecting.

"Enough," I say simply. When she drops her head into her hands her hair falls forward. The spray of gray around her ears seems to have doubled since last night. She mumbles something that sounds like, "Helen promised." There's a lot of this happening at the moment, snatched words that don't make sense.

"What's Helen got to do with it?" I say. "She wasn't there."

Mum looks up from under a messy wing of hair. Only one eye is visible but it's boring right through me. "Wasn't where?"

I try to hide my exasperation. "At Nanna's funeral." I take both her clawed hands in mine, trying not to see the shape of the cage beneath her blanket. "Where else would I have met him? He's a nice guy, Mum. I know it's a bit of an age gap, and you probably don't want a reminder of Jesse hanging around, and, I mean, it's early days anyway, but I've got a really good feeling about him."

Her hands relax in mine and her expression changes again; now she's trying to suppress giggles. Is this what it's been like trying to have a straight conversation with me over the years? "Baby Clay!" she shouts. It's a weird way to describe what must be fifteen stone of solid muscle but I suppose he would've been a baby to her, once.

"He *gets* me, Mum. Let me give it a chance?"

Her shining eyes tell me I'm asking a lot of her, probably too much and I'm on the verge of telling her not to worry, I'll leave it, I'll give him up, when she smiles a smile I know all too well, and only now see the effort involved in it. "Who am I to stand in your way?"

"Thanks," I say. "Your blessing means a lot. Now I just have to get it past Dad." She bites her lips but it doesn't stop them trembling and she lets go two diamond tears. "Don't worry, I'll be gentle with him."

There's another knock on the door. Physiotherapy this time, an hour of exercises that have Mum screaming in pain. She'll be back weeping with exhaustion and for the loss of her leg. It's the least I can do to be here. The nurse pulls off the blanket and hands it to me. I bend down to kiss Mum, closing my eyes against the cage.

When she's gone, I fold the blanket and drape it over the back of the sofa. I'll call Clay in a minute, tell him he can tell the Brames we're seeing each other. They won't want a mini-Marianne in their lives any more than my parents want him. Will it be worth it? I have no idea.

Something catches my eye, spots of white against the bottle-green upholstery. Tiny shreds of balled-up tissue, hard little pebbles this time that have fallen between the seat cushions. I am propelled back to the relatives' room the day Helen Greenlaw came to see me, the still-warm seat, the scattering of tiny paper pebbles.

Mum had been in there before me.

Of course Helen wouldn't come all this way simply to put my mind at rest, but she would if there was more story to get straight between her and Mum. They were both taking a huge risk talking to each other. Helen killed Jesse on purpose, and Mum knows why. And they are covering up for what reason?

Me.

Helen promised.

Both of those women gambled their freedom to keep me in the dark.

They did that for me.

So the choice is mine. I can upset Mum by digging for a truth that might destroy both of us, or I can grow up and admit that we're stronger when the space between us is big enough to hold secrets. Secrets are how you survive.

I cross my legs and stare out of the window at the floodlit trees. Three big lights silver the swaying branches. I see Dad barreling back across the lawn, three shadows tailing him. This is the closest I've ever seen him come to running. I turn out the light, the better to watch him. He disappears, only to rematerialize in the covered walkway that connects the residential block to the physio suite, and there he waits until Mum is pushed in. He drops to her level, kisses her cheek and then takes charge of the wheelchair. He cut short his walk just to push her twenty yards to her appointment. He kisses her head and stays there, inhaling her hair, and she lifts her arm and hooks him into an awkward backward hug that she can't sustain for more than a few seconds. She doesn't see that his face is contorted with the effort of trying not to cry. They are both going to fake it and that's how they—we—will survive.

I know then that I am never going to confide in any man about what I think I know. Not Dad: Christ, certainly not Clay.

I said my brain was a maze. Thoughts charge through it like screaming patients and I realize that those doors that stop me thinking the worst are there for a reason. They are there to keep me safe. I can choose to know, or I can choose to thrive. Lock them up. Throw away the key.

Mum was just doing what she's always done: trying to keep me safe. I know everyone thinks this, but I really do have the best mother in the world.